HERE STAYS
GOOD YORKSHIRE

THE RYERSON FICTION AWARD
The All-Canada Prize Novels

1942
Little Man   *G. Herbert Sallans*

1943-44—No Awards

1945
Here Stays Good Yorkshire   *Will R. Bird (aeq.)*

Day of Wrath   *Philip Child (aeq.)*

HERE STAYS
GOOD YORKSHIRE

by WILL R. BIRD

THE RYERSON PRESS • TORONTO

PRINTED AND BOUND IN CANADA
BY THE RYERSON PRESS, TORONTO

TO MY MOTHER

A COURAGEOUS DAUGHTER OF CUMBERLAND SETTLERS

AND

TO ALL DESCENDANTS

OF OUR YORKSHIRE PIONEERS

Author's Foreword

THIS NOVEL is not written as authentic history. It is, rather, an attempt to tell of the rooting of Yorkshire settlements in Cumberland, Nova Scotia. The writer, J. S. Fletcher, in his book about Yorkshire, states:

It is usually held all the world over that the Yorkshireman possesses certain qualities and characteristics which distinguish him from all other Englishmen. Just as everything that lies within his country has an indefinable atmosphere or colour which is comprised in the word *Yorkshire*, so there is something about the Yorkshireman which clings to him wherever he goes.

It is not his speech, though that never leaves him; it is not his hard-headed fashion of conducting business transactions; it is something which is a part of himself, ingrained in him from birth, and as difficult to name or classify as the fleeting vapours seen far off on one of his own hillsides. He is *Yorkshire*. That is all the outside world can say of him; but in saying so much it says a great deal. Whatever is Yorkshire merits respect and admiration, and demands both with a calm insistence which is typical of a folk who know their own greatness.

It should not be gathered that he is an arrogant fellow. In point of fact he is one of the fairest-minded of men, bluff, hearty and off-hand, of a respectable hospitality. He is serious in his religious beliefs; on occasion he evinces strong emotion.

The Yorkshiremen would not join the king's militia; nor would they support those who stood against the king. Necessity, that of planting crops that they might eat, of building roofs for shelter, of making furniture, beds, stools, tables and chairs that they might have more comfort, occupied their minds to the exclusion of all else, even to the greatness of their adventure. Nevertheless when Eddy's men began looting, irrespective of the householder's interest in the American cause, the Maccan Yorkshiremen presented such a united front that the raiders soon left them alone.

Eddy's force of Maine adventurers, Acadians and Indians, aided by sympathizers from the Fort Cumberland and Cobequid areas, lacked discipline and cohesion to such an extent that their attempts against the fort were pitifully weak. The fort garrison of renegades and misfits did nothing heroic. Outside of assistance given by a few Yorkshiremen there was scarcely an episode worth relating.

A writer of fiction has the privilege of adjusting locations to suit his purpose, and I have used that privilege. Every care has been taken, however, to present the arrival and establishment of the Yorkshire families as accurately as possible. The documents dealing with discharged members of the Royal Highland Emigrants are exact copies of originals in the Nova Scotia Archives; only the names are fictitious.

To the following I am indebted for invaluable data: Prof. D. C. Harvey, Archivist, and Dr. J. S. Martell, of the Public Archives of Nova Scotia; Dr. J. C. Webster, C.M.G., F.R.S. Can. and Edinburgh, Member of the Historical Sites and Monuments Board of Canada; Miss Frances Tilley, of Mount Allison Memorial Library, Sackville, N.B.; Miss Muriel Kinnear, of the Public Archives of Canada, Ottawa; Mrs. M. K. Ingraham, of Acadia University Library, Wolfville, N.S.; Miss Lois E. Fisher, of the History Division of Rochester Public Library, Rochester, N.Y.; and Miss Elizabeth F. Barnaby, of the Citizens Library, Halifax, N.S.

In addition, I must acknowledge help from various descendants of Yorkshire families who have permitted me to scan old documents and letters.

Printed sources consulted include: *The American Invasion of*

Nova Scotia, by Professor Wilfred B. Kerr, Buffalo University; *The Neutral Yankees of Nova Scotia*, by John Bartlett Brebner; *A Book About Yorkshire*, by J. S. Fletcher; *Yorkshire Wit, Character, Folklore and Customs*, by Blakeborough; *Specimens of Yorkshire Dialect*, by J. S. Fletcher; *The Chignecto Isthmus and Its First Settlers*, by Howard Trueman; *History of Sackville*, by W. C. Milner; *The Forts of Chignecto*, by Dr. J. C. Webster; *The Rise of Michael Francklin*, by Prof. W. B. Kerr; *Records of the Lumley Family*, by Dr. Thos. Lumley; and *A Journey through Nova Scotia*, by J. Robinson and T. Rispin.

Contents

BOOK ONE
1772

BOOK TWO
1773

BOOK THREE
1774

BOOK FOUR
1775

BOOK FIVE
1776

The Principal Characters

CHIPLEY, ADAM: A Yorkshire settler.

CHIPLEY, SYLVIA: Daughter of Adam.   Married Matthew Crabtree.

CLEWS, POLLY: Silly girl, daughter of village drunk.

CORNFORTH, JACOB: A Yorkshire settler.

CORNFORTH, AARON: Jacob's son.

CORNFORTH, SAMSON: Jacob's son.

CRABTREE, TRISTRAM: A Yorkshire settler.

CRABTREE, JONATHAN: Tristram's brother.

CRABTREE, MATTHEW: Tristram's brother, a wrestler.

CRABTREE, LANCELOT: Tristram's brother, a hunter.

CRABTREE, ASA: Tristram's father, a wood carver.

CRABTREE, PATIENCE: Tristram's sister.

CRABTREE, MELODY: Tristram's sister.

CRABTREE, MALACHY: Tristram's uncle, the magistrate.

CRABTREE, AMELIA: Tristram's aunt, who became melancholy.

CUTLIP, THOMAS: Yorkshire cobbler, who settled at Amherst.

CUTLIP, SHUBELL: Son of Thomas, a boxer.

CUTLIP, ANN: Daughter of Thomas, deaf from childhood.

DANKS, GIDEON: Giant of a man, who spoke Micmac and rode black stallion.

EAGLESON, PARSON: Clergyman at the fort, fond of drink.

FARING, JUNE: Fugitive from Boston, stranded at Halifax.

FERGUSON, DONALD: Disabled soldier who came to live with his sister.

FRANCKLIN, MICHAEL: Lieut.-Governor of Nova Scotia.

GARRISON, GABRIEL: Peg-legged New Englander settled at Bathol.

GREEN, TITUS: Francklin's land agent at Cumberland.

HODGE, ISRAEL: A Yorkshire settler.

HODGE, EZRA: Son of Israel.

KEELOR, AGGIE: Alluring widow who lived at Amherst village.

KNAPP, SHUBAD: Ex-fisherman who settled at Bathol.

KNATCHBALL, PEREGRINE: The Yorkshire blacksmith at Bathol.

LACEY, JOHN: The New Hampshire man who came to Bathol.

LEMMING, UNITY: Yorkshire parson's daughter.

MARSH ROSE: Indian chief's daughter.

MEEKINS, PETER: Young man who joined the rebel cause.

MULLINS, SETHELLA: Widow with half-wit son who lived near the fort.

MUNCIE, OBED: Militia officer who lived at Maccan.

NILES, HENRY: Settler who lived at Nappan.

O'CONNER, DR.: Ship's doctor driven ashore through drink.

PEAMAN, SALLY: Lived with her grandfather across water from Amherst Point.

PLUMLEY, SILAS: Yorkshire settler who led religious gatherings.

SCURR, REUBEN: A Yorkshire settler, taken by the press gang.

SCURR, JUDY: Reuben's wife, who married again.

SMITH, SOLOMON: Settler who owned a sawmill.

SOUR BEAR: Pock-marked Indian who was ugly-tempered.

TUMP, DELIA: Plump Scottish widow who lived on River Hebert road.

BOOK ONE
1772

I
The Yorkshire Emigration

TRISTRAM CRABTREE plodded determinedly along a
field path leading to a stable at the rear of Banfield,
a Yorkshire village situated a day's ride from the sea.
The winter cold and his sullen determination hardened his
features. He did no more than grunt a greeting to the man
who admitted him at the stable and led him to a nook inside.

"Stay from sight," said the fellow, Paddy Bundy, who
boasted of having been a champion boxer. "If Shubell puts
eye on ye there'll be no fetching him inside. Windmill yer
arms a bit and loosen up."

It was as if he had not spoken. Tristram sat on a bench
and glowered. His mother had been ill for weeks and showed
no signs of improvement. He detested sports as a waste of
time yet had practised boxing for more than three months.
He resolved, as he glowered at the straw, that when he had
beaten Shubell Cutlip to insensibility he would go to Unity
and tell her all he had had to do on her account.

Unity Lemming was the parson's daughter. She was young
and slender and darkly beautiful with a soft slurring in her
speech like a small caress, all one piece of loveliness in his
eyes. There were those who said she did everything for her
father but go into the pulpit in his stead. Everyone was
certain that she wrote his sermons and she was generally with
him when he walked down the village street.

"He's coming 'long t' road," called Paddy in a low tone,
blurred with excitement. "Don't ye say a word till I have
him in."

Tristram sat up and began to remove his jacket. He
remembered the day Shubell, returned from a three-years-

1

service in London, and slightly drunk, received a lecture from the parson. Shubell, hardened by his London experience, yelled defiance. He called the parson, in Unity's presence, a vulgar name.

Someone told Tristram what had happened. He was a heavy man with immense shoulders and arms, swarthy, with thick hairs on the backs of his hands and wrists, with small tufts in his ears, and black shaggy brows. He had hunted up Shubell and tried to give him a thrashing.

Shubell was a hefty youth. He had learned to use his hands with some cleverness, and had courage. He knocked Tristram down half a dozen times before villagers interfered.

Tristram carried marks of the encounter for a week but his pride had suffered most. He was determined to have revenge and the idea burned him until, finally, he engaged Paddy to instruct him in using his fists. His training had been in secret, and now the day of reckoning had come.

"Come in, Shubell, and see the fine fighting cock I've got," called Paddy. "I'll vow it's best in t' village."

"Tha art always bragging," returned Shubell good-humouredly. "Let's see t' chick."

The stable was closed. Paddy barred it, then Tristram stood forth. He was stripped for action.

"Had to be done this way," said Paddy briskly. "This is a private matter that's to be settled and ye'll have fair play. Off wi' yer jacket and waistcoat. Ten rounds to go. I'm acting referee."

Some of Shubell's confidence seemed to return when he saw he was not to be ganged but the stall they were to fight in was entirely too small to provide a boxer with sufficient room. He took his position in the centre and did his best to avoid Tristram's savage rushes.

Paddy's patience had taught Tristram to guard himself but he was still slow of hand and foot. Through the first round he weathered the going nicely but in the second his temper began to have the better of him. He missed badly and took a blow that slammed him against the stall timbers.

It was during the third round that someone hammered at the door until Paddy called time and undid the fastenings.

He admitted Tristram's brother, Matthew, who was but twenty yet had the same breadth and thickness of shoulder that distinguished Tristram, the same swarthy features and heavy jaw. Matthew checked himself as he saw the two fighters waiting Paddy's signal. He watched a round of torrid action, saw his brother take two quick blows in the face and fail to land one in return.

"Time!" called Paddy.

Tristram sat on a milking stool and Matthew bent over him. "Mother wants all o' us," he whispered. "She's had a bad turn."

"All o' us!" grunted Tristram as if he could not understand. He was seething with rage and stubbornness.

"Aye," said Matthew heavily. "She wants all o' us."

Tristram glowered at Matthew. "Tha wait," he ordered.

Matthew nodded. He had always taken orders from Tristram.

Tristram charged his man with ferocity but Shubell boxed him well enough to escape damage until the small space caused his undoing. He bumped against the wall, lost balance, stumbled briefly. Before he could recover a terrific blow felled him like an ox. He lay on the floor, his heels digging at the planks. Tristram scanned him triumphantly, then turned to Matthew. "Coom!" he said brusquely.

Outside, his conscience began to burn him. In his way he loved and admired his mother. She had worked hard as long as he could remember and although on occasion she had used her sharp tongue on him like a long-lashed whip he thought her fair in her judgments. It was her contriving and persistence that had enabled them to save money enough to buy a farm; it was her natural caution that had refused to let them make the purchase while the depression lasted. Her trust, as he knew it, was in the land, the security of the natural round of crops supporting stock that, in turn, became food and, once more, crops; grain and fruit and crops; sheep, cattle, pigs and poultry. These, to her, were the substance of life and all else was folly.

"Coom!" he shouted at Matthew and they began, clumsily, to run.

It would be a fine beechen bowl. Clean beech, free of doty runs and dried properly, was good carving wood. Asa Crabtree could sense a true grain with his fingers and he delighted in getting a block to work on when there was no need to hurry and a man could put his artistry into each cutting.

His draw knife, gouger, chisels, scraper and honing stone were arranged in order on the window sill beside him and his leather apron was filled with fine shavings. Time was when he was afraid of letting any litter reach the floor but now his family said he was childish and let him work as he chose. Jonathan, his second son, brought him all the wood he wanted to carve and saw that he had plenty of tools.

January was a cold month in Yorkshire. A farmer rode by on a rough-haired nag and the breath of both man and beast lifted like smoke in the frosty air. A good day, Asa thought, to stay indoors, though Tristram, his oldest son, had gone somewhere without saying a word about it. Every few days he would be gone most of the afternoon and Asa wondered what he did. Farmers did not work long hours in winter as they did at seedtime and harvest but there were scythe handles and flails to make, rakes and stable forks and ox yokes. Everyone in Banfield could work well with wood or leather.

A gust of wind rattled snow against the pane and more wood was placed on the fire. The ground outside was covered with ice and snow, so different from summer when the buttercup meadows and hawthorn hedges were at their best, especially the early summer when the trees were not in full leaf, when the ashes were still feathery and sycamores splashed the woods with red. The sweaty heat of the year had not arrived but the pulse of growing roots and plants could be felt in a man's blood.

There was whispering in the kitchen behind him but he hunched over his work, pretending not to notice any of their comings and goings. Now he sensed that something unusual was to take place. His sons had not gone to any outside work. Instead they had gone into the inner room as if afraid of something.

He started as Melody, his daughter, put her hand on his shoulder. "Coom in," she said. "Mother's asked for all o' us."

"All o' us!" His wife, who had been strong as a horse, was ill, and he had been barred from her bed. What could she want now?

A slyness crept into his expression. "Does she know tha have paper on Nova Scotia?"

"Noa." Melody shook a finger at him. "Don't tha say a word o' it. Coom now. Matthew has gone to find Tristram. Parson's down wi' ague and can't get. Coom."

Asa did not want to go. He dallied by shaking the shavings from his apron into the fire. Melody's vigour irritated him. She was vibrant with life, with her impetuous hurry, her blazing red hair, her red urgent mouth and the swelling lines of her young body. Even when tired from a hard day in the field her vitality was something to warm your hands at.

She drew him into the room against his will, tugging him along three or four steps before leaving him. There was a fourposter bed in the centre, placed sideways to a crackling fire. On it, her shoulders and head braced by many pillows, his wife was lying. Her bulky figure seemed a mountain under the coverlets; her hands plucked aimlessly at their fringes. Perspiration beaded her flushed cheeks. It glistened on the faint moustache that darkened her upper lip. She turned her head to look slowly at Asa.

He turned away, his Adam's apple bobbing in his scrawny neck, then glanced at her again to see if she were watching him.

"Tristram?" she murmured fretfully.

"Matthew's gone for him," assured Melody.

"He's oop to some lark," mumbled Asa. "Thear's no market t' day."

His oldest daughter, Patience, sat by the head of the bed with a Bible in her hands. He knew she had been reading aloud from it. When she looked at him he went around the bed to where his second son, Jonathan, and fourth son, Lancelot, were standing. He liked them best of all his family, and had pride in them, for they were both over six feet in height, blond and blue-eyed like himself, with soft golden beards.

"I want Tristram," the sick woman said again.

They all, daughters, sons and husband, gazed at the sufferer while she had her eyes closed. When she opened them they glanced at each other, looked out the window, studied a sampler on the wall lettered "God's Name Be Praised," or scanned the dresser and bed as if embarrassed. Asa wished she would go to sleep.

She looked at him again. "Asa," she laboured in her speech. "I'm going. Tha have been a good man—good Yorkshire." She paused to gather strength. "Carve all tha want, but do as t' girls tell thee. Remember."

Her voice bothered him. "I'm carving now," he announced. "Bowl for rye pudding."

"Patience." His wife sounded very tired and he listened carefully. Generally she was in a bad temper after a hard day. "Watch thy father. He'll need new shirts coom May. Read thy Bible. Bake roasts longer than tha do wi' old meat. Go careful wi' butter. Keep thy eyes open—and marry when tha can."

Asa raised his head and watched furtively as Patience placed her hand over her mother's restless fingers. They had strong resemblance. The daughter had the same dark hair and strong features; her mouth had the same immobility of lips that can guard secrets.

"Aye, mother," she said in a low voice. "Are thy feet cowd?"

"Never mind them t' now. Jonty," her voice began to hurry, "tha have been a champion lad. I'm proud o' thee. Don't tha quarrel wi' Tristram. Thee are twenty-four. Pick thyself a steady lass and settle."

Jonathan leaned over the bed to pat his mother's arm. "Don't tha worry over me," he said. "I'll wed when t' reight lass cooms by."

"Lancelot, I want tha to choosen thyself good friends. Get more to market and know prices." Her voice dragged to a whisper. "There's nowt to be had wi' fishing on moors. Tha are no gipsy. Tha worry Tristram wi' t' like. See tha help more wi' t' seeding."

"Aye, I'll do my share." Lancelot's lazy intonation of

voice seemed as physical as the touch of his hand. "Depend on't. I'll be no gipsy."

"Melody." There was a longer pause. Asa shuffled his feet, felt of the bed post. He had never heard his wife talk in such a strain before. Next afternoon he would go to the stable before Melody could catch him. It was warm enough with the beasts. He studied the "Star of Bethlehem" pattern of the quilt his wife fingered and wished he were back in the kitchen.

"Aye, mother."

Asa wondered what his wife would say. About all she had done since Melody was sixteen was to shake her head and tighten her lips for there was not a more magnificent-looking girl in Banfield.

"I'll say nowt to thee, lass, for tha will do as tha will. Thee and Jonty sing. One o' Wesley's."

Jonathan stepped around the head of the bed to stand by Melody. Asa saw her touch Jonathan's hand. He heard her whisper "Lover o' my soul."

When Jonathan nodded she started the hymn, her voice suddenly steady and clear.

Jesus, Lover of my soul, let me to Thy bosom fly,
While the nearer waters roll, while the tempest still is high.

She started to lag but Jonathan joined his strong baritone with her singing and they reached perfect harmony.

"Other refuge have I none; hangs my helpless soul on Thee. . . ."

Asa swayed with the singing, enjoying it. Lancelot hummed an accompaniment until the second verse when he joined in with his fine tenor. Patience sat with the Bible in her lap, gazing at it as if she were among strangers. It was a pity, Asa thought, that she could not sing. Too much like her mother, he reckoned, who could never sing a note.

They sang the hymn through. When they had finished the mother opened her eyes. "That wur good," she whispered.

"Aye," said Asa heartily. "It wur champion."

His wife did not look at him but seemed to sleep at once. He shifted about, looked toward the kitchen, but Melody shook her head at him. The sick woman opened her eyes. She began to struggle for breath. "I won't die—until I've seen him—my lad. Fetch him—tha dolts."

Melody peered out of the window, then shook her head at the others. The silence lengthened until suddenly, as if the vacuum of the waiting stillness had drawn it from her, the mother tried to release a torrent of raving.

"Tha'll not go," she gasped. "Tha shan't. I know what's in thy minds. Nova Scotia. But tha'll stay here. Tristram will promise me—and tha will do as he says . . ."

The violence of her efforts set her struggling for breath. Her voice failed completely. No one made her any answer. They looked away as if she had uncovered guilt among them. Asa wondered if she had seen the paper Melody kept in the dresser. Patience left her chair and moved camphor about the window sill to ease the reek of fever. Jonathan put another stick on the fire.

It seemed a chance to escape from the room but when Asa tried it Lancelot reached for his jacket and tugged him back. "Mother wants us to stay wi' her," he murmured.

"But she's sleeping," argued Asa. The others frowned at him and he subsided. Melody brought him a chair. He was no more than seated when his wife opened her eyes. She glared about her, stared at him without recognition.

"Whear's Tristram?" she wheezed. "Whear's Matthew? I want my own lads. Not these dolts, like their father."

Melody gasped. "Mother!" Her cheeks flamed with embarrassment. She looked at her brothers but they gave no indication of having heard what their mother said.

Asa wetted his lips with his tongue, rubbed his head. He did not like the odours of the room and he wished his wife would not say such harsh things. He shrugged. She had always been that way.

The extended silence made him uneasy. He was glad he did not have to sleep in the room. Being by himself in a small chamber upstairs was a grand experience. He slept with his stockings on every night, and no one knew it. Not even Patience, who was so like her mother.

His wife began shuddering but did not open her eyes.

When she was quiet again Melody said it was time to light the candles. Then they heard the door open, heard sounds of hasty washing at the slop bench. Tristram entered the room, Matthew following. He walked straight to the bedside to touch his mother's hands. She opened her eyes and looked at him but her power of speech had failed. Tristram bent over and kissed her.

There was the barest whisper, yet it was so quiet in the room that each watcher heard it. "Tha—art—ony—one—who—kissed me." She shuddered violently, then relaxed, seemed to sink into the bed. Her hands became still.

Outside, in the dusk, a dog howled mournfully, the sound filtering into the room. Patience pushed beside her brother and bent over the dark head on the pillow. A long moment after she looked around at Asa. "Mother's dead," she said simply.

Asa blinked at her. He spoke in a half-whisper. "She didn't get to say about Nova Scotia, did she?"

The others gave him no heed. He edged to the door, hurried into the kitchen. The next moment he was at work on his beechen bowl. There was much low talking but no one came to him or gave him attention. Presently he went to a dresser in the corner, took a folded paper from the top drawer, smoothed it and, holding it by candlelight, read each word half aloud.

Desirable farm land to be had at or near Francklin Manor, River Hebert, Nova Scotia. Consisting of marshfields which do not require manure, upland of great fertility, mostly cleared, and excellent wooded land. Much of this district formerly occupied by Acadians. May be had at the following attractive rentals: First year, rent free; next five years, one penny per acre; second five years, threepence per acre; third five years, sixpence per acre; all later period, one shilling per acre. All tenants free of land tax.

Passage arranged for respectable Yorkshire families in ship to sail from Scarborough direct to Fort Cumberland, Nova Scotia, some time in March. A reasonable amount of household chattels will be carried free of charge for each family.

All interested persons to be at Banfield Hall, February 17, to meet with Martin Hobbs, Esq., agent for Michael Franklin.

In the night Asa awoke and sat up in bed, remembering. He slid his bony feet to the floor and stood, a grotesque scarecrow in his flannel nightshirt. Then he moved quietly down the stairs and into the little cottage parlour. His wife was there in the coffin he had seen carried in, and he examined its smooth outer surface, felt for the corner joinings. Then he could see his wife, dressed as she was on Sundays, her eyes closed, her hands crossed with the left uppermost, showing her wedding ring. The moonlight made her appear peaceful and resting.

Suddenly he was afraid that she would rouse and see him. He stole from the room and scuffed his stockings up the stairs, a frightened old man.

At the funeral the parson spoke with some fervour, praising the departed as a mother whose life was devoted to the well-being of her family. That evening the Crabtrees sat at their meal without conversation, Patience occupying her mother's chair, until Tristram pushed back and spoke abruptly.

"We'll buy stone for t' grave," he said in his harsh voice. "I'll go after market for prices." He looked at his sisters. "Tha better pick summat to put after name. A line o' Scripture will do, happen it's not too long. T' charge is fourpence a letter."

No one discussed his proposal. The family moved for days as if unconvinced that their mother would not return, then they all attended the meeting with Francklin's agent.

Tristram sensed that his brothers were keen to move to Nova Scotia. He surmised that Jonathan and Lancelot wanted most the chance to fish new streams. Matthew had thrown out a hint about taking land for himself. His proposal did not alarm Tristram. There would be no harm in letting the lad have such thoughts during the voyage over but when the time came he would squash the plan. Matthew was a capable worker and would be kept in the family for a few years at least.

Their talk as they went to the Hall was about the incredibly

cheap rents but Tristram had other thoughts. He saw the
move to Nova Scotia as a means of forcing Unity to marry
him. She had dallied with him for over two years and thought
of ending her hesitancy urged him so that he resolved to do
everything possible to boost the emigration.

To his surprise there was no need of boosting. Silas
Plumley and Adam Chipley, two of the leading farmers, voted
Francklin's bargain better than anything similar offered in
England. Israel Hodge, who pinched his pennies, agreed with
them. After that it was but a matter of signing papers with
the agent. Even Thomas Cutlip, Shubell's father, a widower
who had a good cobbling business, declared that nothing
would keep him from going.

The next evening Tristram went to see Unity, going late so
that her father would have retired. "It's done," he exulted.
"We're going to Nova Scotia."

Unity paled. "Who are going?"

"All o' us. Chipley's and Plumley's and Hodge. A dozen
more from hereabout."

"But not you?"

"Aye, every Crabtree. I coom to let tha know in plenty of
time to make ready. We're to sail early in March."

"To get ready!" she echoed, and her tone caught him
like a slap.

"We'll be married by thy father, proper, afore we go," he
said.

"But tha never asked what I'd do?" Her voice was gentle
enough yet something wound an icy coil around his heart,
and tightened it.

"Unity! Tha'll go?"

"Noa. I can't leave my father."

"But tha are to marry me. Tha promised." Bewilder-
ment washed over his features. "Why can't tha go?"

"I won't leave father. If I went to Nova Scotia I'd never
see him again, and tha know it. Please don't argue when
tha will be gone so soon."

Listening to her, Tristram could feel the slow, uneven thud
of his heart. Every plan he had nourished in his thinking
became distorted, impossible, and he knew she would not leave

her father as long as he lived.   It was a blow he had never
reckoned, and temper heated him.

"I thowt," he said bitterly, "when a lass promised, she'd
go wi' him wherever he went."

"Don't tha say harsh things," she begged.   "It won't help
ony.   If tha don't want to wait for me tha are free to marry
who tha will."

He looked at her as if he could scarcely credit his hearing,
then turned to the door.   "I'll wait," he said hoarsely.
"Tha know I will."

She smiled and he took her into his arms, for he could not
resist.   Her hair was in his eyes, soft as moonlight, and
fragrant.   She looked up at him as if a little frightened—and
his lips crushed hers.   It was seldom that he had shown his
affection with such passion, and she yielded to him.   Then he
tore himself away and flung out into the night, wordless.
Unity stood as he left her, staring after him, as if unable to
adjust herself to candlelight and reality after the violent
rapture of his kiss.

An hour later Tristram was still tramping the road outside
the village, battling impulses.   His pride had received a
terrific shock.   He knew there would be gossip over his failure
to induce Unity to go with him.

The Yorkshiremen sailed from Scarborough during the
third week of March in a fine ship with its name *Duke of York*
lettered grandly on blue-painted woodwork.   There were
sixty-two settlers on board with their peculiar possessions.
There was grain stored in the stall-like cabins, a sack being
used as pillow in every berth to keep the seed dry.   In the
deep hold were chests of drawers, dressers, bedding, crockery,
scythes, reaping hooks, plows, harnesses, everything counted
as a necessity in the home.

Thomas Cutlip was among the passengers, accompanied
by his daughter, Ann, who had been deaf from childhood.
She wore a hood that covered her head to her neck, her father
being afraid she would catch cold in her ears.   Cutlip's sides
of leather, his lasts, hammer, awls, wax, thread and lapstone,
were stowed where he slept.

There was sensation for the Crabtrees at the sailing when

an aunt and uncle from Backfall arrived, an elderly couple entirely unsuited for such adventure. Uncle Malachy Crabtree had been a magistrate in the town. He was togged in velvet small clothes ornamented with silver buttons engraved with his name. His wife, Aunt Amelia, had a sharp nose that protruded from the lace and streamers of her bonnet like a bowsprit.

They had no oven or brewing kettle among their possessions, not even knives and forks. Most of their concern was given to a leather trunk containing Aunt Amelia's best bonnets. Their other worry was the safety of a china chamber of lavish pattern, which had a knitted wool cover over the lid to prevent sound.

Tristram did not welcome the pair. He bluntly told them they were too old to cope with hardships in a new land. He said they should stay at home. They resented him at once. Uncle Matthew stiffly told him to mind his own affairs. Matthew defended the old gentleman, and a coolness sprang up between him and Tristram that would not easily be overcome.

Asa went on board ship with quiet content. The day before leaving he had found a sunny corner of the garden free of frost and there filled an old leather sack with soft earth. He would take some of Yorkshire with him so that he could always see and touch it. His tools were kept in a strong oak chest and he put the sack of earth with them. The key to the brass lock of the chest he placed on a string he wore about his neck, and each time he fingered it he chuckled inwardly, greatly pleased with his secret.

Tristram hated the sea and the ship. He was not ill but a nausea was never far away, making him moody and short-tempered. Stormy weather set in during the third week at sea. There was a sickness that dragged, in some cases, to become a ship's fever, but April turned mild and gentle at the halfway mark. The air grew warmer and the ship became more oppressive to Tristram. He began asking the captain when they would sight land.

He was fathoming the nadir of wretchedness when Matthew hunted him out and tried, mistakenly, to hearten him.

"Coom on deck," he said. "Jonty's got all hands to play roundaboot."

"Noa," grunted Tristram, not stirring. "I want nowt wi' such foolery."

Matthew softened. "Art tha sorry tha coom?" he queried.

"I might be," admitted Tristram. "Happen I'd married and . . ."

He did not go on and they were silent a moment.

"Don't tha mind," cheered Matthew. "It's likely tha will find wife in Coomberland. Tha need a stronger than Unity."

Tristram sprang up in a rage and gave Matthew a buffet that sent him reeling. "Howd thy fool tongue," he gritted. "Art tha daft?"

In the morning Tristram heard shouting and rushed aloft. A night mist had lifted from the sea and on the horizon a faint low line hung against the sky.

"Land! Land!"

The shout was echoed the length of the ship. Yorkshiremen boiled up from below to stare over the pale-grey sea with wonder-struck faces. Even Uncle Malachy was revived by the news. He climbed on deck and croaked a cheer like the crowing of an aged rooster. Someone laughed at him, tremulous at first and then with wild guffaw, and soon everyone was laughing, with many of the women embracing and shedding happy tears. Before they scattered for their first meal of the day everyone stood in a group and their voices rang out, startling the gulls.

> Rejoice, the Lord is King;
> Your Lord and King adore;
> Mortals, give thanks and sing
>   And triumph everymore:
> Lift up your hearts, lift up your voice;
> Rejoice; again I say, rejoice—rejoice!

All day Tristram stood on deck, watching, giving no heed to those crowded about him or their shouted comments, and at noon the scent of land and forest came faintly on the air. There was scarcely a breath of wind but in the evening they saw the harbour mouth and the yellow lights of Halifax became cat's eyes in the darkness. Smells of the populated hillside hung heavy in the dusk and there was a shouting of welcome from wharves he could not see.

A cannon was fired somewhere to announce their arrival. He ate little supper and went back to the ship's rail to watch the shore, to listen to the barking of dogs, the singing of men as they left taverns, and to sentries, somewhere, calling out their rounds. On the wharf some drunken roisterers paraded noisily, howling derision at the ship. "From Hell, Hull and Halifax, Good Lord deliver us," they chanted. Tiring of their antic, they went away but the echoes of their bawlings seemed to hang about the wharf until long after.

It was late when he went below and, strangely, he thought of his mother. She had fought fiercely their idea of emigration, and here they were already. It was just as well, he reflected, that she had been unable to speak to him before she died.

In the morning he could see a dozen ships ranged along the water front. Boats were being rowed up and down the harbour and mewing gulls soared and dipped about them. A long sprawl of buildings lay on the slope above the water. This at last was Nova Scotia. The wide salt sea was behind them. Yorkshire was a memory.

The captain announced that the passengers would go by schooner to Fort Cumberland. The tidal rivers at the fort, he explained, would not admit the passage of large vessels. One schooner would sail as soon as a transfer of the people had been made. A second would go later. If any of the men wished they might walk overland forty miles from Halifax to Windsor, take a ferry to Partridge Island and walk another forty miles through wilderness to the fort.

Tristram saw to it that their belongings were among the first to be moved to the waiting schooner, and stared sullenly when Jonathan and Lancelot informed him that they were walking overland.

"I'd walk too, if I could," said Patience, standing by them. "It would be a champion lark."

Tristram snorted disdain and walked away. Jonathan gave Patience a brotherly kiss and Lancelot waved a hurried goodbye. They left the ship like a pair of lads on holiday, and Patience, watching them, laughed throatily. She felt exhilarated. The world was suddenly a grand adventure. She gazed at the shore line as their schooner got under way. She saw ragged dark greenwoods and bold rock. It looked untouched, primitive, a challenge to civilization. Overhead a legion of gulls wheeled in the free grace of the unfenced sky.

As she gazed, the Nova Scotia coast seemed to fade. She saw instead a flitting kaleidoscopic of Banfield. Her mother's red hands and heated face before the fire . . . the road bordered with fine oak . . . the elder in bloom . . . Tristram reaping golden barley . . . red and white cows standing in the shade . . . candlelight in the windows . . . waving larches in a rainstorm . . . baskets of cabbage on Jonathan's barrow . . . roast beef on the table.

Her every emotion ran its full gamut in the topsy-turvy picture. Then it had passed and there were only noisy sea birds and a fishing boat going home with the morning's catch.

The captain said there would be rain overnight and the wind's song in the rigging began to keen like minor violins. The goods on deck were lashed fast and covered with tarpaulin. By late afternoon the sky darkened. The deck became black and wild and scary, wet with heavy spray, and a lighted lantern was swung below.

The rain came, drumming on the deck as night set in. The schooner swayed and tossed. Someone, alarmed, extinguished the lantern. Asa, in his blankets, cackled with laughter. Blackness ruled. Blackness of varying shades of density. Blackness filled with the thin scream of an offshore breeze. In lulls there rose, pitifully, the moans and retchings of several who were sick.

Toward morning Patience discovered that Melody was awake and together they groped their way on deck. The shower was over but a thin skimming of clouds obscured the stars and the moon was only a dim glow, seeming to take light rather than give it to the world. The schooner, stripped of sail, rose and fell in a swirl of foaming water. Sheets of stinging spray swept over the side of the vessel.

"It's champion!" cried Melody. "Happen Nova Scotia will be like t' night, scary and wild. I'm so glad we coom."

In the morning a bright sun in a cloudless sky transformed the wilderness of the night into a field of tumbling white and blue. The schooner was under sail again, dipping and plunging in gay style. Tristram was sick at last, horribly sick. Asa, on deck with his daughters, chuckled over it, and they laughed with him. The captain said the wind was right for a quick trip up the Bay of Fundy, and he seemed in excellent humour.

II
Overland

JONATHAN AND LANCELOT decided they would be first to Cumberland. They had a brief look around Halifax, and bought a rifle exhibited for sale in a shop window beside a sign announcing that the proprietor could carve, professionally, head stones or hearth stones and also set copper. The rifle was a long weapon, its metal beautifully chased, its English make stamped on the stock. Jonathan added a bullet pouch and powder horn to his purchases, some trout hooks and lines, a knife and a small brass kettle.

"I wouldn't go to Cumberland," the stonecutter said. "Too far from tradin'. You go to Boston and you'll do fine."

"But," protested Jonathan, "thy Francklin coom to Yorkshire and towd thear wur plenty o' champion land for t' taking. Is he honest?"

"More honest than most. Land enough up there, too. But where will you sell what you raise? My advice is, take a boat to Boston."

They laughed at him and set off on the trail leading to Windsor. It was a rough path but they thrilled at the sight of new bushes and flowers, at fiddle heads of ferns pushing through old leaves, at clusters of mayflowers. They saw robins and jays and yellow hammers. Thickets of red maple were in bloom. Tasseled alders shed clouds of sulphur-coloured pollen by little brooks. They heard song sparrows in the bush and the mellow fluting of the hermit thrush. The white bloom of wild cherry and Indian pear splashed against the dark greenery of spruce and fir.

At a tavern they stayed the first night, eating a huge supper of rye bread, milk, eggs and bacon. In the morning

18

they were up early and asked their host about Cumberland. "You suit yourselves," he shook his head. "Sweet land up there, but where's your market?"

The ferry carried them to Partridge Island, a misnomer for a cove, and they were bedded roughly for the night at the log shack of a squatter. He gave them a breakfast of hasty porridge and they left him to follow the well-worn slot of an Indian trail over a ridge leading to River Hebert, from which a water route led to Fort Cumberland.

Late in the afternoon they made camp by a brook, constructing a crude bush shelter. Jonathan gathered dead sticks from a blowdown and placed them cunningly on paper-dry inner bark from a fallen tree. He took out his tinder box and struck the small steel rod on the rifle flint he kept screwed fast to the lid until a brighter spark flew and the filmy bark flared into flame. The fire took life from the dried sticks. The blaze caught hold and sent up curled strings of rusty smoke that smelled acrid and half-sweet.

Lancelot caught four fat trout which they fried in a fashion they had learned on Yorkshire moors, rubbing greasy fingers on their breeches. They drank scalding tea and finished with slabs of bread and cheese. Darkness had fallen when they were done and when they lay on their brush beds they could see a fine moon lamping over the ridge they had travelled.

The novelty of their situation kept Jonathan awake. He could hear the bubbling murmur of the brook and the distant yapping of a fox. Once a whisper of feathers sent a tingle up his spine. It was directly over his head and he saw the broad wings of an owl as it floated across the gleam of the moon. Then it was gone as though absorbed by the night.

When he woke past midnight he replenished their fire for the air held a chill. He could see mist rising from the stream. The morning would be grand and the sun would have summer heat. He snuggled down on his brush bed. It would suit him, he thought dreamily, to live in such a manner, hunting and fishing, sleeping where night found him. It occurred to him, then, that the world seemed a freer place since his mother had died.

The heat of the sun roused them. They ate and pushed on. By noon they were at the home of an Acadian settler, a small cabin in a stumpy clearing. The fellow had his black hair tied in two shiny pig-tails. He was working with a mattock, planting potatoes in loose earth between the stumps.

His chipped-log cabin was undaubed inside, for he said his wife, a smart, dark-eyed woman, would not live next to mud. Three silent children stared at the visitors with the momentary hostility and strange wistfulness of the young, then tried to sit on the same stool in one corner. There was a wide bed at the end of the cabin and a table in the centre. The Acadian placed slab benches beside it and invited his visitors to be seated to a serving of baked shad and boiled potatoes with pork bits as a side dish. His wife made them strong tea and a batch of barley biscuits.

The settlers answered questions in broken English. He had been on his land a few years but he did not own cattle. Times were hard. He had a small boat with which he attended shad weirs and if they liked he would take them part way to the fort. They looked at his small dory and whittled oars, then said they would keep on overland. The Acadian shrugged and went back to his planting.

His wife said an Indian trail that led westward was a short way to the fort, and she scratched with a stick in the soil, showing them a route to follow.

They spent another night in the bush, then pushed on over swampy land where midges stung them like hot needles and black flies reached under their hats, behind their ears, until their arms ached from fighting the pests. At dark they emerged in a clearing. They had reached Menoudie. Across Cumberland Basin's small neck, lay the fort. The settler another Acadian, gave them supper and a bed in his loft.

At flood tide the next morning the Acadian had them in his boat and he rowed them to Fort Cumberland, using a strong unhurried pull with a fisherman's tug at the end of it. He talked about the marshes, called the hay "broadleaf" and described the dykes his people had built.

Jonathan was disappointed in his first glimpse of the fort. The wooden roofs of the barracks shone in the sun but there were no stone walls or towers as he had imagined. Five ridges like long fingers reached toward the Basin, and tidal rivers flowed between the fingers.

They went to a settler's home and were entertained so eagerly that Lancelot was ill at ease. The settler was from Connecticut, he said, and had been eight years in the country. He had a fine, square-built house, with a chimney of brick in the centre contrived to take the smoke from four different fireplaces. The windows were all sashed, and numerous, making it a better lighted home than any in Banfield.

The farmer showed them the roomy cellar under his house, and his barn, clapboarded like the house, with shingled roof and a loft for hay and corn, with huge doors at an entrance wide and high enough to admit a loaded cart.

"Hoam," said Jonathan, "we stack oor grain. Thear is none wi' stable that will take cart inside."

He and Lancelot viewed the country from the highest ground. The marshes were more vast than they had thought, stretching for thousands of acres, their tidal rivers ugly red ditches when the sea had ebbed; the home of countless muskrats that had their homes in little run-offs and silts from the main streams; the nesting place of black ducks. Its smells were salty and strong and a million peepers sang at night from little pools near the upland.

The schooner fought contrary winds for a day and when it reached Cumberland Basin the captain reefed sail and waited a tide so that only Uncle Malachy and a few others were lying in blankets, indisposed, when they finally reached a berth at the fort creek.

Asa shouted and pointed. "T' fort!"

Above them, on a low ridge, was the outline of earthworks. Several buildings were scattered near it and a cart road led down to the creek. On either side of the fort ridge, stretching for miles, was a wide sea of new grass. Thousands upon thousands of acres of marsh.

On a faraway ridge, like another long finger, were squares

and oblongs of planted fields.   Blue supper smoke spiraled from the chimneys of several houses, imparting an impression of domestic security.

Everyone ate their evening meal on deck.   No one complained about cold food and stale water.   They could hear robins on the upland.   Distant cowbells tinkled and lambs blatted in the twilight.   Yellow lights began to twinkle on the ridges.   Finally Uncle Malachy crawled up from the hold. He tottered to the schooner's side and peered about him. "Here we are," he said to Aunt Amelia, who had brought him a stool, "and here we stay.   No man born of this world could induce me to cross that water again."

Aunt Amelia stared at him with widened eyes.   Then she had a quick look about her.   Smells of salty mud flats being uncovered by the receding tide permeated the evening, and the universe seemed filled with frog chorus.   The air had become chilly.

Suddenly she dropped her face to her hands and began to sob, making a rough, gasping noise of it.   Uncle Malachy turned to her nervously.   "I can't help it," she gulped. "I'm so afraid."

It was past sunrise when Melody and Patience, freshened by a quick scrubbing, went on deck.   A seaman was just placing the gangplank in position.   In a flash Melody had removed her shoes and stockings, for the grass was wet with dew.   "I'm going to be first to set foot on Coomberland," she cried.

She raced across the gangpank then, holding her skirts and petticoats free, she ran along the rutted way, jumped a ditch and called out as she saw blue violets in rich clusters. "It's champion land," she shrilled.   "It feels good underfoot."

Asa had followed her.   He knelt and felt the sod with his fingers, rose and inhaled the tang of the marshes as if he were savouring their future.

The Yorkshiremen roused.   Children scampered on the schooner's deck.   Slops were emptied overside.   Tongues wagged briskly.   Tristram began lugging chests and sacks

to a spot for unloading.   He was gaunt and pale from sea-
sickness.   Farmers with high-wheeled carts came down the
trail to remove the schooner's load to the fort barracks.
Melody helped Patience assemble their belongings.   She
looked overside and saw a pair of black-and-white oxen standing quietly, with the marsh wind scuffing cat's-paws in their
neck hair and wind tears rolling down their jowls.   Their
driver stood by, waiting, grinning at everyone, as if he were
offering them an official welcome to a new land.

III

The Indian Basket

TRISTRAM managed to engage the first carts and
thought he would be first to meet with Francklin's land
agent. He glowered with incredulity when he saw
Jonathan and Lancelot coming leisurely to meet him, and
learned that they had been a day in the area. They introduced Titus Green, the agent, a fellow who wore a little smile
on his face as if he had put it there and forgotten it, then
turned to the work of unloading in their unhurried fashion.
Tristram was vastly annoyed by the situation. They
offered no information regarding farms they had seen, so
he asked nothing. He treated Green with civility then left
him to talk with others while he went to visit farms on the
fort ridge to see for himself the fertility of the soil.

He loved good land with a passion almost pagan and was
determined to secure the best. The farmers of the ridge were
friendly, showing him their black-and-white cattle, like
Lancashire stock, their long-legged sheep, their geese and
turkeys; they showed him their upland fields, free of stone,
and the rich black marsh soil that needed no manure.

The marshes were greater than he had thought, but the
area, to him, looked too windswept, too open to the weather.
He did not like the idea of dyking in the spring and fall when
the tides were high, and after one day he had decided not to
settle on the fort ridge.

Jonathan and Lancelot ventured farther afield. They
crossed the marsh and followed an old Indian trail into wooded
areas. At home in Yorkshire when the urge was strong they
would take fishing lines and go away for a day, travelling
through bare flanks of pasture scarred with patches of brown

moor and ling between which sheep strayed up and down to crop short grass. There they had known noisy becks that tumbled over rocky ledges to form deep pools. Sometimes they fished keenly, taking home a fine string of trout; other times they wandered idly over ground dotted with brambles and dogroses until the day was gone. The Nova Scotia woods was, to them, a huge adventure. Their travel from Halifax had whetted their appetite for further roaming, and now that they could move leisurely they saw wild life in abundance, rabbits, porcupines, owls, partridge and a young moose. At night they returned to the fort and slept soundly on the heaps of straw piled for the newcomers on the rough barracks floor.

Tristram had little to say. He was wildly eager to acquire land and plant seed but the indifference of his brothers made him stubborn. It irked him that Matthew, who had always obeyed him, had become sullen. He would not discuss buying with his sisters, for he scorned their knowledge of good earth.

Three days after they were arrived at the fort he returned from a hard day of tramping to have Melody triumphantly tell him that Uncle Malachy had purchased a fine farm with all stock and equipment and several acres already sown. A widower had come from Amherst Point, a second ridge beyond the fort, asking for a buyer with cash.

"Matthew wur first to meet him," said Melody proudly. "He made t' bargain and he wur shrewd. Uncle Malachy said he would have paid twice as much. It's like he will leave t' place to Matthew." She paused, and shrugged. "It is too bad that Matthew had a drink wi' t' man after. They have rum here, and it made him silly."

Tristram was both angry and alarmed. He was irate at the thought of the bargain he had missed, jealous of Matthew's luck, and fearful of him acquiring a taste for liquor. He went at once to find him.

The day was warm and Matthew had been sick on the grass outside the barracks. He looked wretched but he tried to grin.

"Tha should let stuff be," rasped Tristram. "Tha will never get on if tha start to tamper wi' rum."

Matthew's grin faded. "I've found a bargain sooner than tha have done," he taunted.

"I'm fair hurt tha are going wi' Uncle Malachy," rejoined Tristram with the hurt in his voice. "I counted on thee for helping wi' oor farm."

"Aye." Matthew stood and faced him, his breath foul with rum sickness. "Tha thowt me cheaper than hired hand for plans which tha keep to thyself, but tha are mistaken. I'll go my way, and I'm as good a man as tha are."

"Tha have drunk overmuch," flung Tristram hotly, "and it's put silly tongue in thy head."

Matthew swaggered up to him and pushed him roughly. "I'm not so drunk but what I can put tha on thy back," he bantered. "Tha never would have handled Shubell if tha hadn't had him cooped wi' no room to move in Paddy's stall."

It was more than enough. Tristram struck, his blow catching Matthew's shoulder, spinning him around. He rushed, struck again, hitting Matthew in the ribs, hard. Matthew gasped, staggered backward. "Now tha'll have it," he swore, and charged.

He struck Tristram a terrific blow in the mouth. Simultaneously Tristram struck him, but Matthew's blow was hardest and he drove Tristram back under a flurry of wild swings. A girl cried out that the Crabtrees were fighting in the yard. Barrack windows were thrown open. A teamster spread his arms to hold everyone back. "It's a fair fight," he shouted. "Go on, young feller. Knock the devil out-a him. Hit him."

Tristram, breathless, spitting blood, set himself and smashed Matthew back, pounding him on head and shoulders but never getting set for a drive with his weight behind it. They grunted with the thud of their blows. A woman began crying for them to stop. She put her hands over her eyes and made moaning noises.

Matthew was being driven back. He rallied when he felt the barracks wall behind him and drove in with a punch that rocked Tristram on his heels, hit him again and, trying to follow his advantage, ran into a swing that knocked him down. Tristram blundered over him, fell on hands and knees, rose and was grappled by Matthew before he could strike.

Their struggle was like that of yoked oxen, a tremendous straining and wrenching. Then Matthew thrust a leg back of Tristram's, applied a trick he had learned in a fair wrestling ring and hurled Tristram backward. He fell on him and gripped his throat, his thumbs on Tristram's windpipe and his knuckles driven into the arteries under Tristram's ears.

Tristram rocked, tried to arch his back, writhed in agony, but Matthew was like a maddened beast sensing a kill. The teamster and Ezra Hodge tore him loose but Tristram was nearer dead than alive and lay on the ground for an hour, struggling in recovery.

Sobered, Matthew offered no truce or regrets. He let Uncle Malachy take him away to Amherst Point. Tristram was helped to a bunk in the barracks and lay there the rest of the day, his head throbbing, his throat a torture. For the first time in his life he had known fear. It had reached him when he failed to loosen Matthew's grip. His thinking culminated in an overwhelming nostalgia for Banfield and Unity. Remorse burned him until he slept, but the next day his energy had returned.

Some New Englanders told him there was fine rich land bordering the upper reaches of the Maccan River more than twenty miles from the fort. Plumley and Hodge agreed to go with him and explore it.

They borrowed horses and rode, crossing the Fort Lawrence ridge, to Amherst ridge, and on to Nappan. The houses were square buildings with plenty of upstairs room where there were large farms. In the smaller clearings the homes were often little better than cabins.

The land along the river was better than they had expected. Tristram forged ahead and grabbed for himself a choice area. He could scarcely hide his exultation from the others. He had watched carefully as they rode and knew the trail would permit the passage of ox carts.

He returned to the fort in great hurry. "I've bought oor place," he announced to the others as they ate. "Silas Plumley bought near. And Israel Hodge. It's fine soil. I've bought oxen and carts. We'll start tomorrow and t' others will go wi' us. T' place is called 'Bathol.'"

"I'm glad," drawled Lancelot, "that at least we know where we are going."

There was sudden silence. The brothers and sisters gazed at Tristram. He stared back at them. "I'm oldest," he said defiantly. "I've worked most on oor farm. Father can't do business, so I will."

"Thear are six o' us," said Jonathan. "Tha may have biggest share, but tha have no more than a share."

"Aye," flared Melody. "It's best we all know a-fore tha do more buying."

Tristram glowered at her but she met his gaze without flinching. He turned and slammed out of the barracks room.

June had come, with blundering beetles at the windows and moths beating at the candlelight. Rhodora bloomed on the pasture hills. Toad spit and spider webs on the grass were omens of warmer weather. The day was crawling down the fields as the first cart creaked along the fort road. Light yellows and bright greens, dew-washed, glittered as the first sun fingered the upland. A flock of crows rose out of woods on a hill to the east. Dogs on the fort ridge roused and began to bay and bark in alternate fright and challenge.

Six great carts were in the slow-moving procession. The women and children rode in them, settled, sleepy-eyed, among chests and sacks and spinning wheels. The men drove cattle and sheep. Their cries echoed over the marshes. Pigs squealed in boxes on the carts and crated poultry added to the clamour. The hour was thrilling to Tristram; he felt that destiny was guiding him to great achievement.

He watched Jonathan and Lancelot leading cows he had bought and cracking jokes with Melody who sat high on the second cart, her feet kicked free of shoes or stockings. He frowned but said nothing. She was strong and willing, doing her full share of a day's work, but she would brook no curbing from him. So he held his tongue and his glowering was as ineffectual as the cloud shadows that raced over the marsh grasses.

They veered across the marsh to Fort Lawrence. The cows had quieted to tame leading and they caused no trouble at a log bridge that trembled under the carts. The long convoy climbed the ridge, descended to another marsh and crawled toward Amherst. The oxen were panting and flies bothered them. Tristram decided he would rest them at Amherst ridge. He had good beasts and would take care of them.

There was a cluster of wigwams on the ridge, near a small brook. He stopped there so that everyone could view the encampment. The sheep and cattle drank thirstily and the drivers watered their oxen with buckets.

Melody slipped on her shoes and climbed down from the cart. She joined Tristram near the first wigwam and watched Indian children playing in a sand pile. Squaws sat in the sunshine, working with splints, making baskets. One carried a papoose. She looked a sullen creature, with smoke-sore scars about her eyelids, and she turned her back on them. The smudgy small eyes of the papoose unwinkingly watched from under a beaded hood, and the doll-like face was as expressionless as that of its mother.

A trio of younger squaws came with baskets and offered them for sale. They had husky voices. "Shillin'. Buy bas'et." An Indian with a pock-marked face advanced with arrogance. He looked stupid but his eyes were sly under a dirty cap of raccoon fur.

"You new people?" he queried.

"Aye," nodded Tristram, not liking the redskin.

"Goin' far?"

"Twenty miles."

"You trade potato for plant? We give bas'et. Moose moccasins?"

"Noa." Tristram disliked the sweetish Indian smell.

"Any tobac?"

"Noa."

Two squaws wearing cast-offs of linsey-woollen walked near and boldly stared at Melody's red hair.

"Beasts," she muttered, and went back to her cart.

"Two shillin'." A soft voice startled Tristram. He swung about and confronted a young Indian woman offering him a basket with a strong handle, similar to others he had refused. "You buy, please, from me. You fine man."

She walked as proudly as Melody.   Her features were well-made and even.   She had fine white teeth.   Her eyes were dark brown and watched Tristram like cats at a mouse hole. She wore a red jacket and skirt.   Her moccasins were prettily decorated with coloured beads.   "You buy from me," she coaxed.   "I glad you come.   You fine man."

The inflection of her voice set Tristram's pulse racing. He had refused to buy baskets from the others and she asked double the fair price.   Yet he found himself with the money in his hand.   She said 'T'ank you," and their hands met as she accepted the coins.   The touch of her fingers made him tingle hotly.   Then he was irritated.   She smiled, watching as he took the basket and tossed it up to Melody.   "We'll use it for seed potatoes," he called.

"T' Indians are laughing at thee," returned Melody with scorn.   "Tha paid twice what they wur asking.   T' girl just wanted to show what she could do."

"Never mind that," flung Tristram heatedly.   "We need t' basket."

"Tha should have bought it for a shilling, then."

"Keep thy tongue, will tha, lass."

"Noa, I won't.   I never thowt tha would act so soft. They smell."

"Don't tha say ony more."   Tristram had anxiety in his voice.   Every Indian was scowling.

At night they stopped by a farm in Nappan where the Chipleys and a Lother family were building.   The farmer, Henry Niles, was a loquacious fellow.   He said he had lived on his land for many years.   He invited the women to the house for the night and said the men could sleep in the barn loft.

Tristram gladly unyoked his oxen.   The day had been lucky and here was a fenced yard for their sheep and cattle.

Mrs. Niles was a big woman.   Her kitchen was roomy, with plenty of rush-bottomed chairs, but her hand-split table needed scrubbing.   She helped place planks on benches outside the house and was generous with salt shad and rye bread as the women prepared a meal for the entire party. When they had eaten she joined with her husband in finding fault with the country. "The winters are too hard," she said, "and there's little to sell."

"What about pigs?" asked Israel Hodge.

"Hard to fence," answered Niles. "They take too much tendin'."

"But boats will come if there's enough in this country to buy?"

"Maybe. They'll buy pork for the sojers at Windsor. But you'll find it killin' work to clear land. I ain't got half my land stumped yet."

Tristram climbed down from the barn loft before it was light and fed the oxen from Niles' mow. Then he went to the house and asked Patience to rouse the women. They built a fire and had eggs fried and tea made before Mrs. Niles appeared, frowsy and yawning. "Mercy on us," she shrilled. "I never heard of gettin' up so early. You'll tame down after a year in this country. I couldn't git Henry to stir."

The sun had not risen when Tristram headed the first team out of the yard. Darkness still pooled in the hollows but the shadows were slipping from the slopes. As they reached the first upland brook and watered the cattle, the first brightness of the day caught the top of dykes along the river and a lone gull sailed in from the Bay, white and high and clean in the light of the new morning.

The sheep had become accustomed to travel, the ewes following the carts where their lambs were crated. Rests were frequent as the day became warm. Tristram wanted all the stock to be in good condition when they reached their destination. At Maccan a pretty girl rode by on a spirited horse, almost colliding with the carts as she waved to Lancelot. He waved back at her. She swung into a farm lane then reined in to watch the procession rumble past.

"Come back and see me," she called to Lancelot.

"Put a candle in thy window tonight," he laughed. "Tell thy mother I'm to coom."

They followed the Maccan River until they were away from the salt marshes, above reach of the Fundy tides. Wide intervales spread the river valley and the upland sloped to hardwood hills. "We'll soon be thear," shouted Tristram.

"We've forty acres t' Cajuns used to crop and another lot that needs ony t' small bush cleared. We'll be planting afore week's oot."

The trail became deeply rutted around alder swales. They would have two New England families as neighbours, Tristram explained. One was Solomon Smith, who owned a water mill and had a yard piled with dry sawn lumber; the other was Gabriel Garrison. He had a wooden leg, five sons and five daughters.

When they rested he said that their farm was really two holdings, with a vacant house apart from where they would build. He hoped, in a few years, to fence in the second place. Its stable had been blown down but there was a well that could be easily cleaned.

It was during the last mile that they reached a miry brook crossing and the smaller Plumley oxen could not haul their heavy load. Tristram took his team back and ran a long chain from their yoke to the Plumley cart pole. He was proud of the cattle he had bought and of his ability to handle them. They were alike in colour and larger than any other oxen he had seen. He admired them as they rested for the pull, the sweep of their horns, the roll of brawn that backed their yokes, their puncheon bodies and rump muscles.

"T' mud is deep here," said Silas Plumley anxiously. "We should have a third team."

"Tha watch," said Tristram quietly. He made sure of the chain to the pulling pole, reached gently to the middle horns and pulled them down. "Ready, Buck." He kept his voice low. "Ready, Lion. Now!" The great bodies settled into the yoke, quaked with effort, and the cart rolled from the slough, its wheels dripping slobs of black slime.

"Whoa, lads." Tristram stood from his beasts and watched them raise their snow-white muzzles high as they always did after a hard pull, then lower them as their heaving sides became more quiet. "Tha'll not better that pull wi' ony beasts in Yorkshire."

The Hodges turned into a lane leading to a substantial-looking house with a brick chimney in its centre. It had

clapboards on the side and a shingled roof. An acreage of
plowed land was ready for seeding.

"Home!" shouted Israel Hodge, like a boy. "Put t' cows
to pasture."

"They paid hundred pounds for yon place," said Tristram,
catching up with Jonathan, "and they've cattle and sixty
cartloads o' manure to good. Man who had it stayed abed
late. Drank rum first go in t' morning."

"They don't like work," shrugged Jonathan. "Niles keeps
his cows in t' barn so he won't have to go for them in morning.
I towd him he'd have extra bucket o' milk if they wur back to
pasture. He said he'd sooner do wi' less than go oot in wet
grass."

"We'll show them Yorkshire ways," shouted Tristram. He
drove his oxen from the trail to a spot on a horseshoe slope
overlooking the river and sheltered by wooded hills. A small
cellar pitted its centre and wraiths of a path were there
leading to a spring, ringed with flat stones. A dozen apple
trees graced one flank and a red-tipped rose bush survived
near a group of elms that gave it shade. At the top of the
slope, near a stand of dark spruce, an ancient willow stood in
silhouette, life gone from all but a few of its branches.

"My!" cried Melody. "It's more bonny than ever I thowt
it would be."

The site was a beautiful one, though Melody knew its
beauty meant nothing to Tristram. He had seen only the
spring of pure water, the gentle slope providing good drainage
and the natural shelter from north-easters. She gazed and
saw where their house should be, a spot just far enough from
the elms and providing the best view of the river.

"Thear," she pointed, "is t' place for oor house. I'll
mark it wi' posts."

"Give over," snorted Tristram roughly. "Get busy wi'
summat."

Jonathan and Lancelot herded the cattle near the carts
and began some of the unloading. Asa had ridden in the first
cart, seldom speaking throughout the journey. Tristram,
watching him, saw that he was a tired old man. It was
possible that he might not live through a hard winter. It

would be just as well. An old person was of no use on a farm, and how could they enjoy life?

Asa climbed stiffly to the ground and looked around. Then he saw the ancient willow and went up the slope, his hat in his hand, his hair floating like a halo around his bald pate. Finally he stood by the tree and patted it, as if he had expected to find it there. Then he turned to survey the reach of river and intervale.

Melody and Jonathan had watched him. "He always likes a tree," said Melody. "It's like he'll call that one his own, and I hope he does. He'll need summat to keep him from thinking o' home."

"He'll have chance to use his tools when we build," said Jonathan. "All way he's stayed by his chest like it wur filled wi' gowd."

In the moment Melody thought of her mother. They had not mentioned her from the day they left Banfield. None of them had been able to summon much grief. They had had a sense of lifted restrictions that outweighed all other emotions. Patience had seemed thrilled to have authority in the kitchen. Yet they had been glad to leave. When it was still, Melody had imagined she heard her mother's urgings in every corner of the cottage.

Now, in the fading light, as they looked about, she seemed to see her mother's red hands and heated face before a cooking fire, to hear her strident voice. Then the notion passed and she breathed more freely.

They would put up a pole shelter until the crops were in, Tristram said as they unyoked the oxen. They piled goods at the ends of the carts and made beds in the centre; put the tired cows and their calves to sweet intervale pasture. Then they sat on stools around a cooking fire and ate bowls of potato soup.

Over at the left, at easy borrowing distance, the bulk of a small house was a dark blur. Tristram said that a young New Hampshire couple had lived there. He said no more, but remembered everything Solomon Smith had told him. The young settler's parents had lived there, too, and both had died of lung fever. Then the wife had died, and the young

widower left the place.   While he had walked about the area,
exploring, Tristram had found a grave with a wooden slab at
its head.   He had deciphered the lettering: "In Memory of
Jane, wife of Philip Tibbets, who died in child birth, age 20.
Her infant buried in her arms."

Child birth! He had wrenched the board from its place
and hurled it into a bush tangle.   It would never do to have
Unity find such a grisly marking.

It became dark and they were aware of distant cowbells.
The oxen ceased feeding and lay down.   A full moon rose
over the tree tops.   The ewes, tired and nervous in new
surroundings, fidgeted themselves into positions for the
night under one of the carts.   The fowl in the crates quieted.
Tristram stretched and gazed around the moon-whitened
fields, made a rough bed on sacks of seed grain, and slept.

He tried to think of Unity as he drowsed but his dreams
were of an Indian girl with fine white teeth who smiled at him
and said "Two shillin'."

IV
Matthew Wins a Brown Mare

MATTHEW had spent several holidays with Uncle Malachy as a boy and had been a favourite with the old gentleman. He had helped the elderly couple stow their belongings on board the ship. Each day he had visited them. The Chipleys occupied the next cabin and so he chanced to become better acquainted with Sylvia Chipley, a big, blonde girl, who seemed painfully shy.

"Would tha like to walk on deck?" he asked her one evening.

She shook her head but when he insisted she went with him, walking so as not to touch his arm. After a time they rested by the schooner's side and talked about the stars. Soon they looked forward to their evening together.

One night the lurching of the ship slid them together and all at once he was aware of the warmth of her shoulder and hip, of her soft flexing against him. Almost without thinking he put his arm about her and although she tensed she did not push him away. She had tussles with him and he found her amazingly strong. When his hands found her breast by accident she was not too quick to push them away, and the discovery emboldened him. He kissed her, an awkward peck on the cheek, and resolved to marry her.

Nearing Nova Scotia stormy weather sickened several, and Sylvia was among them. She did not recover to any extent and the Fundy voyage was rough. She was pale and indifferent when they landed at the fort, scarcely looking his way. In a week he had forgotten about her.

The farm Uncle Malachy purchased at Amherst Point was on a knoll above the marsh that faced Menoudie. The house

36

was roomy, with plenty of windows.   There was a long barn,
a sheep pen, a shed for carts and a pigsty.   From the road the
place had an imposing appearance, and Matthew felt his
importance as he plowed and harrowed and seeded.   Each
time he rested his cattle he thought of Tristram, and resolved
he would have the better farm no matter how hard he had to
work.

Uncle Malachy, dressed in his velvet small clothes and
carrying a cane, visited in Amherst village, but was soon
content to walk about his farm and marvel at the extent of
the marshes.   The villagers drank too much rum, he said.
They told him he would do the same after a time.   The
eternal wind from the Bay that riffled the marsh grass and
sighed at doors and windows summer and winter, rain in
and snow out, would break his endurance.

Matthew thought such talk but an excuse for drinking and
kept away from the houses.   He never tired of watching the
tide ebb from the great mud flats so that farmers could go with
drag sleds to their brush weirs.   They sold the best fat shad
at threepence, and crow-picked ones for a penny.   Aunt
Amelia baked them and fried them, learned to make a treat
of shad chowder with salt pork and rye bread.   She worked
hard in her fluttery, disorganized fashion and by mid-summer
was so ailing that Matthew decided she must have help.

The nearest neighbour was Gideon Danks, a single man.
He was a giant with a great black beard, standing six feet four
in his bare feet, weighing two hundred and eleven pounds
stripped.   His voice boomed like a drum and his good-
humour was contagious.   He had a farm with snug buildings
but only worked as the spirit moved him.   His boast was that
he had spent ten years among the Indians, learning their ways.
He wore moccasins at all times and an odd cap of wildcat
skins that made him look taller than he was.

"I'm Gid Danks," he shouted the morning he rode into
Uncle Malachy's barnyard.   "I live next door, when I'm
workin'.   Mostly I'm too full of wild meat and Injun tricks
to stand the squeeze of four walls more'n a few weeks at a
time."

He rode a black stallion with thick heavy mane, a strong

brute that kicked and slashed and squealed like a demon under his whip.

"I never like a tame hoss or woman," he roared.

He tied the raging black to a hitching post and strode into Aunt Amelia's kitchen. "You look right snug already," he commented. "It'll take plenty of elbow grease, though, to keep a shine on all this crockery. You thinkin' of gettin' married?"

Matthew shook his head and grinned. He liked Gideon. "I'm young," he said. "Plenty o' time."

"Don't be too sure." Gideon stroked his beard with a flourish. "Thought the same myself and put off lookin'. Here I am nigh thirty and still alone."

He had brought a mess of new potatoes and beans, and needed no urging to stop for dinner. He would be proud, he said, to lend a hand any time. "Every tub has to stand on its own bottom, more or less," he bellowed at Uncle Malachy, "but Christians help each other. Ask Gid anything you want to know. He only lies to Injuns."

Aunt Amelia piled his plate high and he accepted her attentions with decorum. "You'll do fine till winter," he prophesied, "and then you'll wish for Yorkshire. The wind gets the chill of a jackass breeze and the snow drifts six feet on the roads. All you'll see of neighbours is chimney smoke. But if you stick it five or six years nothin' can take you away."

After dinner Gideon walked out in the field to look at Matthew's garden of parsnips and pumpkins and cabbages. "You're a hustler," he praised, "and I'll say you know good earth." He ran a speculative eye over Matthew's proportions. "You're a good size," he allowed. "You ought to be good on a lift. A little more reach and you'd be good as I am."

Matthew's pulse began to beat faster. "Want to bet wi' me," he bantered, "that I can't throw thee two oot o' three?"

"Ho, ho," roared Gideon. "Yorkshire feels his oats. Done, my young rooster. I'll stake my black hoss you can't throw me one out of three."

They doffed hats and jackets and faced each other on the sod beside Matthew's potato rows. Their rush and clinching was a shock of bone and muscle. Their heels dug inches in the turf. They heaved and grunted. Swung around. Wrenched apart. Gripped again. But Matthew, winner of many a bout at Yorkshire fairs, achieved an under arm he wanted and he was like a grizzly in strength. He withstood every desperate counter Gideon could contrive. Then he thrust with hip and heel. Gideon struggled wildly, crashed his full length with Matthew on top. And was pinned, fairly.

"The devil has britches!" gulped Gideon, breathless. "I didn't know the man lived who could do that. You tricked me grand and you didn't learn that in your father's barn."

Matthew helped Gideon to his feet. "Want to try again? I'll change t' bet to three oot o' three."

"Done," puffed Gideon. "I wish I knew that trick with your knee."

They circled more warily than before. Then Gideon charged. Matthew avoided him as he had seen carnival wrestlers do at home, caught an arm and swung his man around. He seized him before he could recover, drove a knee back of Gideon and threw himself, taking the bigger man with him. Before they hit ground his momentum had twisted Gideon underneath. He was again the winner.

"Enough," panted Gideon.

"Tha are strong," said Matthew. "Tha'd soon learn to throw me."

"Don't reckon I'll trouble. You've won my hoss, Yorkshire."

Matthew suddenly realized that Gideon meant what he said. "Noa," he protested. "It wur not fair. I've been trained in holds. Thear wur a wrestler in village back home."

"No diff'rence, lad," boomed Gideon. "I'd taken something of yours if you had lost. We make a bet in this country."

"But I don't want thy horse," persisted Matthew. "I don't ride ony but a quiet beast."

"Then you can't handle my hoss," agreed Gideon. "I'll give you my brown mare. She's a hoss for wimmen. Gentle, and moderate young. I won her in a shoot. She'll do for the gal you marry one of these days. First rainy morning I'll bring her over."

He went to the stallion, waving his arms and shouting. The stallion kicked and squealed. It reared as Gideon mounted, but it had made no attempt to strike at him as Gideon undid the hitching rope. Matthew grinned. The horse, like the man, was a show-off. Powerful, pleasing to look at, dangerous sounding; yet under it all no hostility or mean action.

Oh, Mary Jane came down my lane to claim my lovin' boy; Her eye was wild, her temper b' iled because she'd been his toy . . .

The song rolled back across the field, boisterous, fantastic. Matthew looked at the trampled sod and felt good. He had made a fine friend.

Gideon came with the brown mare. It was a rainy morning and Matthew was resting in his mow of upland hay, listening to the drip from the barn eaves. He had had fine weather for mowing and raking and carting. Uncle Malachy had tried, one day, to swing a scythe, then had returned to the kitchen to help Aunt Amelia. She had grown gaunt as a skeleton and was never caught up with her work.

"Here's Annabelle," boomed Gideon. "Come and git acquainted. She likes a lump of sugar, jist like a gal. There, now, let her nuzzle your hands so she'll know you. Better put her in young pasture."

The brown mare trotted into the field and seemed satisfied. Gideon turned to Matthew. "Like rum?"

"Not much," said Matthew. "Oor folk don't favour hard drinking."

Gideon nodded approval. "Them's right ideas. Too much likker is ruin-ashun. Have a snort of this cider. It perks a man up on a rainy day."

Matthew had drunk ale and north country beer at the Fairs. He took the jug and had several drinks. The cider warmed him, made him exuberant. They tried to outdo each other in swinging by the arms from beams. Before the jug was empty each man had fallen into the hay several times and their shouts scared poultry, squawking, into the rain.

Uncle Malachy came to call them to dinner, and was

astounded. Gideon apologized profusely. Matthew had become sleepy. Gideon took him to the house and put him to bed. Then he sat at the table and ate with great gusto. When he was gone Uncle Malachy went to the barn. He found the cider jug and smashed it against the door sill.

It was evening when Matthew aroused. He went out to the field behind the barn and was sick, then walked the lane until he felt better. The rain was over and the morrow would be fine. He went back to the house and sat at the supper table with his thick shoulders hunched like a man unsheltered in a storm. But Uncle Malachy and Aunt Amelia made no reference to Gideon or his jug.

At candle lighting Gideon rode over on his black stallion. Matthew heard him coming, singing. "Oh, Mary Jane came down my lane . . ." Gideon laughed uproariously as he saw the shattered jug. "Glad you're about," he whooped at Matthew. "I had you on my conscience all the afternoon. I've got to teach you to hold your likker."

Uncle Malachy came from the house. "Can you tell me where I can hire a likely lass?" he asked. "My wife is not well."

Gideon removed his fur cap as if it would help his thinking. "There ain't many likely wenches," he said. "There's an Irish one in the village or you might git Polly Clews. She's simple, but a fair worker."

"Please get me the Irish one," said Uncle Malachy. "I'll pay a fair wage."

Gideon rode off at a thunderous rate and was gone an hour. "No luck at all," he boomed as he returned. "The Irish girl's gone to work at Maccan, and Polly won't come. She lives in a house back of the village, if you want to try coaxin' her."

Aunt Amelia had heard Gideon in the yard and in the morning she began working again, stating her resentment against any girl coming into her kitchen. She said the rain had bothered her nerves but the sun had brightened her, and Matthew let it go at that.

It was the next day that he saw Polly Clews. She was a well-made girl with yellow hair and china-blue eyes. Her dress, of calico, was too small for her, had ripped under the arms.   It outlined her firm high breasts.   She was barefoot and had been picking blueberries.   When she stopped by the fence and stared at him he thought of Sylvia Chipley.

"Good day," he said.   "Art tha Polly Clews?"

She nodded.   Her wooden bowl was filled with berries, cleanly gathered.

"Can tha do cooking?"

She nodded, watching his face.

"Washing?"

She nodded again.

"Would tha work for us?   We live in yon white house." He pointed.

Polly shook her head.   "I'm silly.   Pa says I'll never have good sense."

"But tha can work.   Will tha coom?"

She wriggled her toes in the grass.   "Would you like me?" she asked, and giggled.

"I'd like tha to help my aunt," he said.   "Tha look strong."

She giggled more.   "Pa says if I were strong in my head as I am in the back I'd be good as two girls."

"We'd pay tha ten shillings a month," coaxed Matthew. "Will tha coom?"

He suddenly wanted her and it was not entirely of Aunt Amelia that he was thinking. Polly was a half-wit but she had a woman's allure.   He was not sure of his intentions but he wanted her at the house.

She shook her head.   "I'm twenty.   I want to git married." She turned her fine straight back to him and walked away with unconscious grace.

Uncle Malachy was caught in a heavy shower in late September.   He had found blackberries on the marsh and was there with a bowl when the downpour began.   His jacket was drenched through at once and the day was cold.   When he reached the house he was shaking with chill and Aunt Amelia was so flustered that it was half an hour before she made him a hot drink.   By night he was in a fever and Matthew asked Gideon to ride to the village for the medico, Danny O'Conner, a rum-sodden ship's doctor driven ashore. O'Conner came, sober and gruff, and said he had been called too late.

Hot bricks wrapped in flannel were placed at Uncle Malachy's feet and mustard poultices were applied to his back and chest. He was given bitter herb potions and kept warmly covered but he steadily grew worse. In delirium he held a hearing of a gipsy roost robber at Banfield. Then he threshed about under the blankets, demanding that Gideon be sent for. Exhausted, finally, he lay in a stupor. At noon of the third day he died and Aunt Amelia collapsed from over-strain. Matthew went for Gideon. The big man returned with him and moved with exaggerated care. He washed Uncle Malachy's frail body and prepared it for burial as decently as a woman would have done, then sat by the fire and turned a roast of beef expertly.

In the morning Aunt Amelia refused the breakfast Matthew offered her but Gideon took the platter of eggs and bacon and went up the stairs. Matthew could hear his rumbling voice overhead and when he came down the platter was empty. "I kin handle old wimmen, Yorkshire," he boasted, "but gals of an age I want to marry has me beat. I wonder why a man is made that way."

He rode to the fort and induced the parson to come and conduct the funeral. They buried Uncle Malachy in the Amherst cemetery, on a slope out of range of the marsh wind. Crickets sang under the pole fence near-by. Swallows were leaving and there was goldenrod along the cart trails. Choke cherries were ripe and a west wind blew white mare's tails over the blue fall sky. Parson Eagleson, a bony man with a nose whittled by marsh winds, let himself go with a sermon strung on high-sounding phrases, as if he had known Uncle Malachy's fondness for them.

When they returned to the house Aunt Amelia did not want to go in. Gideon whispered that she should be humoured for a time and told Matthew to fetch her a chair. Matthew hurried inside, stopped and stared. Someone was sitting on a stool by the fireplace and a bright blaze revealed a red ribbon in her yellow hair. It was Polly Clews.

"I've come," she said, and giggled.

V
Melody's Bowl of Milk

MELODY CRABTREE'S most treasured possession was her mother's Bible. It was bound in calfskin and had a heavy silver clasp. Its entries went back over half a century but there were two she knew best. The first one was dated "June 20, 1743." It read: "Married this day Asa Crabtree, of Banfield, County of Yorkshire, England, to Hannah Scurr, also of Banfield, by Rev. Henry Perkman. A fine day. Forty-two sat to dinner." The second entry she knew best was on the next page. "Born February 10, 1753, a daughter, Melody Crabtree. A stormy night and hard labour."

She kept the Bible wrapped in an old petticoat so that its covers would not become marred, and promised herself often that some day she would begin and read every chapter in the Book.

Their life in the pole shelter thrilled her. She did not mind sleeping in the cart until the seeding was finished. It was fun to boil clothes over an open fire by the river, and at the same time keep an eye on the dark-wooled old ewes and their white-fleeced and inquisitive young lambs. She sang and whistled, morning and night, and laughed without restraint when Tristram, blundering to bed in their make-shift lodging, upset their precious store of salt so that it was spoiled.

The next morning she went to the Garrison home to borrow. Patience was timid about such an errand and the men had no time for it. A dog yapped and raced with a bevy of children that ran to meet her. "Ma," they screeched, "here's a woman come."

Mrs. Garrison appeared from her house as her husband

emerged from his stable. He was a round little man with a wooden leg painted a dark red. His woollen shirt was dark with sweat and he looked as if water were hard to come by. His wife towered inches above him. She greeted Melody warmly, saying she hoped the Yorkshire folks had come to stay.

Melody mentioned her errand. Gabriel Garrison removed his hat with elaborate politeness and said they would be glad to loan anything they possessed, even one of their "rabbits." He patted the nearest child on the head and evinced his pride in his brood.

Mrs. Garrison sniffed. "He's free with his tongue, Gabe is." There was a squall from the kitchen and she returned with an infant tucked under her arm. "Come in and set," she invited. "This one needs nursin'."

She enthroned herself in a home-made chair, opened her dress and set the baby to nursing. It puffed and squirmed, feeding noisily throughout the conversation. "You've purty hair, dearie," said Mrs. Garrison. "My, you look fresh." She sighed. "I were like that when I married Gabe. Do you like it here?"

"Aye, we do," said Melody, wishing she had the salt.

"It's bad in winter. I were riz in town and I don't ever git used to it. Anybody courtin' you, if I may ask?"

"Noa," said Melody, flushing. "Could I have t' salt, please?"

"Certain you can." Mrs. Garrison raised her voice as the infant squalled. "Laviny—come and git the salt for the lady. There's so many jars I never kin remember which is salt, but Laviny knows. Her and Molly jist about run the house. Molly's fourteen and she's learned to read from her pa. She knows some Injun words, too."

"Are there Indians around here?" Melody remembered Amherst.

"They come and go. You'll have them droppin' in for bread and 'lasses. Pa swaps with them. He gits axe handles and baskets. There's one he don't like, a bad-tempered one with pock marks. The rest is welcome."

"We won't feed them," decided Melody. "We never gave onything to t' gipsies at home."

"Injuns is diff'rent.   I'd treat 'em civil."

Laviny brought the salt and Melody accepted it gratefully. She was pleased when Molly, the most attractive of the family, walked a way back with her.

On their first Sunday at Bathol, Jonathan took the rifle he had purchased at Halifax and pampered it with rag and oil.   "Want to walk in t' woods?" he invited Melody.

"This is no heathen land," said Tristram harshly.   "Put t' gun away."

Jonathan put it away.   "Meat wouldn't keep onyway," he said.   "I'll wait till fall.   But we'll have oor walk just t' same."

Melody sang as they went up the slope.   The people at the fort had told her about the sugar maples.   They were trees with sweet sap, and farmers notched them in spring so that the fluid ran into bark containers.   The sap, boiled long enough, produced a syrup sweeter than honey.   She wanted to see the trees.

It was cool and quiet as night in the woods.   Brown rabbits crossed their path. They found a trail and followed over the hardwood ridge.   They saw the maples, gashed with many scars.   But the path ran eastward and across a barren, then to a brook where two trees were felled to serve as a bridge.

They rested in a glade warmed by the sun.   Star flowers and pink-veined wood sorrel were abundant.   The long, dreamy notes of the wood peewee were mingled with sharp calls of olive-tinted flycatchers.   The day grew almost sultry and Jonathan pointed to white thunder-heads gathering over the hardwoods as they heard the hollow cries of the black-billed cuckoo or "rain-crow."

A clump of raw ash stumps offered evidence of intruders who used hatchets.   "This is oor land," said Jonathan.   "It's Indians who cut trees.   Thear is plenty o' ash so we'll say nowt.   We have trouble enough wi'oot t' Indians."

"Trouble?" Melody stopped walking.

He nodded.   "Aye.   We'll have to settle wi' Tristram sooner or late.   He has all t' money.   None o' us know how much.   When t'hoose is oop we'll have a settlement."

Melody's heart beat fast.   She could remember the fight

Jonathan had had with Tristram over Unity. For years Jonathan and Unity had played together, and then Tristram had started to press his attentions. They were only in their late 'teens but Tristram was nearly full grown. He had tried to crush Jonathan with sheer weight and strength, but Jonathan had been too quick for him. It was in a field where none could see but herself and she was too frightened to run for help. Time and again it seemed that Tristram's ferocity would triumph, but he was tired and cut and bleeding when their father chanced that way. Jonathan, unmarked, was far the fresher, and would likely have won.

"What makes him so?" she cried. "Thear's times, Jonty, when he don't seem oor brother."

"He's like Matthew," said Jonathan, relaxing to whimsical humour, "and they fought."

They went back to the clearing to find Silas Plumley at the pole shelter with his Bible in hand. The threat of rain had passed. Abel was there, sitting silent as usual. "We've waited for thee," said Silas. "It's t' Sabbath and we can have a service here if tha will lead t' singing."

Melody saw the Hodges in the background. There was Israel, his wife, their sons, Nathan and Ezra, with Mrs. Plumley and Hannah, her daughter. They nodded cheerfully. Silas had a sonorous voice and he read with fervour from the Psalms. His listeners sat on stools, benches, chests, or the ground, and every head bowed as he prayed.

"Oor Heavenly Father we coom before Thee in humble spirit to thank Thee for Thy mercies and benefits received. We ask a continuance o' Thy rich blessings. Thee has browt us safely o'er a great distance and Thee has given us guidance to a goodly land. Grant us strength and health for t' tasks before us, and wisdom in oor judgments. Help us earn oor daily bread. Forgive us oor trespasses as we forgive them that trespass against us. Sustain us when we are weak. In Thy name we give oor thanks. Amen."

Then they sang. Lancelot's clear tenor held the high notes and the music rolled over the fields so that cattle raised their heads to listen.

Tristram worked early and late, working his oxen to the limit. He sowed his seed with greatest care, selecting the plots for the different grains. The others gave no opposition to his planting schemes but with the choosing of a site on which to build they were different. Melody had placed small stakes to mark her selection and when Tristram tried to ignore her Jonathan faced him.

"We'll have say o' t' house," he announced. "Tha have done seeding as tha wanted, and we said nowt. Now it's oor turn. I've talked wi' carpenters from Maccan and they will coom and help us. T' house will be whear Melody wants."

Tristram gazed at them in turn. He stood as if realization of what they said were a tremendous effort. The silence extended, became grim, then he surrendered. "It will do as well thear as ony place," he said indifferently, and walked away.

It was easy to clear the cellar and enlarge it. Then Garrison came and built a wall of heavy stone hauled from the river. Tristram yoked the oxen and drew timbers from Smith's mill. Asa, Jonathan and Lancelot worked with the Maccan carpenters at the framing.

A day was set for the raising. Everyone in Bathol attended, as well as a dozen men from Maccan. With them was Peter Meekins, a young man with red hair, handsome in a rough way and bold enough with it. The women came, riding farm plugs, bringing baskets heaped with food.

The joists and timbers arose as if by magic. Melody felt a leap inside of her as the first rafters swung into place. Here was their home and what was to happen would happen. It was being built where she had chosen and she would not leave it unless there was strong need. The pounding of hammers filled the air. Boards passed from hand to hand. The sun was hot and dry. Locusts sang by the woods and the men said hay would ripen early.

The next week Michael Francklin came to Cumberland, visiting the fort and every village. It was said he also visited the Indians. Melody thrilled when she saw him ride into the field to talk with her brothers. She baked barley biscuits and a salmon Lancelot had caught at the river. When Francklin came in she made her best curtsey.

"Melody!" He rolled her name on his tongue. "For a week I've met newcomers but not a prettier lass have I seen in all my travels. Lucky will be the man who finds your favour, and sore his trials if he does not please you."

The others gazed as if they did not understand and Tristram frowned darkly, but Melody smiled as she tossed her chin and did not permit herself to become confused. "I hope," she said pertly, "that tha do not think it easy to flatter me."

"Not at all," laughed Francklin. "I'll visit again, with your permission, and see if I am not right in my judgment."

He complimented Patience on her deftness with kettle and ladle, talked with Tristram about seeding and with Jonathan about Yorkshire moors. He lingered after their meal to admire Asa's carving and a salmon spear Lancelot had fashioned. When he left he had them feeling he was an old acquaintance.

The Maccan carpenters stayed at their work and the last shingles were on when Tristram finished stacking his upland hay. Then the neighbours came again and raised the barn, boarding it in and laying the floor of clean yellow planks in a single day. After supper Jonathan hung a lantern to a beam and Garrison produced his fiddle. The younger folk shuffled the "half-moon" and "scamperdown" with such high spirits that Mrs. Garrison's infant awoke in the new house and cried. Her husband bounced around on his wooden peg and predicted that the first-born in the home would be a boy, and that Tristram would be the father. The men cheered and Tristram went outside, looking surly as a bear.

They forgot him and danced again, with the young men eager to have Melody as a partner. She tried to be impartial, but there was high feeling until Solomon Smith, who was celebrating his fiftieth birthday, grabbed her in hairy arms and kissed her, saying he would be the first in Bathol to have that pleasure. Melody was taken by surprise, but she set him back on his heels with a slap to the chin and Garrison roared, pounding the floor with his stump, that you could not blame either of them for what they had done.

It would have ended fine enough if the dancers had let it go at that, but Peter Meekins tried to kiss her, saying he would not be outdone by an older man. Melody pushed him away fiercely, fought herself free and ordered her hair, her bosom rising with deep and angry breathing. Abel Plumley, looking on, had seen enough. He snagged Meekins by the collar, dragged him outside and flung him heels over teacup. Meekins fell awkwardly, striking his head on a stick and Mrs. Plumley had to burn a feather under his nose to bring him back to consciousness.

A dozen voices told Meekins he had received what he deserved so he sulked a while, then told Melody that he was sorry. She gave him a smile and danced with him again but watched her chance and thanked Abel for his interference.

The broad pine boards of the house floors were laid by Jonathan and by the time tall fireweed was brilliant among tangles of raspberry bushes near the mill the Crabtrees had moved in. It would be some days before the upstairs was finished completely but Melody picked a room under the eaves that overlooked the river and was so happy the first night that she could not sleep.

She made a favourite of Molly Garrison but she romped with the others as well and learned to use a moosehide sling as well as the boys. Mrs. Smith, a thin woman nourishing a chin whisker, often came with Mrs. Garrison, to admire the new house, especially the fine cupboards and closets that Jonathan and Asa had installed. They talked of cooking with Patience, watching her make frumity of hulled wheat boiled in milk, then showed her their method of doing it with buckwheat. They taught her to make Yankee butter by frying scraps of fat pork and mixing the result with molasses, and to cook a treat of Indian pudding from corn, suet and maple sweetening. But with Melody they joked about the young men of the settlement, telling her Peter Meekins' father had died and left him a fine farm, well stocked, with only an old mother to keep house for him; they admired her red hair which, they said, matched Peter's.

Tristram built a log shelter over the spring and Melody kept bowls of sweet milk there. Neither she nor Patience would adopt the New England way of letting it set until the cream could be lifted like a pancake. She was getting a bowlful for dinner and had placed it outside while she filled the water bucket when she heard coarse drinking sounds. She dashed outside, thinking a pig was loose. The pock-marked Indian she had seen at Amherst had the bowl to his lips and was drinking with loud sucking noises.

"Tha filthy brute!" she blazed.

He continued to swallow so she wrenched the bowl from him, slopping milk over his jacket and breeches.

"Get from here, tha dirty dog," she ordered. "Don't tha dare coom again."

The Indian glared at her. "You poor squaw," he sneered. "You no good."

His glare startled her. She pointed to the road.

"Go," she said tightly. "Go!"

He made no answer but stepped back of the shed for a musket he had stood there. Then he turned and went toward the woods.

The men had not come from the fields for dinner so Melody ran to them. "T' Indian wur here, t' ugly one wi' t' pock marks," she panted. "He drank oor milk from t' bowl. I took it from him and spilled doon his breeches. He looked he would kill me, and he had a musket."

Tristram was greatly disturbed. "We must be careful," he said, "else they'll burn us oot."

"Aye," said Jonathan. "Don't tha be feared, Melody. We'll watch place ootside tonight."

It ended with their calling Garrison over for advice. "Let it drop," the one-legged man advised. "You don't want this fine house burned or your cattle killed. An Injun is bad when he gits a grudge on you."

Jonathan and Lancelot took turns watching the buildings for a few nights but nothing happened to alarm them. Then Garrison promised he would see the pock-marked Indian and persuade him to be peaceable.

The last of September was warm and balmy. Melody discovered a blackberry thicket over the hill to the east and took a bowl there an afternoon when the air was still and locusts sang from old poles. She was gathering the luscious fruit when a moist hand was clamped over her mouth and she was held, helpless, as a gag of leather was thrust in her mouth and bound there. She lost the bowl and berries as she twisted violently, kicking and lunging, and had a look at her captors. One was the redskin who had taken the milk and the other was an evil-looking brave who smelled like an animal.

When they had walked her well into the woods the gag was removed. Melody retched and was sick. When she was ready to go on the Indians walked with her between them. "Tha will be sorry," she gasped. "My brothers will catch thee."

"Do same with them," came the retort. Both Indians patted their muskets significantly. "Mebbe shoot 'em."

Melody saw they were on a path she and her brothers had travelled many Sundays, and she was heartened. "You need plenty stick," said the pock-marked Indian savagely.

They reached the barren, crossed it and located a cache of dirty blankets, an iron kettle and ladle. "You carry," they ordered, giving Melody the lot. Then they turned in a new direction that took them away from the brook.

Melody pushed from her mind every tale she had heard of white women being taken captive by Indians. She concentrated her thinking on escape, watching their direction.

A spruce partridge scurried from their path to the shelter of a windfall. Another joined it, like a half-alarmed fowl in a henyard. The Indians put down their muskets and ordered Melody to stand quietly. The pock-marked one took a hatchet from his belt and cut two sticks to use as clubs. With these in hand they stepped forward. One partridge ran among brown fern. The mate of the pock-marked Indian pursued it, passing from sight around some windfalls. Melody let the blankets drop on moss without making a sound.

She snatched the hatchet from the pock-marked Indian's belt. He turned swiftly to seize her but she was quicker. She struck him on the head with the flat side of the weapon. The blow tingled her arm, sounded harsh. The Indian's knees buckled under him and he slid down in a heap. Melody turned and ran as the kettle she dropped rolled against a tree.

She flung the hatchet away, gathered her skirt and petticoat high and ran as she had never run in her life.   The second Indian had chased his bird from view.   She plunged through thickets, heading toward the brook and was sobbing for breath when she blundered onto the trail leading to the bridge of two trees.

The find encouraged her.   Not a sound had come from the woods behind her.   She did not know how far she had run but was sure the second Indian would be hot on her trail as soon as he had examined his companion.   She slowed, thinking.   The Indian would overtake her long before she was through the maple grove on the far side of the barren.   It was a stretch of at least a mile and a good path to follow.

She reached the barren, and stopped.   They could not track her on its sun-dried sod and upthrust rock.   She turned to her right and circled back to the woods and crouched under a hemlock.   Her heart pounded like a mad thing and she was shaking with exhaustion when she saw the Indian.

He emerged from the woods and continued over the barren at a steady jog, carrying his musket.   She saw that his speed was deceptive.   He seemed to skim over the ground.   Then she started again.   The pock-marked Indian followed the other, trotting doggedly.   He looked neither right nor left and she knew that both Indians were sure she would keep to the path.

When they were gone she headed directly for the brook. She knew it would lead her out to Smith's mill.   It was getting dark under the trees and the hardest part of her travel was ahead of her, but her courage was revived.

She found the brook and there was no time to look for a dry crossing.   Plunging in, she waded to her knees, slipping on stones and splashing.   The chill of the water set her teeth chattering and then she was across, scrambling through low-branched hemlock and spruce thickets that tore her clothing and forced her to detour again and again.   She nearly lost the brook once and had to stand and listen until she could hear it.

The last light vanished and the woods became inky black, eerie, menacing.   Branches slashed at her face.   Brush tore her stockings. She fell many times. Soon she could only advance slowly, groping her way with outstretched hands. Something bounded from a thicket beside her and crashed through the bush in wild flight. A limb ripped her dress from her shoulder, causing her to cry out as she wrenched away.

A fox yapped somewhere in the darkness. An owl hooted. Stars appeared, but they make the darkness under the trees more intense. A jumble of windfalls barred her way and she climbed among them, not daring to veer from the sound of the brook. Snags caught at her torn dress, made greater rents. She slipped between fallen trees and in her frantic struggle tore free from her skirt. She caught her hair in a bush, tugged free and fought into a thicket that resisted her strongly.

There did not seem to be any opening. She tried again and again, then shut her eyes and drove in, shoving, making her way by sheer strength. The undergrowth was a maze of tough limbs that impaled her petticoat. She tore free only to be snagged again until she was fighting in a frenzy and she finally emerged in a glade, sobbing and gasping, naked save for her shoes and remnants of her stockings. She was bleeding from a dozen scratches.

A glimpse of the moon helped her. The woods was more open and she began running. A field appeared and she saw a light. It was reflected in water and she knew it was Smith's millpond. She had reached safety.

She waded the brook again, ran across a field and climbed a fence to gain their own pasture. Far away, toward the river, she heard shouting and recognized Jonathan's voice.

"Melody! Melod-ee! Mel-o-dee!"

She tried to answer him but her throat would not function. She reached the barnyard, then the kitchen door. Strength drained from her and she clung there as Patience and Tristram came running. She tried once more to lift the latch, then sank on the step. Patience's cry sounded far off and then she knew no more.

When she roused she was in bed and Patience was bathing her bruises and scratches. Mrs. Garrison sat beside her, rocking on a chair. "The poor dear! The poor, poor dear! Her purty face! Oh, the dear!"

Melody stared as if she were talking in her sleep. "T' Indians got me," she gasped. "They took me to woods. They gagged me. I hit him wi' t' hatchet. I hid by t' barren. Then I waded t' brook. Thear wur beasts in t' bush. I'm hungry."

They fed her with broth and when she had eaten she fell asleep, muttering and crying out so that Patience stayed beside her and, in the next room, Jonathan and Lancelot sat and listened.

In the morning she was normal again, but her body ached. Tristram was like a madman. He went to Solomon Smith and asked him raise an armed party but the millman talked him down. They could not afford hostilities in so remote an area, he said, and it would be better if Melody went elsewhere on a visit until there was no further danger.

Silas Plumley was going to Amherst for spikes and nails with which to build his house and Jonathan asked him to take Melody along to Matthew's place. Word had come of Uncle Malachy's death, with a message from Matthew asking that one of his sisters come and help with looking after Aunt Amelia.

Jonathan went along with them as far as Maccan, with his rifle over his arm, but they saw no Indians. They stayed the night with Henry Niles and his wife greeted Melody warmly, keeping at her avidly for every detail of her capture. "Injuns," she snorted, "are dirty as pigs. They pestered me years ago till I took to puttin' physic in cookin' they was always beggin'. It cured 'em after a while."

Niles said the ill-feeling would iron out if the Crabtrees would send some gift to the tribe. "I got in wrong with 'em once," he grinned, "so I killed an old ewe and give 'em the carcase entire. They took it keen enough and we've been good friends ever since."

He had a pitcher of rum on the table in the evening and he tried to persuade Plumley to drink. In the candle light Melody watched the shadow of his queue nodding up and down the pitcher, and the bulk of his wife as she leaned over the table. When, finally, the Niles couple began arguing, Plumley went out, saying he would sleep in the barn loft. Melody asked for a tallow dip and crept up to a room she shared with the Niles children. Down below the parents squabbled until far into the night.

Before noon the next day Plumley let Melody down at Matthew's lane. She thanked him and ran to the house. The kitchen door was open and someone was tending a bake kettle at the fire. She paused and stood, wondering. The person was a well-made girl with yellow hair and stupid blue eyes.

"Good day," said Melody. "Is Aunt Amelia here?"

The girl stared, pop-eyed. "Yes, miss," she giggled. "She's outside. I'm Polly Clews and I work for Matthew."

Melody went around the house and saw Aunt Amelia at the garden fence, her arms resting on the top rail as she looked over the marsh. Melody called to her but she did not stir as she made slow response.

"Tha have coom too late," she said dully. "Malachy's gone."

"We were very sorry to know," said Melody. "I've coom to visit thee."

Aunt Amelia left the fence and kissed Melody. "Be happy while tha can," she sighed. "It's a sad world."

She looked over the marsh again. "Some days Malachy calls to me from over thear. I do wish I knew what he says."

"Who's t' lass in t' kitchen?" asked Melody, to change the subject.

"Polly Clews, poor soul. A good worker but clumsy wi' my china. Matthew hired her."

"Did Matthew put his grain in alone?"

"Mercy, no. Gideon Danks helped him. Tha will like Gideon. He's on t' next farm, a fine gentleman. Rum's his worst fault. Matthew drinks wi' him sometimes. I wish he wouldn't."

Matthew came to the house at noon. He greeted Melody awkwardly, finally kissing her. He was burned darkly with salt winds and sun, and his shirt was ragged. He looked as if he needed a wife more than anything else in the world.

"Is Tristram plowing?" he wanted to know. "How much hay has he stacked?"

He asked endless questions about the crops, the cattle, the sheep, the barn and the new house. "Do t' others take orders from Tristram?" he wanted to know. "What is thear share in t' farm?"

Melody shrugged and said she did not know. Matthew's jealousy of Tristram was as apparent as the broken hat of woven marsh reeds he wore.

They went in to dinner and Melody watched Polly become so flustered that she broke a bowl. The girl kept looking at Matthew and she giggled whenever he spoke to her. In order to ease the situation Melody helped with the serving, and told Matthew her experience with the Indians. He listened gravely.

"I'll get Gid Danks to coom over," he said. "He's lived wi' Indians and he'll know what to do."

Gideon came for supper. He gazed at Melody with frank admiration. "Matthew's a mean one to hold back news," he roared. "He never let on he had your like in his family. No wonder the Injuns run off with you."

"That pock-marked Injun is bad medicine," he mused. "They call him Sour Bear, and the name fits him. The smelly one is harmless. Don't you worry none. Gid risked his hair with Injuns half a dozen winters and he kin talk muskrat Micmac. He'll find out what'll soothe 'em best. This Sour Bear ain't related to the chief and he'll have to bide by what they say or git out on his own. The chief is decent enough but his squaw has more whims than an old maid. Please her and you'll please him, and that's the way to put a blister on Sour Bear, but it'll take some thinkin'."

He talked in his booming way until Polly had finished her work for the night and crept away to bed in a corner of Aunt Amelia's room. Then he jumped up.

"Come and put your eyes on Annabelle," he roared. "I'll bet Matthew's forgot to mention the mare."

They went to the pasture and Gideon roared out his story of losing a bet. He whistled and the brown mare trotted from the darkness to nibble a lump of sugar he carried. Melody thrilled as the mare nuzzled her.

"Like her?" queried Matthew.

"I could love her," said Melody. "She's such a lady."

"Then she is thy mare. She's too light for me and I've nowt for her to do."

"I were tryin' to put the words in your mouth, man," shouted Gideon. "A blind granny could see they go together."

Melody was up at sunrise. She found a sleepy Polly trying to get the fire going and tried her best to make friends with the girl. Polly was sullen, however, until Matthew came for his breakfast and then she brightened fast enough, filled his plate first and tried to catch his attention.

Matthew saddled the brown mare and Melody rode to the marsh with him, back again on the cart trail and around the stubble fields, exultant in her possession of Annabelle. Gideon came over, riding his stallion. He made the animal rear and strike for Melody's benefit, said his hay could rot for all he cared, that he was off to parley with the Indians. Melody thought he was drunk but he dismounted fast enough when she told him that Aunt Amelia was in the doldrums and would not leave her room.

"I'll bring her down," he shouted, making a great do-do as he went up the stairs. He came down with Aunt Amelia in his arms, smiling feebly. She told him he reminded her of Malachy in everything he did.

Gideon came back at night. "The chief ain't too bad," he reported, "but his squaw needs some sweetenin'. None of them like Sour Bear, so that's in our favour. Marsh Rose, she's the chief's daughter, has a fancy for your brother. He bought a basket from her, the chief says, and paid two shillings. You should see her. She's real handsome."

Melody pretended that she knew nothing about the basket. She became tired of Gideon's talk and went to bed. She dreamed that she was in the blackberry tangle and Sour Bear's hand was over her mouth. She snatched it away and awoke. Aunt Amelia was bending over her, a gaunt ghost in her night gown. "I'm looking for Malachy," she whispered.

Melody put her to bed again and stayed with her until she

slept. On a narrow board bed against the wall Polly snored
on her back as if a thunder clap would not wake her.

The house was dirty. Polly prepared the meals but she
made no effort to scrub floors or bedding. The next morning
Melody heated kettles of water and set to work. She put
everything soiled to the tub and strung the fence with washing. Gideon came to dinner and when he went out he stared
at Melody's display, then whistled and ran toward his horse.

A pounding of hoofs heralded his return. Melody, looking
out, saw him ride to the fence and gather in Aunt Amelia's
best pair of lace-frilled drawers. He flourished them wildly
as he saw Melody watching, yelled and was gone. She could
hear his roaring voice long after.

"Oh, Mary Jane came down my lane . . . ."

Matthew was too far away to call so she brought the rest
of the wash in when it was dry and heated the smoothing iron.
Hot and tired, she had lighted the candles when Gideon
returned.

"Leave it to Gid," he howled with laughter. "The old
squaw danced like a cow when I give her the drawers. They
tickled her fancy better'n a keg of rum. She promised she
would lay into Sour Bear and run him out of the country, and
she's one to keep her word. Make yourself a plain flannel
pair, ma'am, and they'll do jist as well as them frilled kind."

Melody could feel the hot flame on her cheeks. Aunt
Amelia had put an edge on her nerves and this hooting man
roused her resentment. She flared and told him he was no
gentleman. Gideon stared, then slapped his knee and shouted
approval.

"You've got your dander up, Miss Melody. You look
purtier'n ever when you're mad, too. One look at the hair
and I knowed you had spunk."

She tried to stay angry but he made his words laugh at
everything and everybody. Then Aunt Amelia came down
with her best dress and bonnet on, saying she was going to
Backfall for the evening, and it took all their tact to change her
decision. Matthew arrived, shouting for his supper, and Polly
began to giggle. Melody helped her put food on the table

then slipped away to her room and there, like a child, cried into her pillow.

She was wakened in the night by Aunt Amelia prowling again and after putting her back to bed she could not sleep. A rooster crowed for midnight and that meant rain for the morrow. She heard it begin toward dawn, a steady pattering on the roof that lulled her into long dreamy rest.

In the morning Matthew sat around the kitchen making leather hinges for a flail. He was morose until Gideon came over and beckoned him to the barn. Soon they were shouting with laughter and Melody knew they had been drinking. They were ready to joke about anything as they ate dinner and Matthew slapped Polly's thigh and pinched her as she passed him. It set her to giggling without restraint.

Melody went upstairs and tied up her bundle. "I'm going home," she said.

The men stared at her. Matthew, suddenly contrite, followed her outside. "Wait till tomorrow," he begged.

"Noa." She was furious as she saw Polly peeping from the door. "I'm going now. How can tha put hands on that silly creature?"

Matthew's dark skin reddened. "Mind what tha say," she snapped.

Gideon came and joined them. "Give her rein," he boomed. "She's too skittish for a tight check. She'll come back." He called the brown mare and saddled her. Matthew watched without protest as Melody mounted. "Good-bye," she said briefly, and rode out of the lane.

The rain had changed to fine mist that beaded her bonnet and cloak but she headed down the trail to Nappan without hesitation. A mile on the way, the mare pricked up her ears and Melody, looking back, saw that Gideon was following on his black stallion.

Dusk overtook her at the Bathol intervales and then she heard Gideon riding nearer than before. Light was shining from windows of the new house so she put Annabelle at a faster lope only to have Gideon overtake her at the lane.

"I've something to say, miss," he boomed in the darkness, "and you'll listen or I'll turn you around right here."

A lantern appeared, coming from the house, and Melody
defied him.

"Tha will not take me back, now or ony time, big as tha
are.   What have tha to say?"

"It's this, Miss High and Mighty."   He tried to be humor-
ous but there was pleading in his voice.   "You've a wrong
idea of your brother.   You can put all your mad on me for
the little drinking he's done.   If you've a bee in your bonnet
about him and that soft wench you're doing him wrong, but
if you leave him there to winter with her and Aunt Amelia
whatever happens will be on your own head.   Now you've
heard my say and I thank you for bein' so kind."

He was wheeling the stallion around when the lantern
was suddenly held high and there was Patience, with a jacket
of Jonathan's around her, gazing in wonder.

Melody recovered first.   "This is my sister, Patience,"
she said.   "Mister Gideon Danks o' Amherst Point.   He
made sure I coom safely."

"I'm proud to know ye, miss," shouted Gideon.   "Matthew,
the rascal, never let on he had sich handsome sisters.   Whoa,
there.   Hold yourself, boy."

The big black reared and pawed the air, snorted, squealed
and tamed again as if cowed by masterful hands, a magnificent
animal in the lantern glow, ruled by a magnificent rider.
Melody saw the admiration that washed over Patience's
cheeks and heard the excitement in her answer.   "I'm proud
to know thee, Mister Danks.   Won't tha coom to supper?"

"Thank you, miss, but I promised Matthew I'd see him
again tonight, and it's a goodish ride home."   He paused.
"The old lady is ailing, so if you can find it convenient to
make her a visit soon it'll be a Christian act."   Then he
slackened rein and the stallion was away on the trail like a
mad thing.

Patience looked after Gideon until he was gone from hearing
around a bend in the road, then turned to Melody.   "Is he
married?" she asked, not even waiting to query about the
brown mare.

"Noa," flung Melody.   "He's had Matthew drinking until

he's like a stranger.   He has his horse act that way to make thee scary and if he wur not so good to Aunt Amelia I could hate him.   Besides, he isn't a gentleman."

Patience nodded as if she had not heard.   "Thear is a chicken missing but I'll not bother looking further.   Coom and tell me about Matthew.   Ezra Hodge is going to Amherst tomorrow and I think I'll go along wi' him."

VI
Tristram Borrows a Rifle

THERE was no man from Yorkshire who could plow a
better furrow than Tristram Crabtree. The breaking
of soil held for him a lasting fascination. He loved the
aroma of broken earth and he was proud of the perfection of his
work. When he rested his oxen he gazed about him and
admired the view. The land he had chosen was the most
fertile in Bathol, of that he was sure.

In his mind he counted every animal they owned, cattle,
hogs and sheep. Then he reckoned a year's natural increase
and calculated how long it would take him to have herds and
flocks that would bring a substantial income. He frowned
as he saw his brothers at work building a fence. He had
made his decision regarding them. He would drive them to
another part of the country. There would be no quarrel,
if he could avoid it. He would not talk with them nor let
them know his plans. Already he had ceased asking them
to do any work. He would force them to see that he had
taken charge and that they were unwanted.

The June weather was perfect. A blanket of shimmering
quiet hung over the intervales. Even the river ran softly.
He spoke to his cattle and started again, smelling the good
earth, treading its springiness, exulting in his power, his
intelligence. He would have his seed sown and there would
be rain. He could sense it in the stillness. Then there would
be sunshine again.

At the end of the furrow he rested and looked at the
abandoned farm on the left. In time he would own it as
well. After seven years, the official at the fort had said.
He never spoke of it for he did not want either of his brothers

to settle there. He hoped they would go from Bathol. He would let them have a few cattle and sheep, a pig or two, at any time, if they would but go from the place. He would not give them a shilling. They, nor Patience, nor any other knew of the money hid in a small leather bag, buried under the roots of a gnarled spruce on the hill.

His mother had taught him the value of having two purses. She kept one in the dresser and the family knew to within a few shillings of how much it contained. They went to it when there was need, placed money in it after a sale at the market or elsewhere. But she had a second purse. It was hidden under the stairway in a spot she had contrived with amazing ingenuity, and into that purse she had slipped odd pounds over so many years that she and Tristram had talked of buying a better farm than any in Banfield.

He had the purse still with him. Their holdings at Bathol, the materials for the new house, their equipment, had been purchased with money accrued from the sale of their livestock at Banfield. When his brothers were gone he would use his extra money to buy more gradely stock, a team of horses and harness, to build a second barn. There would not be another like him from Amherst to beyond Bathol. This was his dream and he nourished it with his daily thinking.

The river made an elbow turn at the corner of their farm, to Smith's mill half a mile on. A trail over the upland to the mill shortened the haul as they carted lumber for the house and barn, but Tristram had discovered a shorter path leading through the corner of woods. It crossed a brook so he felled a tree and used it as a bridge. Fear of the Indians kept him from telling his family about the short cut.

The frame of the barn was almost completed when the carpenters demanded a better stick for the ridgepole. It was a hot afternoon and the last load of hay had been stacked, the oxen unyoked and put to pasture. Tristram started over the path to Smith's mill. If Smith had the proper timber he would go for it in the morning.

His shirt was drenched with sweat and it was airless under the trees. He thought of the brook in the woods with relief. Several times he had gone there on Sunday afternoons to wash himself clean of the week's perspiration. A long pool angled into a glade away from the current so that the water was no more than pleasantly cool. He removed his clothing without hurry, let himself down on the gravel bed and was preparing to splash his neck and shoulders when a slight sound caused him to rise and look toward the far end of the glade.

He stood without moving. There was only the gentle murmuring of the brook. All bird song seemed hushed. Not more than thirty paces from him, on soft sod in the shade of a pine, stood an Indian girl, entirely naked.

She had been bathing and her satiny skin glistened as she used wild grass as a towel. She was long-legged, beautifully made and her every movement was filled with effortless grace.

Tristram was caught by the spell of her presence. He watched, fascinated, as she posed and twisted leisurely, drying her body. His eyes feasted on her as desire maddened him. He went forward with splashing, smiling as she looked at him like a startled deer. Then she, too, smiled, dropping her handful of grass.

"Good day," her voice was soft as the coo of wood pigeons. "You look fine man, sure. You buy bas'et? Two shillin'."

Tristram halted and swore as none of his brothers had heard him. Then he went on. The Indian girl was Marsh Rose from whom he had bought the basket and she was laughing at him, trying to provoke him.

He leaped to the bank, caught her, unresisting, to him, the coolness of her flesh inflaming him like liquor. He was crazed with lust and Marsh Rose cried out, half in fear, for him to be gentle.

An hour later, at the woods edge above Smith's mill, Tristram halted to fight himself back to normal. Remorse had sickened him until he was almost unnerved. He had left Marsh Rose by the brook without a word, never heeding as she called after him. His conscience tortured him, shouted at him that he was now unfit to marry Unity. He needed all his strength of will to go to Smith and inquire about the timber.

He walked back by the cart trail, resolving he would not

go again by the path through the woods. As he travelled he refused to as much as look toward the trees where Marsh Rose might be hiding. At the supper table he was morose. He did his chores in silence. Far into the night he lay awake with his guilt. He grew haggard. After Silas Plumley had another service on Sunday, Tristram took a goose quill, ink and paper from a chest and wrote to Unity.

August, 1772.

My Dear: This comes to let you know that distance or length of time since we parted has not made me forget you. We have a good place with many acres of cleared land, a fine house and a barn to be raised soon. Also another fifty acres alongside which will serve as a second farm if need be. This is good country and all that is troublesome is a small fly called a miskatoo which is plenty near the marshes. I am writing to you my dear to ask you to come to me. If you will come I will be a kind husband to you and have for you as good a house as at Banfield. O would I were in place of these lines so that I might make you understand my need, for I cannot live well as I am. We had a good passage here and were healthful, being sick but a few days. The people here are inclined to be friendly. They are of a different persuasion in religion with ye Church of England the fewer. My dear if you could but read my heart with these lines I know you would come quickly. My want for you is so great that my work is hard and there are many mistakes. Spinning wheels are dear being twenty shillings a peece English money. Ye guney pays for three and twenty and fourpence but there is a dollar that is 5s. All linen cloth and woollen cloth is very dear but they are weavers and work their own both linen and woollen. I ask you, Unity, to come to me quickly and pray you be guided by my love which is stronger than before.

TRISTRAM CRABTREE.

If you write to me you must direct to me at Bathol near Fort Cumberland.

A few days after Marsh Rose went along the river trail with baskets to sell and without his wishing it his eyes enjoyed her curves and litheness. He tried hard to drive thoughts of her from his mind, and won his struggle, but there were other days and he went several more times to the pool in the woods before he entirely mastered himself.

When Sour Bear came to the spring house Tristram was afraid. He blamed the Indian girl for causing him harm. He cursed his folly and tried to convince himself that it was she who would have to answer for their sin.

It was different when Melody was missing. Then rage ruled him for a day. After that he hated Sour Bear with an intensity that grew stronger as the summer passed. Garrison reported the Indian as being in the woods beyond Smith's holding, and Tristram determined that if chance offered he would have revenge for the wrong done him.

Marsh Rose came again with baskets, encountered Tristram in the field. "Why you scare'?" she teased. "Me many time' more by brook. You not come?'

"Tha fool," he gritted. "Don't coom here ony more."

She made no reply but stood looking after him with a gaze that followed him to the house.

"That's t' one tha bought basket from on Amherst ridge," said Lancelot. "Don't tha know her?"

"We've had enough o' Indians," said Tristram grimly.

"Garrison gets along all reight wi' them," said Jonathan.

"I'm not Garrison," raged Tristram. "Let them stay wi' him."

When Melody returned with the brown mare he asked her many questions about Matthew's farm. It irked him almost beyond bearing to think that his brother had gained such a holding with so little effort. He tried to think of some verse of Scripture that would scorn a man having that which he had not rightfully earned, but he had a limited knowledge of the Bible, and no inspiration.

The last turnips were put into the cellar. Late October tightened the frosts and wild geese honked in the sky at sundown. Tristram amazed Jonathan by asking if he could learn to use his rifle. He said he wanted to go hunting with Solomon Smith.

Smith had come over to talk with Tristram. He said he had killed moose every autumn when they were in good flesh and it had annoyed him to find Indians camped near his wood lot.

He wanted someone to go with him in his hunting, as one of the Indians he had seen was Sour Bear, and he mistrusted the redskin. Tristram agreed to go. A hope that he might in some way be able to wreak his vengeance on the pock-marked Indian made his decision.

The long rifle was of the finest English make, its butt plate, trigger guard and muzzle band of polished brass, its stock dark walnut, smooth as satin. Jonathan watched with interest as Tristram fired his first shot with surprising accuracy. Tristram had keen eyesight and he held the rifle steady. He listened patiently to Jonathan's instructions about the use of a powder gauge, tamped his charge well, and could place a bullet within a ten-inch mark at ninety yards.

He hunted with Smith for three days while the dead leaves underfoot were too noisy to permit them to get near moose. The fourth day it rained. The trees were a-drip and wild grass soaked them to the waist as they circled back of a beaver meadow to a moose run. They kept their rifle primings dry with birch bark breech covers that Smith fitted to each weapon. They saw no Indians. Smith said they would not hunt in a rain but would crawl under some cover and build a fire.

Toward the end of the day Smith suggested that they separate in order to travel opposite sides of a "run" of mixed birch and poplar. Tristram agreed. He was bone tired, wet to the skin and impatient to be done with moose hunting.

It was the smell of damp wood smoke that jerked him to a standstill. He stood a moment, unbelieving, then had thought to step behind cover of the nearest tree bole. The smoke curled upward from the grey brush of a blowdown. When his eyes had become accustomed to the gloom Tristram could detect a clutter of green brush forming a shelter against the windfall. It was so small that it would not hold more than one redskin.

Tristram looked around him. It would be necessary to detour if he were to get past without being seen, and he dare not go far from the defined glades and hardwood thickets that marked the sides of the "run." Before he could move an

Indian crawled from under the brush and stood erect. It was the pock-marked savage—Sour Bear.

Tristram experienced a strange exultation. The wretch had been delivered to his hands. It was meant that he should be the instrument in rendering full justice in the interests of decent settlers. He would avenge Melody.

The Indian began picking up sticks for his fire. Tristram removed the birch bark from his rifle breech. He looked to his priming.

Sour Bear stared under the trees as if some sixth sense warned him of peril. Tristram lined his sights on the Indian's chest and pressed the trigger. He had an awful fear of misfire but the report thudded heavily under the dripping hemlocks. The redskin dropped his armload of sticks and sank down on his haunches. He poised there as if rigid, toppled sideways and lay with a leg twisted crookedly. He had not uttered a cry or groan.

Tristram reloaded with care and had not finished when another rifle report, dulled by the dampness in the air, echoed from some area not far away. In a moment he was running under the trees, not thinking of the tracks he might leave, and not until he reached Smith did he remember the birch bark he should have replaced on his rifle breech.

Smith shouted to ask if there had been more than one moose. "Noa," called Tristram, suddenly cunning. "I didn't see more."

"You never hit him then," declared Smith. "He crossed right over in front of me, and I missed him. We've had bad luck."

It was late afternoon when Tristram reached home and gave Jonathan his rifle. "I've had enough o' tramping," he said shortly. "If we have ony moose meat tha will have to hunt it."

Jonathan brought out his oil and rag. "I'll wait," he said, "until it freezes more. Then Lancelot will go wi' me on a real hunt."

Tristram ate a hot meal Melody prepared for him and went up to his bed. He was morose because he could not put from him the thought that he had done a terrible thing.   He finally compared himself with Samson, who had slain in a righteous cause.   A man had but to trust in Providence, he reasoned, and circumstances made opportunity, and opportunity made circumstances in a never-ending cycle of progress.   He had avenged Melody and now, he reflected, he would give her a decent share of stock if she would keep house for him until Unity arrived.

His thoughts turned to Unity.   He needed her to rejoice in the capacity of the land he had tilled.   Beyond that, he needed a progeny to take up the plow when he had finished and in their turn beget descendants.   If this were done as he visualized good Yorkshire blood would widen their holdings until they had richer land than any other in America.

He turned on his side and let fatigue overtake him.   The loft was warm from the all-day fire in the chimney that passed back of the low rope bedstead on which he slept.   Above the roof the wind hooted softly in the chimney mouth; the sound brought a sense of December cold and storms, a sense of thick plank roof and split shingles.

A skiff of snow in November placed a clean sheet over the barnyards and fields.   Taking advantage of the markings in the woods Jonathan and Lancelot rigged a twitch-up for rabbits and caught a brace overnight.   A hard frost held the snow and when Garrison came over he skidded lively enough as his peg struck an icy spot.   He told Jonathan that the Indians had been to his house the day before and they were quite willing to go hunting with the young white men.

"What is this?" demanded Tristram, and the atmosphere in the kitchen was no longer friendly.   "No one from this house will go wi' Indians."

"Noa!" mocked Lancelot.   "Are tha 'fraid o' them?"

Jonathan looked at Asa carving by the window, and at Melody.   "No one in this house takes orders from thee," he said with a quietness more challenging than a shout.   "We have said nothing about thy comings and goings, and tha will have nowt to say to us."   He turned to Garrison.   "We will go wi' them whenever they coom for us," he said.

"Then thear is but one thing," said Tristram, the skin

around his mouth feeling stiff. "Thee can go but tha will not coom back."

Lancelot sprang up, pulling a bench from his way. He had become a fine figure of a man, more powerfully built than Jonathan and inches taller than Tristram, with a red-gold beard that enlivened his appearance like a jaunty hat. Jonathan sprang before him. "Hold thy head, lad," he said deeply. "Let me talk."

Lancelot waited, standing in the centre of the floor. Asa put his carving knife on the window sill. Garrison nervously backed toward the door, trying to make no noise with his wooden stump.

"We have worked for one home," Jonathan said with the same quietness, "and no one in it has more say than another. Matthew has left it, but he has sent me a signed paper which gives to myself and Lancelot his share in what we have. If thear is ony trouble, t' one who makes it will leave. We will go hunting wi' Indians or who we like. We will coom back ony hour, day or night. If tha make a single move against us we will put thee from this house and tha will not be allowed in again. Nothing here is thine, not a beast, not an acre, as long as oor father lives. Tha have handled money that was not thine, wi' oot t' reight. Now we are finished wi' thy high-handed ways."

Tristram's rage flooded him so that hammers beat at his temples. His muscles tensed and every nerve trembled for action; but he did not move. He was no coward yet he knew his brothers would handle him without mercy, and the story of it would spread through the country. He turned to the fire and did not offer any reply.

Jonathan began talking with Garrison as if nothing had happened. They ate supper in a silence that made Asa more nervous but when it was over Melody began joking. Lancelot responded and soon they were singing Yorkshire roundelays with a gaiety that made Jonathan join them. Tristram went to his bed. He was too dazed to think. He had forgotten the shooting of Sour Bear. It was an episode of the past. It was his future that had received a terrific blow.

The next morning two Micmacs knocked at the door. They

looked intelligent and smiled at Melody through the window as they waited for her brothers to make ready to go with them.

Tristram watched from the stable until they were gone. All night he had lain awake, thinking. Then he came to the house. "How long will they be gone?" he asked.

"They do not know," said Melody, putting wood on the fire so he could not see her expression. "They want to learn camping in t' woods and thear is no hurry to coom wi' meat."

There was another tapping at the door and she opened it to admit Molly Garrison, mittened and wrapped, her nightdress in a neat roll under her arm. "Pa said I was to come," she said, and her smile showed her appreciation of the visit. "I'm to stay overnight."

Melody helped her unwrap and Tristram knew she was talking for his benefit. "Tha can stay till t' men coom back from hunting. We'll have a champion time."

Tristram waited until he had her attention. "Art tha wi' them or will tha help me?" he queried, trying to make his voice kind.

"I'm wi' Jonty in onything," she said crisply. "This is oor home."

"It's mine," he said heavily. "Can tha manage if I go a few days?"

"Aye," she answered him. "Art going hunting again?"

He flushed. "I'm going to Patience, and Matthew. Thear will be some bargain made. I've worked harder than ony. We'll have it settled."

Melody faced him and he felt a barrier rise between them. "Tha will go on a fool's errand," she said cooly. "Matthew gi' me t' paper wi' his share for Jonty and Lancelot wi'oot ony asking. He hates thee more than ever Jonty will do. He would not let thee in his house."

He stared at her.

"Patience will not help thee," she added. "She has always liked Jonty more than thee."

VII

The Amherst Whipping Post

POLLY CLEWS went about her work in stolid fashion, often letting Aunt Amelia call her a dozen times before she would answer. She was strong, however, in carrying wood and water and had the knack of making the most of a joint of beef, so Matthew let her be. Her giggling at anything he said vexed him, but he did not want to be without her.

It was hard to finish harvesting. He had to keep watch on the house, fearful that one or both of its occupants might leave. Gideon furnished the only respite in the drag of the evenings. He came often, bawling his song, praising Polly, cheering Aunt Amelia.

One Sunday afternoon he did not come, and the day hung heavy until Aunt Amelia had exhausted her tantrums and gone to her room. Matthew went looking for Polly. He found her in the garden asleep beside the rows of poled beans, stretched out like an animal. She was lying relaxed, half-turned on her stomach, her face flattened in the grass, the curve of her hip higher than the point of her shoulder, her legs and feet bare.

He sat beside her and tickled her feet until she woke, yawning, saw him and giggled. She was wearing an old dress Aunt Amelia had given her and, he saw, very little else. A rent showed her smooth pink skin below the shoulder and when he tickled her there she let herself drop back in the grass and looked up at him with an odd animal expectancy. As he stared, hesitant, she put her arms up and pulled him to her.

Matthew came to himself when he heard Aunt Amelia calling from the house. He left Polly fumbling to smoothe

73

her dress and went to the kitchen. "I want supper," the complaining voice met him. "Malachy wants me to have a good appetite."

Patience, when she came, transformed the house. She cleared Polly home at once. She had none of Melody's dash and deftness but her planning was better. Room by room she cleaned with thoroughness, unsparing herself or her scrubbing brush, and Matthew came home to meaty stews and puddings that had become little more than a memory. She conjured dainties that won Aunt Amelia's confidence and she fastened the old lady's door each night so that she could not get out. With Gideon she was quiet, unobtrusive.

Matthew's relief was immense. He felt a new man, was glad Patience had got rid of Polly. He snugged his stables for the winter, brushed and banked the house. He was away for a load of brush the morning Aunt Amelia slipped out of the back door and was gone for an hour before Patience missed her.

Shredded fog came in with the tide and clung, like tattered ghosts, blanketing the upland, and when Patience discovered the old lady was not in her room the road to the marsh was lost in swirling vapours. She called loudly and her voice, tremulous and quivering, carried on the soft, limitless cushion of fog, but there was no answer.

The long brass dinner horn hung inside the door and Patience seized it. Its far-reaching notes seemed to echo and re-echo in the grey mist. Soon Gideon came across the fields, his black stallion running. "Anything wrong, miss?" he shouted.

"Aunt Amelia's gone." Briefly she told him of her search, and that the old woman's best dress and bonnet were missing.

"The devil has britches!" gasped Gideon. Then he swung his stallion in a prancing circle. "If she'll answer me I'll find her in no time."

"Tha will only scare her more if tha go down marsh road on that horse," protested Patience. "Tie him to fence and I'll go along wi' thee."

"Right, miss. You've a smart head," he shouted.

The cart track seemed to end beyond the barn, vanishing

in the fog. Soon they were in a world of murk. Everything was unreal. Smells of the wet stubble and marsh ditches were depressing. The mist beaded moisture on their clothing. When they stopped to listen they heard no distinct sound but an indefinable faraway murmuring. "It's the tide, Miss," said Gideon. "I hope she's not reached the flats."

Matthew drove into the yard with his load of brush, unyoked his oxen and saw the stallion. He went to the house and shouted. The fire was low and no preparations had been made for his dinner. He ran up to Aunt Amelia's room and looked in. It was empty.

Outside, he called for Patience, then ran down the cart road at a lumbering pace, seized with a premonition of something dreadful about to happen.

He heard Gideon when he reached the marsh, called to him and found him, with Patience, soaked to the knees from tramping through reedy grass. They shouted in turn but no one answered them. There was not as much as the call of a seabird. The only sounds were the bubblings in the ditches and the whispering rush of the tide over the mud.

"Tracks, man." It was Gideon, the hunter, who thought of them. "Why in tarnation didn't we look when we came down? If she were on the road and kept on to the mud we'll see where she went. A gull can't walk on the flats without leaving toe marks."

They hurried together over broadleaf stubble stretched in brown scythe ridges to weeds that bordered the flats and there found the imprint of Aunt Amelia's best cloth shoes, tracks leading straight out from the shore.

The tide was near. It came in little rushes, swirling greedily into every hollow. Matthew saw that Patience was shaking with chill.

"Go oop to house and warm thyself," he urged. "We'll stay."

"T' mist is getting thin," Patience pointed. "We'll be able to see."

The muddy water was rolled to full depth a long time before they found Aunt Amelia. The tide had brought her in. Her

Sunday bonnet was gone and her grey hair floated free but she still clutched Uncle Malachy's cane.

Gideon went for Parson Eagleson again and they buried Aunt Amelia beside her husband on a cold blustery day, then went back to the house and sat by the fire. Matthew was sobered by the tragedy but made no effort to put from him the thought that he now had property of his own worth as much as the entire holdings of the rest of the family. He wished Patience or Gideon would mention it but they sat still until he sensed that they were only interested in each other.

His woodlot was on the far side of Amherst village. The winter settled with savage frost. It darkened windows in houses and cabins alike, cattle crowded each other for warmth and Gideon said the women grew home-made looking. Patience dipped wicks for the year's supply of candles and snow birds came to yellowed patches by the stable door as snow drifts piled higher and outbuildings became laced together by snowshoe trails.

Then the storm abated and the sun put a blinding glitter over the marshes while men and ox teams made snail-like progress clearing a road through the village and to the dark woods beyond. In a week there were roads to the windswept marsh trails ironed smooth by hay sleds and splattered darkly with the droppings of oxen. Matthew whetted his axe, yoked his oxen and early of a morning set off to fetch his next year's fuel.

Gideon went along with him, tutoring him in the art of getting the sleight of an axe on a hefty beech bole, in felling and limbing a tree so that it could be neatly yarded, and in making use of brow poles to load his sled when alone. They dinnered the first day in a spruce grove but the next noon Gideon boldly rapped at the last house by the wood, inviting themselves to a warm fire and comfortable table. Their hostess was Aggie Keelor, a vivacious widow who eyed Matthew appraisingly and insisted on his coming every noon to eat with her.

"It's a pity you ain't ten years or so older," chuckled Gideon when they were back at their loading. "She'd be a bargain, my boy, and no two ways about it. The next man she takes will enjoy good vittles and he'll be an old one before he'll ever use a bed warmer."

Matthew grinned at his chaff but when Gideon had gone to his own wood cutting the widow seemed tongued with honey, she knew so well what a man wanted to hear. She admired the way Matthew handled his oxen and his industry in getting the best beech and maple for firewood, then patted his shoulder timidly, saying he must be very strong. Each day she put away the bread and cheese Patience had packed for his dinner, substituting hot meals and mince pies that nourished his appreciation of her abilities. He began spending longer noons in her kitchen and at Christmas took her a bottle of French perfume Aunt Amelia had kept, unopened, in her dresser.

Gideon helped make Christmas a cheerful day. He brought Matthew a fat turkey that Patience cooked until its skin had turned to crackling and then stuffed with rice and raisins. They ate it with some ceremony. Gideon told his best tales of living a week on an undersized porcupine, making soup of all but the quills and feet. Then he opened a bundle he had brought and presented Patience with a fine Lincoln-green cape with scarlet lining, surprising her so that Matthew grinned broadly.

"Tha didn't think owd Gid wur a Santa Claus," he teased, "or thear'd been a stocking oop by t' fire."

Patience stared at the rich beauty of the cape. Her lips quivered. "Mister Danks, tha shouldn't . . ."

"Art daft," Matthew broke in, dreading any show of emotion. "Gid wants to do it. Howd thy tongue till next Christmas, then surprise him wi' some pretty."

"Reckon I will," Patience smiled.

"If you want to do something for me," roared Gideon, "drop that handle of 'mister.' Call me Gid, like Matthew."

Matthew hooted his appproval until Patience turned on him. "Whear did tha go wi' t' perfume Aunt Amelia treasured?"

"Ho," shouted Gideon. "I feared as much. Aggie has him on her string. She is fifteen years older if she's a day, but she knows her tricks."

When he went back after New Year for wood Matthew ate

his lunch by his sled. The next day Aggie baked him a rabbit cake and carried it over to him herself, looking a plump boy in her jacket and stocking cap. She appeared so hurt at his passing her door that he went again as usual for his dinners and within a week had pulled her to his knee and kissed her. Then it was hard to get back to his work and after that she seemed to be dancing in every bush he passed.

She was nearer forty than thirty, no doubt of that, but, he argued in his mind, her years of married life had not hidden the girl she had been. Her soft dark hair tied in a neat bun had sheen and sparkle and her sturdy body had been kept trim by her passion for work. She was lonesome, she said, and her's had been a hard life. Matthew went hot and cold as she cried a little and, in February, he tried to tell Patience that a difference in ages did not matter so much if the woman were healthy. She heard him with a silence that was discouraging and told him he should make inquiries in the village about his Aggie, that the simpler a man was the better tears and soft soap worked, and no doubt the widow in her scheming had used both.

Matthew went sullenly to bed with a sleet storm rattling at the window. Everything had an icy coating in the morning but he went to the woods as usual and during the forenoon slipped awkwardly as he trimmed a log, slashing a wicked gash in his foot. He bound it hurriedly with his scarf, rolled what logs he had on his sled and drove to the widow's yard. A broad-sterned farmhorse was tied at the hitching post with a bearskin blanket strapped in place as if the visit might be a lengthy one. His foot throbbed as he hobbled to the house and entered as he had become accustomed to doing. But no Aggie met him. The door to her room was closed and as he stood he could hear such goings-on that, for the moment, he neither moved or spoke.

"Not so free with your hands," giggled Aggie, "or I'll be calling young Yorkshire from his chopping. He'd take you apart if he thought you were over bold."

"You're a smart one to have strings on him," laughed a man's voice, and Matthew recognized the sauve tone. He remembered the man at Fort Cumberland when the Yorkshire folks had arrived, walking around, listening, sleek and mild-mannered, his head cocked to one side like a robin considering a promising worm hole, putting a mild word in now and then on Francklin's behalf. Titus Green, the land agent, was making a visit in keeping with his reputation. "I thought you'd promised yourself to that Aulac farmer?"

"Not yet, Titus, though I have my hopes. But I'm not chancing another winter alone, and Yorkshire, green as he is, will be better than no man at all."

Quietly Matthew closed the door and hobbled back to his sled. The air was biting cold and he could not walk to get warm as the hardwood runners of the sled screeched on frosty snow and a rising wind swirled drift tops into the sled ruts. The cold had worked into him like porcupine quills when he reached home and his wind-nipped face, drawn and tight, set Patience into a flurry of action. She boiled a kettle and undressed his foot, bathed and bandaged it before a dozen words passed between them. Then she whipped herself into a heavy jacket, went outside and stabled the oxen as quickly as he would have done.

"Gid says tha have plenty o' wood hauled," she said as she went back to him. "Thy greenhide's sotted wi' blood. Pity tha didn't stop and let t' widow dress thy foot?"

"Howd thy tongue," ordered Matthew, uncomfortable. "I've nowt to do wi' her."

Patience closed her lips primly and went on with her chores.

Gideon came over in the evening and concern filled his voice. "You need a hoss to ride," he roared. "There's a chestnut for sale, cheap, by another New Englander who's pulling up stakes and getting back to his Massychusetts on the first boat that comes to the Bay. I'll get the hoss, saddle and all, at half price, come you give the word."

Matthew gave the word. He had a notion he wanted to visit other communities, and a horse was needed in case of emergency. Gideon, elated, went away the next day and returned leading a hefty young nag that had plenty of ginger and yet was easy to ride. Matthew made a few riding ventures on the marsh trail and as his hurt healed took longer rides. A slushy March day when crows were exploring dirty snow between rows of corn stalks and all hay stacks had been hauled from the marsh he rode into Amherst village and saw a mob of men and boys around the whipping post.

He had sledded past it during the winter, a weathered timber with a crosspiece, set deeply near the main pump and ringed with dog tracks, but had never thought of it being put to use. Now a slack-jawed wretch was spread-eagled to the beam, yelping with every cut of the lash that left angry welts on his bare, bony back. The onlookers shouted ribald suggestions to which the constable with the whip offered apt retorts as he carried out his duty with more show than vigour.

"What's his crime?" Matthew asked of an oldster as he reined in outside the yelling circle.

"He took advantage of Ned Clews's silly girl, that Polly," grunted the oldster. "Serve him right. They ought to alter him and be done with it."

"Caught him proper, eh?"

"Nope. Polly squealed on him. She were workin' for him while his wife had a youngster."

Matthew looked again as the constable, having finished his task, loosened ropes and let the culprit sink down to whimpering misery. Then he turned the chestnut and rode away, forgetting why he had come to the village.

The snow left in mid-April when wild geese honked overhead of a night and first greens crept along the marsh ditches. The first Sabbath in May was mild. Matthew saddled the chestnut. He togged in his best with fine grey woollen stockings Patience had knitted for him, in decent pegged shoes, clean jacket, his hair in a pair of tidy pigtails. He rode through Amherst where ducks swam in ditch puddles, then swung eastward to the Chipley farm at Nappan. He had not seen any of the family since they left the fort barracks. Mrs. Chipley kissed him a grand smacker as Adam pumped his hand. Sylvia came to greet him and he could scarcely wrench his eyes from her to answer questions.

She had grown a hearty woman with clean skin and hair like corn silk. "I'm glad tha coom," she said without a hint of shyness.

"We've wondered all winter why tha didn't coom over."

Mrs. Chipley fussed about him as if her delight were unbounded. "Reckon tha waited for fine weather to come?"

"I had no horse till this spring," explained Matthew. "Here's t' first place I've rode."

"We hope tha will keep coming, then," cheered Mrs. Chipley. "Young folk hereabout are not like oor kind in Yorkshire."

Matthew looked at Sylvia. "It's a champion fine day," he said. "Would tha show me about?"

Sylvia flung a shawl of blue over her shoulders and led out to the orchard. The ground was still spongy with late thawing but there was a wide view of oblongs of plowed land that drained to the marsh. Matthew stood with her and felt he was back in Yorkshire with the scent of hawthorn hedges blowing over the field, with wood pigeons calling from the groves and cows lazying by rows of pollard willows. He told her of his empty house and his dread that Patience might leave him.

"No woman wants to wither on t' virgin bush," he said with great seriousness, "and she be getting on. Have tha heard o' more to coom from Yorkshire?"

She tossed her head, saying she believed that if he waited there might be some likely wench he would admire, freezing him so that he had not recovered his wits when Mrs. Chipley called them to dinner. They had a fine Yorkshire pudding and dried-apple pie. Mrs. Chipley filled Matthew's plate twice and when the meal was over took him to see a Job's Comforter quilt Sylvia had completed, fairly hovering over him. It was all very fine, but he worried most of the afternoon for he had no encouragement from Sylvia herself until he was mounting the chestnut to go home. Then she prettily put her arm through his, saying she hoped he would come again to gather some Mayflowers with her, which would be at their best the next Sunday.

He made an answer of sorts, so confused that he was half a mind to turn back and make sure he had said he would come. Then he rode home like a warrior returning from conquest. Gideon was with Patience. He had helped her milk the cows. "It takes a longish time on a hoss to reach that wood lot of yours," Gideon teased. "How's the widow? We figgered she were showin' you her settin' hens."

Matthew only grinned. The widow was not even a twinge to his conscience. Polly Clews would be far away and long ago when he was married, and he would be a good husband. Sylvia's eyes held the same heart-disturbing blue but there was no longer any indecision about her lips; she would have her man toe the mark all right.

The week was fine so he plowed early and late, getting a fair start on his planting, but he stopped early enough Saturday to carry water for heating after the supper dishes were cleared. He took a tub to his room, a bowl of soap and a towel. Then took his time and had a thumping fine bath. He hurried chores in the morning, shaved with care, changed his breeches and rode away on the chestnut as if time were at his heels.

He saw Sylvia a-watch for him at the lane end and glowed with purpose but the cat got his tongue when her father appeared and walked him to a shed to show him twin lambs an old ewe had disowned. Then it was Mrs. Chipley wanting to show him the beginning she had made with her hollyhocks so that it was noon before he had had more than a nudge from Sylvia, and that he had not understood. Mrs. Chipley was a person of vast knowledge, knowing the correct planting times, the moons for pig killing, the bee moons and berry moons, moons when cattle became ill. She discussed them all as she served pork with sauce of winter apples, and onion pie, while Matthew only listened. When chance came he almost carried Sylvia outside to wherever she said Mayflowers were in bloom.

"I thowt tha mother would never give over," he said. "All week I've been thinking a proper way o' speaking what's in my mind. Now thear's nowt but singing, like an empty tea kettle."

He doubted at first that she had heard him with more than her ears but she smiled. "Art happy to be wi' me, so that tha sing?" she plagued him. "If a man asks t' reight question, his own way will do."

It was as though she knew what he was thinking about.

"Reckon it will," he blurted. "I'd like to ask thee to be my wife."

"Nowt could make me more glad." He felt her calmness flow out against him as he took her into his arms and her kiss set him back on his heels.

"Tha art champion," he stammered, collecting his senses. "Coom to house and I'll speak wi' thy father."

Adam gave them his blessing in a voice that would have done Gideon credit and Mrs. Chipley mourned that it was the Sabbath else she could have begun selecting what linen and china would be Sylvia's. They had a tasty supper of warm honey and barley biscuits and then it was decided that Matthew would stay the night. Adam read his Bible and they had prayers. "Nine o'clock and to bed," said Mrs. Chipley, handing Matthew a tallow dip.

He took it readily enough, pleased with his day. Sylvia gave him a kiss. Her room, she said, was next to his and if he would rap on the wall in the morning she would be up as soon as he was. He promised, but it hindered his getting to sleep at once.

They were married on Saturday. Matthew had his hair trimmed and neatly clubbed. He bought himself a fine serge jacket and a three-cornered hat. Gideon and Patience came on horseback, amazing everyone, for the big man rode a plug as docile as the grey mare Patience handled. "I swapped my black for the two of them," he shouted. "It's the best hoss trade I ever made."

The parson was in good voice and the ceremony passed without a hitch. Mrs. Chipley had a trestle table put outside and it was loaded with edibles that put the guests in good spirits. Matthew sweated under congratulations while Sylvia seemed as cool as her mother. A group of young men came on horses to join in the fun. They sang with great gusto and Matthew noticed their leader was a handsome young man with red hair, who winked at Sylvia until her cheeks burned darkly.

"Who's yon rooster?" asked Matthew, and Sylvia's coolness returned.

"Peter Meekins from Maccan," she whispered. "He's a gay one at a party."

The celebration lasted long after candle lighting and it was late when the silver and pewter had been scoured and put to place, the house set in order. Then Adam had prayers and the newly-weds went to bed.

They left in the morning with Matthew's ox cart piled with Sylvia's bedding and other possessions. The day was fine. Patience, they reckoned, would have dinner waiting and they looked ahead eagerly as they neared the farm. But the door was latched and the fire had died to hot ashes. A meat stew had vapoured into coolness. Matthew thundered up the stairs to where Patience had slept. Her bed was made and the room brushed clean, but her bundle was missing. He went down slowly.

"She said nowt o' leaving," he shook his head, "but she's gone. Tha will have to get first dinner thyself."

VIII
The Sack of Gold

IT WAS COLD in the stable but Tristram spent the greater part of two days there, after his brothers had gone hunting with the Indians. He was thinking. He could not endure the atmosphere of the house. His father kept peering at him as if he were a stranger. Molly Garrison avoided coming near him. Melody chatted with her father and Molly. She did not speak to Tristram except to answer any question he had.

Tristram went to see Silas Plumley. He told how he and his mother had handled the farm money at Banfield and made plans for seedtime and harvest while his brothers had never shown any real interest in their work. Then he described his finding the farm at Bathol.

"Aye," agreed Plumley, "tha have done well. Tha have picked best land oop here. Tha will get on."

"How?" cried Tristram. "T' family are 'gainst me."

He poured out his troubles, telling of his brothers hunting in the woods with miserable savages, telling of Matthew signing over his share of the farm to them.

"Tha can do nowt about that," declared Plumley. "Matthew has t' reight to do as he will wi' his share." He sighed. "It does not seem possible that trouble could enter a Christian home in such a manner. T' Lord will help thee."

"It will take more than praying," gritted Tristram, "to change my brothers. T' place is mine."

"Noa," Plumley shook his head, "it is not thine, nor can be unless tha buy oot t' others."

"How much would they ask?" Tristram dreaded high prices.

"What tha paid for land and stock. Divide in shares. Ony man would call it just."

"Will tha help me?" begged Tristram. "Tha talk wi' them. I'll not ask a share but will pay full price for t' others."

Plumley stared at him. "Whear can tha get t' money?"

It was a question Tristram had known he would have to meet some time. "I have a friend who will loan," he said. "I have had t' offer a long time."

He left Plumley in good spirits. The money in the leather sack under the gnarled spruce was more than he needed to buy out the family. He would go for it when arrangements were completed, and not before. The skiff of snow under the trees would betray his mission.

Plumley visited Melody and Asa the next day. When Jonathan and Lancelot returned he went and saw them. Tristram waited in the stable. The suspense, though, became too great for him. He followed over to Plumley's house.

"Tha should be thankful tha have Christian brothers," said Plumley. "They towd me of thy ways wi' thy father, and thy buying wi' oot telling ony o' thy plans. Tha have been wrong, but they forgive thee."

There was sternness in Plumley's voice but Tristram gave it little heed. He had not dared hope that his brothers would be agreeable.

"But Melody will not agree wi' them," continued Plumley. "She wants to know whear tha will get money."

"What has my getting t' money to do wi' her?" demanded Tristram, raging. The girl had always daunted him, and he feared her wit and tongue more than the rest together. "If I bring t' money, is that not enough?"

Plumley pondered. "It should be," he decided. "If tha will bring it I will make oot t' papers for signing."

Tristram took his axe and went to the woods. He went to the old spruce and reached under the roots. The cavity was filled with snow and ice and old leaves. He had to use his axe to clear an opening. Then he touched the leather sack and had soon wrenched it free. Its weight thrilled him. He took the bag and went over to Plumley.

The strings of the sack were so knotted that he was unable to undo them. Seizing a knife, he slashed them. Then he stared. Speech was stricken from him. It was incredible, impossible. The bag had spewed small stones on the table. There was not a coin in it.

He knew that Plumley was speaking to him but heard not a word the man said. In his mind he went back over the procedure of his getting the sack. He had placed it in his chest when no one was around. He had buried it when no one saw him. Whoever had taken his gold had been cunning as a fox.

"What is it, man?" Plumley shouted. "Speak oop."

Tristram sagged to a stool. He felt physically sick. It took all his strength to make a statement.

"I have been robbed."

"Robbed?"

"Aye. I had this sack filled with gowd, and hidden. T' gowd is gone."

"Whear was it hidden?"

Tristram told him. Fury began to seep into his veins and before he had stopped he was shouting.

"Calm thyself," commanded Plumley. "Tha can gain nowt wi' rage. Tha did wrong to put sack under tree. Tha should have had it in t' house whear t' family knew. Thear is no need for an honest man to hide money from his brothers."

His words drummed against Tristram's thinking but gained no entry. His money was gone. The stark fact dominated. He could prove nothing. If he told the truth his family would be more against him. Worst of all, he would be known as dishonest, and he dreaded such a name. To own the biggest farm in Bathol was his ambition, but he had equal desire to be looked upon as the settlement's leading citizen.

He stumbled from the house, leaving the sack on Plumley's table. He went back to the crooked tree and explored thoroughly the cavity. Then he returned to the house.

"I cannot buy," he shouted as he entered, startling Asa so that the old man sprang from his chair. "I have no money. I thowt I had but it is gone. Thear is nowt I can do."

His brothers gazed at him, and at each other. They said nothing. Melody went on with her work. Tristram went up to his room. He lay on his bed for a day, unable to think clearly, stunned by the catastrophe that had overtaken him. He rejected calls to meals. He could hear the murmur of voices below and felt that his family was discussing him, but he did not care. He did not suspect them of robbing him. Matthew might do such a thing but he knew that neither Jonathan nor Lancelot would touch a penny that was not their's. It was the Indians, he decided, and he was fiercely glad that he had shot Sour Bear.

The next day he rose as usual and went about his chores. He worked slavishly with wood-getting and waited feverishly for spring.

IX

The Devil has Britches!

PATIENCE liked Gideon from the moment she first saw him in the lane at Bathol. She went to keep house for Matthew so that she might be near Gideon, and she made her plans to stop his drinking.

The first rainy morning after her arrival she saw Gideon come across the field with a jug in his hand and a moment after she was in the barn looking for eggs. She talked with the men until Gideon put a ladder to a corn loft where he knew no hen would nest. She persisted in his searching the cow stalls. Before he knew it she had him carrying water for her kitchen. One errand led to another. It ended with Gideon staying to dinner and both men sober.

She had deep apple pie with a crust Gideon declared melted in his mouth but they did not notice her leaving the kitchen after she had provided them with extra slices. The jug was gone from under a beam when they were back in the barn and Gideon roared approval she could hear from the house.

A few days later Patience put the jug back in place but the next rainy day Gideon came to the house and showed Matthew how to make larrigans from greenhide with the hair turned inside. Three pair, he reckoned, would put a man through the winter.

Cutlip came around with his cobbling tools to make Patience a pair of shoes for winter wear. He said Ann, his daughter, was working out while he was away from home, that her deafness was neither better nor worse. Word from Banfield was that half the folks from that district were coming to Nova Scotia the next summer.

His gossip was to Patience like a Yorkshire visit but she

was not in the least homesick.   There was plenty of work to keep her occupied and she knew she was happier than ever she had been at home with her mother forever saying do this and do that.   In the evenings Gideon was over.   She sat with her knitting, listening to his tales, knowing many were for her hearing, tingling with every inflection of his outdoor voice.

One Sunday when Matthew was sleeping she slipped outside in the crisp fall air and with hens trailing hopefully after her walked around the barn to a plank seat Uncle Malachy had built overlooking the marsh.   Many times she had gone there to watch sunsets over the Basin and she was surprised to see Gideon in the seat, apple cores on the grass showing how long he had been sitting.

"I thought you might be out," he grinned.   "I've seen you here other Sundays."

He talked, then, of wild geese he had seen on the marsh, of teal and red-legged ducks, blue heron and plover.   With his homely phrasing he painted her a picture of far-reaching expanses of grass and reeds beyond meandering little rivers which cut through sodden land that seemed to rise and fall and breathe with the daily tides.   He talked of sunrises he had seen when spring floods covered the old grasses and sky and land seemed aflame with red and golden fire, until she saw with her own eyes.   She was chilled and the heat of the sun was gone before she realized how long she had sat with him.   He did not try to detain her when she rose but went to the house with her like any farmer's son a-courting.

When she tried, at first opportunity, to thank him for his gift at Christmas he hushed her with a hug and kiss as warm as any youngster's, but instinct told her his actions were not merely the immemorial way of a man with a maid, and she began to watch for his comings.

They seemed far apart after the New Year when the men went to their wood cutting and her work narrowed to yard paths and outhouses.   It was then she thought of the cider jug.   She found it still in its place, tightly corked.   Curiosity raised the jug to her lips.   She had several swallows.   Her veins warmed agreeably.   An hour later she felt so good she did a small jig on the barn floor before tossing forkfuls of chaff and hayseed to birds that came each day from the woods back of Amherst village.

The cider afforded tricky pleasuring. She had tampered with it a second time one morning when the hay loft began to tilt alarmingly and her legs gave way as she tried to reach the door. She was creeping on hands and knees when Gideon put his head in and stared at her like a man unsure of his senses.

"Are you hurt?" he rumbled, and he reached to help her. Then he sniffed her breath and cattle jumped in their stalls as his merriment boomed and echoed. "The devil has britches!" he roared. "You're tight, miss. You've sampled Gid's home-made like a youngster when the folks are away. Ho-ho, but you've a shine in your eyes now."

He laughed and crowed and she laughed with him because her head would not stop spinning and most of her bashfulness was gone. He picked her up and carried her to the house and she begged him to stay with her, telling him she wanted him more than anything else on earth.

When she awoke the fire was low and Gideon gone but she was on the sofa with a blanket tucked around her and the outside chores were done. Shame tore her as she remembered, vaguely, her babbling tongue and when Gideon came over in the evening, bringing a faint but stimulating aura of woods and horse and frosty weather, she could not look at him at all.

"Wine ain't got much spread to it," he whispered, "but cider sure drowns a misery. I took the jug home and I'll bring it back, full, when you give the word."

"A bargain," she caught at him. "Wait till I do."

The first Sunday Matthew went to court Sylvia seemed immeasurably long to Patience. She put on her bonnet and went down the drying cart track to the marsh, gathering blue and white violets. Then she returned and was at the seat behind the barn when Gideon came with a great armful of Indian pear bloom he had gathered for her.

It was a wonderful morning. Juncos were in the weeds of last year's gardens and song sparrows were in the bush. Tree swallows were after midge and Mayflies, and along the brook back of Gideon's barn they could hear the rattling cry of a kingfisher. The sun was warm and Patience could feel her pulse hammering. She wanted Gideon to put his arms around her and hold her tightly while he said words that would end her loneliness.

Something held him in check. She could see the wish in his eyes but he said everything except what she wanted to hear and in late afternoon when he had gone she walked back to the kitchen with her wilted flowers, crying with disappointment. She knew he lacked courage to speak his mind and discouragement went with her as she did her work.

Gideon was back before she had lighted her supper fire. Her heart gave a great leap. She knew, intuitively, he had come with strong purpose but when he looked at her it was as if his words dried up inside him. She laughed, and it was not a nervous laugh.

"Tha coom to ask me to marry," she said, "and I will." It was as if she had borrowed some inevitable moment from their future when they had lived together long enough for all artifice to vanish.

He took her in his arms with rough tenderness. "You've saved my life," he said. "I never knowed Gid Danks could lack so much nerve. We'll git hitched the day you're willin'." Then he laughed. "We'll put a stir to Matthew's courtin'. Will you stay till he finds what he wants?"

"Noa," decided Patience, and swirl of ideas spun her mind. She entertained one for several seconds and coaxed it along as she noticed the sheer happiness shining through his perspiration. "If we could get, I'd like to be married at home. Thear's nowt would please father more."

"Then," said Gideon with grim resolve, "I'll swap my black hoss for a pair I've had eyes on. We'll save time by ridin'."

Patience was worried over Matthew. He had taken her work for granted and was too like Tristram to worry over her future. He would be upset when she told him she was marrying Gideon. When he came home excited and worked through the week like a man possessed she said nothing.

When he invited them to his wedding she still did not tell him her news, but when they returned from Nappan she packed her bundle and the next day rode home with Gideon. She was apprehensive of their reception but every fear soon vanished. Her brothers kissed her as they had not done in years, even Tristram, at first greeting, seeming to be emotional. Jonathan had Gideon telling his hunting tales in no time. Melody held her as if she would never let go, and her father patted her shoulder timidly, saying he hoped she had wintered well. Tristram, gaunt as a winter-starved steer, asked if she had quarreled with Matthew. When she assured him she had not, and told him of Matthew's wedding, he went from the house, enveloped in sullen humour.

They had supper in style and Gideon was in his best form, his booming voice startling Molly Garrison to jumping each time he laughed. Then Melody called Patience to her bedroom.

"I'm so glad tha have coom," she said. "Happen Molly hadn't stayed wi' me this winter I'd been a shivering goon. Summat happened about Tristram. He towd Silas he had money to buy us oot, then took over a bag wi' nowt but stones in it. We thowt he might be turned in t' head. He's said nowt to ony about it. He's saying he'll take land alongside, and does nowt but glower, coom Sunday or Monday. Jonty and Lancelot have been champion but father's feared o' Tristram. It's been a devil's recess fair enough."

She held to Patience and sobbed as if her endurance had crumpled but when she was rested she said a good cry was what she had needed, and they went back to the kitchen to talk over the wedding as if their happiness were complete.

In the morning Gideon rode back to Amherst Point, commissioned to invite Matthew and Sylvia as tactfully as he might and to bring himself back the day week. He came in new broadcloth jacket and breeches. Matthew, he said, had received the news with gladness. He had sent over Aunt Amelia's prize chamber as a wedding gift.

The wedding was a grand affair. The Bathol settlers came in force to the last Garrison baby so that the parson was obliged to perform the ceremony outside the house. A group of young men arrived from Maccan and joined in the festivities. A roaring bonfire was built in the cart lane and a fiddle made merry with such airs as "Pea Jacket" and "Faith-ful Shepherd" while some of the men danced like animated bears. Melody said, loudly, she had not known grown men could act so crazy when Peter Meekins, with a steer's head before him and a cow's tail tied to his belt behind, galloped and roared and pawed the earth. But Gideon joined in the roaring out of various ditties, accepting good-naturedly the jocose admonitions of married men to a groom.

It all ended suddenly when a rider came tearing up the road and pulled in with his horse well blown. "Hast heard t' news?" he shouted. "A ship's in at fort wi' Yorkshire on board. 'Nother coom, too, and waits tide to reach wharf."

There was a great clattering of voices as the party ended. Jonathan and Gideon carried buckets of water to blacken every cinder in the roadway. They said "good-night" cordially and went to their beds.

X
Lancelot's Bear Cub

SOME inherited strain in Lancelot's blood gave him a true
hunter's instinct. Ancestors with brass-studded leather
shields and inadequate spears, relying largely on their
wits as they pursued a stag or wild boar, had passed along an
instinctive understanding of creatures of the wild and an
inherent love of the forest. His first woods thrill at Bathol
was on a Sunday afternoon when he watched a black bear
pleasantly engaged in ripping open a pine stump in search of
honey. Sometimes he went walking with Jonathan or Melody
but more often he roamed by himself. He gained confidence
in his sense of direction as he roved farther each Sunday,
getting to know hardwood knolls where wild plums fruited
abundantly and beechnuts brought grouse and squirrels in
the autumn; glades where mountain ash and moosewood grew,
succulent undergrowth by lily ponds where moose tracks were
like cattle trails.

At one such place he watched a bull moose suddenly emerge
from its wallow of liquid mud. The huge animal moved with
scarcely a sound to a path where it stood, savouring the wind,
its great ears thrust forward to catch the slightest noise.

Puzzled by its sudden flight, Lancelot remained hidden and
saw a young Indian moving with incredible quietness on the
trail of the moose. He rose from his hiding with imitative
silence, noting with amusement the startled gaze of the
Micmac. "Art tha after yon bull?" he queried.

The redskin darted a quick look about him. "You alone?"
he asked.

Lancelot nodded carelessly. "I wur just roaming t' woods."
The Indian relaxed. They sat on a windfall and began a

guarded conversation that ended in friendship.   Joe Paul, like Lancelot, was a solitary rover, ten miles from his wigwam at Maccan.   He led the young Yorkshireman to several beaver dams and to other haunts of moose.

It was dusk when they separated at a hill near the great willow and agreement was made for similar excursions.   Each Sunday they explored new territory and the Indian's tutoring was invaluable.   Lancelot began to observe every sign of thicket and wood path, to interpret the clamour of jays and crows.   So it was that he noticed Tristram take the short cut through the woods to Smith's mill.

He found the path for himself readily enough, followed it to the brook and saw that Tristram had bathed there.   The next hot afternoon he told Jonathan about the spot.   They slipped away from their work and were hurrying on the path when Lancelot, leading, put up his hand.   His quick ear had heard a twig snapped under hasty tread and he pulled Jonathan to hiding as they saw Marsh Rose emerge by the far end of the pool and strip herself to nakedness with amazing celerity.

Then she idled on the grassy bank, studying her reflection in the water and, quite obviously, watching the path.   The brothers stole back the way they had come and it was easy for Lancelot to find in a fringe of birch saplings the bower from which the Indian girl had watched the farm.   "Tristram!" said Jonathan grimly.   "Aye," nodded Lancelot, but when they went back to their work they said nothing to him of where they had been.

Lancelot was delighted when Jonathan suggested that they get an Indian to act as guide and go on a long hunt.   He asked Garrison his opinion, and the little man thought it a prime move.   "Nothin' pleases a redskin more than showin' a white man how smart he is in the woods.   'Sides, you kin pervide yourselves with meat for the cost of lead and powder. Let the Injuns take an odd rump or so and they'll think they are well paid."

"Thear is one they call Joe Paul," said Lancelot cautiously. "Could tha get him?"

Garrison wrinkled his nose and spat.   "Nothin' easier."

He scanned Lancelot's blue eyes.   "Are you sure you don't know that Injun yourself?"

"Happen I do," said Lancelot shrewdly, "it's best tha make t' bargain."

Paul brought with him a brave who looked older than himself and spoke little English.   They camped the first night near the cranberry vines of an old beaver meadow and grey jays hovered around them as their camp-fire sent flickering light among the trees.   Tomas, the older Indian, built a tipped-brush screen to throw heat on their beds of spruce boughs.   A lug-pole of ash carried their cooking kettle and savoury odours of a thick meaty stew added to the hour. Tomas smoked in silence when the meal was ended but Paul examined Jonathan's long rifle with eagerness.

Every sound of the forest came distinctly on the frosty air and as the moon climbed into the sky, its light increasing, they heard a restless moose come out on the meadow and saw the beast, painted black against the hazy white of the snow-covered reeds.   The Indians gazed without excitement, saying the animal was a cow and they would not kill until they had found a prime bull.   Then they curled up like dogs in their blankets and slept.

Tomas could read trails in the snow with a sureness that was like magic to the Yorkshiremen.   In a week they had shot many partridge and small game.   The Indians showed them how to stretch pelts, how to build a bush wickee-up in a storm, and how to snare foxes and mink and otter.   They killed a big moose near home and carried the meat to the woods at the top of the hill.   Joe Paul bid them good-bye with some ceremony.   Then the redmen were gone under the trees, leaving only their dark tracks in the snow.

Jonathan and Lancelot took to the house an Indian hunter smell of wood smoke, raw skins and balsam, wild and sharp and disturbing, but Melody made much of their success. She cooked moose steaks as tender as young Yorkshire beef and spent evenings trying to master the smattering of Micmac that Lancelot had learned.

In the spring Jonathan went over for a day to the abandoned farm and helped Tristram clear its well.   The water was good and was easily reached with pole and bucket. Tristram announced he would move to the house and start a home for himself. Lancelot was busy tapping maples. Melody boiled the sap he gathered and made a syrup that Asa loved. The snow had gone. Soon the woods had a sharp savour of aromatic buds and sappy twigs and pungent young leaves.

The day Lancelot knocked the wooden spiles from notches he had made in the maples he was startled by menacing sounds in the gloom. A black furry head defied him over a windfall. It was a mother bear. Her cub, squealing with fright, had upended itself in a brush tangle.

Bears were a threat to sheep, so Lancelot hurried to get the long rifle he had leaned against a tree. He shot truly and the old bear sprawled beside the blowdown while the cub whimpered in terror. Her hide was spring ragged so Lancelot left the carcase where it lay. He caught the cub, rolled it in his jacket and took it home. Melody helped him teach it to take warm milk and bread, and it entertained them with such droll antics that the settlers came to view it.

It was kept in a strong log pen that could only be opened from the outside. The day Patience was married everyone admired the cub. Gideon reckoned it would fetch more than two pounds hard money at Halifax. The next morning the fastening bar was on the ground, the door open and the cub gone.

Lancelot searched the nearest woods but found no trace of it. Then he set off, belatedly, for the fort to greet any Banfield folks who might have come in the two ships.

BOOK TWO
1773

I

The Coach Without Wheels

ASA LIKED the grain of Nova Scotia pine and spruce. It was hard for him to understand that he might cut down a tree almost anywhere he fancied, and he stored every piece of timber saved from the house framing. Putting shelves and cupboards in the new house was a joy for him. He kept a pile of pine blocks under his bed. Often at night he would reach for a smooth block and fondle it till he could sleep again.

Jonathan and Lancelot were kind to him. They admired his cleverness with tools and praised his carving. Melody would often kiss him as she had done when a ten-year-old. She kept his big chair by the window and saw to every comfort for him. But it was different with Tristram. They seldom spoke to each other and Asa sensed that his oldest son had no patience with him. The idea grew until he avoided Tristram whenever possible.

His favourite spot for dreaming was at the big willow. He had taken there his sack of Yorkshire earth and inserted it in a plot large enough to stand on. He felt himself back in Banfield when his feet were planted on it and it pleased him greatly that no one had guessed his secret.

He was back of the big willow one day when he saw Tristram go into the woods as if he were looking for a pole to cut. But at the woods edge Tristram stood and looked back with a furtiveness that made Asa instantly alert. When Tristram was gone under the trees Asa moved silently into a space nearby, sank to his knees and could see his son halted by a gnarled spruce.

It was impossible for him to detect what Tristram was doing

so he lay hidden until Tristram was gone.   Then he went to the tree and explored a cavity under its roots.   His hands encountered rubble at first but soon he had found a leather sack.

Asa trembled with excitement.   He drew the sack from its hiding and replaced the rubble he had disturbed.   Then he went a distance into the woods and opened the leather bag. Chickadees came very near him for the old man was silent. He gaped in amazement.   The sack was filled with gold coins.   He tumbled them on moss and counted.   There was more than two hundred pounds in hard money.   He had not seen as much in many years.

For a time he tried to think, then he went back to the big willow and buried the coins in his earth.   A quirk of craftiness set him to filling the sack with small stones.   Then he drew the drawstrings tight and knotted them thoroughly. Chuckling to himself, he went back to the spruce and restored the bag to its hiding place.   For a few days after he thought of telling Melody about his find, and then he forgot it.

The deep snow was bewildering but he did not mind the winter.   He was engrossed in making a long chain from a pine stick.   He worked daily by his window.   He had seen a wooden chain once with sixty links, and it was his ambition to make a longer one.   He told Melody that when it was finished he would put it on exhibition at the next Banfield fair.

When the chain was finished some twist of memory fastened his mind on the Yorkshire coach in which he had ridden many times.

"Happen I had wood," he said to Jonathan, "I'd build a coach, like t' one that run to York."

Jonathan looked at the rude cart track that followed the river.

"Whear'd tha get wheels?" he questioned.

"Down to Backfall coom next winter," said Asa.   "Tha knows it will take a longish time to build a coach."

"Aye," agreed Jonathan.   "I'll get thee all t' lumber tha need."

Days on end the old man seemed to sit by the window and

dream but his knives were fashioning pieces that became whip-holder and baggage rail. A king's crest was carved to show that the coach carried mail. In May he had the axles finished. Jonathan drove strong posts in the earth beside the sentinel elms and across them the axles were spiked solidly. Then, bit by bit, the framework of the coach grew. Asa smoothed each part lovingly, hummed ancient Yorkshire airs as he worked and, when resting, thought the Bathol stream the river at Banfield.

II

Gov'ment Trouble

WHEN Tristram heard that two schooners had come
with Yorkshire people a thousand hopes rushed
through his thinking. There had been no letter from
Unity but it was not likely that she would have written if
she were coming. It might be that she was already waiting
him at the fort, sure that he would have had word of the ships.
Abel Plumley had a horse he could ride and he secured promise
of it before he tried to sleep, going across the fields after the
wedding guests had gone home.

In its pen the bear cub whined softly, prelude to an outburst
of complaint. Tristram's nerves jangled. He let himself
out from the kitchen door and the cub, listening, made no
further protest. A sledge for stake driving rested by the
spring shed and he picked it up, hefted it nicely and took the
bar from the door of the pen. The cub scampered out into
the moonlight and there was only the sound of heavy iron
crushing soft skull.

The blow knocked the cub into the chips by the kindling
block but Tristram snatched up the small carcase before it
could bleed. He ran in his bare feet to an old woodchuck
burrow in the pasture and thrust the small bundle far inside,
then trod down the edges until the entrance was blocked.

When he was back in his bed he was able to sleep soundly
and he said nothing of what he had done in the morning.

The barracks at the fort were crowded with families. More
than one hundred Yorkshire settlers had arrived and Titus
Green was busy as a dog burying a bone. Tristram's heart
leaped as he saw Jacob Cornforth, a Banfield farmer. He
shook hands warmly.

"Happen tha have word of Unity," he said. "Did she coom?"

"Noa," said Cornforth. "She's not coom. But her father's dead."

"Dead!"

"Aye. First o' winter."

"Then she could coom. Did she say nowt about it?"

"Ask Emily." Cornforth nodded toward his wife, a solid, hearty woman with reddish hair.

Apprehension prodded Tristram. He went to Mrs. Cornforth with reluctance. The big woman was not one to mince words with any person.

"Whear's thy folks?" she demanded after greetings. "Happen we'll find land whear tha live."

"Tha couldn't do better than coom to Bathol," said Tristram warmly. "Did tha see Unity?"

"Aye." Mrs. Cornforth's lips tightened. "I've a letter for thee." She scanned him with critical eyes. "Tha should not fight wi' thy brother."

His fight with Matthew!

He flushed and made no answer. Small use to protest that his brother had been drinking. So he waited her pleasure in giving him the letter, telling her that if her family would come to Bathol the settlers would assist them in every way.

The letter was the first Unity had ever written him, and was brief.

TRISTRAM—Your letter to hand and I am pleased that God has prospered you in Nova Scotia. It is with full heart I tell you that father has passed to his reward. I cannot pay rent longer so will sell what I have and go to live with an aunt in Backfall. It hurts me to know you have quarreled so bitterly with Matthew. No good can come while there is ill-will between brothers and I earnestly pray that you will be reconciled before long. There is nothing more that I can write at this time. UNITY LEMMING.

Address care of Eunice Lemming. Backfall, Yorkshire.

Tristram read the letter three times, and stared, unseeing, about him. If only he knew who had written to Yorkshire about him. He would beat the man to a pulp, even if it were Matthew himself. Then his rage spent itself and he talked with the Cornforths again, urging that they see Bathol for themselves. Finally he unhitched his horse, mounted and rode from the fort.

At Amherst village he tied the nag to a post and had a meal at the tavern. No one at the fort had invited him to eat with them. A frowsy slattern served him meat poorly done, but he ate without comment, paid his toss and mounted again. Outside the village he slowed his horse to a walk and rode, thinking, until he was at the Point.

Matthew's house looked far in from the road but he saw Sylvia in the yard feeding fowl, and as he watched, a woman came from the adjoining farm, using a field path. He stopped his horse. The woman was Patience. He had forgotten that Gideon owned the next farm.

He turned his horse boldly into the yard. The women looked at him, and at each other. "Good day," said Sylvia calmly. "Art looking for Matthew?"

Patience looked up with quick gaze. "Tristram—is father sick?"

"Noa," he said gruffly. "I've been over to fort."

"Matthew's thear," said Sylvia. "Did Unity coom?"

He had expected the question and her tone told him that she had not written anything to Unity. He looked at his sister. "Noa," he said harshly. "Someone took trouble to write her more than wur needed. Happen I find oot who, they'll settle wi' me."

He saw no fear in Patience's eyes, and relented. "I've coom," he said with great effort, "to make peace wi' Matthew, if tha think he will."

Neither woman answered. They were looking toward the road. He turned and saw Matthew riding in the lane.

Matthew pulled rein when he saw who awaited him and walked his horse into the yard. Tristram faced him fairly. "I've coom," his voice was strained, "to tell thee I am sorry for my temper, and to ask thee to forgive me." Then he added, almost pleading. "Wilt tha, Matthew?"

Matthew's glance dropped from him to the watching women

and Sylvia's hand pressed his knee, urging. He put out his hand. "I forgive," he said simply. "Put oop thy horse and stop to supper."

They shook hands and Tristram tingled with the warmth in the hard grip Matthew gave him. His urge was to get back to his work but he put it from him and dismounted. He would see what furnishing Sylvia had in her house that had belonged to Uncle Malachy. Gradually elation spread over him. Matthew was joking as if nothing had happened between them and Patience let gratitude shine in her face.

He resolved to write to Unity, and after they had eaten asked Sylvia for materials.

"My dear," he put thought into each line, "your letter duly handed me by Emily Cornforth. It is with sore heart I read your lines for I have long waited your reply. My prayer is that you will not grieve overlong now that you are alone but will come to me and share the home I am now making ready. It is a new place apart from the rest of my family, so you will be mistress entirely. This day I have made peace with my brother, Matthew, and all is well with us. Indeed I am humble to think there ever should have been trouble. Oh my dear, this land is rich in all grains and roots but nothing will bring content if you do not hasten to join me. In my work I think of thee and no other. It may be that the Cornforths will take up land near us. My dear I am sure you would be happy with so many old friends about us. Please take passage in the next ship that will come and if money is lacking I will repay any loan. TRISTRAM CRABTREE."

He sanded the ink carefully and called Patience. "Tha can read what I have written," he said, "if tha will put encouragement in."

Patience read the letter.

"My dear," she wrote below his lines, "I add my prayer with Tristram that thee will come to him. He has truly made peace with Matthew. The people here are a fine folk and the land is good. I have married lately and sign myself PATIENCE DANKS."

It was Gideon who took the letter. He would ride to the fort, he said, and send it with the ships. Thanking him, Tristram noted how marriage had changed the man. Gideon had his seeding done, his fences mended, fine cattle in his pasture. He had a snug home, better than the one that would receive Unity. Tristram surveyed Matthew's holding. It, too, was better than he would have at Bathol. The house was large and well built. Resolve burned him. As sure as there was sky above him he would one day have a better home than either of them. He would do it. Nothing could stop him.

When Tristram reached Nappan it was evening and the Lother young men, with Adam Chipley, were entering Niles' house. They called for him to stop.

"Have tha heard t' news," shouted Adam Chipley. "Thear is trouble. Coom in. Tha can stop t' night wi' me."

The invitation cheered Tristram, but word of trouble worried him. He hitched his horse and went in.

There was such a hubbub within the house that at first it was hard to discover the reason. Henry Niles and his large wife sat on one side of the table with a jug before them. A stranger was with them, a red-faced man with dirty hands and a greasy jacket. Adam Chipley and two Lother young men, Benjamin and Rufus, had stools along the wall. Across the table sat a small man with a beard so high that his head looked all hair and whiskers. Beside him, in contrast, his wife bulked, an Amazon with drooping breasts like batter cakes, her arms and wrists ponderous. She and her husband had mugs beside them and their excited tone indicated that they had emptied them more than once.

Tristram stood, looking about him, seeing two milk buckets, unwashed, on a bench by the fireplace, a pup cowering in a corner, pop-eyed youngsters peering from the loft.

"Pull up a bench," shrilled Mrs. Niles. "This stranger is Sim Gilbert from outside of Boston. These two," she nodded at the couple across the table, "is Jake Gold and his missus from the next farm. Sim, you begin over and tell the trouble that's started where you've been."

Sim poured from the jug into a cup he kept in his hands and drank with his head back like a fat rooster. He hiccoughed. "I swan I never thought there could be any place so iggerent of what goes on. There's been talk of trouble more'n a year down where I come from, and you didn't know. Why sojers is everywhere and there's fresh talk of getting an army to match 'em." He wagged his head as if such ignorance baffled his credulity.

"Trouble," repeated Rufus Lother, a big lad with a back like a barn door. "What trouble?"

"Gov'ment trouble. That's the kind of trouble." Sim sucked a last drop from his cup as Mrs. Niles moved the jug out of his reach. "It's the gov'ment that's made it. Our folks ain't goin' to put up with any more bullyin' from Britishers. We're all bred from emmygrants but that don't mean we ain't got rights good as anybody. The start was at Rhode Island last year when they burned a schooner belongin' to the gov'ment and damn' near killed the officer."

"For what?" said Chipley.

"Trouble, man. Don't ye understand? It's gov'ment trouble."

"Do tha mean Rhode Island is rebel?" Rufus Lother had contempt in his voice.

"Rebel be damned. They're levelers. No high and mighty lobster back is goin' to come over here and tramp us in the dirt. We're goin' to have a free country."

"Sojers don't bother us here," said Gold. "We're free as anybody."

"You're payin' tax if it's tea up there in that caddy," snarled Sim, looking at the shelf. "Who give them blasted Britishers any right to tax our tea?"

"Over hoam," said Adam Chipley, "tha pays a shilling tax."

"Home's not Ameriky," flung Sim. "We don't ask what they pay or don't pay. It's what they try to make us pay. I'll wager there ain't been ten pounds of tea drunk from Maine to Boston."

He paused and watched with apparent fascination as Niles drank thirstily from the jug. "That's right." Niles wiped his mouth. "Where does the tax money go? You tell 'em we'll back 'em in Nova Scotia. If we all stand together what can a few sojers do?"

"We want no trouble with sojers," protested Gold. "We'll stay out of it."

"Good thing you ain't up in my country, mister," said Sim. "They're makin' it rough for king's men." He looked at Tristram. "Are you a Tory?"

Tristram eyed him coldly. "We have nowt to do wi' ony," he said.

"There'll come a time ye will. It don't take a prophet to see there's a heap of gov'ment trouble comin'. It'll spread down here."

"It can't," said Gold stubbornly. "We'll mind our business."

Mrs. Niles took the cup from Sim and poured it brimming full. "Who are you speakin' for?" she demanded, drinking with hearty swallows. "I have kin over in Concord and I aim to take their part against any Britishers."

Gold gave her a sombre look. "If a person's hankerin' for trouble they'll allus find it, no matter where they're livin'."

"Are you tryin' to say I'm lookin' for trouble?" Hostility flamed across Mrs. Niles' horsey countenance. "Just because you're a wormy little . . ."

"I'll thank you to keep a civil tongue in your head, Maggie Niles." Mrs. Gold had a voice as deep as a man's. "Jake's said nothin' but gospel truth."

Colour flooded Mrs. Niles' features. "I said your husband was a wormy . . ."

She did not say further. Mary Gold rose with remarkable agility for one so bulky and fetched her hostess a resounding slap across the mouth.

Instant action ensued. Mrs. Niles attempted to retaliate in like manner and tipped the table in her lunge, as Rufus Lother caught up the candle. Her husband rescued the jug and was left holding it as Sim, losing support of the table, went down heavily, breaking the cup. Gold skipped away from danger, and stepped on the pup in the corner, causing it to yelp dismally. Overhead the youngsters began bawling.

Mrs. Gold made no retreat. She faced her enemy with grim courage and took such toll with straight punches to the midriff that Mrs. Niles was driven back to the wall. Tristram rose from his bench to avoid collision. The empty milk buckets rolled to the floor and gave Mrs. Niles inspiration. She scooped one up and clapped it neatly over her opponent's head.

It fitted so closely that Mrs. Gold staggered like a decapitated hen, affording Mrs. Niles excellent opportunity to drive in with destructive jabs. Her eagerness for a quick victory was her undoing. Mrs. Gold achieved a firm grip on her linsey-woollen dress, raised her knee and drove it into Mrs. Niles anatomy.

Mrs. Niles withered under the assault. She tried to escape. It was her dress, however, not Mrs. Gold's grip, that yielded, and she pitched against the wall, her dress torn to the waist and her flabby bosom revealed.

Adam Chipley pulled open the door and went outside. Tristram followed him, the frightened pup bolting past his legs. He untied his horse and led it to the Chipley home. Behind them they could hear slams and screechings as the battle continued.

There was a light in the kitchen and when they went in Lancelot was seated with Mrs. Chipley. Tristram stopped short. "Happen I had better go on," he said.

"Rubbish!" snorted Mrs. Chipley. "We have two extra beds, and tha are not strangers."

"I was to see Matthew," said Tristram, watching his brother. "I had supper wi' him and Sylvia."

Lancelot started. "That will please Sylvia," said Mrs. Chipley.

"I'm goin' to t' fort," said Lancelot. "T' bear cub's gone. Did tha see it when tha got oop?"

"Noa," said Tristram frankly. "Tha knows I never look at it."

When the crops were in, Tristram's barn was raised and, in the same week, there was a second raising for the Cornforths. They put up a big house near the Garrisons. There were more raisings. It had been a good year. The rains had been early, the hay season dry and the ripening sun a heartening sequence. The yield of grain and roots exceeded all expectations. Barns and cellars could not hold the year's bounty.

Peregrine Knatchball settled near the Cornforths. He put up a log smithy and ox frame, built a small cabin. The Garrison children flocked to watch him work his bellows, for he had plenty of shoeing of both horses and cattle. Reuben Scurr was a cousin of the Crabtrees. He had worked as a hostler at Backfall. The Hodges helped him put up a cabin near them and Jonathan made him a table, benches and a bed. Reuben was an easy-going fellow with no knack of tools and small liking for too long a day with axe or plow. His wife, Judy, took life as she found it, made no complaint. She called on Melody and admired her fine kitchen, yawned like a sleepy cat when she had had a good dinner and joked with Lancelot. She was a big, handsome woman with a well-fleshed body and fine strong legs and she watched Tristram with increasing interest when he invited her to inspect his house.

Her praise of it, and the new barn he had built, heated his blood and as she laughed and jollied with him in his kitchen she gave him a picture that crept into his thinking for days afterward.

III

The Cattle Drive

THE MAPLES flamed and dropped their leaves; birches took on golden colours, the oaks their red and brown. In the alders grouse drummed in the afternoons, reverberating throbs that rolled out to end in a confused whirr. Along the Bathol intervales cold night mists were slow in burning up before the morning sun.

Jonathan watched the cows come filing through the yard gate, their bellies wide with feeding, their flanks rounded with a filling of water from the brook. Behind them, in the pasture, the two-year-olds poked about uneasily, anxious for a bed in the stable. Ezra Hodge stood with him.

"They'd bring top price in Halifax," he said. "Over't Windsor they said a drive sold in one day. There are ships in t' harbour wanting beef."

"They're gradely cattle," assented Jonathan. "Pity to butcher such champion beasts. We couldn't hurry them."

"No need," argued Ezra. "There's feed along and t' weather will howd fair this time o' year. We'd rest at Partridge Island. T' ferry would make two trips wi' t' beasts."

They organized a cattle drive. Nearly every Yorkshireman at Bathol had fatted steers. A drive down the hogback to Partridge Island would be less than forty miles, and after the ferry crossing there was but another forty miles to the market. Careful driving would keep fat on the steers, and they picked the three big Cornforth boys, Aaron and Samson and John, both the Lother brothers, and Reuben Scurr.

The drive was gathered at the river ford and the cattle bawled and milled about the meadow, smoke of the drovers'

113

fires making them uneasy, so the first day's drive was a short one to River Hebert. The second day was better. They pastured at noon in the last deserted Acadian clearing where apples were ripe in abandoned trees and red-tipped rose bushes still survived.

The drovers ate their bread and cheese where they sat watching the cattle, drinking in turn from a spring. The scent of sun-heated spruce mingled with the reek of cattle droppings as they started on. In the thick growth the trail seemed airless. Squirrels chirred drowsily, careless in the heat. When they were still the silence was thinly threaded by the chirping of birds that waited for the noon warmth to pass.

The drive filed out in a long, restless string, making it imperative that the drovers keep pace through the bush on either side. Flies irritated the steers to violent brushings against the trees. The hour was exhausting to both men and beasts. Suddenly the herd stopped, its leaders snorting anxiously.

"Bear," said Jonathan tersely. "T' smell will soon go."

The men made careful excursions along each flank of the nervous cattle, calling in reassuring tones. After a time they urged the drive on. It was still alert but soon regained confidence.

They reached Partridge Island without mishap. It was dusk, an evening poignant with the scent of clover and smell of the sea. The cattle grazed a day before the first load was taken to Windsor. Jonathan went with it, leaving Abel Plumley in charge of the second lot. He took with him Aaron and Samson Cornforth, Reuben Scurr and Rufus Lother. After landing they moved their cattle to a hill near the Windsor ford. There was plenty of grass in open land spotted with hazel groves. It was apart from the village with no pastures near.

The ferryman cautioned them that Windsor drovers would be so jealous of such fine cattle going to the Halifax market that they might try some mischief in the dark. The York-shiremen listened soberly, deciding on an all-night watch. Scurr and Aaron Cornforth took over the first period, walking to keep themselves awake, checking any steer that tried to leave the herd. Then Jonathan took over, with Samson Cornforth to help him.

The cattle were still, lying together in dark groups, and the only sound was the faraway hooting of an owl. Jonathan sat on the higher ground, watching and listening. The hard heat of the year was gone and this was the kind of quietness that came when the earth slowed down and steadied itself for winter. He felt an edge in the small wind, the edge of coming rain. There were no insect murmurs; no twittering birds. The moon had risen. Its light silvered the grass stubble about him and lay on the knolls like a depthless mist. It was the kind of a night when the land gave up its thick scents of straw and stacked grain; of stubble field and dyke banks; of barn yards and sheep pens. It was new country to him but he could catch each smell distinct and clear from the others. A night like this, he thought, was all a man could ask.

One of the steers raised its head and looked toward the nearest thicket. On the far side of the herd Samson trudged back and forth like a drowsy soldier on an accustomed beat. Jonathan was seated at the edge of a small hollow in which the other men slept. A tuft of hazel bushes gave him cover from any prowler in the woods.

Each man had cut for himself a stout cudgel of hardwood, withy and green. Jonathan picked one up and squirmed his way across the lowest ground, taking advantage of every clump of weeds or grass as Joe Paul had shown him in hunting. He reached the wood, peered into its shadowy depths. Samson still plodded his round, the moonlight making him an elongated figure, but the steer had risen.

Jonathan ghosted forward among the small trees, making no sound on dew-wet moss, until he was at the rear of any possible intruder. Then, gripping his stick ready for action, he crept on.

An apparition rose before him, feathered and paint-streaked. It stood and whispered, holding a long musket at the trail. A second savage materialized from a fern bed, his neck ringed with raccoon tails, a heavy brass pistol in his hands. Then a third appeared, gliding in from cover of a spruce thicket. The trio whispered together, pointed. They were at the fringe of the wood and by raising and looking Jonathan saw that Samson had missed him and was coming around the cattle.

The three Indians crouched. "Jonty!" Samson called softly so as not to disturb the herd. "Where art tha sitting?"

"Here!" shouted Jonathan. He leaped ahead and struck, knocking the musket from the nearest redskin, jabbing with his cudgel to upset the savage with the pistol. It exploded with a loud report. Then the brave who had lost his musket grappled with Jonathan and they rolled on the sod. Samson charged in among the trees, shouting. The cattle heaved up and began running, tails over their backs. The men in the hollow, sleep-dazed, stumbled from their beds, clubs in hand, in pursuit.

Jonathan's first thought was that his attacker would have a knife, and he flung him over and pinioned him so strongly that the Indian gasped and relaxed. Samson weighed over two hundred pounds and could move swiftly. The pistol shot galvanized him to a leaping charge, and gave him direction. His cudgel knocked aside a musket barrel as a flint missed fire and the next instant he had crashed his enemy to earth with a foot to the stomach. His speed tumbled him among the hummocks but as he went down he seized a befeathered figure that sneezed from powder smoke and groped for the brass pistol.

"Mercy," panted Jonathan's victim. "Yer killin' me."

"White Indians!" grunted Samson. He had snared the pistoler and in a trice he retrieved the speechless recipient of his kick to the midriff. He rose with them, dragged them out to the moonlight.

Running desperately, the other men had kept the herd together and gradually the cattle quieted. No other disturbers appeared.

"What have tha there?" gasped Scurr.

"Speak oop," ordered Samson. The man he had booted was still limp so he gave his second prisoner a shake.

"Wait. I'll t-t-talk," moaned the fellow, his teeth chattering. "We were hired to scare yer cattle, so help me, and no more."

Jonathan gave his man to Scurr to hold, went back and found the musket that missed fire. "Draw the load," he ordered and the wretch, shaking, rolled a ball from the muzzle.

Scurr and Aaron trussed them with ropes brought for troublesome steers. The fellows begged for their lives, swearing they had been hired by drovers to scare the Yorkshire cattle, to kill a few and to make the Yorkshiremen think they had been attacked by Indians. They groaned and shivered on the wet grass and the kicked man was wretchedly sick.

The rest of the cattle came over on the morning tide and the drive went on. At Windsor Jonathan handed over their prisoners, their feathers sadly bedraggled, their paint smeared fantastically by Rufus Lother who had acted as their guard.

The officer at the blockhouse ordered the culprits in irons. "Francklin's trying to build up a cattle trade," he said, "and he's special fond of you Yorkshire men. These chaps will wish they'd never been born."

Word of their capture spread ahead of the herd. At noon they rested near a brook and farmers came to view the cattle. "Watch your step in Halifax," they warned. "The press gangs would work all night to get a few hands like your lot."

It began to rain that night, causing the cattle to huddle together in a fenced pasture a settler rented for two shillings. The men slept in the loft of the farmer's barn. Only one man at a time kept watch of the herd, crouching under a thick spruce with a fire beside him to beat off the chill.

Buyers met them outside the town, eyed their herd and offered prices that even Ezra Hodge had not expected. They kept on till they reached the market. There they sold the cattle, getting paid in gold before they would part with a single steer. It had been a long road and tiresome. They obtained beds on the floor of one room in a tavern, for the town was crowded, then slept as if the end of the world had come.

When they roused the next noon the rain had ended. A rising wind was drying town paths and whirling leaves to soggy burial in ditches. Ezra Hodge said he wanted to buy

some amber soap for his mother. Lancelot wanted a good
rifle if he could find one, then some ribbons and perfumery to
please Melody. Each man wanted something so they
travelled to all the shops.

Lancelot had luck in his search. At the headstone carver's
little shop a fine rifle was offered for sale, a weapon of comparatively small calibre, not so long in the barrel as Jonathan's,
but with a reinforced chamber and counter weights near the
muzzle to eliminate upkick.

The stone cutter gave them grim warning. "The press gang
will be on shore afore dark. They'll pay an extry bounty for
men of your size. You had better be gone from the town."

He gave them no idle rumour. Tall masts showed at the
water-front and seamen in wide-legged sailors slops gave them
hard stares as they filed along the streets and made little
excursions into taverns. At dusk they found they were being
trailed by a tough-looking bully in tarred hat and pea jacket.
He was following them, they decided, to see where they would
turn in for the night.

"After me, lads," said Jonathan, boldly entering "The
Golden Ball," a tavern they had avoided because the rates
were a sixpence more than they cared to pay. Serving
maids gaped open-mouthed as they entered and a negro handy
boy squeezed himself to a corner.

They sat to a good enough dinner of beef and onions, with
tarts and blueberry pie to finish, and coffee with lump sugar.
Then Jonathan paid the bill and tipped the kitchen wench a
tanner to let them out the back door. It opened to an alley
running to an upper street and in five minutes they were back
to the tavern where they had slept, and where their stout cudgels were stowed under their blankets and cooking utensils.

"We'll start in t' morning," said Ezra Hodge, "and be well
quit o' this town. We want nowt to do wi' press gangs."

"Hisst," said Scurr, by the window. "They're at it
already."

He was right. Mixed cries like a shrilling of excited gulls
came faintly to the tavern attic and when they listened they
could make out the words. "Press! Press! Take cover!
Press!"

The yells rose and ebbed as the gang worked along the water-front and after a time died to no more than occasional shouts. A moment later the tavern keeper came up the steps, his face pale in the candle light. "Press gang's after you lads," he palpitated. "They've searched 'The Golden Ball' cellar to top, and they'll be here. Better go 'fore they come."

Samson Cornforth pulled forth his cudgel. "Let them coom," he growled. "None will get oop t' stairs."

"Please, men," begged the proprietor, "yer can't hold them off. They'd go back and bring fifty hands if need be. I've seen 'em put twenty men in a stable loft to bring out a pair of Dutchmen."

Jonathan and Ezra rolled up the blankets and gear. "We'll put stoof oot by t' rock top o' hill," they said, "and coom back." They knew it useless to try and keep the Cornforth and Lother men from the excitement.

Each man left his bundle where it could be snatched up quickly, then they hustled back through the darkness. They were slipping again by the back way to the tavern when a lantern's gleam eddied around a corner, throwing light into the alley. A half-dozen burly seamen led by a swaggering giant in a three-cornered hat peered at them and roared like dogs springing a bull. "At 'em," bellowed the giant, and swung an oak stretcher to fell Aaron Cornforth.

His attack was sudden but he slipped in stinking slops underfoot as a woman, with hair like a witch's disorder, screeched warning as she leaned far out from a window overhead, and Aaron put the big bully asleep with a crack of his cudgel that sounded cruel enough. One seaman fell over his leader and lost his piece of oak. Samson reached out before he could scuttle backward, picked him by the scruff of the neck and thwacked his head grimly against the nearest wall. The rest of the gang backed away, whispering together.

"Happen tha don't want new hands," bantered Aaron. "Why don't tha coom along?"

"Watch," screamed the woman. "A gang's gettin' behind, without light."

There was a rush in the dark and the advantage was with the new gang for the Yorkshiremen were in silhouette against the lantern glow. Lancelot, in the rear, however, had heard the scramblings and he, with the Lother boys, had been watching, keeping their eyes turned to the murk.

They parted and let the first fellows near, then struck together, each dropping his man. That much Jonathan saw, then all was confusion. There were at least ten bullies in the flanking party and five survivors at the front, fortified with an issue of rum and promise, no doubt, of a free day ashore if they brought in their catch.

He saw big Samson, disarmed by a tricky blow, stoop and heave a stunned seaman, bodily bowling a trio of the enemy off their feet; saw him regain his cudgel and flatten an assailant with a sweep that knocked his legs from under him; saw Aaron bang an opponent to the wall with his fist, and saw Ezra Hodge hit the fellow so that he dropped forward, out on his feet. Then a bloody head, hatless, reared before him, and hot breath snarled seamen's curses. He struck with his fist, his weight behind it, and felt the man's nose bones crush under his knuckles, was thrust against him by surging bodies, saw him cracked hard with a stick end, and then was heaved on.

Samson and Aaron were behind him, eager for new targets, but above their shouts he heard the shrill woman again. "Run, Yorkshire. A new crowd's coming up the street."

Jonathan jumped over several unconscious seamen to the alley opening and looked down the hill. A score of lanterns bobbed unevenly and half a ship's crew seemed in the mob.

He jumped back and yelled warning. Overhead the slattern screeched like a lunatic. In the alley a concerted rush headed by the Lothers and Samson mowed everything down and Jonathan, following, tripped over squirming casualties until he was in the clear.

"Coom!" he shouted. "We can do nowt! There's a hundred men after us!"

Panting, jostling together in the dark, they ran, through a field, up a hill, and away with their bundles. Wild yells hung over the town and lanterns appeared as far up as Citadel slopes. But no pursuers appeared on the cart roads leading to the farms. The seamen would not risk any mêlée out in the blackness of bush and stubble field.

"That wur a champion go," chuckled Aaron Cornforth. "I've a lump like an egg whear stick caught me, but it wur worth it."

"Hold oop," panted his biggest brother, John, a slow man like Abel Plumley. "Art counted us?"

Jonathan felt his bowels pucker. They gathered and counted. Ezra Hodge, Lancelot, Aaron, John, Samson, the two Lothers and Abel Plumley.

"Whear's Reuben Scurr?"

None of them had seen him, when they tried to remember. He had got his man in the first rush that came from the rear, and then had seemed to vanish.

"Thear's nowt we can do now," said Jonathan. "They'll be like hounds round a fox hole till midnight, thinking we'll coom back after him. We'll bed somewhere and watch road till toon's quiet."

A stack of hay near the cart ruts made an excellent outpost and they bedded together in their blankets, with one man keeping watch.

The late moon was up, struggling with a dank fog, when Jonathan wakened Lancelot and climbed down from the stack with him. They slipped away without waking the others and were in the field back of the tavern before they realized it, the fog deceiving them. It was impossible to see anything in the alley but after listening a time they were sure none of the press gang lay in wait. They probed with their sticks and found nothing. The street was a ghostly ravine and the mist so thick that lanterns near the water-front were no more than lighter spots in the gloom.

Jonathan tapped with his cudgel against the side of the house, the sound echoing oddly. He pounded again and the window overhead was raised. "Yorkshire?" They could see no more than the blur of a face but they were sure it was the woman who had given them warnings.

"Aye," called Jonathan softly. "Did tha see a mate o' oors after?"

"They took one of yer crew. The devils lugged him off like he were dead. Watch yerselves. They've been back twice, talkin' bloody murder.   There's too many of them'll be no good the next fortnight."

"Do tha think oor lad wur dead?" asked Lancelot.

"No bloody fear.   Ever know them hellions to bother with a stiff?   They've had him strung up.by his thumbs afore this, makin' him tell how many's in yer mob and where yer goin'. My advice is that ye get from Halifax."   She paused coyly. "If yer have a spare shillin' I'll let one in the back door till daylight, and that's best I'll do."

So they would string Scurr up and make him talk!   Jonathan and Lancelot ran until they reached the stack.   "Down wi' thee," hissed Jonathan.   "They took Reuben and happen they'll get horses and try catch us afore we reach Windsor."

Sleepily the Yorkshiremen slid down from the hay, Aaron swearing he had stiffened with hurts he had not had before he slept.   They set off briskly in the fog and long before sunrise were far into the woods beyond the town, sweating freely and swinging their clubs, half hoping a party of man-of-war lads would overtake them.

They had breakfast by a brook and slept in the bush until the sun's heat bothered them, then pushed on until they reached a tavern.   Several mounted travellers passed them on the way but none had ventured questions.   A young man at their table stared at their cuts and bruises and gulped his food nervously.

"Ony news in t' toon?" asked Jonathan.

The lad swallowed hastily.   "Plenty.   The press gang got a bear by the tail last night.   They had some farmers in an alley but more'n twenty of the ships men had hell banged out of them.   They say these drovers used clubs better'n the gang could handle their stretchers."

Samson paused over his beef and gravy.   "Like sticks yonder?" he queried, pointing to their assorted cudgels stained with blood and alley slime.

"I-I think so," stammered the lad, his face crimson.   "There was an awful row about it along the water-front but Francklin's given orders that no Yorkshiremen are to be pressed, so that's the end of it."

It was wet and cold as they trudged over the Boar's Back

to River Hebert and Lancelot shot a young moose they surprised in a thicket. They cut off the best parts and lugged the portions rolled in the hide until they reached an Acadian's cabin. They stopped with him the night, drying their clothes and blankets while his black-eyed wife cooked the moose steaks and pots of mealy potatoes.

The ground froze hard overnight and ponds skimmed with ice but they stripped and waded the river where they had crossed with the cattle and at night all had reached home.

Jonathan and Ezra went to Judy Scurr's cabin. She sat dry-eyed as they told her of the press gang taking her husband. "I'll take his wages for t' drive," she said dismally. "Heaven knows he wur poor enough provider ony time. Now they'll feed him on t' ship but what will I do?"

Tristram was given a third of the money received for the Crabtree cattle, and the payment was so unexpected that his emotions were shaken. "Take oot thy wages," he insisted, his conscience on fire. "Tha took cattle to market."

His brothers took out a small fee. "I'm moving over to my house," he continued. "I'd like thee to say what is mine."

He heard his brothers talking with Melody and in the morning the sharing was made, a dividing of cattle, sheep, pigs and poultry. He was given the best team of oxen, a spare yoke and one of the carts, the bed in which he slept. He would have to procure his own pots and pans, his baking kettle, flails, axes, forks and plows.

It was fair enough. Lancelot loaded the cart with split firewood before Tristram took it, and again the act roused Tristram's feelings.

"Tha art too good," he said huskily. "It is more than I deserve."

"Tha art oor brother," returned Lancelot.

It was too much for Tristram. He put out his hand. "I've done thee wrong," he said. "Will tha forgive me? I killed thy cub and put it in hole oop pasture. I could not sleep for t' whining, but I should not have done it."

"Aye," said Lancelot. "Summat dug it oot o' hole t' week after, and I saw."

Tristram gaped at him. "Tha knew it wur me?"

"I reckoned it wur. Jonty would not do t' like."

"Did tha tell others?"

"Noa. I thowt tha would be 'shamed enough to have it on thy mind, and I didn't want Molly to know Yorkshire folks would do t' like."

"Tha are reight," said Tristram humbly. "I'm shamed and sorry. Wilt tha forgive me?"

"Aye." They shook hands strongly and Tristram felt better.

He had money enough to buy what he must have for the winter and had made a table and stools for his kitchen. Preparing his own meals was another matter. He had never had the patience to attend a cooking kettle and for a while he fared badly. Then he developed a boil on his shoulder and went to Mrs. Plumley, asking a remedy. She made him a poultice and gave him warning.

"Tha needs a woman to cook thee plenty o' vegetables. Happen tha go living on bread and meat tha will have boils all winter."

The thought worried him. He borrowed a horse and rode to Amherst to buy crockery and to hire a woman for house-keeper. There were none to be had. As he rode back he turned into Judy Scurr's yard, tied his horse and went into her cabin. She was sat by the fire combing her fine yellow hair and she gave him warm welcome, putting her kettle to boil and insisting that he stop for supper.

"Staying alone will be t' death o' me," she told him. "Thear isn't another man I'd sooner have call."

"It's not for pleasure I've coom," he said gruffly, "but Reuben is my cousin. I'm sorry for what has happened."

"Tha art kind to say it," returned Judy, watching him so closely that he felt his face flush. "It heartens me to know that thear is one man who cares about my position."

They watched each other a moment and then she cried out for him to sit himself down.

He sat down, uncomfortable enough, and watched a smile begin back in her eyes, spread across her high cheek bones and quirk a corner of her red mouth; it was an inviting smile that made him think of her sitting across his table every day, warm and companionable.

Her chest was in one corner, her shawl and bonnet hung from pegs. There was a little crockery on a shelf, some onions and corn dangled from the rafters and dusty-looking apples draped in festoons; these seemed the extent of her possessions.

"Would tha coom to my house?" he questioned.

He saw the leap in her eyes. "What do tha mean by that?" Judy spoke as if she had selected and tasted every word before using it.

"I need a housekeeper, a woman to cook and wash and look after milk. I'll pay a fair wage and tha'll have a warm home t' winter."

"Nathan Hodge says tha have a parson's daughter promised. Happen she'll coom?"

"Not till spring. I tried to get a woman at t' village today. Then I thowt o' thee."

"Not till then?" It was the same provoking smile. "I've been thinking o' thee all t' while."

Tristram disciplined himself. "I'm pledged to be married and I'll thank thee to remember it. But if tha want to earn thy keep and a few pounds extra I'll move thy chest in morning."

She sobered. "Done. I'm a married woman, or widow, and have to keep my own respect. Mrs. Hodge said it wur a pity I couldn't work for thee. She's a good woman so she'll think t' worst. But if tha don't mind her, I don't, and I'll be ready when tha coom."

He went for her in the morning, moved everything from the cabin including a musket, powder horn and bullet mould that Reuben owned.

Tristram had two bedrooms in his house, with both doors opening from the top of the stairway. He put Judy's chest and bed into the unoccupied one, carried her fresh water from his well and made up a brisk cooking fire. Then he went to his stable to attend his chores, taking plenty of time so that his dinner would be ready when he went in.

Judy called him sooner than he expected, and he was pleased. They had said at the fort that she was lazy but his potatoes and roast beef were done to a turn and she had made a tasty sauce from apples he had gathered from an old French tree near the house. Her skin was clear and she looked a wholesome woman as she sat meekly enough at his table and filled his plate.

In the evening she sat by the fire with knitting, clicking her needles industriously, not speaking unless he spoke to her, and when an hour had gone took her candle and went primly up the stairs, saying "good night" as casually as Melody would have done.

It was a week before Tristram went over to see Jonathan about making a new road back to their different wood lots. He sensed a coolness in his brothers. Melody was more frank. She came from the house to face him. "Tha will never have Unity if tha keep Judy Scurr in thy house t' winter," she flamed. "She has a poor name and tha know it."

Tristram scowled his resentment. "Get me another, then. I'm paying her a wage to cook and wash and make butter. No one else would coom."

"Then get Molly to stop wi' her and howd thy decency. We've too good a name here to have tha shame it."

He retorted that Judy's sense of decency was as heavy as her own, then flung off. A fine thing, that, having a young girl tell him what to do. Molly Garrison indeed. She had hung around the winter before, whispering in corners with Melody, watching him whenever he came in as if he were an animal not to be trusted. He would never have a Garrison brat in his kitchen.

Judy eyed him in the evening. "They don't want me here, thy folk," she said suddenly. "I went to borrow yeast from thy sister and she wur no more than civil. Happen I'd better go?"

"T' devil tha will!" he cried. "Do no more borrowing from her. I'm as good as they and tha know it."

Her bright blue eyes dropped, almost demurely. "I know tha art headstrong," her voice softened, "but why don't thy sister trust me?"

"There isn't ony why to it," he retorted. "Do thy work and think no more o' ony o' them."

Jonathan and Lancelot joined with him in cutting the new road to a grove of winter-naked beech and birch and the weather grew bitterly cold so that the river froze over, making dark ice that glinted at sunrise. They chopped and felled trees within hailing distance of each other, loaded together, ate beside the same fire at noon, but at Christmas Tristram and Judy were not invited to the bigger house.

Melody's action galled Tristram, though he made no mention of it to Judy. She made for him a raisin pudding and cooked the goose he brought her as if she were glad they were alone. When they had eaten in the evening she went to her chest and came down to him with a dark stone jug.

"Reuben wur saving this for today," she said brightly. "If he's alive I'll warrant he's thinking o' it. Have a drop wi' me. It's champion rum."

He scowled at the jug, remembering Banfield. His father had been an easy-going man, leaving the matter of discipline largely to their mother, but in one thing he had been adamant. No strong liquor was ever allowed in his home and he had forbidden his sons ever to indulge. Sometimes Tristram had thought him fanatical on the matter, but he had rarely gone to a public house.

"Tha shouldn't have browt it here," he said. "I'll not have rum about."

Judy poured herself a mugful and set another for him as he watched her.

"Thy father is 'gainst it," she said. "He has towd thee to leave it alone?"

"Aye," he nodded, "and I have."

She sipped her drink thoughtfully. "Do tha know why?"

"T' stuff is good for nowt," he shrugged. "It's ruined many."

"It has that," she assented. "If tha can howd thy temper I'll tell thee how it ruined thy father."

He stared at her. "Art crazy? My father had nowt to do wi' drink."

"Will tha howd thy temper?" persisted Judy.

Her seriousness made him uneasy. "Aye," he grunted. "Have thy say."

"Thy father wur one o' t' finest men ever in Yorkshire."
Judy let her mug alone. "He wur more handsome than
Lancelot, a champion lad wi' every person. My mother towd
me o' him and that's how I know. He coom to Backfall Fair
to buy cattle and wur wi' some who had him meet thy mother
for a lark. Keep thy temper, now."

She chose her words with such care that she was slow in
speaking. "Thy mother wur a kitchen wench at t' 'Cock and
Sparrow.' She wur sharp and had her eye open for ony man.
Summat wur done that got thy father alone wi' her and she
coaxed him to drink. He'd never touched more than ale and
she mixed t' dram so he wur slopped proper, and went to bed
wi' her. He wur fearful shamed coom morn but she let on it
wur a joke. A month after he got word she wur wi' child by
him so he coom to Backfall and married her. His family
would have no more to do wi' him so he got work at Banfield
wi' a farmer. That's how he started. Tha wur born in
seven months."

He sat and gazed at her. "Tha art daft," he said heavily.
"Tha said he married her month after?"

"I did that," owned Judy. "She fooled thy father, same
as many a lass has done wi' a man. Did tha ever see Barney
Scurr, over at Sliderpool? He's thy father, and Matthew's
to bargain."

"Tha lie, woman!" Tristram rose from his chair in rage but
Judy's calm assurance sat him back in his seat.

"Tha know I don't," she said. "Ony grown person in
Backfall will tell thee same story. Now tha see why thy
father wants nowt to do wi' drink."

Tristram turned from her and watched the fire. Things
he had heard in a sly way, as a child, came back to him. He
remembered going to Backfall with his mother and their
meeting a big hairy man she called "Barney." A whirl of
other memories began flooding his thinking, but he refused
them.

He swung about, glared at Judy. "Tha howd thy tongue
o' this to ony," he said fiercely. "Happen it's true, there's
nowt to be gained by telling."

"I've towd none but thee," she answered him, "and I've

known it since I wur a child. Can't tha get it into thy head that it's for thy good and nowt else I've towd thee? There's no harm in a dram wi' a man who can howd it, but no one can blame thy father for his way o' thinking." She drew her mug toward her and emptied it with obvious enjoyment.

Her move unsettled him. He began to see why his father had been such a crank about hard liquor, and now that he understood he could not see why he should not take a glass like anyone else. His father had been weak to be trapped so easily, but he was no gangling boy afraid of being sick. He took a mouthful from his mug, swallowed, smiled at Judy. The stuff was not bad at all. Warm little runlets commenced coursing through him. He drank the mugful.

Judy laughed merrily. She put a log on the fire, giving him a poke with her elbow as she went by. "We'll have a bit o' jolly after all," she said.

She refilled his mug and hovered near him. "It's a frowsty night and if tha face freezes sour tha will scare cattle wi' it come morn."

Her gaiety jangled his thinking. He drank another mugful. When she went on with her joshing he tried to assert his authority but Judy laughed at him until tears ran down her cheeks, and her hilarity reached him. He began grinning, then rose. An irresistible impulse made him move toward her so that in a trice she had slipped into his arms. He held her there and found her surprisingly solid for all her soft appearance.

"Now tha are like a real man," she exclaimed, "but remember thy sister does not like . . ."

"Never tha mind her," he choked, and his uncertainty left him. He would do as he pleased in his own house. She put her lips to his and the fragrant warmth of her mouth crazed him and he strained her to him as her finger tips closed over the back of his neck, played there and imparted new passions to his brain.

It was late when he roused in the morning and he could hear his cattle uneasy in the stable. He felt for Judy but she was gone from his bed and when he went downstairs she had the fire going and was before it, her nightdress hiked up shamelessly to warm her legs.

"Thy cattle are bawling for fodder," she yawned. "It is well that Christmas is over."

He stared at her and went outside to his work. His head ached vilely and the sickness reached his conscience. An urge to clear Judy Scurr from his premises racked his mind but gave way when he went back to the warmth of the kitchen and found her dressed with his breakfast on the table. She had found time to brush her hair and tidy herself and as she sat across from him, her clear skin glowing with health, her wide generous mouth ready to quirk a smile, part of his wretchedness left him. It was late to go to the woods for the day but he got his axe and worked with such energy, cutting and splitting frost-filled beech, that he perspired freely. By night all the nausea of his drinking had left him and he had ironed his conscience to submission.

IV
The Redhead

GIDEON DANKS said that Sylvia was as pert as a red heifer and plump as a butter ball. He vowed that Patience was the only other woman he had seen who could do as much work between daylight and dark, and still keep her temper. Matthew liked to hear him say it. He was proud of Sylvia. Her mother was old and wrinkled and coarse-handed but when she wanted there was an indestructible dignity about her, and Sylvia had inherited some of it. She was so strong that after a hard day she would whistle little tunes as if she were beginning the morning.

It was her even temperament that pleased him most. No matter how badly the day might go she held her peace and there were no arguments waiting in his kitchen after a hard day in the field.

In July she told him she was with child and he was mightily pleased. He could think of no finer picture than a strong young boy on Sylvia's knee, gurgling with her good nature, putting up baby arms to him as he came in. When Patience came over the next day he met her in the yard and told her, boastfully, that she would be an aunt before she was a mother. Gideon was coming along the path and he heard.

"Don't crow till daylight, young feller," he grinned. "I might be placing a bet t'other way."

A thin sweep of colour went over Patience's face but she made no comment. Gideon waited until she was out of earshot, then spoke in a different tone.

"I shouldn't have yapped like that in front of my wife," he said, shaking his head. "It's all right to have such talk between you and me but a man should respect wimmen."

131

Matthew gazed at him dumbly. "Tha sound like a parson," he ejaculated. "What's coom over thee, man?"

"Nothin's come over me, son," returned Gideon, his voice hardening slightly, "but I think it best for you and me to pick our words when our wives can hear. This is a rough country but it costs nothin' to be decent."

Matthew grunted, and left him. He wondered if Gideon were wanting to quarrel with him. The feeling was gone by evening. Sylvia had baked him a deep mutton pie. He went to bed and forgot the day, dreaming happily of his crops. Sylvia was being extraordinarily good to him. He had eaten well and his stomach and his heart were full.

His barley field edged bushy growth running down to the marsh, and in September he mowed the grain. In late afternoon he worked near the line of scrubby spruce, and heard his named called.

"Matthew!"

He stood and peered. A face stared at him from the cover of the evergreens. It was Polly Clews.

Her cheeks were dirty and streaked with tears. Her dress was a single ragged garment, too short for her thick bare legs.

"Pa said I were to come to you."

"Coom to me! Why should tha coom to me?" He gazed anxiously up the slope toward his house.

She stooped back of the bush and picked up a bundle. It was a baby wrapped in a dirty blanket.

"Pa said you were to take my brat. He beat me cruel."

"Get from here!" Anger tightened his throat. "Tha have nowt to do wi' me and thy father knows it. Get from here."

Polly made no move and her infant began a tiny wailing.

"Pa said you were to take it. He said it were your own."

"Thy father is a bloody liar. Take thyself oot o' here." His fury heated him, yet he dare not raise his voice.

The girl made no rejoinder but stood, watching him dully, giving no attention to her child.

"Go!" He looked around again. "I'll have t' constable coom for thee, and thy father as well."

Polly's mouth opened at the word "constable," but she did not speak. Matthew turned and went up the hill. Blast the girl! An hour before he had had every reason for happiness. Now she had given him a dread that would stay with him.

He went from the field to his barn and stayed there, watching. Presently he saw Polly. She was scurrying among the bushes, going toward the village like a hunted thing. She had left her brat for him.

It cost him effort to go to the house for his supper. Sylvia never had looked more lovely to him and she was so busy with the bake kettle and his meal that he was able to compose himself. He ate and went out to his milking but as he carried the full buckets to the kitchen he thought he heard a wailing from the field. It startled him and he knew that if he did not go and find the baby he would be hearing the sounds all the time.

It took him but a few minutes to find the pitiful bundle, wet with dew and scarcely wriggling. He carried it to the house and gave it to Sylvia. "Polly Clews left this under a bush," he said gruffly. "She wur crying about her father beating her."

Sylvia undid the bundle, and gasped. "Ride for t' doctor. Quick."

Matthew thundered into the village and routed O'Connor from the tavern. "It's Polly Clews's brat she left in a field. Coom away, man. I'll pay thee."

"There may be little I can do," said O'Conner, "but the fee pulls me into service. This shyster will not give me a sip of his rotten beer on credit."

He spoke truly regarding the infant. Neglect and malnutrition had sapped the tiny creature's vitality. It died in his arms as he took it up for examination, and he put it away from him as if Death's bony hand had tapped his shoulder.

"Let Ned Clews bury it," he advised. "It's another of his mistakes. He should never have let Polly go from under his roof. I'll thank ye now for my fee and then I'll be out of your way. Heaven rest ye, and good night."

Ned Clews lived in a miserable shack at the back of Amherst village. His wife had died of abuse and cold, and his sons had left him as soon as they were able to forage for themselves.

At Matthew's hail Ned came from his hovel and stood outside, hostility glinting from his rat eyes in the light of the guttering candle he carried.

Matthew slid from his horse and dropped the reins over the hitching post. He carried the bundle he had brought into the shack and laid it on the dirty bed Clews had been lying on. "There's thy daughter's babe," he said. "She left it under bush by t' marsh. O'Conner says tha art to give it decent burial."

"Me!" Clews spat the word. "Who the hell you givin' orders? You're the Yorkshire that had her workin' at your place. I know yer. Wot's more, yer the father of that brat. So look after it yourself . . ."

Matthew seized the fellow in an iron grip, shook him until his head seemed like to fly loose. "Shut thy bloody mouth!" he roared. "Tha art a liar and a blaggard to boot." He pitched Clews against the shack wall, watched him slither, gasping, to the floor. "If tha tells ony dirty lies about me I'll bash thy dirty face."

"No—no. I'll not. So help me. I'll bury the kid." Clews begged for mercy, afraid to get to his feet. "I'll not say nothin'."

"Mind tha don't," grated Matthew.

He rode back and was slow putting the chestnut away and had to force himself to go in and face Sylvia. But she was still busy with clearing up for the night.

"T' poor thing's better off," she said softly. "T' girl wur here this afternoon and I could see she wur silly when she wanted to leave t' babe."

Matthew could feel his heart pounding. So Polly had been to his kitchen and all the time he ate supper Sylvia had probably wondered about the baby, or had she? Women with child were often moody with their own thoughts, so Molly Flannigan, the midwife, had said when he questioned her about attending Sylvia. He watched her as she puttered around with the final chores and was grateful when she made no further mention of Polly.

Next time he rode into the village he saw O'Conner, only slightly drunk, beckoning him. "Ye scared Ned Clews wit-

less," he hiccoughed. "Had him beggin' me to be witness to
his buryin' that brat proper alongside his wife. That Polly
of his has gone 'way up the fort ridge, livin' with a Cajun.
She'll breed, too, and what an unholy litter there'll be."

When the cattle drive was organized Matthew wished he
could go but Sylvia's condition kept him at home. She could
not do the work about the stable and she roused him one
night in November, crying for him to hurry for Mrs. Flannigan. Sleep-fogged, he mounted the chestnut and was away
for the midwife before he began calculations that left him
startled, dumbfounded, incoherent.

The baby was born before morning, a lusty boy, and Mrs.
Flannigan was well pleased with her work. "Not half the
trouble I expected," she told Matthew, "and a great handsome
lad."

He looked at her as if he were in a stupor and she jogged his
arm. "Ye look like a man not sober. Bide a bit and I'll
let ye look at your son. He'd make any man proud."

Matthew gazed at the bundle she brought him. His
glance went over the puckered visage to the hair. It was
thick for a new-born babe—and it was a bright red!

It was afternoon before he made himself go in and see Sylvia.
She turned her head, saw him and smiled, her arm around her
baby beside her. She was not afraid.

"Isn't he a bonny lad?" she whispered.

He nodded and stood beside her, still silent, then sat
down.

"Tell Patience," she said. "She'll be glad."

He nodded again, unable to speak.

Quietly, without disturbing her baby, Sylvia put out a hand
and touched him. Matthew took it, pressed it. He edged
his chair closer and gradually all that had seared him began
to lessen, dissolve, become vague. He saw her close her eyes
over tears.

"Matthew, coom closer."

Her voice was a whisper from painfully deep in her throat.
"I—love—thee—truly."

He bent and kissed her, and when she looked at him he
nodded. Mrs. Flannigan came in on tiptoe. "Out ye go,"

she ordered, her eyes shining. "Holdin' hands like new-promised! Do ye know ye've been half an hour?"

Gideon and Patience came over in the evening and Mrs. Flannigan proudly took them to see the baby. Matthew hunched himself away from the candle light, waiting Gideon's outburst. But there was none. "A fine boy," he said heartily. "We'll have him a cousin to play with come spring."

Then he talked of word that had come of more trouble at Boston. "The king's men ain't liked up there, they say, but who cares? It's a thunderin' long hoss ride from here."

Matthew nodded, scarcely knew what had been said. A little nagging had begun at the back of his mind. Someone with red hair . . . singing at his wedding . . . Peter Meekins . . . Sylvia whispering "A gay one at a party." He remembered how Mrs. Chipley had gushed over him. A sense of injustice nipped at him but he fought it and controlled it, put it away. Before the hour ended he was in good spirits again.

After the New Year he and Gideon went for wood again, but Matthew ate his dinners cold until he discovered that Aggie was gone from her cabin and a young Irish couple were there in her stead. So he ate with them and warmed himself at their fire until one name in their gossip jerked him to attention.

A party of young men had organized, they said, to persuade settlers not to join the Cumberland militia. Governor Legge at Halifax had tried to put every man to bearing arms, but it was a free country. "They'll be callin' on ye," said the young Irishman. "Peter Meekins has a devilish delight in opposin' the gov'ment, and a smooth tongue to git ye lookin' his way."

"I'm no rebel," said Matthew. "Let him keep from me."

A late afternoon in February he was hailed in a snowstorm as he followed his heavy sled past Amherst tavern.

"Hi, Yorkshire. A word with you!"

Matthew halted his cattle reluctantly, for the storm was gathering fast.

"Come in and have a drink, man, while I put a word in your ear."

Something in the gay tone pulled Matthew around—and he faced Peter Meekins.

"Speak thy word here," he said slowly, scanning his man.

Meekins was tall as himself, but not heavily formed. He would be quick, though, with his hands and feet.

"The storm has shortened your patience, eh, Yorkshire. Well, I won't keep you. All I want is your word that you'll not join Legge's bully milishy, and you can go."

"Can I now?" Matthew stuck his ox whip in the snow and pulled off his heavy mittens. "Listen what I say. I'll join what I want for all thy kind will stop me and if tha trouble me again tha will regret it."

Meekins' breath was heavy with rum. He looked at the knitted woollen cap Matthew had pulled over his ears, and jeered. "A little more of that, my fine Yorkshire, and a few of us will stick your head in a snow bank and cool it, Cajun cap and all."

He had not the words from his mouth before he jumped to call for cronies but Matthew slid out his foot and tripped him neatly, caught him as he rolled to escape and hurled him back toward the sled.

There was ribald singing in the tavern but no one looked out. Meekins fell, sprawled in the sled ruts, scrambled to get up and was thrown against the load of beech logs. His hand groped for his belt and Matthew saw a knife as he gripped the man's arm. He held it and twisted until Meekins groaned and the blade dropped in the snow. Not a word more had been spoken; there were only the smothered sounds of Meekins' body against the logs and on the hard-packed road.

"Pull a knife, will tha!" gritted Matthew. He pushed Meekins, struggling and kicking, against the load, bending him backward, pinned him there and beat him with his knuckles, hitting him again and again with jarring, punishing blows that left Meekins helpless.

Sated, he picked the man up and carried him to the tavern door, kicked it open and slung him inside, returned to his sled and set his uneasy oxen on their way. There were wild shouts behind him and he saw one or two dash into the storm to look after him, but no man took up pursuit and he went on, a huge satisfaction swelling his veins and spreading through him like warm drink.

When he was home Mrs. Flannigan had gone to Patience and that night a fine son was born to her, a boy with a short tuft of hair as black as his father's, and Gideon whooped and cheered on his way over with the news in the morning until Sylvia's baby woke and cried in fright.

"We'll have the parson christen the pair when it comes warm," boomed Gideon. "Patience has named our lad already, Asa, after her father, and good enough name for a prince. Had time yet to pick a handle for your youngster?"

Sylvia looked at Matthew. "We'll call him Adam, after father."

She had not mentioned it before and Matthew tingled. He was sure she was the smartest woman he had ever known.

BOOK THREE
1774

I
The Windsor Bull

THE SPRING of 1774 was early in Nova Scotia. Tristram went to the maple grove at the back of his wood lot and gathered buckets of sap that Judy boiled to sweet syrup. His winter's work was represented in a huge pile of beech logs drying for fires for the next twelve months, and his cattle had wintered well, but he was worried when Niles rode from Maccan and asked him not to join the Cumberland militia.

He had thought many times of the man from Boston who had talked of trouble. "Thee talk like a rebel," he growled. "We want none in this country."

"I'm no Tory," said Niles, "and I do my own thinking. The Britishers had better let us alone. That old fool of a Legge will need more than milishy one of these days."

"Art daft?" said Tristram sharply. "I'll not have to do wi' treason."

"But ye won't join Legge's crowd?"

"Nor any other. I've planting to do, and so have thee. Never mind owd Legge."

Niles stepped nearer and lowered his voice as if he were speaking secrets. "Do ye know they've been holding meetings this winter over on the fort ridge, and they are ready to take arms if there's need to help Boston?"

"To go there?" Tristram was amazed.

"Might be. More likely to help Boston when they come here."

"I don't like such talk," frowned Tristram. "I'll tend my farm, and tha do same."

Niles rode away but he had startled Tristram. At night

141

Judy added to his worry. She had had a dream, she said, three nights in a row, of soldiers fighting in the Bathol intervales. It was the first time in her life that such a thing had happened to her but it was a family gift. Her mother had dreamed a thing three times and it had come true in detail.

The next day he went over and talked with Silas Plumley. Silas said he had listened to Niles, but had not been impressed by the man's argument. "Some may be wishing to side wi' t' rebels," he said, "but they are few. A dozen like Niles would make a stir in ony place."

Tristram felt more assured but as he was leaving Silas asked him if he had had any word from Yorkshire.

Tristram started. "Noa," he said slowly. "Have thee?"

"Aye, and thear will be four hundred to coom this summer. We'll have a Yorkshire o' oor own, please God."

The old man looked around the intervales. "We have much to be thankful for, wi' two fine harvests and t' land warm so soon. Ony man in this settlement should be happy, if sin is not wi' him."

Silas was deeply religious and Tristram wondered if the words were not for him. He wished, as he had so many times, that he had not taken Judy into his house. His thoughts made him sit sullen through his supper and the next day he shouted savagely at his oxen. In the evening he again held to moody silence.

Judy watched him a time then brought her jug from the chest and poured him a mugful of rum. "I heard a frog last night," she said, "or was it thee talking wi' thyself? Take a sip and get t' hump off thy back."

It was in him to refuse but he let her persuade him and the rum soon set him to roaring that he was as good living as any man in Bathol and Judy had her own time getting him to bed. He was sick before morning, retching an hour outside the house, cursing the liquor and his own stupidity. Judy let him be and slept beyond rising time so that he bellowed for her to get her lazy carcase out of bed and make him breakfast.

Her slowness was deliberate when she came down, maddening him.

"Move thyself, woman," he shouted. "Are thee awake?"

"Don't tha shout at me," she defied him, "or tha will get thy own breakfast. I'll take nowt from thee, and it's best tha know it."

Tristram sprang up from his table. "Get gone, then," he roared. "Never mind more in my house."

"Not so fast, Mister Crabtree." Judy's face was white as she threw down her ladle. "Thee'll not put me from thy house in my condition. Tha has done as tha pleased all winter, and now thear's others will see tha use me fair."

He stared at her and his feverish lips cracked with dryness so that he wetted them with his tongue. His rage ebbed and he thought of Silas. "I did not know thy condition." He sat down again. "Happen it would be better if we wed."

Judy picked up her ladle and colour came back to her cheeks. "When tha wish," she said briefly and went on with her work.

Tristram could not calm himself. He went across the field to Abel Plumley and asked the loan of his horse. "I want parson to coom and marry us," he said humbly.

"Parson's coming this day week to marry Hannah and Nathan Hodge," said Abel. "Thee can wait?"

The news surprised Tristram. He had thought Hannah would marry Lancelot. "Aye," he said tersely. "We'll wait."

He left word with the Hodges, noting grimly their surprise as he mentioned Judy, and went back to his work. He had sinned and now he would make everything right. Judy was a widow and he would give her proper standing in the settlement.

Judy smoothed her only good dress, cleaned her worn cloth shoes, prinked her hair and sat, ready for the parson, an hour before Tristram put on his coloured waistcoat and broadcloth jacket. She had almost a bride's eagerness as she watched from the window but it was Abel instead of the parson who rode into the yard.

"Father wants thee to coom over and be married after Nathan," he invited. "All thy folk are thear, and they want thee. Mother says it will make a champion party."

Tristram's heart leaped. His people wanted him! Yorkshire blood was thick and strong.   He and Judy would be as respectable as any in Bathol.

"We'll coom," he shouted, and kissed Judy to smiling.

The weddings were long but everyone was in good humour and Mrs. Plumley was kind to Judy.   Jonathan and Lancelot talked with her.   Melody sounded sincere as she wished them both happiness.   Silas had killed a young steer for the occasion and after the huge repast Tristram heard with interest that Matthew had become a father sooner than was expected.   He treasured the fact, gloated over it.   They could say nothing of him, then, for everyone knew that if Unity had come to him there would not have been any living with Judy.   He convinced himself that any blame there might be regarding his actions must rest on Unity.

He and Judy walked home in the dusk to attend freshened cows that needed milking, and their joy seemed complete. It had been the first warm day with spider webs spinning across sunlit spaces at the bush edge and juncos exploring old bean vines in the garden.

"Art happy?" he asked.

"Surely thee knows."   Judy squeezed his arm.   "Happen tha has a chance to village," she said, "will tha get me new shoes?   These coom apart when parson wur done."

"Aye.   Tha will have new shoes.   I'll buy them in Windsor. Ezra Hodge has asked me to go wi' him to buy a bull.   It's best we have gradely stock.   I'll have t' best cattle in t' country."   He hesitated.   "Jonty will tend t' stable till I coom back, so tha be careful o' thyself."

He was glad she had spoken about the shoes.   He did not want her going around in bare feet like a New England woman. She was his wife and he would be a leading man of the community.   Already he could visualize great herds in his pasture, a new barn to hold his grain.

Ezra had written to a farmer in Windsor who was said to own the best stock in the province and he had the promise of two fine bulls.   He would buy one and Tristram would buy the other.   They would take them over by ferry to Partridge Island and lead them through the woods over the hogback.

The Hodges were shrewd farmers and industrious.   They

had put logs to Smith's mill the year before in order to have lumber for Nathan's house and barn, and they sold their pork to the fort garrison at Windsor, sending it around by schooner. They had pens of fine black and white pigs and it seemed to Tristram at times that all they spoke of was pigs, spring pigs, farrow sows; roast pork, salt pork, smoked ham, bacon, pig's knuckles; it was as if pigs turned to pounds and shillings and Hodge stomachs cried out for such delicacies as only properly raised pork could supply.

Neither he nor Ezra carried a musket. They had but a brass kettle and their blankets, their flint and steel for making a cooking fire.

The farmer at Windsor drove a close bargain. He had a fine three-year-old bull in prime condition, with sleek black hair and a depth of shoulder that Tristram admired. The other animal was a yearling of promise, offered at a much cheaper price. Ezra bought it at once. Tristram had only small reluctance as he paid more than he had expected for the larger bull.

"Now," said the farmer, "leave the beasts to feed and come with me. There's going to be excitement. A wagon's come from Halifax with a chest of tea, and the magistrate's got it at his house. The crowd's after it."

About thirty men and boys were in front of a white-washed house, shouting at a man who stood on the porch.

"Keep back," he ordered. "You'll not have the tea. That's all there is to it."

"Burn him out," yelled a voice. "We're for liberty. Burn him out."

"The man who makes a move to do any burning will rot in a Halifax jail," warned the magistrate. "Take care what you do."

The mob shuffled uneasily, those in front edging back to escape recognition. Then a man caught up the wagon pole and pulled. "Here's the tea cart anyway," he yelled. "Give a hand, lads."

They ran the wagon back to a hollow and, in the dusk, wrenched the pole from the axle, smashed the wheels and body. It was done in a few minutes and when the magistrate, with a lighted lantern, came to the hollow every man scurried away in the darkness.

"A brave lot," blurted Tristram.

"They dumped three boatloads of tea in Boston harbour last winter," the farmer said. "It's different there."

"A fool waste, that," retorted Tristram.

"Waste for them that bought it," said the farmer. "Why should we pay a tax on our tea?"

"Howd thy peace," ordered Tristram. "Threepence on tea is nowt to anybody."

The farmer eyed him sourly and went off to his house, growling like a dog unsure of a stranger. Tristram and Ezra took their bulls and led them to a farm near the ferry slip from where they could start early in the morning. They had a good crossing and before noon were on their way over the hogback.

The three-year-old was full of mettle. They had two strong ropes to its nose ring. Tristram held one rope and walked ahead and Ezra, leading the yearling, held to the second rope in the rear so that the older bull, irked with the loneliness of the wilderness and the constant travelling, would not charge its leader. At night they tethered it between stout trees and Tristram watched with pride as the powerful animal, disdaining the yearling nearby, pawed the earth and shattered the silences with mad bellowing.

"Yon's an ugly devil," remarked Ezra. "Tha will need a strong pen."

"He's champion," gloated Tristram. "I have seven cows to breed, and not one of his get will I sell."

It was the third day when they reached home for Tristram refused to hurry his bull, letting it feed a morning on sweet grass at the first clearing near River Hebert. When they reached the Hodge farm Ezra put his yearling to pasture and went on with Tristram for the three-year-old had become more sullen and the men had to be on their guard.

Judy came to the door and watched them put the animal in the barn.

"Did tha ever see better?" called Tristram exultingly.

He had no echo from Judy. "I wish tha had never seen

t' brute," she said dully. "Give him chance, that one will kill."

Tristram laughed at her in great good humour. "Thee would be feeling same if tha had ring in thy nose and were pulled on't here to Windsor."

He had brought her shoes with silver buckles, solidly sewn and Boston cobbled, a comb and a gay shawl. In a moment she was smiling. She put the shoes and shawl on and paraded before him, filling his eyes with pride and making him feel that his days lost from planting were worth while.

The next weeks Tristram worked early and late, sparing neither himself nor his oxen until his work was in hand. Then he gave a day to the raising of Nathan Hodge's house. The frame was reared, roofed over and floored before nightfall. Kettles were boiled over an outdoor fire and a huge supper served.

Judy had helped make the food ready and as she sat with Tristram he sensed an expectancy in the gathering. Ezra Hodge had not been at the raising. Neither had Samson Cornforth or Abel Plumley. Yet no one mentioned their absence and he was wondering about it when the creaking of carts in the distance put an end to the meal. Three loaded ox teams could be distinguished in the dusty trail shadows and they came to a standstill as men and women rushed to the carts, crying greetings.

Tristram stared. No one had told him that Yorkshire people had arrived at the fort. No one had hinted at it. He saw Abel Plumley finally drive on, a family huddled on his big cart with their belongings about them. He stood with Judy out of the light and no one called to him. Ezra Hodge was the driver of the next cart and he had a family with him that, someone called, he was taking to live a time in Reuben Scurr's cabin. Judy squeezed Tristram's arm at the mention of Reuben's name but he gave her no heed.

The third cart rolled along, and Samson Cornforth was its driver. Some woman from Banfield was seated by him and she saw Tristram.

"Unity Lemming's at fort," she cried. "Art tha not to meet her?"

"Howd thy tongue," Tristram heard Samson say roughly. "Tristram's married."

"Aye," called another voice softly. "That's his wife wi' him."

"I'm sorry, Tristram," called the newcomer. "I did not know."

There was a sudden silence. Samson started his oxen with shouts that were unnecessarily loud and commanding. A man of the family of newcomers who had been talking with Silas Plumley shouted that on the morrow he would visit every Yorkshire family in the place. Then he ran after the cart. No one else spoke.

Tristram turned, picked up his pod auger and hammer. "Coom along," he said gruffly, and Judy followed him into the night.

The new faces and voices from Banfield swept him with bitter thinking, made Judy an alien. All the weight that had been on his conscience returned and settled heavily. In his mind he saw Unity at the fort. Waiting him. Watching each cart coming over the marsh. Questioning. Getting an answer that struck her like a blow. He winced at thought of it.

"Am I walking too hasty?" he asked, aware that Judy had not spoken. "I forget thy condition."

"Never tha mind it." Her voice was brittle. "It's not wi' me as I thowt."

He stopped so suddenly that she bumped against him. "Tha art not wi' child?"

"Noa, man, I'm not." Her voice was sharp. "Art tha stopping here or cooming home?"

She went into the house and to bed, leaving him with the chores, and as he worked all his acquaintance with her revolved in his mind until it was rancid with suspicion.

In the morning he did the milking, then brought the buckets to Judy and stood, gazing at her like a man driven to the devil. "I wish," he said surly, "tha had never been born."

Judy said nothing but the blue in her eyes darkened and her mouth tightened in an ominous line.

His glance inspected her, saw that her neck needed washing,

her hair combing, that her bodice was stained yellow at the armpits with perspiration.

"Tha art a dirty wench," he went on. "Wash thyself, woman, afore handling milk."

"Dirty, am I?" blazed Judy. "Tha clod, wi' thy body smelling weeks afore thee bothers to fill a tub. I'll take no tongue from thee."

"Slut!" he shouted. "Shut thy dirty mouth!"

"Tha knows many sluts," shrilled Judy. "Happen tha can tell why a squaw coom to house a week by, wanting thee and no other?"

"Devil take thee!" roared Tristram, and he slapped her.

Judy caught up a heavy wooden cream ladle and struck him in the face, the violence of the blow snapping the handle off short.

Her assault drove him back and he upset a bucket of milk over the floor. Livid with rage, he called her a foul name and lurched to seize her but Judy, her eyes flaming with hate, snatched up his butcher knife. It's edge was like a razor blade; he had honed it himself.

Tristram halted. "Put that down," he rasped.

"I'll put it in thy belly." Judy was like a coiled rattler, "if tha dare lay hand on me again."

She was strong as a man, far quicker than he, and determined. He looked at the upset bucket. "Calm thyself, woman," he said contritely. "Give over. We're both plagued wi' temper. Let's no more o' it."

Judy gave him no answer but she put the knife on her stool and began mopping up the milk. One cheek was bright red from his violence, the other was dead white. He watched her a moment, then turned and went out.

The weather was strange, unsettled. It poured rain a day and stopped suddenly, then burned the land with windless midsummer heat so that oxen sweated and panted, needed careful handling.

Tristram built a new trough in his yard beside the pole enclosure covering the well. He could hear the bull in its stall stamping and twitching the steel chain fitted to the nose ring, irritable in the heat and quiet. Once he left his work and went in to look at the animal.

"Rest thyself, lad," he spoke gently. "It'll be cooler coom night." The bull turned to look at him. Its black hide glistened; the muscles of its great neck bulged in a lump. Its eyes, shot with changing lights, seemed to emanate smouldering temper.

"T' heat frets thee," said Tristram. He reached in and unfastened the chain from the ring. "That will make thee more content." There was a strong gate to the stall, made with hewn poles, and he tested it briefly, then went back to his work.

He was making the watering trough with three wide planks as bottom and sides and had nailed a block at one end when he heard a quick snapping of wood and the bull shot into the yard to stand, stiffly, its head lowered, shining black in the sun.

Tristram spun around. "Get back thear," he cried. "Get!"

The bull trotted towards him, its hoofs clopping on the yard gravel. Tristram edged into the well shed. A fork was leaned there and he seized it as the animal came barging against the trough. "Get!" he shouted, and struck the fork smartly on the bull's rump.

The bull launched itself about in a savage rush and Tristram evaded by dodging around the shed. "Judy!" he called. "Judy!"

There was no rush this time but a slow sidling chase that drove him around the small shed and into it. The bull snorted and charged in at him.

Tristram put up the fork but the handle snapped in his hands. He seized the brute's horn as it wedged shoulders in the doorway, but was thrown in a corner as the bull surged and carried in the door posts of the shed. He seized the nose ring and wrenched with all his strength, but was driven backward in a wreckage of poles. The roof dropped on them. There was a terrific report, deafening him. Pain tore through him. Horrid breath snorted in his face. Then he became unconscious.

When he roused Jonathan and Judy were dragging him from beneath a carcase that almost covered him, and warm blood seeped through his clothing. Its rank odour sickened him but it was the agony of his hurts that made him groan. His chest felt crushed and his back had been strained. He was one mass of bruised flesh.

"Judy saved thy life," said Jonathan. "She pushed t' musket till it touched bull's head and she wur quicker than ony man could be."

They made his bed in the kitchen and Judy bathed his hurts. His whole world was pain, tearing, surging, flooding through him, but Judy's hands were more gentle than ever his mother's had been and when she had finished some of the burning had ceased.

Then her fingers caressed his cheek, lightly, and she smiled.

He looked up at her. "Tha art champion," he gasped, and clung to her hand.

II
The Family Bible

ASA'S COACH took form slowly as he worked at it during the winter. Melody talked with him about each detail until she knew the identity of each stick he whittled. Most of the time he thought he was in Banfield. Melody had begun a flower garden and he delighted to help her cultivate roses she transplanted in the spring, to trim a honeysuckle bush for her, to plan a spot for hollyhocks and pinks and Sweet William.

When Tristram took Judy to his house Melody was scandalized. She urged Jonathan to go to his brother and protest. Finally she went herself and when her venture brought little success she was cool with Judy. When a month had gone by she relented and one day when Tristram was in the woods she called at his house and spent an hour with Judy, being friendly, disregarding Judy's lack of response. When she was leaving she said carefully. "If tha marry Tristram coom spring I'll be champion glad to have thee for kin."

Judy nodded. She said nothing but she had the look of one who had made some strong resolve.

Winter vanished. Wild geese rode the skies northward. Swallows returned. A soft warm rain left the sod under the elms dotted with worm holes. Melody and Asa attended the rose bushes. Tristram went to Windsor with Ezra Hodge. The next day Judy came to borrow sugar, half afraid, half challenging. Melody greeted her warmly, drew her into the kitchen, sensing it was company, not sweetening, Judy wanted. She induced her to stay to supper, gave her a warm mince pie to take home and urged her to come again the next day.

Judy came readily and, to Melody's amazement, became

friendly with Asa, admiring his coach, and their flower plot, telling him how to sweeten sour earth with hardwood ashes. He went with her one day to Tristram's house and explored it eagerly as a child, staying the afternoon.

Another day he and Judy went up the slope to the big willow tree and were there a long time. The next month there was a big storm that roared in with thunder and lightning and ended in a downpour that soaked the thirsty earth.

In the morning Asa went up the hill and stayed until noon. The big willow had been struck by lightning, its top shattered to litter over the pasture. In the afternoon he went with his axe and commenced chopping, cutting the stump off even at a height near his shoulder.

It was the second day before he had finished it as neatly as he wished and then he began hewing the sides, making a square of the stub and smoothing the front to a perfect finish. He took his chisel and hammer when he went back the third day and Melody saw him cutting letters deeply into the soft wood. She went up the hill and could read the inscription before she was near it.

"Here Stays Good Yorkshire."

"Father," she cried, "what's yon for?   It's like a graveyard post."

"Aye," he said. "Here's a champion place to bury, top o' this hill. I want tha to have me put here when time cooms."

He would say no more and when she went to the house Mrs. Garrison had come over. The big woman wagged her head sorrowfully.

"It's too bad your pa's teched like that.   Puttin' up a thing like a headstone is bad luck any time, and doin' it afore there's a grave is sure to bring death.   I'd root out the stump and burn it."

They gave her no heed. Asa finished the coach and sat in it for days, talking to himself as he rode, in fancy, to York and many towns. Some days he went over the hill to the wood and spent a hard hour chopping a big spruce or pine to see them topple into a ravine by the brook.

"Let him be," Jonathan said, when Melody told him about

it. "He hasn't strength to chop many and there's plenty o' trees."

Melody became restless and at last rode to visit Patience and Gideon, knowing that Molly could attend the house until she returned. Gideon roared a welcome as he saw her ride in the lane, put Annabelle to pasture and declared she should stay a month. He had his farm in good order. Patience looked younger and happier, yet more quiet. She glowed with health and under her loosened bodice her breasts, heavy with milk, rode easily. Her pride in her baby was great. She said little but Melody sensed that here at last she had found complete satisfaction, embodying Gideon and all she had ever been, giving her work purpose, so that she took each day with a small spoon, savoring each moment.

Matthew's face had lined until he looked older than Jonathan. He asked after his brothers and father but seemed indifferent about his son. He boasted mildly about his farm work. Gaspereaux had run in the river with the Indian pear bloom. He and Gideon had taken more than three barrels with their dip nets, so that though the splitting, gutting and salting were long finished, the smoking was still going on in a small shed that reeked of the fumes of green maple.

Melody told them of Tristram's fight with his bull, of Judy saving him, and of Jonathan and Lancelot going over to his farm to finish the planting.

"A younger beast would have been better," shrugged Matthew. "He wur always wanting better than ony neighbour."

Gideon came with exciting news one evening. "Boston port's been closed a week. No traffic in or out. King's men and ships watch to make sure. Folks there tolled church bells and put flags at half mast but the port's tight as a shut barn door."

The Indians had left their camp at Maccan so Melody rode home without dreading the wooded stretches. Gideon had said that Sour Bear quit the tribe without any farewells.

When she passed through Maccan a musket shot startled her. The report rang over the river so that the hills carried the echo. Peter Meekins and some of his cronies had blazed a fat hemlock with a broadaxe and, using charcoal, had sketched a picture of George the Third for target practice. They waved at sight of Melody, and Peter sent his wild hooting after her, patting his mouth like a real redskin and scaring Annabelle into furious running.

The next afternoon when she was alone Melody took a horn of ink from the shelf and a goose quill pen. She opened her big Bible to the glossy pages with border ornaments of cupids and marble columns, the centre spaced for the recording of births and marriages and deaths.

"His name is 'Asa,'" Patience had said when Melody was admiring her baby. "Will tha put it in thy Bible?"

"Aye, I will that," Melody had promised. "I'm keeping t' Book for all o' us."

Patience had pulled open her bodice and given her child a breast, treasuring him as he patted her with fat baby hands. "Sylvia won't ask thee," she went on, "but will tha put t' date ahead for her baby? It would be pleasing to her."

Melody scanned the entries in the Bible and wondered how many were correct; it was only a mother who knew the father of her child. She turned the page and wrote there the marriages of Tristram and Matthew and Patience, put the births in proper sequence, and young Adam's with a respectable date, then closed the Book. In the space after her own birth she would place the records of Jonathan and Lancelot and herself.

Asa asked about Patience and was immensely pleased to know she had named her baby after him. He whittled a jumping jack of pine and said it was for young Asa's first birthday. When she told him about young Adam he did not seem to understand, saying, finally, that he must have a day at the market in order to know what was going on in the village.

The next morning Melody missed him. Jonathan went in search at noon and found his father dead in the coach. The old man was looking through the window as if to see the turn ahead. He was dressed in his broadcloth coat with stiff collar, his frilled shirt and white waistcoat that he had taken from Melody's chest without her knowing. On the seat beside him he had a number of his carving tools wrapped in an old kerchief; he had gone prepared on a journey he anticipated.

They buried him on the hill by the willow stump, with every hoe and harrow in Bathol stilled for the afternoon. The slopes were lined with neighbours and Silas Plumley read a Psalm in a shaking voice that stilled every youngster, and prayed till many of the women were sobbing.

"I wish he could have heard," whispered Mrs. Garrison, holding her youngest. "There ain't a parson could have done better."

Jonathan carved deeply on the willow stump. "Asa Crabtree. Age 72 years." Melody planted flowers on the grave. Then she penned in her Bible: "Asa Crabtree. Died June 14, 1774." She remembered him as he had been when she was a child, patient, never speaking an angry word. And she added: "A good husband. A kind father. A gentleman."

III

Confession

TRISTRAM, unused to sickness, to being crippled, was restless as a colt haltered the first time. He fretted until he had his bed by the window where he could watch the planting of his fields, and then worry still stayed with him. He was unhappy with the thought that he would be greatly indebted to his brothers, and was certain the crops would not do as well without his attention.

Then he began to think of Unity. Each time Judy attended his hurts her gentleness made him wonder how careful Unity would have been. Some days he groaned in anguish as some of his old dreams were revived and he thought of how he had planned to have her with him. Judy did not seem to notice his moods. She gave every care to her tending each wound and cooked him every treat at her command. She talked when he wished, and was silent when he wanted.

His back was getting better when one day he saw a squaw coming in the yard and shouted to Judy to close the door. He did not want to have to look at the creature, he said, and he wanted no baskets.

Judy went outside. The squaw, she saw, was of the intelligent type of Indian, and she came as if she had some purpose.

"I want to see your man," she grunted.

"Tha can't t' day." Judy shook her head determinedly. "He's sick in bed."

"Sick? Him big strong man?"

"Aye. But he wur hurt by bull. He's in bed and tha can't see him."

"He give me something. Me want dress, five, ten shillin's."

"Noa," declined Judy. "He can't give thee onything."

"You his woman?"

"Aye. I married him. Why do tha ask?"

The squaw came nearer. She studied Judy's face. "Him in bush with my daughter. She have baby."

"Tha lie!" Judy's heart seemed to pause in its beat. "Thy daughter wur never here."

Quickly, but calmly, the squaw told of Tristram buying the basket from Marsh Rose, and of her being surprised by him at her bathing. She related every detail with a candor that impressed Judy.

"Me want something," finished the squaw, and she seated herself by the house.

Judy tried to make talk about other matters until she had control of herself. Then she went into the kitchen. "T' squaw won't go," she said quietly. "She's begging for summat to take wi' her."

Tristram had heard the murmur of voices outside and old dread swept over him. He had a fear of any dickering with the creature.

"Take a shilling and buy a basket," he said quickly. "Take oot thy kettle and let her drench her gizzard wi' tea. Give her summat to eat."

Judy took the food and drink. Then she went to the shelf where Tristram had some silver and took five shillings in coins. "She has no baskets," Judy had no tightness in her voice, "and nowt else to sell, but it will be best to give her five shillings."

Tristram stared at her briefly, and nodded. "Aye. Give it her, and tell her not to coom back."

The squaw had wide eyes that looked honest as a child's. She took the money with some dignity, then struck a plaintive note and wrapped her voice around it. She wanted some clothing for the baby, she said, and could not go without it.

Judy took out a flannel petticoat she could ill afford to spare. "That's all tha can get," she said decisively. "It will be no use to coom again."

The squaw accepted the petticoat. "Plenty time next year," she said, and went away.

"Did she say who she was?" asked Tristram. He was trying to see some trace of suspicion in Judy's glance.

"Noa," said Judy. "She wur like t' rest o' them. Begged more when she had what she asked. I towd her that wur all she'd get from thee."

"Tha art champion," said Tristram, greatly relieved. He felt Judy had saved him from some embarrassing situation and through the rest of the day he thought about it. Her killing the bull had saved his life. He forgot about Unity and watched Judy in the candle light.

"Tha art a champion lass," he said suddenly. "Tha art too good for me."

Judy came and sat by him. "Tha married me," she said. "I must do what I can for thee."

Tristram's emotions set his mind in a turmoil. He was sure that Judy would be wondering about the squaw calling and being so persistent in her demands. His fears rioted in his thinking until he suddenly reached for her hand.

"I'll confess to thee," he said huskily. "I hope tha will forgive me. I've a sin I'll carry to myself no longer, and if tha can believe me it will be end o' it."

Judy nodded, but said nothing. He plunged into his story, making no mention, however, of his buying the basket at Amherst. "T' lass wur thear by t' pool," he cried. "She knew I wur coom to wash and she tempted me. I sinned but it wur her fault. Now, will tha forgive me?"

He was shouting as he finished and Judy patted his cheek. "Calm thyself," she murmured. "Aye, I forgive thee. If tha will keep from them now t' past will not matter, and tha wur honest to tell me."

IV

A Piece of Birch Bark

JONATHAN took Asa's chest for his own and in its corner found a leather bag with his name written on it. He felt it part of the reason why his father had always kept the chest locked and the key on a string around his neck. He opened the bag and found a note. It had been written during the years when his father was clever in everything.

"Every shilling in this bag is mine. It did not come from my farm. It was not earned in any part by my wife, nor did it come from her people. It was sent me by my father on his death. I pass it along to my son, Jonathan. God grant that he will be strong to make his own way in life."

Three hundred pounds! Jonathan walked the hill by the willow stump and did his thinking. Then he borrowed a horse and rode to Maccan. To the east side of the village there were many acres of cleared land. A New Englander there had died and his widow was anxious to sell the holding. The cabin she occupied was falling down about her. She sold eagerly, the farm, her husband's horse, a cow, sheep, chickens and a pair of steers ready for the yoke, for half the money Jonathan had taken with him.

It was a fine locality. He would not build near the site the New Englander had chosen but in a sheltered spot where land like a long footprint led in between wooded slopes, a stumpy clearing with a spring so cold the water made his teeth ache. The American had cut down the trees and burned them. He had hacked into cultivation the rich earth between the blackened stumps. Now they were rotted enough to be torn loose with oxen and all the little valley could be given to the plow.

Jonathan was glad he could secure a home for himself. He would build and equip his house; farther than that he could not visualize. At the various winter gatherings he had enjoyed himself but there was no girl that attracted him, just as there was no lad who interested Melody. Lancelot often said they were destined to live to lonely old age, and sometimes he wondered if there were any truth in the statement. Of one thing he was certain. He would not marry simply to have a housekeeper.

His moving would leave Lancelot as the one to carry on with the home, and it seemed but fair, though he remembered that Patience had assigned her share of the home to Melody. The thought caught him that Melody might need more in her future than sharing with a sister-in-law, and he decided that he would make over to her his share in the farm, then trust to matters being all for the best.

He was on his horse, riding away, leading the borrowed one, when an ox cart creaked into view. It was loaded with Yorkshire possessions. He stopped and waited. Samson Cornforth was driving the cattle and the people in the cart were from Banfield. They shouted at him but he scarcely saw them. His gaze was on Unity Lemming, who sat among chests and bedding as if she were stranded and desolate.

"Eh, thear, now. Jonty Crabtree," called the farmer. "Tha look champion. It's like cooming hoam to see thee and Samson. Happen tha will be settled near t' place we're going?"

"Aye, it's not far wi' a horse." Then he added. "I'm settling here."

"Here!" echoed Samson.

"I've bought this land." He pointed to the clearing. "I'll have house oop afore snow cooms."

"Oh, Jonty!" Hearing Unity's voice again made him think of tall Banfield wheat in summer; of the cool stream where he had helped her gather mint; of Sunday mornings at the chapel. "Isn't it a lovely place. It's like at hoam."

Samson's face lighted in a speculative grin. He rummaged in the cart and dragged a saddle to view. "If thy spare horse is quiet," he suggested, "tha can let Unity ride?"

It was incredible.   An hour before his planning was vague.
Now Unity rode beside him, bringing back the dreams and
ambitions he had had as a boy, talking so brightly of nothings
that he sensed she wanted to know the hard and bitter truth
that awaited her.

"Tha knows Tristram is married?" he ventured.

"Aye.   I heard at fort."

"Reuben Scurr wur taken by press.   Judy wur keeping
house for Tristram.   T' parson married them."

"He fought wi' Matthew?"

"Aye, but that's ower.   Thear is nowt between them now."
She patted her horse's neck.   "I'm glad he married Judy."

"Glad!   Did tha not want him?"

"Noa."   She looked at him fairly.   "I coom to tell him we
would never be wed.   I will say it to him when I see him."

Jonathan's wonder rose.   "He has no quarrel wi' ony o'
us?"

She shook her head.   "It is not that.   I wur first wi' thee,
Jonty, and you know how he fought wi' thee."   She reddened
and looked away.   "I wur no more than a fearsome child,
and I did not want thee quarrelling.   It wur easier, then,
to go on wi' him, and father towd me to do."

So!   Jonathan's heart gave a great leap.   His thoughts
were in tumult.

"I wur but a lad," he said kindly, "and foolish headed."

She ventured to look at him, and he smiled, his heart pounding the more.

"But I wanted thee more than ony other thing on earth.
That is why we fought so bitter."

Unity looked away again.   "It pleased father," she said,
"and I wur glad o' that.   Happen thear had been no move to
Nova Scotia I would have married Tristram when father
died."

"It wur his quarrel wi' Matthew that halted thee?"   Jonathan could not hold back his question.   Patience had told
him of Tristram's rage against someone who had written to
Unity of his fighting.

"Noa."   They were alone on the trail for the ox cart had
halted for a rest and they had gone ahead.   "When he wur

gone I could think, and I knew. He had been so urgent
I had not thowt about myself. It wur then I began remembering thee, Jonty."

Jonathan wanted to touch her with his hand to be sure he
was not dreaming. She pointed at a goldfinch hovering over a
ripened dandelion, its plumage bright in the sun. "T' man
I marry will see that. Tristram never had time."

They rode side by side along the river trail where a dozen
sand peeps bobbed and ran on the banks; by a yellow warbler's
cottony nest in wild honeysuckle. Then they rode through
the Bathol woods where the tin trumpet of the wilderness, a
red-breasted nuthatch, shrilled his "yank-yank-yank," and
the fluting of the hermit thrush was faraway music.

It was seldom they spoke. He had thought she would have
a flood of questions and there were many things he wanted to
know; yet it seemed that having her with him made a time too
happy to be interrupted with talking.

He went with her to the Cornforths, helped her dismount
and took the saddle from his horse. Unity put her hand in
his. "If tha will coom again," she said, "I'll borrow t'
saddle."

The settlers said there was not another summer like that
of 1774, a long interminable season of cloudless days with
nights of heavy dews and small showers. There was lush
growth everywhere. Hay was gathered and stacked. Berries
were picked by the bucketful. Potatoes were early. Ox
carts creaked summer long hauling planks and boards and
other sawn timbers from Smith's mill. Four steep-roofed
houses, slanted to shed snow, were erected in Bathol.

Then, in the middle of harvesting, Jonathan had his raising,
and soon had finished his house. He bought bellows and
kettles, crockery and bedding. In the winter he would fit
shelves and make a mincing tray, a churn, wooden ladles and
bowls, wash benches, buckets, noggins and piggins. His
barn was raised when wild fowl overhead hinted of winter.
He moved in the hay for his cattle and sheep, built a strong
pen and acquired a pig.

The next day he bought a black mare with a white star on
the forehead and rode to Cornforths in Bathol. Emily Corn-

forth answered his rapping, looked at his two horses and called Unity. She came from carding wool, saw him and stood, her eyes searching his.

"There's no need to borrow," he said quietly. "I've bought thee a saddle."

Emily Cornforth smiled, and went indoors.

"Will tha coom to see my house?" he added.

Unity nodded and went for her cloak and bonnet.

He helped her mount and they rode by fields where crows hunted the stubble. The air was brisk but they talked little until Unity cried out as she saw the house, its shingles and clapboards so new and clean in the sun, the trim peeled log shed over the spring, the new barn and the fence of peeled poles. Every chip had been cleaned from the grass; everything was in place.

"I would know," she said, "this place wur yours if tha had not towd me. It has something different from ony other." Then she looked at him. "Why did tha bring me here?"

"To go on whear I left off wi' thee, if tha art willing."

"Willing, Jonty!" It was a cry. "I'd give heart's blood for thy words alone, never mind this hoam." She slid from her horse. "Howd me tight, Jonty. Say tha want me."

"I want thee, Unity, for my wife. I have always wanted thee."

He put the horses in the stable and they lighted a fire in the new house. He had bread and sliced cold beef so they boiled potatoes and Unity made tea.

"I'll make thee bowls coom winter," he said, "and snow-shoes to use."

She cupped her chin in her hands. "It would be terrible to wake," she said, "and find I've dreamed this. I've but a pound to my name, Jonty. It took rest to pay passage here—hoping tha would remember."

Jonathan, watching, saw her eyes were moist and he saw want come to her. He went around to her and kissed her. "Jonty," she breathed. "Tha art good." She clung to him with strength that surprised him, and when she laughed her lips were full and heavy and red so that he thought of her when she was sixteen, and told her so.

They rode back to Bathol and told Emily Cornforth their happiness. "Praise God for his goodness," she said. "Tha art a lucky man, Jonty."

Jonathan rode to Amherst to buy jacket and breeches. He had to pay the parson a pound to ride from the fort for the wedding and on his return rode in to tell Patience and Gideon the news and invite them to the wedding. They could not go, they said, but they were mightily pleased. Gideon rushed outside and threw his rush-plaited hat higher than the barn, shouting his delight, until Patience came out, smelled his breath, and dragged him inside.

"Blow me cold, Jonty," he roared, "but I thought you were cut out for a bachelor. I've never seen a lad so easy-going among a flock of pretty chickens, and now I understand. We'll pick up the visitin' habit when you're settled, you can bank on that."

Melody rode Annabelle around the settlement collecting flowers and made the prettiest bouquet, Mrs. Cornforth declared, ever put together by woman's fingers. The Cornforth men built an arch of red maple boughs and Jonathan took his place under it with Unity. Melody and Lancelot stood near and it seemed strange that no other members of his family had attended.

They were a fine couple, and there was no tomfoolery after. Jacob Cornforth saw to it that no rude jokes were passed by the men while his wife kept a check on any sly looks among the married women. Afterward they sat down to a feast that outdid anything in Bathol's history. Garrison brought his fiddle and set the young folks to dancing.

At its close Jacob shouted that an Indian was at the door asking for Jonathan. The Indian was Joe Paul and he had two muskets to sell. The Government at Halifax, trying to keep the Micmacs loyal, was giving them arms and powder, which they sold cheaply to Yorkshire buyers.

At Christmas Jonathan and Unity rode to spend the day with Melody and Lancelot. Melody roasted a goose and stuffed it with onions. They had a rich pudding with maple flavouring. They sang songs and talked of old days at Banfield but Jonathan could see that his brother had something nagging his mind. When they went to get their horses Lancelot said. "Joe wur wi' me hunting moose this fall, back o' Smith's by a run. We found what wur left o' that pock-marked Indian who took Melody in woods. He'd been shot a year ago. By surprise. His musket wur under windfall whear he wur sleeping."

"That is bad," said Jonathan. "What did Joe think?"

"He would not believe that Smith would do it."

"Happen it could be a mistake?"

"Noa. There wur coil o' birch bark fitted wi' peg at tree whear person stood to shoot."

"Birch pegged?"

"Aye. Joe says it wur to cover rifle breech from rain, but it won't go on rifle Smith carries."

Jonathan nodded. "Then tha can't blame him, and I'm glad o' it."

Lancelot took something from a beam. "I made 'nother birch same size as we found. Happen tha think o' it, try it on thy rifle."

Their glances locked but no name was spoken. When he was home again Jonathan took down his rifle and slid the bark over the muzzle until it rested around the breech snugly. Then he shook the weapon, turned it about, but the bark stayed in place. It fitted perfectly.

BOOK FOUR
1775

I

The Liberty Pole

THE WINTER of 1774-1775 was the coldest remembered in Nova Scotia. Word came to Cumberland that the harbour at Halifax was frozen over so that teams drove back and forth to the Dartmouth side. The frost came with the New Year. At Bathol the river was frozen so that only a rumbling came from its tomb but as the cold increased the ice cracked with whip-like snappings. A sort of fog came in the night, but vanished as the sun rose above the tree tops. The day grew clear and colder, calm for the most part but with occasional gusts, brisk little breezes that presaged bitter weather to come and sometimes merged into miniature whirl-winds that swirled the light snow blindingly. Road ruts were frozen hard as steel.

Lancelot hurried back from his rabbit snares and looked in at the stable. Frost glittered on beams, lay white on ledges behind the cattle. He forked plenty of straw for bedding at night and made sure that no doors were fastened insecurely. He and Melody sat up until late, loathe to leave the fire, listening to cold starting timbers to snapping.

In the night he went down to the fireplace and raked the bed of coals, lifted a tremendous green maple backlog and bedded it firmly against the throat of the chimney. Beside it he laid another log not quite so large and in between piled dry beech hunks. Soon the steady sighing draught kindled a clear sheet of flame that ran up the back of the chimney and from it genial heat beat far back into the room. He basked in it a long time, and the next day did not venture into the woods.

There was no sound at night in the little valley where Jona-

than had built his house and the still dead cold of the place
was appalling.   An old pine at the edge of the wood split
with a report louder than a musket shot.   The diamond
window panes were coated with frost and the door latch was
whitened not ten feet from the fireplace.   Unity and Jonathan
cracked and shelled beechnuts.   When it grew late Unity
combed and braided her hair before the fire, standing there
in her nightdress so that the light showed him the shadow of
her body.

He filled a warming pan with hardwood coals.

"Jonty, darling, do we need it?" she laughed.   "I thowt I
could warm thee".

"It's to take off first chill," he cried, and as he slid the pan
back and forth between the blankets his heart warmed with
happiness.   Unity had never complained of the deep snow or
of cold.   She was cheerful the day through and grand
company.

The wind poured itself over the marshes, arctic, clear and
steady.   It seemed quiet because it no longer came in rowdy
gusts but in one continuous blast that drew the last warmth
out of every creature out of doors.   Overhead the stars
blinked in a frosty carbon blue.   In Amherst village everything was frozen into crisp metallic hardness.   In the nearest
bush large white Arctic owls from the north hunted shivering
rabbits.

Tristram put off getting his wood until February when the
cold eased so that doors did not squall when opened and a man
dare slip a hand from his mitten when outside.   He worked
then with great energy so that by the time the snows softened
he had all the wood he needed.   The spring came early, as
if repenting the winter.   The sun dried the hillsides for plowing and harrowing a month ahead of time.   Bright greens ran
along the intervales.   Willows lost their furry sprouts and
began tentatively to leaf. Swallows nested early. Silas
Plumley went over to see Tristram.

"Thear has been more rumour o' trouble," he said.   "I
have talked wi' Jacob Cornforth and Israel Hodge.   They
have said tha would be best man to ride to Amherst and

find what is true. We are away from news here. Tha are better than others who would be hot-headed."

Tristram's mind was in turmoil as he listened. He did not want to leave his planting, but it would be worth it to be recognized as the leader in Bathol. The suggestion was like wine in his blood. If he could not quickly attain the property he wanted, he could have the position. Judy had been kind with him and life was very good.

"Aye," he said. "It's poor time to leave worked ground, but thear would be folly in not heeding talk o' trouble. I'll ride in morning."

He had bought a fine riding horse and made good time to Gideon Danks' farm. Gideon shouted that he was sweating like a June bride as he carted manure to his potato field. He put up Tristram's horse and then they watched a rider enter the lane, a whiskery man spare-legged as a crow, mounted on a white horse lean as himself.

"It's Michael Healey, the magistrate," said Gideon. "He looks like he's eat the Book of Job."

"Good day to both of you," hailed old Michael. "Have ye heard the news from Ameriky?"

"No," grunted Gideon, winking at Tristram. "What's the tale this time?"

"There's been fighting at last. A mob fought the soldiers at Lexington and Concord in April—I've had it from Halifax by letter—and a terrible lot of the king's men were killed."

"Killed! By a mob?" Gideon pulled his beard, considering. "How would ye be explaining that?"

"I don't," snapped the old man, picking white horse hairs from his breeches. "Bad news is bad news. That's all there is to it." He looked at Tristram. "Where are ye from?"

"Bathol. I'm brother o' Matthew."

"No need to tell me," agreed Healey. "I hope the news wakes the people up all over this country."

"Wakes them up to what?" Gideon had grown impatient.

"To the fact that we have vicious irresponsibles among us who would like to get treason started here." The old man's rage put huskiness in his voice. "That's why I've ridden to every farm hereabouts. There's a meeting in Amherst tavern tonight for everybody and that misguided Sam Rogers is to do the speaking. I'm asking, gentlemen, that you'll attend and," he calmed himself with visible effort like a hen that had swallowed a hot pellet, "use your voice and influence at the proper time."

Gideon looked at Tristram. "We've been denned most of the winter," he grinned. "A mite of fun won't do harm. We'll be there."

Tristram watched a hen lead a brood of yellow chicks to the manure pile Gideon was disturbing, then he nodded. He had news already to carry back with him, but it would be worth losing an extra evening to watch what manner of meetings were being held. He had heard that Jerry O'Regan, proprietor of the tavern, was not an honest citizen, but he knew nothing of Rogers or any others.

The village was dark when he and Gideon and Matthew rode to the tavern. Wails of a pair of tomcats daring each other to battle dominated the quiet outside. A dozen horses were tied to the hitching rail but the tavern's shutters were closed and only a murmuring of voices came from within. Tristram looked well about him as he tied his grey to a fence apart from the rail. One horse was a blooded creature he had seen on the trail several times. It belonged to the redhead at Maccan they called Peter Meekins, and he felt they were to enter where they would be entirely unwelcome.

The tavern was a clap-boarded building with additions to both sides giving it the look of a squatted fowl with wings outspread. At its rear two outbuildings stood guard, double-barrelled privies that were one of O'Regan's many boasts.

A drumming of hoofs down the trail held them outside until five men appeared and Tristram's heart leaped as he saw Jonathan, the Lother brothers and Adam Chipley. He had done no foolish thing in coming.

They filed in with Gideon leading and odours of sweaty wool and tobacco filled their nostrils. More than twenty men were seated against the walls and on long benches at the rear of the big room. At the front O'Regan worked feverishly behind a row of copper beer pots and pewter tankards.

Back to him, occupying the floor, was a man with a broad dark face and hard eyes, all of him stocky as a blockhouse.

"Sam Rogers," whispered Gideon, and Tristram had a second look at him before he glanced again at O'Regan. The tavern keeper had a board on which crude letters had been scrawled and now he placed it on a shelf so that everyone could see. "Sons of Liberty," read Gideon. "Now wouldn't that give ye goose pimples?"

Rogers heard him and his hard eyes glinted. "Anyone not liking our name is free to go," he said.

"Hear that now," retorted Gideon. "A visitor from over the marsh has come and is tellin' us in the village what we may and may not do. Perhaps he can say what would stop me from bein' free to come and go?"

"Easy," warned Tristram, remembering Silas. "Let's find what's afoot."

Rogers looked as if he would send hot retort. Then he swung away and waited while O'Conner, with no more colour than rusty liver spots on his dried-up cheeks, ordered drinks for himself and a crony. Tristram watched O'Regan set out two brass-bound leather mugs, add rum and sugar to a pitcher of beer, plunge a red-hot mulling iron in it and hold it until the hissing stopped. Then he sprinkled the drink with cloves and cinnamon and poured the mixture into mugs. O'Conner's companion scoured the corners of his mouth with a prodigious tongue and as he raised his drink Tristram recognized him as Cutlip, the cobbler.

He saw Yorkshiremen from the Fort Lawrence area, and from Sackville, Gold and Niles from Maccan near two devil-may-care fellows with Meekins.

"Get seated, please," said Rogers. "This meeting will come to order." Then he looked at a corner where sat Michael Healey with his spindling legs tucked under his seat as if he were ashamed of them. "Friends of the cause," he went on, "we're invited for this evening but I see that many others have attended."

He paused as if to ascertain where his lead had taken him and Healey nodded. "A tavern's a public place and honest

citizens have a right to know what's going on when there's
so much treason in the wind."

"Treason!" Rogers' voice tightened. "I don't like the
way you use that word. There are too many king's men
mouthing the same while our brothers are being murdered by
British redcoats. Is it treason to want a fair chance of trade
and the electing of honest men to govern us?"

"Has anybody in Nova Scotia been murdered by lobster
backs?" asked Gideon. "Is anybody bothering you over the
marsh?"

Rogers looked through him and over him and away from
him. "No men worthy of the name will stand idly by while
their brothers are being oppressed. The Sons of Liberty
showed what they could do at Lexington and Concord and
that's only the beginning. Nothing will stop men who fight
for justice, but if we join them victory will come much sooner."

"Victory! Liberty!" A short dark man had jumped to his
feet. "What drivel is this I hear?"

"Obed Muncie from Maccan," hissed Gideon. "A good
man, that."

Muncie talked passionately and Rogers could not shout
him down. Liberty—they had it! Where on earth had they
more or could they have more? Every man was free to act
entirely on his own responsibility. There were no compul-
sions, no oppressions. They had only such crack-brained
fools as might rise in their midst, wild animals and the forest
to contend with. Freedom to trade? How long would they
have trade if England's ships quit the sea?

Adam Chipley took up where he left off. "Thee prate of
taxes," he glared at Rogers. "But tha know nowt o' them.
We are from Yorkshire and have paid in a year more taxes
than you do here in ten, and no talk against it. Tha have a
bluster over threepence on tea, and nowt else. We paid a
shilling a pound on tea wi' oot a growl. Man, thee are tempt-
ing Providence when tha try to stir oop trouble in a land the
Lord has so richly blessed."

"Enough," yelled Rogers, and Peter Meekins pounded his
bench with a bung starter. "Give over. Let this meeting
proceed."

"Proceed where?" Muncie popped up again. "What authority have you to come to this village to spread sedition?"

Rogers spraddled his heavy legs as if to weather a gale. "By what authority is Boston port closed to honest traders? What authority sent soldiers to shoot down men for wanting fair government? We'll make our own authority, before the same thing happens here."

Then he pointed to the lettered board on the shelf. "I move," he challenged, "that we set up a liberty pole in this village to show our brothers our true stand in their cause."

"I second the move," yelled Peter Meekins.

"All right," said Muncie. "Stand, those who are for it."

Tristram counted easily. There were twenty-seven men in the room, counting O'Regan, and but eleven were on their feet.

"Against it," bellowed Gideon when the eleven sat down, and he jumped up. "There ye are, mister over-the-marsh. Tuck yer tail atween your legs and get gone. Sixteen good men against you, and twice that many would be here if they knew the deviltry you have on foot."

Rogers stood, waiting, and they quieted to hear what he would say. He looked at Meekins. "The Sons of Liberty have heard it moved and seconded that we raise a liberty pole in this village. I ask them—and no others—to vote by raising their right hand."

Eleven men put up their hands. "Carried," declared Rogers. "Is the pole ready?"

"It is." Meekins and his pair led the way outside and every man followed. "We've a pine tree flag as well."

A long peeled stick had been laid well back of the privies and now they dragged it forward as O'Regan carried a lantern.

"That's good-lookin' lumber," shouted Gideon, seeing a hole had been dug near the whipping post. "Too good to be mishandled. What say, lads?"

His leadership was all that was needed. Matthew joined the big Lother lads in a rush to seize the stick. Meekins tried to flourish his bung starter but Gideon caught his arm and wrenched the weapon from him. Tristram let the excitement move him. He bowled over one of the young men with Meekins. Chipley, old as he was, attended to a third. In a trice they had possession while Gideon barred Rogers from lending a hand. He looked him bang in the eye.

"You've listened to too many dirty shirts from Maine," he roared. "It's addled your thinking. You better tend your farm and forget this foolishness or you'll be ridin' a pole one of these days 'stead of tryin' to put it up. Next time you run afoul of this village you'll be in real trouble. That's true as the Book of Genesis."

Rufus Lother came out of the tavern with the "Sons of Liberty" board in his hand. He split it with a wallop against the hitching post then flung the pieces toward the privies. Rogers stared at him as he went slowly to his horse. "You men have had your night," he said bitterly. "The next time will be our turn."

Tristram rode home the next morning, feeling important. He went to Silas, and that night the men of Bathol gathered to hear what he had to say. He told them of the fighting that had happened in the American colonies, of the attempt to hoist a liberty pole at Amherst, of the danger of men like Rogers stirring men to mad undertakings. His audience gave him respectful attention and he went back to Judy feeling that he had been elevated to the leadership of the community.

II
The Stranger

MELODY was glad the winter had gone. It had been lonesome without her father carving by his window, with only young Molly to keep her company while Lancelot was away at his wood cutting. Her restlessness had driven her to organize many social gatherings in the settlement. Several of the farmers had acquired horses and winter roads were easily made. Knatchball, the smith, hammered out steel shoes for wide sleds that could easily carry a dozen persons on a smooth snow track. Each evening they went to a different home. The singing of old Yorkshire songs was hearty. Everyone played games with zest. Why should they not be merry? Meat barrels were full after half the winter was gone. There was plenty in every cupboard. There was every promise for the future.

Spring brought some ease to Melody's strange moods. She enjoyed hearing sap birds calling in the hardwoods, and it was grand to boil maple syrup to thick sweetness they spread on the snow. It was exhilarating to go bare-headed in first days of May, gathering pink and white Mayflowers. Then came the glamorous blossoming of the Indian pear, runs of smelts in the river, wild geese dropping to feed on the intervales, and first robins. It was lovely out of doors in the spring twilight with the many birds she had encouraged flying about to announce their return to her feeding stations.

She rode the river trail one morning simply to enjoy the air. It was as dewy and fresh as only June can be. Larks whistled over the intervales. Woodchucks made new burrows. Bluebirds flitted on pasture hills.

A stranger came walking toward her and she felt a twinge

of the worry that some women of the place had begun to carry. He turned to face her and she saw that he was tall and quick and lean, with strong hands, and the eyes and forehead of an imaginative person.

"I beg your pardon," he began, and he had the gentlest deep man's voice she had ever heard, "but can you tell me where Mrs. Philip Tibbets lives?"

A quick tremour chased through her entire frame. "Art tha a relative?" she asked.

"She's my cousin," he smiled. "More than that, she mothered me for nigh on seven years."

Instinctively she put a hand down to his and tried to soften her words. "Thy cousin is dead," she said, "and her husband is gone. If tha will coom to my house I'll tell thee all ony here in Bathol knows."

It was after he was in her kitchen and she had told him of Tristram moving on the farm because no owner could be found that she saw how pale and hungry he looked.

"I have milk in t' spring house, and new barley bread," she said hesitantly. "Would tha eat if I fetched?"

She smiled as he looked at her, and had his smile back. "I've not eaten since yesterday," he said. "You see, I have no money."

Melody hurried to the spring house with the look of a person in a dream, as if she had slept and climbed a hill to find him in the lonely world beyond. He was not strange to her. He was twined into her being from before the start of her memory; of that she was sure.

"Tha will stay here," she said as if her words were final, "and we will see what my brother will do."

"Will do?" he echoed.

"Aye. He has not paid ony person for t' farm. If tha art kin . . ."

"No." He smiled and reached for his hat. "I have no claim of any kind and it was not for that I came."

"Then," she said, before he could say more, "I ask thee to stay because my brother, Lancelot, is in need o' a man to help wi' t' seeding. Will tha stop wi' us and give a hand?"

He seemed to search the pockets of his mind and the room was quiet, thick with his gratitude and embarrassment.

"I'll stay a time," he finally agreed, "for it's long since I've had the pleasure of meeting one like you."

The uneasy look stayed with him so after he had eaten a hearty meal of cold meat and bread and milk she walked him up the hill to show him the willow stub and her father's grave. Then they sat in the warmth of the sun and talked.

His name, he said, was John Lacey, and his home had been in New Hampshire. His father had been a disabled ex-officer of the British army, and his mother had died when he was ten years old. His cousin, Jane Lacey, scant years older than himself, had come to keep house for them. They had lived well under her management until a lad from the next village had won her with tales of rich farmland in Nova Scotia being granted to settlers. She had married him overnight, and vanished.

Jane had written, John said, telling of a neat home they had at a place called Bathol, where crops were good and a river ran by their farm. She had signed her name with a flourish "Mrs. Philip Tibbets," and had begged him to visit them if ever he had opportunity.

The years dragged after that, then came the trouble. A mob came to the house to threaten his father. There had been pistol shots. The door was crashed in and the house set on fire. John's father had been shot and killed. It had been touch and go with John but he had escaped with a wound over the ribs.

Then he had travelled to Nova Scotia, being lucky enough to fall in with a small schooner's crew needing a man and not given to asking questions. They were running a load of Tories to Nova Scotia and he had landed at Windsor, paid his passage by ferry to Partridge Island, then walked overland.

It seemed to Melody that they had scarcely sat down before Lancelot was at the house, calling for his dinner. She scurried to meet him, breathlessly told him what she had done.

He stared at her. "Why, lass, I've never seen thee so stirred. Tha look as if tha art in love. Don't tha fret. I'll bid him stay."

There was no argument about John staying. He seemed starved for company his own age and for a week they talked late each night.

"I'll never go home again," declared John. "My father never bothered any man, and I saw what people did to him."

Melody listened intently to every word John spoke. His voice remained in her ears when he was out of her sight. She studied the shape of his head, the strong curve of his jaw, the traces of boyish freckles still on his forehead. She gave heed to nothing else.

The night of his arrival she had scarcely slept. She had but to close her eyes and she could see him as he stood on the road, asking her his questions. In the morning she was not tired, and when he appeared she called "John!" without thinking what she did. He had laughed softly, gleefully, then had said "Melody."

When he had gone to the field with Lancelot she had heated water and filled a wooden tub. Standing in it, she had scrubbed herself clean until her skin shone. When she had dried herself she put on clean, fresh clothing. She had prettied her hair.

When the men came to the house at noon she had flushed as John looked at her, and when they were gone again she rushed to the small mirror kept in her chest and studied herself tensely. One night as they sat in the dusk not troubling to light a candle John's hand touched hers, and she had let it stay. She could sense his start in the darkness, and then his hand had closed over hers with gentleness. The contact had made her tremble.

During the second week John became more pale and the day the last of the potato sets were in their rows he buckled at the drag sled and lay there writhing in pain while Lancelot ran with great strides to reach him.

Melody came flying from the house at Lancelot's call and they carried him to bed. Before the next night O'Conner rode in with his worn saddle bags and, with Melody holding a tallow dip to give him light, probed for and removed a pistol ball.

"There ye are, my dear," he exulted. "The O'Conner still

has his clever hand if he's neither drunk nor sober, but how the divil this buckaroo could travel with such lead jammed between his ribs is beyant my knowledge. Now I've made a bit of a hole in him and it's up to your sweet self to keep him quiet until he's healed entirely. Do you hear me?"

John lay white and still as she dried the sweat that had beaded him as O'Conner worked, and his smile was faint. The doctor put on a dressing, explaining every move to Melody, and showed her how to remove it. Then he led her to the door.

"If your heart flutters while yon lad's about," he said in an attempt at whispering, "you'll do well to keep him on his back an extry week or so. He's come a fairish distance on his nerve and nothing less. Feed him and keep him in bed if ye have to steal his breeches."

Melody gazed at John's lean prideful head with the skin hammered tight to the bone and needed no further urging. She made him meaty broths and stews and stayed with him whenever she thought he wanted her near. She was there the day Tristram came over, saying he had heard it rumoured that a man had come to claim his farm.

Tristram had begun to look like a middle-aged man and she had no way of telling what was going on behind his lined and sweat-brightened face, but she spoke when John said he had no claim, and poured out his story.

Tristram's face set like granite. "Have tha onything in writing to prove thy tale?" he asked.

"Nothing," said John.

"No one else would ask it but thee," flamed Melody. "Tha art living in his cousin's house and tha know it. Thy conscience . . ."

"Never tha mind my conscience," interrupted Tristram. "I'll pay for farm to ony who coom wi' proof. Is that fair?"

"It's fair," said John, "but you mistake me. I have no claim on the farm, and am not looking for any. I wanted to see my cousin, and nothing more."

"I am sorry, then," said Tristram with sudden gentleness, "for she is dead."

He left without a word to Melody, and John was very quiet after he had gone.

When he had strength to walk again John's health returned. He sat in the sun and put on a layer of tan. He ate puddings and greens that fleshed his ribs and filled out the hollows in his face. He was over six feet in height and almost as big as Lancelot. Melody, watching his every move, thought that he grew.

Word came around that Silas Plumley and his wife would celebrate their fortieth wedding anniversary with a party. It was a busy time of the year but the people went with gay hearts, saying they needed something to perk them up against the steady run of rumours from Maine. Garrison had honed his fiddle to fast jigs and every man sleeved sweat from his face before he had made many rounds on the floor.

John went with Melody and Lancelot. He was shaved cleanly and he wore a clean new shirt that Melody had given him. She treasured the look he had worn when he accepted it. "No other girl," he had said, "ever gave me anything in my life, not even Jane."

Melody wore her best stockings and a chip bonnet that Patience had said was a bold affair. It gave Melody a provocative appearance that she felt she needed. Never once had John given her a hint of his feelings toward her. He seemed on guard against any impulse or emotion, but he laughed with the rest when the Garrisons arrived, Gabriel whacking his oxen along the trail while his large wife issued orders from a moored-down rocking chair she occupied in the cart.

"May I have the honour?" asked John, when there was a cleared space in which to dance.

Melody swung to him without troubling to answer and then she was whirling among the couples with a lightness that stilled tongues of the lookers-on at the doorways and windows. John was feather-light on his feet and the music of Garrison's fiddle seemed to lift his toes. When they danced a second time nearly everyone stepped aside to watch and Melody was more happy than she had ever been before. "They are watching thee," she whispered.

"No," breathed John, "it's you they admire. Am I not

interfering with some good lad? Please remember that I'm unacquainted."

"Thear is no one," said Melody, as if she could sing it over and over for his ears. "No man has ever courted me."

"Then will you be my partner for the evening?" John spoke wonderingly, as if her lack of suitors were beyond his power of understanding.

There were games besides the dancing, and a bountiful feast. Silas Plumley and his wife then stood together and received the compliments and wishes for their future that every settler wanted to express.

"I'm proud to have thee at our house," said Silas to John when he and Melody were making their turn. "Tha will do well to stay wi' us in Bathol, for I have never seen Melody looking more happy than she is this night."

John was quiet again as they walked home. Lancelot was not with them and it was a beautiful night. Melody took John's arm without hesitation and in every way gave him encouragement to say the words she believed he held in his heart. But they were to the lane and he had not spoken other than to comment on the kindness of those he had met. She could not suffer longer.

"Art timid of me, John?" she queried.

"Timid!" He stopped and they faced each other. "Why do you ask?"

"Because I thowt," she faltered, "tha might . . ."

"Yes?" he said softly. "Say it, Melody."

"Want to court me." She could almost hear Patience' shocked cry but she was desperate.

For a moment he looked at her with the awe of a man watching dreams come true, and then his arms were around her.

"I love you, dear," he whispered. "I have loved you since the day you first spoke to me on the trail."

Melody did not know after whether they had stood a moment or an hour on the trail. She was in such an ecstacy of happiness that long after Lancelot was in and sleeping she still sat by her bed without a light, seeing as clearly as in bright sunshine the days and years ahead. Sometime she crept into her bed but it was long before she could try and sleep.

Lancelot wakened her with his shouting. "We're late," he called. "Get oop, lass, and make breakfast. Whear's John?"

"John!" She looked out at him.

"Aye. He's not in house. I've been all about. He's gone."

Gone!

Melody thought she never would be dressed. She rushed to John's room. He had lain on the bed, resting, but had not slept in it. The only reminder of him in the room was the worn shirt he had removed when she gave him the new one.

An hour later she and Lancelot faced each other.

"Tha must have said summat to him last night he did not like," insisted Lancelot. "T' man would not leave for nowt."

"He towd me he loved me." Melody's tears rolled unchecked. "I never wur more happy."

"Wur tha talking o' being wedded?"

"Noa. He wur not asking me."

"Then it's like he's gone," decided Lancelot. "He has not a shilling, so how could he ask thee to wed?"

"Why not?" The colour drained from Melody's cheeks. "Do tha think I would wed for money? It is no matter to me what he has." She grasped her brother's arm. "Will tha go and find him?" she pleaded. "Else I'll saddle and go myself. I cannot bear it wi' oot him."

"Calm thyself," soothed Lancelot. "I have to go. Muncie, at Maccan, is militia officer. He sent word last night to muster at t' fort. I'll clean t' rifle and go. It's like I'll find John afore noon."

"Will tha send him to me?" Melody quivered with grief. She wrung her hands and gazed unseeing at fowl waiting to be fed. "If tha don't I can't stay here. I'll go and seek him and I care not what tha say or think. I want John and nowt will stop me findin' him."

When he was gone Melody moved as in a dream. She let the fire die to gray ashes. She ignored the breakfast dishes and the milk in pails where Lancelot had left them. Her routine chores were forgotten. She walked through the house and out again as if unaware of what she did, then climbed the hill, bare-headed, her red hair glistening like fire in the sunshine, until she was by the willow stub.

She looked back.

Her glance swept over the young green of the planted fields, the intervales with grazing sheep and cattle and the long, lazy windings of the sun-kissed river. She looked down the hill at the square-built house and its setting of flowers, shrubs and tall elms. There was a feeling of permanency about it, of immutability; she felt it would always be there.

"It does not matter," she murmured, dropping to the warm grass. "It's thee I want, John. Why did tha go?"

III

The Muster

LANCELOT rode with Aaron Cornforth, Tristram and
Abel Plumley. They talked little for their errand was
not to their liking. Here and there along the way other
farmers swung to the trail behind them as if each had waited
to be sure he would not be the only one to leave his day's
work untouched. Each time a new man appeared Lancelot
dropped back to speak with him and ask if a stranger had been
seen on the river road. No one had news of John. They
reached the fort and he had not gained any information. It
was as if the man had vanished in thin air.

"Here's t' milishy officer," called Aaron, pointing to Muncie.

Muncie's eyes lightened as he saw the Bathol men. "I'm
proud of you," he said to Lancelot. "You've done well to
have so many come. There's no more than a dozen from this
side of Amherst and not a man has put his name to the roll."

Lancelot pulled Tristram aside. "Happen thear is summat
wrong wi' this business," he muttered. "We should not be
first names in t' book."

A clean-shaven man with strong features came to them.
"Are you men joining the militia?" he asked.

"Happen we do," said Lancelot defensively, "what will tha
do about it?"

The stranger smiled. "Not a thing, friend. Your speech
tells me you are Yorkshire, and I have some for neighbours."

"Tha sound like a Scot," said Lancelot, more amiable.
"Art tha joining t' militia?"

"No," said the stranger. "My name's Allan. I've a farm
on this ridge and I've no hankering to go to Boston."

186

"Boston!" Lancelot was thunderstruck. He remembered the tales John had told him of the place.

Allan looked around him carefully. "I'd likely have a constable calling for me if they knew I'd passed the word on, but I've just come from Halifax and I know what's happening. Governor Legge's asked his men to sign on all they can into the militia, and then the lot's to be drafted for Boston."

"Not for me," swore Aaron Cornforth, listening. "I've no wish to see Boston."

"But if you put your name on their roll . . ."

"Devil take t' roll," roared Aaron truculently. "Coom on, lads. Get thy horses."

Lancelot made no move to stop them. Tristram growled that he did not understand or like such methods and before the others were unhitched he was going to his own horse. No man had intention of leaving his farm on such a mission.

There was a schooner at the fort wharf so Lancelot rode over. It might be that John would reach it and offer his services. When nearer, he saw that the craft had experienced some serious adventure. Part of a mast was shot away and a cannon ball had made an ugly vent amidships.

"The captain's in yon house," pointed a sailor who gazed overside at the bared mud flats. "We had a mate and two others nigh killed. It were Fundy fog that saved us, else we'd be at the sea's bottom now."

Lancelot turned his horse slowly. He seemed on a fruitless errand but he went on. Melody's proud face contorted in grief had touched him deeply. He was still stunned to know that features normally so beautiful could be so strained with hurt. There would be no holding her if he went back without some hope. So he rode to the house.

A farmer's wife, her back bowed with years of hard labour, gazed up at him as he stood by the door.

"We've a fair hospital inside," she wheezed. "The mate will die, ye can count on that, and the others will take a month to mend. Come and see them," she added tiredly, "if ye want. The mate's in the first room."

Lancelot looked down on a thin, pinched, unshaven face,

with its eyes partly closed.   The lips moved fretfully.   "Who is it?"

"I've been to muster at fort," said Lancelot, wishing he had not made the intrusion.   "I'm from Bathol and coom to see . . ."

"Bathol!"   The sufferer's eyes opened wider.   "Do you know it?"

"I live thear," said Lancelot crisply.   "I'm Yorkshire."

"Oh, then you wouldn't know."   The eyes closed again. "I lived there once.   My name is Tibbets."

Lancelot started.   Philip Tibbets!

"It's God's grace I've found thee," blurted Lancelot. "Tha know John Lacey?"

In hurried but careful words he told of John's coming to Bathol in search of his cousin, his story of what had happened at his home, and his sudden leaving that morning.

"Happen he has a lass elsewhear," he finished, "and could not tell my sister, else his lack o' money made him go."

Tibbets put his head back on the pillow and stared up at Lancelot.   "Hurry," he gasped.   "I want two things.   Bring the notary from the fort, and promise you'll bury me at Bathol—beside my wife."

"I will that," promised Lancelot, wondering where he would hire a cart.   "I'll be back reight soon."

The notary said he had become accustomed to unusual happenings so he did no more than purse his lips and state his fee when Philip Tibbets signed over his holdings at Bathol to John Lacey, entire and without any restrictions, as from the day.

When the notary was gone Lancelot was given a purse of otter skin filled with gold coins.   "It's for John as well," whispered Tibbets.   "Tell him to freshen the slab at the grave."

Lancelot stayed the long afternoon beside the bed with Tibbets' high and rasping breathing filling the room with ugly sound.   Sometimes there was a pause and there seemed no heart action, but the pulse would leap and flutter again and the dying man would draw in great agonized gasps.

It became dark in the room and a slight wind stirred at

the windows. The tired woman looked in at the door and said the tide was turning. When she was gone Lancelot began counting the spaces between the gasping battles for breath. He counted on without end. The breathing did not come.

At the fort he made enquiries. John had not arrived there. No one had heard of him. He hired a farmer who owned a small cart to take Tibbets' body to Bathol, had a few hours of sleep, then saddled his horse.

Drowsy birds were cheeping and gray dawn fingers groped through the trees as he reached Bathol. The stars dimmed overhead. Then the sun lifted in a bank of amber haze and he turned in at the farm lane with a heart more heavy than the bag of otter skin tied to his belt. He was more afraid of meeting Melody than of anything else he had known in his life.

Melody stayed on the hill. Large blue butterflies fluttered near her and she could see tiny snails and froth on the grass stems. A lark lifted itself and sang from a hiding place of height. Crows cawed at some rendezvous across the pasture. There was a clean washed feeling in the air.

"John!" she murmured in pain that would not leave her. "Why did tha go?"

She thought of the way he had reached for her as they stood in the farm lane, of the warmth of his arms, his tenderness, and her body shook with sobs. Presently she quieted and lay with her head on her arms, trying to analyze love as she had seen it.

Never would she want a man to endure her as her father had patiently borne with her mother. She thought of Sylvia, going to Matthew with a child not his own. Of Tristram living with Judy, not sure that Reuben was dead. Then she thought of Gideon's devotion to Patience. They loved each other, she decided, in strong measure, but theirs was not the love that had come to herself and John.

What did love mean? It meant, she told herself, going with a man down into the places of his life, his success, his failure. It meant everything. The best and the worst— the rough and the smooth. Couldn't John know that?

Didn't he recognize love when it came to him? Or had he, before . . .

She turned and sat up, stared, unseeing, at the grey, weathered stub, rose to her feet, staggered until she put out a hand to steady herself.

"No!" she cried, so that a squirrel chirred nervously from brush nearby. "Not that! Please."

She sank again to her knees, covering her face with her hands, her mind whirling with unreality. John had not talked of himself. His talk had been of his father, of the rebels and their raids on those who had been their neighbours. Not once had he mentioned his own career, his work or his ambitions. Perhaps he was already promised?

She tortured herself with imaginings, then the squirrel's clamour became more shrill, and she looked up.

She stood.

John was coming from the woods. He looked haggard but he smiled as he saw her, and began to hurry. Her lips moved without sound. She saw the light in his eyes. He still wanted her. She tried to cry "Please, God, make time stand still. Make this moment last. Let me have it long. This is what I've lived for."

"John!" One small word.

"Melody!" His answer.

"Whear did tha go?"

It was long after that he answered, and in the time he had held her, strongly, firmly, as if he would never let her go. Her heart had pounded madly and he had hurt her arms, but she endured the hurt gladly. Then he said.

"I had to think, alone." He kissed her, and released her. "Let's sit," he said. "I must talk with you."

Fear wrenched at her. "Say quickly, John. Have tha someone else?"

"None. There has been no other, Melody."

"Then why . . ."

"Because I've nothing, don't you see. And it will be so long before . . ."

She flung against him. "Noa, say nowt," she cried. "We have home here. Wed me. If we have each other it is all

I ask." She pointed to the house. "I picked t' spot, John. Jonty and I planned t' kitchen and t' windows, t' place for garden. My father smoothed every board in cupboards. I love t' place like tha cannot know—but I'll walk from thear today never to see it again if tha will have me with thee. Can't tha see?"

He waited quietly until she was finished. "But I'm not even a good farmer," he said. "I don't know about planting grain and training cattle. We had but small ground at home."

"What did tha do?"

He looked at her, held his knees with clasped hands and leaned backward slightly, a posture he had used the first day she took him up the hill.

"I was to be a doctor," he said. "I studied medicine and I worked three years with the man at home, but I'd sooner farm. I have only a small packet of instruments I brought with me. It just happened I had them in my jacket pocket that night. I hid them in your barn. Where is Lancelot?"

She told him, then she smiled again. "John, tha will be t' best in this settlement if tha will stay. Thear is no doctor here to Amherst, and tha can farm as well. It is thy duty, don't tha see. Now we will go to house and have dinner. Then we will talk no more until Lancelot has coom."

In late afternoon they went to the hill again and sat in long silence as the day faded and the magic of the summer evening possessed them. The smell of the river intervales rose to them, and robin song permeated the dusk. Her hand held his, stroking it in a comforting way as if she were suddenly the older and wiser of the two, until the robin stopped singing and night chill dampened them. Then they went to the house.

Melody heard Lancelot ride into the yard in the morning. She was up and building a fire, with John helping her, when Lancelot entered the house.

He stared at them as if they were unreal, then his face was wreathed with relief. "Tha art my neighbour, John," he said, extending a paper. "I welcome thee to Bathol. This sack is thy property as well."

John took the paper wonderingly, drew Melody to him and they read it together. They looked at the otter skin purse, at the fatigue showing on Lancelot's face as he told his story.

Then John said softly. "It must have been meant to be so. I'll be a farmer here and Melody will be my wife."

Lancelot grinned, some of his old boyishness creeping to the surface.

"That's best news," he exulted. "I've heard this day."

IV
Luck of Titus Green

THE WEATHER stayed warm and dry. More Yorkshire families were established at Bathol. Then there
was another cabin raising at a new clearing across the
river. Everyone treated the newcomer, Shubad Knapp, with
great good humour, for he was a cod fisherman turned land
hungry, but when he produced an old brass compass at the
raising and made them place the cabin sills due north and
south, square to the earth itself, no one laughed. He was
having his front door face north-easters, and he stuck to it
even after Solomon Smith showed him he was wrong.

They put up his logs as he wanted, then, for it would be
easy to change in another year. The woman made a feast
of shad chowder, caraway cakes and blueberry turnover, which
ended the day. They liked Knapp's patient little wife.
She had come from a town on the coast of New England and
she could not get the fright of a strange land and wilderness
from her eyes.

Reuben Scurr came back in October. He came in the night
to Matthew's house to beg something to eat, saying he had
left a schooner at the fort wharf. Sylvia made him a meal,
then flinched and felt sick when Reuben peeled off his filthy
shirt to show them a back livid with raw scars that criss-
crossed closely as strips on a custard pie.

"A dozen times they laid it on," he gritted, "and for nowt
else but t' knocking they took in t' alley. It wur talk o' t'
ship and a dog's life their bully officer gave me until I'd like
to die after three dozen laid on in Boston harbour for nowt
but their bloody sport. When I had strength back I went
overside one night. It wur a hard swim. I wur like to puke

my innards oot when I reached land.   A lad lugged me to his kitchen, but it wur weeks afore I could walk about.   Then I went oot one night and met that swine o' an officer wi' a lass on his arm.''

Reuben paced the floor as he pictured the happening.

"Happen that lass is running yet," he grimaced.   "She wur off like a singed cat when I had my grip on t' officer afore he could open mouth.   I gave her no heed.   It wur champion to have tha dirty scut in my hands.   I have scars on my back that'll stay but he has a face that will not get him more fancy-nancys.   I bashed his nose flat.   T' rest is a long tale, but here I am and here I'll stay, in Coomberland.''

Matthew told him about Judy marrying Tristram, and Reuben sat with a strange look on his face.   "Did she now.'' He paused.   "I thank tha for giving me t' word.   She wur in proper hurry.''

He went on next day and found his cabin in good repair for a family of newcomers had just moved from it to a new house. Soon he had established himself.   He worked odd days for Ezra Hodge and his only company was a yellow pup.

Tristram heard of his arrival.   He was astounded.   It seemed that whatever he did turned out wrong.   He went to Silas Plumley.

"It wur no sin for thee," pronounced Silas.   "Tha thowt her a widow, and she might well have been.''

"What will I do now?'' blurted Tristram.   "It's busy time o' year.''

"Aye,'' nodded Silas, "but tha must take her back to Reuben.   Thear is only t' reight way to do.''

Tristram rode over to see Reuben.   They shook hands gravely.   "I am glad,'' said Tristram, "to see thee.   I married Judy but she wur sure tha wur dead.   I would not have done it had I thowt else.   Now I will bring her back to thee.''

"Noa,'' said Reuben shortly.   "Tha can keep her.''

Tristram's blood heated.   He had been reluctant to lose her at first, and now he was determined.   "She's thy wife,'' he declared, "and tha cannot refuse.''

He rode home slowly.   Judy had saved his life when she shot the bull.   She had waited on him with every care.   He had appreciated it so much that he had had her jug filled with wine.

She liked men, there was no doubt of that. She had kept her hair neatly brushed while Jonathan and Lancelot were getting in his crops. On Sundays when Lancelot came over she would put on her best shawl and shoes, prinking herself until he had to admit that, next to Melody, she was the finest-looking woman in the country.

When he could work again and had no inclination to fool with her of an evening, her mood changed. "I want a horse," she told him. "Thee are able to ride as tha want, and winter's a time to get to know folks. I'll not be cooped oop here to fatten like a hen till snow's gone."

Tristram had thought it a fair request. He had sold enough cattle to buy her two or three horses if need be. So he rode to Amherst and had Gideon help him buy an able nag no longer young but trustworthy for a woman to handle. A saddle went with the bargain and Judy was delighted. Before Christmas she had visited nearly every home in Bathol, and had been to Maccan.

Sometimes she was late getting back but she made no explanation and Tristram did not ask for one. It was not until March that she stayed away for a night, not coming back until the next noon when she rode into the yard as blithely as if she had been gone an hour.

Tristram had waited up for her, wondering if her horse had fallen on icy road, then he had not rested easy. "Whear have tha been?" he demanded. "Did tha horse fall?"

"Not wi' me," she laughed. "I wur to see friends in Maccan and stayed too late. I've coom to do churning else I'd stayed till tonight."

He thought of Jonathan and Unity at once but because Judy's voice had tightened he did not say more. Judy acted as if she had had a gay time. She sang ditties all the afternoon as she plugged the dasher up and down in the wooden churn, flicking the lid off occasionally to see if butter were forming.

A week or so later she was gone another night, coming back with raisins enough to make a black-eyed Yorkshire cake, good as ever his mother had baked. She placed it on the table with some ceremony, joshing him as when he had first known her, stirring him so that he took her in his arms. "Tha art a funny lad," she said, then kissed him with her eyes squeezed tight as if she were trying to give him the whole cool depths of her.

It was not until they made ready for bed that he discovered she was mildly drunk on red wine she had brought home with her.

When the maple sap began running she stayed at home, boiling all he could gather until she had a thick syrup that, stirred briskly for a time, set firm, becoming a light-coloured sugar more delicious than anything he had ever tasted.

"However did tha learn that?" he queried. "It's champion stoof."

"Uriah Benwood made it oop in Vermont. They cooked it in proper big pots wi' fat pork on string to dip and keep syrup from boiling over."

Uriah Benwood!

Tristram had been warned of the fellow. He was said to be shiftless as an Indian, unreliable, but clever enough if he wanted to be.

"Do tha know him?" he had growled.

"Aye. He wur by road when I coom along."

"Keep from him," he had ordered. "I'll not have thee talking wi' his like."

Judy had given him a look that had words behind it but Melody had come over and there was no quarrel.

In June Tristram rode with her to Amherst and bought her a fine cape, black shoes, a sprigged bonnet and laced velvet bodice that became her perfectly. She thanked him heartily and as they rode home they stopped to rest at Jonathan's and he was amazed at the warmth of Unity's greeting to Judy. They talked as if they had become intimate friends. Sometimes he worried, wondering how much Judy would tell her.

When he was home again Tristram made up his mind. Judy seemed to watch him for some hint as to where he had been but he said nothing until morning when he saddled both horses and brought them to the door.

"Get all tha have," he said briefly. "Tha are going back
to Reuben. I'll take thy chest later."

She studied him as if she were looking into the back of his
mind and seeing there dark thoughts that had festered like
an old wound. Then she went to her room and packed her
belongings with care. She got Reuben's musket and powder
horn and laid them beside her chest, went down and to her
horse, mounted and rode away without looking back.

They saw Reuben by the river bank, fishing, the yellow pup
beside him.

"Helloa," said Judy. "I've coom to thee."

He looked up without interest, drew in his line. "What
for?" he asked. "What do tha want?"

"She wants thee," said Tristram.

"I'd never have gone wi' him if I knew tha wur alive," said
Judy.

"Tha didn't wait overlong," shrugged Reuben, standing
up.

"Tha can take her onyway," said Tristram flatly, and Judy
slid from her horse with the bundle she had packed.

"Noa," said Reuben stubbornly. "I'll not."

Tristram turned his horses. "Tha have to," he grunted.

Then Judy broke into brittle laughter. Reuben was gone.
He had caught up the fish he had taken and was hurrying into
pasture brush, the pup at his heels.

Judy watched him go from sight and tears rolled down her
cheeks. "Tha can go," she called to Tristram. "I want no
more o' thee."

Sounds of a horse coming along the trail held them both
silent. Then they saw that the rider was Titus Green. He
pulled up and bowed.

"What is this?" he questioned. "A parting?" He was
looking at Judy's bundle and the empty saddle.

"Aye," said Judy. "I'm leaving him." She pointed to
Tristram. "If tha know of a place I can work I'll go wi'
thee."

Tristram saw the calculation and greed that leaped to
Green's eyes. It was not unmixed with lust. He kicked his
horses and started back to his farm. At a turn he glanced

back. Judy was mounted on Green's horse, and Green walked
beside her. No doubt, Tristram thought gloomily, his head
was buzzing with ideas that did not auger well for Judy.

Reuben took his musket readily enough when Tristram went
over with it and the chest in his ox cart, but he would not have
Judy's chest in his cabin. "She's not cooming here," he said.
"Tha can take chest whear tha like."

Tristram wanted to avoid trouble so he stored the chest
at Israel Hodge's, and hurried home.

Melody came over and helped him with a churning and then
he knew he would have to get a woman to do his work. She
said, looking into the butter tray. "Parson will give thee
paper that tha art free to wed. Have care whom tha court
this time."

"I will do," he shrugged, resenting her tone but glad of her
help.

"Tha can have Molly to get thy meals and do churning, but
she'll stop wi' me."

His temper flashed but he caught back his refusal before it
could be formed into words. "Aye," he said. "Have her
coom."

It seemed as if Judy's going was the beginning of disaster.
It had been hot and dry right through September that year.
Heat lightning flickered around the skyline, with no rumble
of thunder or smell of rain. Grain was stunted and scanty.
Hay was a light crop. Berries wizened. The eleventh Garrison child was born and Gabriel declared it was no more than
half the size the others had been at birth.

The ground at Bathol was baked hard and dusty and many
of the settlers waited for rain before starting their fall plowing. But not Tristram.

No man watched the drought more anxiously than he.
Often, before dawn, he had stepped outdoors in bare feet to
feel the air. All day he watched the sky. The last thing at
night he looked at it, and he concluded finally that when the
weather changed it would stay changed. So he plowed.
He yoked his oxen at daybreak each morning and plowed
until the sun was hot. The dew helped lay the dust, he said,
and he had too much work ahead of him to be idle.

It began raining when Tristram finished digging his potatoes the first week in November, and there was not another fine day in the month. Instead of the golden autumn sunlight thick upon the tree tops like light through amber glasses, there were clouds that hid the sun, and driving rains that made many potato fields a sea of mud. Only a few farmers had their plowing done.

Tristram lived days on a string without seeing any other person than Molly. There was no improvement in the weather. Day after day the wind held the chill of a jackass breeze; and fog, slow and penetrating, wormed its way over Bathol settlement, feeding its claminess into every building. Wives looked anxiously at their meal barrels and began to say that the family must live on its fat until the spring.

Every daybreak in November seemed to come cold and harsh, trailing slow streaks across the sky, hinting always of snow. A schooner put in at the fort to load with beef that was killed in a day or so at the ridge. Another came, and another, before there was danger of ice to prevent them. All those who had good cattle to sell, now had money in their pockets. Tristram went with the drive from Bathol and had a sharp argument at the wharf. His quarrel was with John Allan, the Scot he had met at the muster. Allan spoke against their selling the meat, saying it was going to feed soldiers who were killing American farmers who dared want the liberty of governing themselves.

Tristram shouted him down. Later a mate on the schooner that had come from Halifax said that new militia and tax laws had been passed by the government. "You'll find," he said, "that you're not forgotten in this neck of woods. Wait till they have you drillin' in the snow."

The selling of the cattle removed all surplus beef from the settlement. Tristram began to wonder about it when he was home. He had some pork, however, and a fair lot of potatoes and turnips. There would be no want in his house but it might be touch and go if he had not been careful.

With the first icy weather he took his horses to Knatchball to have them shod. It was a bitter day with the wind whistling up the river and not so much as a crow in sight.

"I'm glad tha coom," said Knatchball when he had set to work. "Silver's hard to coom by this year and I need more flour in t' house."

He beat out a shoe and sparks splattered against the wall and died out. One of the Garrison boys slipped in and huddled on a bench by the slack tub watching, pop-eyed, as the smith doused a shoe.

"Thee living alone?" asked Knatchball, pumping his bellows leisurely and puckering his eyes against the red glare of the forge. "Making butter and all?"

Tristram glanced at him sharply. The smith was a giant of a man, known to be absurdly devoted to his small wife and their brood, but he had no more imagination than an off ox.

"My sister, Molly, works for him," piped the lad on the bench, grabbing a thin slice of frog that Knatchball pared from a hoof. "She makes butter."

Tristram let the answer do for a moment and then he said. "She's young. Happen tha know of a woman?"

Knatchball nodded, and looked at the youngster. He finished nailing on the shoe then sorted others to find a mate, his huge hard hands pawing over the cold iron as if it were warm. Tristram, waiting for what he would say, noticed the smooth hollow worn in his hammer handle where the thumb pressed.

"Aye, and a champion one, too," he said finally. "Heard o' her when I wur over wi' boat to fetch coal." He pointed his hammer at sacks of shiny black soft coal taken from the old French pit at Joggins beyond Menoudie and boated around on the tide. Then he piled a scoopful near the fire, scraped some of it to the blaze and set his bellows going while black smoke rose and hung under the rafters, sucked now and then toward the opening made by a loose board shingle on the roof, and as often puffed back again. "A widow."

Tristram stepped to his black horse and patted its rump, then looked at the boy. "Did tha see her?" he asked.

"Aye, and she's young as thee. Scottish, for all she cooms from Ameriky, but smart as if she wur raised in Yorkshire." He sloshed a shoe in the slack tub and gazed at Tristram abstractedly. "She has two young wi' her."

Tristram made no remark. He went to the door and listened
to the wind whipping snow particles around the smithy,
looked back at the flickering glow of the forge as the Garrison
boy pumped the bellows with concentrated care, and made up
his mind.

He went over and stood by Knatchball. "Whear does she
live?" he asked.

"Over t' river. Little house. Second oop t' trail from
Francklin Manor."

"What happened her husband?"

"He wur drooned in t' Bay. Fishing boat." Knatchball
punched holes in another shoe.

Tristram paid for the shoeing. "What's t' widow's name?"
he asked.

"Delia Tump. She looks healthy for ony man. Happen
tha is over t' river call in. It's lonesome whear she lives."

It was the next week when Tristram put his horse across the
river where ice had not formed and rode up the trail at a plodding gait, watching for the house the smith had described.

He saw the children outdoors, hovering like small partridges
in their grey homespun, no more than big enough to toddle
and yet trying to get a fire log to the doorstep. The older, a
girl, pushed the boy ahead of her as she scrambled to the
house.

There was a small log barn, but, he saw, no cattle were in
it for there was no manure heap outside; a small pig, by the
sound, squealed mournfully for company or food, probably
both.

Tristram tied his horse to the hitching post set primly by
the path and knocked on the door.

It was opened at once as if the woman had waited with her
hand on the latch and he saw that Knatchball had not exaggerated. Delia Tump was young-looking, with a fine, firm
figure and a complexion high-born ladies would give their ear
bobs to attain.

"I'm Tristram Crabtree, from Bathol," he spoke with decent
assurance. "T' smith towd me to call if I wur passing this
way."

"Did he gi' ye my name?" asked the widow, drawing herself

up as if she wished to appear more matronly and full-bosomed.

"He did. Mrs. Delia Tump, he said."

"Then we're acquainted. I haven't much to feed a man but I'll fry pork if ye will wait."

"Thear is no hurry," he said. "Tha will not be having thy dinner yet." He went in, smiling at the children who regarded him with candid inspection.

"It won't make much difference aboot dinner," she said. "I'm warming a bit o' rabbit stew for oorsels. We have to go sparing wi' potatoes if we are to get through the winter."

She put sticks on the fire with a care that he noticed, and he remembered he had not seen much of a woodpile by the door.

"Thear will be pinching by all o' us," he observed, his habitual impatience urging him on. "It wur thinking o' t' hard winter browt me over. I'm needing a woman in my house, and sort I want are hard to find."

"Are they noo!" She said it with dangerous calm. "Perhaps it is that ye are ower particular?"

"Not at all." He hastened to make amends. "It's just that I want a respectable woman. Neighbours talk if they have a chance, as tha must know."

"They do," she agreed, helping her boy unwind a scarf from his shoulders. He was a sturdy little chap with eyes bright as his mother's. "Were ye thinking o' me?"

He flushed. "I wur. I had it in mind to ask tha to coom and keep my house t' winter and . . ."

"And?" she prompted.

"Happen tha wur suited we might wed."

"And if not?"

"I would pay thee a fair wage while tha stayed."

She looked at her children. "Art tha used to bairns?"

"Noa," he admitted, "but I'd like well to have them."

There was a sincerity in his voice that seemed, inexplicably, to reach through the widow's bargaining demeanour. Her lips trembled and she began twisting her apron in her hands.

Tristram gazed at her in embarrassment. "I did not mean to say onything unkindly." His voice was low. "I would use thee fair."

The little boy began to whimper and his alarm helped the woman regain her control.

"Ye said nothing unkind," she managed. "It was yer offer that made me unsteady. I'll be honest wi' ye and say we have no more in this house than will do the month out, nor as much as a shilling wi' which to buy more. Ye can see what yer offer means."

He nodded. "Then I'm glad I coom, and I'd have thee know—Mrs.—" he fumbled for her name, "that I've no wish to take advantage o' thee in ony way. If tha do not like my ways I want tha to tell me, so I can do summat to please thee."

It was well he had not put off his going to find her for the day after he had moved her over, the river froze with tricky ice that stopped all passing over with carts.

Melody came to meet the widow, and was her friend at once. The children forgot their shyness and went back on the path with Melody so that at long last there was passing to and fro between the houses and Tristram began to find himself in the bigger house of an evening, listening to Delia and Melody discussing the merits of goose feathers for a pillow or the trick of filling a pig's bladder with lard.

Obed Muncie sent Tristram word that all the men in the settlement were to report at the fort for muster and that a colonel had come from Halifax to talk with them.

The Cornforths, Abel Plumley and Lancelot rode with him as they left Bathol. It was a chilly day with wet snow balling on the horses' feet, making them travel slowly. The country seemed dead, with only a few crows investigating bare spots along the river. All the way they saw tracks of other horses, and dogs barked as if their excitement grew with every passerby.

They collected Jonathan as they went along. At Amherst Point, Gideon and Matthew joined them. Every man was wondering as tempers tightened. "Why did the dunderheads wait till winter to muster?" snorted Gideon. "We'll speak to this colonel. We'll ask who's brain has softened."

When they reached the fort they were amazed at the number of men inside the grounds. Every one had a rifle or musket; some had hatchets and knives. Powder flasks, mostly contrived from cow horns, bullet pouches, and leather-covered bottles were carried by various straps and slings. Thick grey stockings were gartered over breeches. Woollen wristlets and mittens served to remove drops that gathered at the point of every nose. Dejected-looking farm plugs were tied at the hitching rail with folded blankets strapped over them to serve as saddles, but the majority of the men were decently mounted.

There was a hush to the talking when a colonel appeared outside the barracks and stood on planks cleaned of snow. He was accompanied by a young lieutenant in flashy jacket and tall fur cap, who wore a sword. Obed Muncie spoke with them and started to call the roll.

"Wait, my friend." John Allan stepped forward as a murmuring arose. "What is the meaning of all this? We're a long way from Halifax—except when they want something, and I represent these people in the Assembly. I demand an explanation."

"You'll get it quickly enough." The colonel's voice was as chilly as the day. "You hold no authority with the military, Mr. Allan. This muster has been called by order of the governor."

A louder muttering ran around the waiting men and the colonel shouted for silence. He did not get it. Instead there were loud calls for Allan to have his say.

"You've come at a wrong time," there was triumph in Allan's voice, "and you will listen to us."

"Fool!" yelled the lieutenant, gripping his sword. "Obey your superior."

The crowd surged toward him. "Get him," someone yelled. "Show the snob who's a fool!"

"Hold!" It was Allan who checked them. "Keep your heads, men." The pushing and yelling stopped as the crowd looked at him. Then he turned to the officers. "Don't call any man here a fool," he said seriously, "unless you are ready for the consequences."

The lieutenant's face became rosy but the colonel looked more grim. Muncie, looking very pale, had not the wit to say anything.

"Now," there was hardness in Allan's voice, "we'll to business. I charge you, sir at your personal peril, not to try to draw a man from this part of Nova Scotia."

A chorus of assenting shouts burst from the assembly and the men crowded closer, hemming in the colonel and his aide. Tristram noted that most of the yelling was done by the New Englanders; scarcely a Yorkshireman opened his mouth.

The colonel surveyed them with cool courage. "I haven't come to cause trouble," he said. "You refuse to muster, and I'll report so to the governor. There is nothing more to do and you may all go home."

"Wait," called Allan. "We came in disagreeable weather to answer your demands. Now you can help us at Halifax."

The colonel shook his head. "That I cannot do. If you wish to make a petition of any sort, that is your privilege. But you will have to present it yourselves." He bowed stiffly and re-entered the cheerless barracks, the lieutenant following closely at his heels.

"Drag that young rooster back," shouted someone. "Let's have some fun."

"No!" blazed Allan. "Nothing of the sort. We'll draw up a petition, and we'll have it read at Halifax, too."

"Aye," yelled a man. "Give it to 'em, Allan. We're for liberty."

The men milled about, arguing, cursing, blowing noses, stamping to knock the chill from their feet.

"Let's go home," said Abel, but Tristram shook his head. "We want to hear the petition," he said in a low tone. "I don't like Allan any more than I do t' colonel."

Some men climbed on their horses and rode away, the majority of them Yorkshiremen. The Acadians, swarthy little men in plain homespun, remained, and Tristram saw they were getting instructions from Rogers.

Allan soon returned. He was energetic all right. He began to read a defiance of Assembly and all its powers.

"Noa," shouted Tristram.

"Noa." The Cornforth men followed his lead and others took up the cry.

"All right, Yorkshire, we'll write it over." Allan seemed anxious to gain their favour.

When he returned he read a long statement assuring Halifax that the loyalty of the Cumberland people remained as before. "But we're saying," he explained, "that we want a suspension of the Tax Act, and the dissolution of the Assembly that passed it and the Service Act. Why should they want to call every man into the army? Do you want to leave your wives to get your winter's wood?"

There was angry hooting.

"Then come along and sign this petition," he shouted.

The Acadians stepped forward as if a signal had been given. Abel stirred uneasily, and Lancelot spoke up. "Art signing?" he asked Tristram.

"Noa," said Tristram decidedly. "I'm for hoam."

Every man from Bathol followed him to the hitching rails. "Won't any of you sign?" They turned to find Allan beside them.

"Noa," said Tristram. "I don't like t' way t' Cajuns jump to do as tha say."

"Do you want to drill, then, and go to Boston?"

"Noa. Neither will I help thee stir oop trouble."

Allan swung on his heel, said no more. There was no sun and snowflakes began to eddy about the frosted barracks. "There'll be a storm afore night," prophesied Gideon and they kicked their chilled horses into a canter down the slope leading to the marsh.

V

The Powder Horn

TRISTRAM liked the widow's children, Jeannie and Jacky. They had a fine Christmas. Delia did wonders with roast pork and a turkey and Melody made them maple candy. Lancelot had carved trinkets for the youngsters and Tristram surprised everyone by producing a bow and arrow he had made for Jacky.

Both children followed him around the yard at his chores and Jeannie was eager to climb on his knee in the evenings. Tristram grew fond of her. Her soft fragile warmth reached some part of his nature that Judy's most subtle blandishments had not reached. Her adoration expanded his ego, made him more sure of his personality.

Delia watched with shining eyes. She was clean and efficient and cheery, making every potato and pat of butter spend full way.

Food was scarce after the New Year, causing much borrowing. The men hunted but moose seemed to have vanished from their usual haunts. Even rabbits were scarce. During the latter part of January it snowed for two days, then a high wind cleared spruce of their white loads as it whined through the trees. Snow birds came in flocks to the barnyards. A new snow began to fall when the wind went down—a driving storm of dry, hard flakes.

Lancelot went over to Tristram and said the men of the settlement were going on a moose hunt. It was to be a big affair, with as many as possible in the party. Those who had no muskets would draw handsleds with which to bring back the meat and every man would carry a skinning knife and hand axe.

Tristram laced his feet into larrigans made from cowhide and dressed himself warmly. He examined his musket, then took a powder horn Delia had given him at Christmas. It was trimmed with red wool and had a fine whittled plug.

They set out slowly in the loose snow. The drifts were deeper than anyone had expected; the wind was keen as a knife. Before night the cold had worked into them. They built a shelter in the lee of a tangle of blowdowns and lighted a fire. They had not seen a sign of game, not so much as an old track. The limbs of the blowdown were brittle as glass and Tristram reckoned it was twenty below.

They started out with daybreak and reached a hardwood knoll. The wind whipped harsh snow particles that cut their faces and travelling was slow for windfalls made each mile three hours long. A light snow began falling in the afternoon and when it thickened they made camp. They huddled by another fire, turning first one way and then another to get warm. In the morning a pot of soup, made from a ham bone and snow water, put sap into their legs. Within the hour they almost fell into moose-trodden paths. The yard had been travelled that morning; there was frozen dung barely covered by frost. They had reached good hunting.

Six men in the party had muskets; the other four had but their axes. They remained at the rear. The "yard" was an intricate labyrinth of paths leading to every corner of browse and cover. It had been trodden to the depth of a man's shoulders. Tristram stood by one trail as Lancelot whistled, and pointed.

Each man peered. Not a hundred yards away the dark backs of three moose were visible. Then an old bull reared and plunged into deep snow, kicking the loose drift into a cloud.

"Chase them!" roared Aaron Cornforth, and every man started as fast as he could travel on snowshoes.

The moose broke from the paths as Lancelot and others cut across to the turnings. The big animals floundered and leaped desperately but the snow was deep and the crust not strong enough to carry them. There was a shot, and wild shouting. Then another shot.

Tristram saw a moose plunging to his left. It was a big cow and she seemed to sink to her neck at every landing. He turned in pursuit. Another moose came after her. He saw Lancelot racing at incredible speed on his snowshoes, saw him gradually near the fleeing animal. Then he heard the thunderous report of a musket behind him, whirled, and saw Abel Plumley shoot a moose that had almost followed his tracks.

The heavy report of Lancelot's rifle rang out. He heard his brother's shout. "Three we have. Watch afore thee, Tristram."

Tristram, bewildered by the shooting and shouting, swung again, and saw a bull moose rising in great leaps, floundering desperately. Ezra Hodge, who had but an axe, had headed the beast on a runway, and now Lancelot had sent it plunging in a new direction. Tristram braced himself, dropped a mitten, took aim. The bull plunged again. He could see the fury in the bull's eye, hear its harsh snorting.

He pulled the trigger, and the concussion of the heavy recoil almost threw him backward. The musket ball thudded into a tree. The bull had lunged downward and was entirely unscathed. Now, headed once more by Ezra, it came directly for Tristram.

"Load, man!" shouted Lancelot.

He wrenched the whittled plug from his powder horn, tried, frantically, to loosen the powder. It had frozen? He pounded the horn.

"Watch out!" shouted Hodge.

Tristram turned. There was nothing else he could do. He ran as fast as he could on his snowshoes, reached a path and fell into it headlong as his brother's rifle slammed heavily again.

There was more shouting. Tristram, badly jarred, managed to free himself, and get up. He peered over the bank. Lancelot and Hodge were beside the moose, waiting until its struggling ceased. They looked at him, and Lancelot had the powder horn, examining it.

"Too bad it's frozen," he said. "That wur close run for thee."

Tristram nodded. He was glad he had not broken his snowshoes, but he was more than grateful to Lancelot. It had come to him that he had not put any powder in the horn, and if the fact had become known he would be derided in every kitchen in Bathol.

But every man was busy. Five moose were down and knives sliced and axes hacked at bone and muscle. Before noon the sleds were loaded. Then slices of steak were impaled on slivers and partially fried by a fire. Rubbed with salt, the meat made good enough eating. The wind had gone and the travelling home was comparatively easy.

Lancelot said they should take some of the meat to Shubad Knapp, so he and Aaron Cornforth went with steaks and boiling meat as well as a few potatoes. They found the Knapps gaunt from lack of nourishment but still proud. Shubad said they were grateful for the potatoes as well as the meat. Their own had long since been used and they had but his wife's three hens to sustain them. It was the cold that had lowered their morale. The cabin was not warm. Frost would creep in at night when the fire was low and they would lay in their bed not fully awake but suspended in a dreamy awareness of sound and of the nipping cold. Sometimes they did not rouse until their breath froze on the blankets. Then Shubad would quickly get out and start the fire going in a prodigal blaze. He would heat water to boiling, throwing in handfuls of cornmeal and a pinch of salt, making a scalding mush that quickly distributed heat through their chilled bodies.

"Tha should have musket for hunting," said Lancelot. "A porcupine is better than nowt for a stew."

Shubad agreed, and Lancelot took over an extra one owned by the Hodges. He told Tristram what he had done, and mentioned it again two weeks later.

Tristram was feeling kindly toward his brother though neither had spoken again about the powder horn. He said he would go over and see the Knapps that evening, taking with him a loaf of bread and some salt beef.

He shouted when he entered the cabin clearing for there was no light behind the frosted windows. He went to the door and shouted again, then saw tracks, newly made, going from the door, and waited. Shubad might be in bed.

There were no sounds of stirring. Alarmed, he went in. The fire was low, an hour's burning, he thought, and no one was in the bed. He looked at pegs on the wall and saw the clothing was missing.

He replenished the fire and became more disturbed when he saw no musket in the cabin. At last he carried a torch outside and found Hetty Knapp's tracks leading into the woods. They looked as fresh as his own and he followed them. Soon he saw Hetty on her knees, tugging at her husband's body, and called to her.

She heard him, he saw, but her eyes held no intelligence. He knelt beside Shubad, but rose quickly. The man was dead, frozen like wood. He picked the woman up and carried her like a child, and she offered no resistance. He took her to the cabin and built the fire to roaring. He made a drink of hot ginger and she swallowed most of it. Then, as the heat reached her flesh, she began calling pitifully for her husband.

He pulled her bed near the fire, put on more logs and ran to Smith's for help. Mrs. Smith came with him. She removed Hetty Knapp's clothing and tried to rub warmth into her body but she moaned until morning when she quieted to tiny sobs. Then she whispered once. It was something about her hens, but they could not understand, and while they waited for her to say more she sank to the same stillness that held Shubad in the snow.

Tristram and Solomon went back on the trail she had made. She had dragged Shubad a considerable distance and the story was plain on the snow. The sailor had found a bear's den. He had roused the animal and killed it with a shot at close range. Starved for meat, he had cut himself too heavy a load. On his way he had tripped over a hidden root and in his fall had broken a leg.

They saw the marks he had made as he crawled, still trying to take some of the meat with him. Then the cold had gripped him and, in his weakened condition, there had not been much suffering.

Tristram looked for the hens and Mrs. Smith showed him

three wishbones.   They had been lying on the window sill, placed together as if Hetty had not dared make a wish after peering outside.

There was nothing they could do about a double grave until warm weather came.   They placed the bodies together on the bed and left, closing the door quietly as if the inmates might awaken.   No one spoke until they were out by the river road.

VI
Melody's Bargain

IT TOOK the man from the fort ridge three days to bring Tibbets' pine coffin to its resting place at Bathol. John and Lancelot had talked with Melody until she had agreed that nothing would be said to Tristram of the deed to the farm until after her wedding. Then the wedding was planned for later in the summer, as it would not do to have it too near the burial of Tibbets, and Melody needed a wedding gown.

Tristram came from his house with harsh greeting when the cart was in his yard. His gaze hardened when Lancelot explained but he offered no opposition as they went to the small glade where three graves could still be distinguished under old grass and weeds. He made no offer of lending help or spade to dig the grave. He did not go near as the burial took place.

After it was over and the man with the cart had started on his long trek back to the fort John spoke his mind.

"There will be trouble with your brother," he said, "and I want none at the beginning. Will you wait one year, Melody, before we tell him to move?"

It was hard for her to agree. Tristram's attitude toward John had angered her almost beyond control, but she saw the wish in John's eyes, and yielded. Lancelot breathed more freely.

"I'll have more time to look around for myself," he said. "Don't tha leave me to getting my own meals."

The wedding was the affair of the year in Bathol. Melody had Unity help her select the best material to be had at Amherst and the making of the gown was a long week of trial and fittings. Parson Eagleson rode from the fort to perform the service and had already toasted the bride a few more times

213

than were suitable for his position. But there was no more than his hiccoughing to mar the ceremony and the feast that was spread on the benches placed near the elms even astonished the expectant Gabriel Garrison.

"I never knowed so many puddings and pies could be baked at one time in this settlement," he vowed. "There'll be full stomachs for a week to come."

It seemed that every person who could walk or ride a cart was there. Melody was afraid of riders from Maccan, remembering the red-headed Peter Meekins, but he did not appear.

"No need to worry, miss," boomed Gideon, catching her glances around the gathering. "There'll be none to worry you. Any you may be thinking of have joined with trouble makers over on the ridge, and they're after bigger shows than a wedding."

Tristram asked what the rumours were. He was not cordial with John but he had come to the gathering.

"Talk of an invasion," roared Gideon, not caring who heard. "Them Maine squaw men seem to think all they need do is walk over, and we'll throw open our doors. Allan hints about turnin' the Injuns on us, but I told him two can play at that game."

"Indians. To burn us oot?"

"That's what they'd like, but I know the tribe and they don't like Allan as well as he thinks. No one here will be burned out by Injuns. You can mark that on your shirt tail."

The women chattered about Melody, and Mrs. Garrison had a hearty cry, saying she could not help it as she had never seen a more handsome bride in her born days. John was the recipient of warm congratulations. He laughed with and at Gideon until they were firm friends.

"I reckon," chortled Gideon, "you'll live here a spell. One thing, you've plenty of house room and that's as sure as rum's a comfort or," he caught Patience's eye, "leastways it was."

"Yes," said John easily, "we'll live here a time. I want to learn about farming."

"Titus Green will rent thee land over t' river," said Tristram in his hard voice. "Tha can put oop cabin and start wi' axe and hoe, same as others."

"Perhaps tha will go soon," broke in Melody, unable to check herself. "Tha can have first pick from Green."

Tristram darkened with quick temper but gave her no reply. Garrison rasped the strings of his fiddle and the awkward moment was past but Tristram left early and omitted to take his leave of the bride and groom.

By autumn Melody was glad she had made the bargain with John. Though the drought was not encouraging they had had a good year on the farm, everything considered, and her happiness was supreme. Her only wish was that her father had lived to know John.

In early October she and John rode to visit Patience. The benison of a mellow autumn day lay on the farmlands and marshes of Amherst Point. At Bathol they had ridden in misty gloomy weather and it was like seeing another country. A film of Indian summer haze hung low in a grove of beeches still holding their coppery leaves but the crimson flags of the maples and the yellow banners of the birches had been struck in surrender to the frost, leaving a skeleton of naked branches on the hillside. Smoke curled lazily from chimneys. Cattle, late in pasture, stood in groups, enjoying the warmth of the sun. Sheep wandered restlessly, searching for succulent grass.

Gideon saw them and shouted greetings. He came to meet them at the lane end and his great voice lowered to a considered whisper. "Don't talk much about the rebels," he said. "We live too near the fort and Patience is one to seize a worry and nurse it."

It was as they rode home three days after that John's horse reared and threw him as a bear crossed the trail. He alighted in such a way that his foot was broken. Melody, frantic with apprehension, had Jonathan ride to Amherst for O'Conner. The medico was neither drunk nor sober when he arrived so he did a fair job of repairing the damage, contriving a sort of cast that would serve. He said the only dependable cure would be John's keeping the foot out of action for the winter, and Melody declared that if no limp resulted his imprisonment in her kitchen was worth the fright she had received.

BOOK FIVE
1776

I

The Victory Ride

IN APRIL Parson Eagleson rode to Bathol for some christenings, and he married Tristram and Delia. Melody and Lancelot went over as witnesses and hushed the children to gazing. Delia looked as young and happy as Melody herself, being dressed in a short-gown of blue calico. They sat to a fine dinner and after Eagleson asked the blessing he said that an invasion was a certainty.

His tirade worried Tristram, and it ended with his riding to Amherst Point with Lancelot to see if anything new were known. Matthew and Gideon made light of the rumours from America while they were in their kitchens but when they were outside their tone was different and it was easy to see that worry was perched on the backs of both men, caught there like little long-clawed monkeys between their shoulders and out of reach.

The snow had gone from the marsh and the winter's sled tracks had melted to dark ice. They were looking at the first signs of green when a clatter of noise from Amherst village came on the wind. Horns were shrilling. Dogs were barking. Someone fired a musket.

They rode to the village and pulled up to see Peter Meekins with three young men of his type driving a chaise with six horses. Meekins had a flag of liberty thrust up beside the calash top and was blowing a dinner horn until his cheeks looked fit to burst. One of his mates had a horn of different key and together they made such clamour that the village dogs were yelping in a frenzy.

"Victory!" shouted Meekins. "Give a cheer. The British had the daylights knocked out of them at Bunker's Hill.

The Sons of Liberty beat 'em. Give a cheer. Let 'em know in Maccan that we're comin'."

No one gave a cheer. People watched them in silence. Gideon looked at their chaise, at the deep road ruts and flooded ditches. He muttered to Matthew and motioned for the others to follow him. They rode back to a small bridge, took up the poles and threw them on a pasture.

Blasts on the horn told them that the chaise was coming. Then there were wild yells and the chaise was halted. Gideon rode up to the spot. "The devil has britches!" he boomed. "Look what the thaw's fetched out."

There was no room for the chaise to turn and Meekins swore that he would make someone eat crow before the year was out.

"The poles for the bridge is here in the pasture," yelled Gideon. "Try and git 'em."

Meekins climbed down and unhitched the four leaders. They had to separate each pair and lead one horse at a time to the rear of the chaise, where they were hooked up again. Finally they took off the first pair and after much labour the chaise was turned by hand. Then they drove back to Amherst. The horns were forgotten and Meekins looked back, shaking his fist.

O'Conner appeared, mounted on his scrawny nag. "It's a pleasure to ride out to something other than a confinement or a youngster with colic," he pronounced. "John Allan's got smallpox and he's rugged enough to take my treatment. The fee he pays supplies my spring tonic of brandy slugs and dandelion tea. There ain't a mortal dose better for the blood and lately I've been so belly sick I can taste dog hair."

"Give Allan plenty of physic," advised Gideon. "He's been tight as a new pair of shoes, sufferin' from liberty cramps. You ought to relieve him."

"Parson Eagleson's laid up, too," returned O'Conner owlishly. "I've got to tighten him, though. He won't hold a morsel of liberty diet." He stared at Tristram and winked. "They give him too much gin punch over't the fort the other night and put him on his horse, facing the rear, led the beast home and rapped on his door. His missus came out. 'Oh, my dear,' she cries, 'but you are well cut.' 'You're right, as always,' he hiccoughed. He pawed around, trying to get hold of his horse's neck. 'They've blessed well cut this nag's head off.'"

They went to the tavern to warm themselves and a man with something vaguely familiar about his appearance walked up to Tristram.

"Tha wur a good man in Paddy's little stall," he said with unmistakable challenge. "Do tha want to try a fair go now?"

The man was Shubell Cutlip, looking a stone heavier and very fit. Tristram stared at him, and backed away. "I want nowt wi' thee," he said shortly.

"Let be," interrupted Matthew. "Tha art t' better man wi' thy hands."

Tristram went out and mounted. His pride had been hurt and as he rode home he cursed himself for having ridden on such an errand.

II

Poverty Row

JOE PAUL came for Lancelot in the autumn of the dry
year and asked him to go on a moose hunt. Joe looked
prosperous enough with a new hatchet Francklin had
given him. His father had been given a fine long red soldier's
coat with only one button missing. Francklin had talked
with many of the Indians, he said. He asked them not to
fight against the English.

The dry summer had concentrated game in areas where
there were springs and lakes, and the second night found
them near a floating bog at the foot of a lake where a pair of
stake drivers boomed their strange notes. Little saw-whets
sat on low limbs near their camp fire and gave their queer
calls, and devilish moans and croaks came from roosting ravens
in a pine grove.

The next day was too warm for hunting so they fished at
a brook and caught trout that Joe cooked in embers without
cleaning. After they were done he split them down the belly,
gutted them, removed the skin and cut the fish into two
portions. Lancelot thought he had never tasted anything
quite so good.

"Bad times," grunted Joe, wiping his fingers. "Allan say
British no good. Say Indians fight with Americans."

"If tha art wise," said Lancelot, "tha will stay in woods
and do nowt. T' British will send over soldiers by shipload
till war's over."

"Allan give gallon rum for us," said Joe. "Promise help
us if we help him. My fader tell him go way."

The bitterns were noisy again the next day, their "o-o-m-p
up" in soft booming notes carrying a long way, and Joe said

no other hunters were around. They travelled slowly and saw a small cow moose taking last bites from lily pads before leaving her feeding. The swamp they skirted was edged by low growing maples and huckleberry bushes through which a grumbling porcupine pushed its way.

They reached the tip of a bog barren that Joe pronounced an ideal place for calling moose. He had cut a strip of bark from wire birch and rolled it cornerwise into a horn about four inches wide across the larger end. It was a megaphone that imparted an animal quality to Joe's voice as he imitated the basic mating calls of the cow moose.

Lancelot listened intently. He had been hunting with Joe for three years and had learned many surprising things. The bawls, whines, moans and pleadings that Joe made seemed to run on a scale of the letters "e-u-r." For a long time the morning was still and frosty with vapour rising from low swales and brooks, then Joe grew taut.

"Bull come," he whispered.

It was a bull all right. Joe's bark talk floated and echoed over the wilds and was answered by what sounded to be gurgling grunts, something like an axeman chopping a log. They could hear the big animal as its hoofs plopped in and out of the bog, but it circled them and broke from crimson maples and green-black spruce at a point too far away for a good shot, striding out on a drier part of the bog bright with tiny maples and myriads of white millers fluttering to dry their wings in the sun's heat.

Joe stopped his coaxing and let the moose go, watching it slash an evergreen savagely before they rose and let themselves be seen. Even then the bull was in no hurry and swung about several times to eye the intruders. Finally it took to cover and they went on idly until an otter, disturbed at its fishing, snorted and dived.

They made camp and stayed lazily on brush beds. At dusk they heard geese in the sky, going southward, and the fluting of snipes and plover, on the same trail. A harvest moon poured a silent silver flood between the trees. Joe spoke. "No hurry, you, me, this hunt. Maybe no more long time."

Lancelot nodded and drowsed. Their fire of pine knots from old blowdowns sent out grand heat. The sky was clear and high, the stars brilliant. The tang of frosted bog grass and reeds and a clutter of Joe Pye weed was pleasant to the nostrils. Joe had roasted a pair of partridges in Indian style. His stomach was warmly full and satisfied.

Yet something in Joe's manner pricked at his instincts and at midnight he sat up. Joe was mending the fire.

"What tha said bothers me," said Lancelot. "Are tha going away?"

Joe nodded. "Injun talk we go by Shepody and be there when American come."

They killed a fine bull near Bathol and carried the meat home. Lancelot told Tristram what Joe had said, and they both talked with Muncie. He invited them to his house for an evening and asked Tristram to bring Delia with him.

Tristram felt honoured. Mrs. Muncie had the reputation of thinking herself a bit above the rest of the people of the place but might not be as bad as pictured.

The Muncies lived in a fine big frame house well in from the cart trail with Balm of Gilead trees at the front. A coloured man who had waited for them until he was slate grey with chill, took their horses and Tristram used the shining brass door knocker.

Mrs. Muncie met them graciously enough, making the proper fuss over Delia. She carried herself with plenty of starch and wore a gown of blue camlet that set off her full figure. Her complexion was good. Tristram resolved that he would provide Delia with a gown as good or better.

"I've heard of you, my dear," Mrs. Muncie said to Delia. "You must have your husband bring you more often. There are so few around here with whom I can be intimate."

She had a dignity gained by those who live long on the resources of their minds and was obviously proud of her establishment as she served them with a steaming rum seasoned with cloves. The big fireplace had an oven built in at the side. On the wide mantel were a silver tankard and candlesticks of pewter. Polished brass warming pans were in the corner with numerous long-handled skillets and spiders.

A rack of clay pipes hung above and a fine brass tobacco jar was on a ledge convenient to Obed's wide armchair with leather seat.

Obed wore a turkey-red waistcoat for the occasion. He was serious and began talking of the Indians at once.

Mrs. Muncie began embroidering a night cap and drew Delia aside for conversation.

Obed went to his desk for a paper. "I have here," he said, "the names of the families this side of Amherst and including the village. It adds up to one hundred and fifty-six able-bodied men. Out of the lot there aren't twenty, counting the Acadians at River Hebert, who aren't loyal."

Lancelot heard water splash in a slop jar somewhere overhead and started as he remembered Obed's daughter. She came down a few minutes later, moving into the room with the fluid grace of a deer stepping out of a thicket. She was straight and slim in a full-skirted dress of dark green taffeta. She was looking at him and at him entirely, with blue eyes deep enough to make a man dizzy. Her brown gold hair flowed softly and she carried her head cocked a little to one side.

"You are Lancelot," she exclaimed. "I saw you years ago. I'm Naomi Muncie."

"You forget your manners, young lady," reproved Mrs. Muncie, introducing Delia and Tristram. Then she looked at Lancelot, her voice like warm honey. "Naomi finds it so lonesome at times that you must forgive her being headlong."

"That I'll do," laughed Lancelot.

The young woman was as female as Eve. Her eyes, very slowly and deliberately, went from his fine blond beard over the width of his shoulders and down the straight length of him, then her smile took sweetly malicious form over white teeth. "You're handsome, too," she said.

There was a general laugh, then, at Lancelot's expense and he experienced strange thrills as she chatted with him.

"I think," said Obed, "I'll take word of the Indians to Michael Healey. He'll know what moves to make before Francklin gets here in the spring."

A bit of oak ribbing seemed to go out of Mrs. Muncie's

vigorous back and the buttons down her bodice front were agitated by her breathing. From the hearth rug a black cat rose, stretched, and arched its back, then subsided into blinking at firelit pots on a crane swung from the heat.

"There is no use to worry," said Obed. He looked at Lancelot. "If there is need of a good man to do a king's errand, may I count on you?"

"I will answer when time cooms," said Lancelot cannily. He gave his attention to Naomi and she had a kind of ease with him when he left, as though she had settled the question of him and his future, and had shrugged off many worries that made other girls exhaust themselves.

There was no mention of a king's errand, however, until the next April when Michael Healey rode in one evening. "There's a man named Eddy stirring up trouble," he said, producing a packet fitted into a weasel skin, "but if the message in this reaches proper hands at Halifax there'll be more soldiers to our fort. Will ye travel the hog back to the ferry afore someone's posted to stop couriers?"

"To Halifax?"

"Yes, to Francklin himself. I'll give ye ten pounds. That will make it a matter of business and no more."

It was shrewdly said. The adventure appealed to Lancelot, and ten pounds in hard money could not be earned more easily. He nodded. "I'll start in morning."

He crossed the river in his small boat and was on his way by sunrise, his rifle under his arm, sliced cold meat and bread in his pocket. The day was warm and ferns were lifting among old leaves. Trails were translucent with light. Fox sparrows worked in a low thicket of birch. Old bear marks on a tree were higher than any he and Joe Paul had found. Something in the air made him think of Naomi Muncie, and he wondered that he had not stirred himself to see her during the winter. Instead, he had stayed with John and Melody, enjoying their company to the full.

By night he was at the home of an Acadian settler, a small cabin in a stumpy clearing. Lancelot was served a hearty supper of salt shad and boiled potatoes and he slept in his

blanket on the floor by the fire. The next morning he was
away early and wind and tide favoured him at the ferry.

Luck remained with him. A drover hired him to help with
a small herd of steers, paying for him overnight at the taverns
and asking no questions. They reached Halifax on a Monday
afternoon, prodding the steers past the Common where tents
of every size were spread on all available ground. Grey
washings draped on scrub bushes. Smoke from outdoor fires
hung heavy on the air.

"Ye'll have a time to find a bed in this place," said the
drover. "Watch yer step after dark. There's a hard lot in
town."

Uniforms were everywhere, red coats and green ones and
blue ones, and white breeches, black gaiters and cockaded
hats. Lancelot remembered the stone-cutter's shop where
he had bought his rifle and found the place.

The stone-cutter looked up at him, considered, wiped his
nose. "I've seen ye before, sure as Job had boils, but I can't
recollect your name."

"Tha never knew it," said Lancelot, "but I bought this
rifle from thee. I'm from Coomberland."

"Is that a fact. How's the lay up there? King's men or
rebs?"

"Both," grinned Lancelot. "Yorkshire keeps oot, and will
do."

"And ye came to Halifax to see the sights in April?"

"Not unless tha call Francklin one o' them. Whear can
I find him?"

"At Golden Ball. Give the darky in the taproom a shilling,
and he'll take ye up to the man himself."

"Can tha tell me, then, whear I'll find a bed for t' night?"

"I can that, and one without bugs in it, which is sayin'
plenty. Ye can rest yer bones on my blankets here if ye'll
keep the shutters closed and the door bolted till I'm back in
the morning. It's a pair of months since I've visited some
cronies I have, and I'd like to make use of your need. Every
room and garret in this town is crowded twice over and folks
is so starved ye can't find a cat about. They've been used in
soups and that's the truth."

The man knew what he was talking about. The shilling acted potently and soon Lancelot was shaking hands with Francklin. He gave him the weasel skin packet, and told him about Joe Paul. They talked until candle lighting time, then, as they parted, Francklin gave orders and a servant led Lancelot to the dining-room. He was served hot steak pie and pudding. Before he was finished a messenger handed him a note and five pounds in cash. The note read: "I know we can depend on good Yorkshire."

In the stone-cutter's bed Lancelot heard a few passersby then slept soundly until the sun was shining in the morning and the stone-cutter, bleary-eyed as an owl, was hammering at the door. Lancelot admitted him and the fellow was snoring in the bed before he could as much as remove his shoes.

Lancelot cleaned his jacket, washed and left the shop, being careful to close the door behind him.

It was easy enough to get breakfast as few were at the tavern. He had bacon and eggs and tea, then had a look along the water-front. It was all confusion. Sailors were eating meat pies at a booth. Some dirty little shops, so small that they let down a part of the wall to serve as a counter, were already doing business. A fat old woman was selling lobsters from a barrow, answering, with shocking profanity, the joshing of passersby. Pipkins of wine were being loaded on carts drawn by rough-haired horses. From warehouse doors came a reek of spices, rum, whale oil, fish and tar, and sweaty, unwashed workers.

He headed out of town by a route that took him by a long medley of shelters reaching from a lane at the south end of the street. Such shelters were everywhere below Citadel Hill, blocking alleys and yards, but here were shacks made of over-turned carts mounted on hogsheads, of poles supporting tar-paulin walls, with brush and pole privies at the rear and slops washing down the ditch at the front.

Thousands of refugees had come from New York before any provision was made for them.

Smoke seeped from divers vents in the hodge-podge of roofs. An ailing infant wailed as if unattended. Men in

ragged garments moved about with a beaten look, carrying
piggins of water and armloads of sticks for pitiful fires that
might heat corn mush for breakfast.

A woman came out of a tent to offer him a silver cloak clasp
and a silver-handled fan. She asked five shillings as if she
had no hope, so he gave her ten and she thanked him tear-
fully. Others saw the purchase and before he was from the
spot he had a silver hair peg, a gold locket and a wedding ring.
Three of his pounds were gone without regret and he was glad
to breathe fresh air as he found a path leading to the Windsor
road.

A last shack of planks had an old moose hide serving as a
door. As he glanced at it a girl stepped outside in shoes tied
with string to keep them together. She stood as if she had
no errand, and time had ceased to matter. She had wheat-
coloured hair, hollowed cheeks and a firm, freckled little
nose. Her dress was a draggled garment too roomy for her
slimness and frayed at the hem. Her neck was thin so that
he could see a tiny pulse beating and the look in her smoke-blue
eyes gave him such an impression of absolute poverty that
he was shocked. Her age could only be guessed; she might be
fifteen or twenty.

Lancelot stopped. "Tha look hungry," he said uncertainly.

"Hungry!" It was as if she had to rouse herself to see him.
"I've been hungry for a month." It was a simple statement,
without cadging or complaint.

"Have tha no food—whear tha live?"

"None," she said tiredly.

"Then put on summat and coom to tavern wi' me."

She bent over and retied one of the strings holding her shoe
together. Then she straightened as if she had done some
thinking, and studied his face. It was as though she saw him
for the first time and when their glances met he saw her grow
taut, then slacken.

"What are you wanting?" Her voice was tired, but held
enough hope to encourage him.

"I want to see thee have a good meal, and I'll buy thee food
to bring to thy folk. I want nowt else."

Her eyes widened. "Where are you from?" she asked.

"Bathol, oop in Coomberland.   I coom to toon yesterday wi' cattle.   Will tha have breakfast wi' me?"

"I'd like to," she said slowly, "because I believe you're real, but I've nothing more than a cloak to wear."

Lancelot stared, incredulous.   It had not occurred to him that a person could live in Halifax in such want.

"Wear thy cloak, then," he said, and paused.   "If tha have others. . . ."

She shook her head.   "There's only me."

Then she went back into the shed and came out with a ragged cloak of a quality once better than any Melody owned. The moose hide was left pushed aside and he saw the only furnishings in the place were a bed of sorts and a stool.

They went down the slope and her torn shoes caught on stones and flapped whenever she lifted them too quickly, but she gave them no more heed than if she had worn them all her life, and she turned into the first small tavern they reached as if odors from its kitchen lured her in.   Half a dozen carters were eating at a table.   They looked around, winked at each other and went on eating.

A serving maid came and Lancelot ordered bacon and eggs and wheat bread and honey and hot chocolate.   Then he looked at the girl with him and could see the way her nostrils dilated when the aroma of sizzling bacon reached them. "My name is Lancelot Crabtree," he said quietly.   "I'm from Yorkshire, coom to live in this country."

A platter of eggs and bacon was placed before them.   He could see the girl tremble as she took her helpings, but hunger could not force her to ill manners.   She ate as daintily as if she were in silks and he a fine gentleman.

He made a pretence of having his own breakfast and she gave no protest but when she had finished the eggs she sipped her chocolate and peered at him over the rim of her cup. "I'm June Faring," she said, "and I'm from Boston.   We were driven out and our place burned.   My mother died years ago.   I kept house for father, but he's gone."

"Tha have had a hard time," said Lancelot softly.

"He was sick when we came here.   When we could find a room it had no heat and he died of lung fever.   Our goods had

come in a boat, but I never found them.   Nearly all we had
was stolen the day he was buried.   I had some rings and
twelve shillings, and when they put me out of the room I went
to that shack, because no one else claimed it.   I borrowed a
kettle and washed what clothes I had—and they were stolen
from where I put them to dry."

She ate the bread and honey while she talked and he
watched the perfection of every movement with knife and
spoon and ladle, noted the little veins in her wrists, the
shadows under her eyes, the slant of her jawbone, the pulse
in the nook where her collar bones met.   She drank a third
cup of chocolate without haste, and sat the empty cup down
with a little sigh of satisfaction.

Then she leaned forward to look at him.

"I may live to be an old woman, if my luck has turned,"
she said, "but nothing will ever make me forget this meal."

He sat and looked at her, every word she had said swinging
through his mind in husky-sweet cadence, his impulses surging
so mightily that he could scarcely keep a tremor from his own
voice.

"Do tha trust me?" he asked.

The first faint tinge of colour he had seen touched her
cheeks briefly.   "I do," she said.

"Would tha let me buy clothes for thee?"

He saw her start.   The tired note came back in her voice.
"For why would you buy me clothes?"

Her eyes searched his face.

"How old are thee?" he asked.

"Nineteen past.   Why?"   Her voice was quicker and he
saw her breathing wait on his answer.   It was that that gave
him his courage.

"Because, happen tha would agree, I'd like to take thee to
Bathol wi' me, and if tha went I'd like to ask thee to marry
me."

For a moment she sat with no trace of expression in her
eyes, as though her thoughts had leaped over him to something far away.   The serving maid came to their table and,
eyeing the empty dishes, asked if they would have something
more.   "No thank you," she said politely, and then he saw

her eyes fill.   Quietly she put a thin hand across the table and, as unobtrusively, he took it, pressed it gently in his own.

He saw the terriffic battle she was making for control, and wished he had waited until they were alone.   She rose from her chair and they went toward the door, stopping briefly as he paid the account.   Outside, she held to his arm and they went up the hill again until they were by a house with its shutters closed and no one was in sight.

Then she went into his arms, her body shaking in a long crescendo, racked with sobs, and he had to bend his head to catch her whisper.   "Dear God, I'll never forget You again."

He held her until she had calmed herself, every quiver of her thin body reaching his heart.

By noon he had bought her clothing and shoes, a bonnet, a cloak, and had seen Francklin again, getting the loan of horses to ride to Windsor.   A schooner there, Francklin said, was taking an officer to Cumberland to recruit for Legge's regiment.

Lancelot thought such a man would have poor results but he held his peace, thinking only of the chance to reach the fort.   It took them the best part of a week as the schooner's captain was not sure of the tides but the voyage was not rough and June's natural good health returned.   Lancelot's happiness steadied.   He had been fearful of change in June, thinking she had been overwhelmed by his kindness and not altogether responsible for her emotions.   But she declared she had been as sure of him when she had seen him fairly, as he had been of her.   It was love at first sight, she said, adding that her father had said it was often the most enduring. She had colour in her cheeks when they landed and he had discovered that her slim frame had the close weave and strength of whipcord.

Parson Eagleson married them at the fort, fuming as soon as the ceremony was over about an officer come to recruit soldiers in a community where every man was needed to keep the rebels in check.   Lancelot gave him scant attention. June was his wife and nothing else in the world mattered.

A web of song from robins and bobolinks and larks hung over the marshes and early May was at its best as they followed the cart trail to Fort Lawrence, Lancelot carrying his rifle and the bag he had bought for her extra clothing. At noon they sat by a tree, eating bread and cheese. They could see a long way and no one was near them. June said her feet heated in her new shoes. She took them off, and her stockings, saying the marsh road with its soft grass was gentle to the touch.

It was late afternoon when they reached Matthew's place for they had been in no hurry. The sun had dipped until it rested above tall dark firs in Gideon's pasture and a horizontal shaft of cloud glowed like a bar of red-hot steel.

"Look!" cried June, pointing. "A promise of fine weather."

There was a faint winnowing of wings overhead, swelling in volume, raising, coming to a stop, apparently from the shaft of rosy cloud, and a snipe came down with a sickle-like sweep.

"Good luck is wi' us," shouted Lancelot. "A snipe at sundown is best thear is."

Matthew drove his cattle into the yard, saw them and shouted. "This is my wife," said Lancelot proudly. "We've coom from Windsor by schooner."

"Tha wur always one for surprises," Matthew removed his hat in a bewildered manner. "Coom in house. Art tha from Windsor?"

"No," said June. "I'm from Boston."

Matthew stared at her as if the fact could not penetrate the bull hide of his senses, then led the way in.

Sylvia greeted June warmly. "How did tha get to know her?" she asked Lancelot.

"We met in Halifax and I asked her to coom wi' me." He told them, briefly, her story. "We wur married at fort,' he finished.

"Why didn't tha wait," shouted Matthew, "and coom here?"

"We couldn't," said Lancelot. "I've to see Healey, and I want to get home."

He laughed at the expressions of Sylvia and Matthew. Their appreciation of June was as apparent as their effort to comprehend the need of haste.

Gideon and Patience were invited over and Gideon roared

such praise that he set his son to wailing. "No wonder you were in a hurry to git spliced," he hooted. "She's too purty a girl to have the lads see while she's single." He turned to the squalling infant. "Young feller, you can't out-yell your father yet, and your mother'll git mad at both of us if you don't stop tryin'."

"Tha have a sweet lass," Patience whispered to Lancelot when she said goodnight. "She's quality."

June held her courage until she was alone with Lancelot. Then she slumped as if the last reserve of her strength had been spent. "Hold me tight," she begged. "I'm afraid I'm dreaming. Tell me I can't wake up in that shack. Make me know it."

They visited Unity and Jonathan the next day, riding borrowed horses, then went home to surprise Melody and John. The next morning Melody waited her chance to speak with Lancelot. "It didn't seem tha could be as lucky as Jonty," she said tremulously, "and tha have. June's champion. Tha couldn't have found a better in Yorkshire. I wish father could have seen her."

As the days passed June's natural assurance returned. Her eyes began to glow. Colour crept into her cheeks and stayed there. The resiliency of youth triumphed. Her bones ceased to dominate and before the end of the month her body was well fleshed, her frame was firm and strong and she had a vitality equal to Melody's.

Aaron Cornforth came riding into the lane one day and shouted that a company of soldiers were at the fort making it ready for defence. "Eddy's run, family and all, to Ameriky," he shouted on. "He said he'd be back wi' an army o' invasion. If he does it will go hard wi' us. Tha never saw such a lot of good-for-nowts as are at fort. Jail rats and t' like."

III

Deserter

MATTHEW was a proud man when Sylvia told him she
was with child again. He thought young Adam a
healthy infant but was vastly pleased to know he
would have a son truly his own. Gideon came over on a
Sunday, with Patience and young Asa, and as Sylvia was
making ready for dinner she glanced out the window and made
clicking sounds denoting interest mixed with dismay.

"It's Francklin, from fort," she exclaimed. "Give hand,
quick, wi' dishes."

Patience scurried to help her and Matthew opened the door.
Two horses were tied to the hitching post and Parson Eagleson
stood with Francklin, looking meachy enough in his jacket
with ornate cuffs.

"We are champion glad tha coom," said Matthew, making
introductions. "Sit thee down and have summat to eat."

Francklin made himself at home with natural tact. He
talked of the crops and the weather. He praised Sylvia's
meat pie until she was rosy with pride, and begged them to
excuse him calling on the Sabbath, but he wanted men.

"To 'list, do tha mean?" said Matthew, surprised. "Noa,
I've my farm to tend."

"If we don't defend this country there'll be no farms to
tend," thundered Eagleson.

"Anyhap," put in Gideon, "we've both got ridin' hosses, and
muskets. If the rebs come around here you can depend on us".

"That's encouraging," said Francklin, "and I'll remember
it."

"There," roared Gideon, as Francklin rode away, "goes a
man with brains."

Shad taken in weirs at Menoudie provided a cheap dinner. Matthew acquired a boat and took turns with Gideon in attending a weir they placed. Sometimes when the day was warm they would go together and would swim in the shallows on the Menoudie side as the tide came in.

July came with hot days and frequent showers, and Matthew went down his marsh trail to the boat to bring up his oars. They had taken up their weir and it would soon be haying. He was amazed at the way the marsh broadleaf had grown. He would be all the fall getting it cut and stacked. It could not be compared with upland hay but was fine to mix for winter feed.

He was bending over the boat when a voice said, roughly. "Drop them oars!"

Matthew swung about, ready to attack.

"Better not, mister." He stopped. He was looking into the muzzle of a new army musket and the man behind it had grim appearance. "Step back and don't make me nervous. I'd as lief shoot as not."

There was no need of threats. Matthew had never handled firearms and his lack of experience made him fear them. The menace of the pointed barrel dried the sap in his legs and blanked his wits. He stepped back.

Gideon had said plenty about the misfits in Goreham's garrison after he had made a visit to the fort, but here was no drooping lad or cranky oldster. The fellow was hearty of chest and shoulder and had a look of determination. His coat was faded and torn as if he had slept in it on the marsh for more than one night, yet he managed a jaunty air.

"Plague take it," he said. "Why did you come? Now you've got to go along with me. Else you'll be ridin' hell for leather to the fort, wantin' a reward for reportin' a deserter. Get the boat into water, quick, and climb in."

Matthew pushed the dory free from the bank, then took a seat in it as the deserter stepped on board.

"Use them oars. Head for the other side, and no monkey tricks."

Matthew rowed. He held direction by keeping his eye on the pole fence that ran between his farm and Gideon's. He

wished that Sylvia or Patience would appear at the back of
the buildings and see that he had a stranger in his boat.   They
would know where he had gone.

They were well across to the Menoudie side when the
deserter ordered him to stand and move back.   "I'll do the
rest of the rowin'," the man said.

Matthew rose with care but a tremendous thrust pitched
him overboard.   He splashed heavily, submerged, threshed
to the surface.   "Ye can paddle the rest of the way," said the
man in the boat.

The water was heavy and full of the rank tang of brine.
Its first numbing shock slid over Matthew and he felt warm.
In a panic to keep afloat, he kicked free of his shoes and
wriggled from his thick shirt and breeches.   He was quite
blown before he had wit enough to let his feet go down and
test for bottom.

His toes touched slippery mud.   He settled to his shoulders
and began wading.   A little later he climbed out on a grassy
bank, wiped his feet of mud and let the sun warm him
luxuriously.

The place where he rested was hidden by bushes from the
rest of the shore and not until he stood up did he see that the
fugitive had landed near the first farm, leaving the boat there,
dragged up on the bank.   There was an open field beside the
spot so the fellow would likely have to come along the shore
to the cover of woods before heading toward River Hebert.

A sudden noise broke the day's stillness.   It was made by
a cart on some road through the bush directly beyond
Matthew.   Wooden axles screeched like hinges of Gehenna.
Matthew came to life as he heard the familiar sound.   If he
could reach the man with the cart they might be in time to
head off the deserter as he went through the nearest spruce
grove.

He plunged under the trees, trying to make a direct line
toward the cart road, and making no sound on the moss and
dried spruce needles.   The cart came to a halt as he was well
up the slope and, too late, he saw he had run into the path
of the man with the musket.

The fellow came along at a jog, peering toward the farm,

and Matthew hid as well as he could behind a tree. The man trotted past him and, acting on sudden impulse, Matthew leaped at him from behind.

He was short in his spring but he had a grip on the fellow's jacket and jerked him around so violently that the musket dropped to the ground. In an instant they were struggling and Matthew was hard put to hold his own in spite of the advantage of surprise. A blow on the cheek made him hang on desperately in a clinch before he could use a wrestling hold. Even then it was nip and tuck before he had his man down and could pin him to surrender.

"I'm done." The fellow gave up suddenly. "Ye needn't do more."

Matthew pulled him to his feet. He was bruised but he felt good. He had not matched his strength with any one in a long time, and the deserter was no easy mark.

"Get along wi' thee," he ordered, pointing to the cart road. "To farm. Push me from boat, eh? Tha'll wish tha hadn't tried it."

The man made no reply. He plodded dejectedly toward the buildings near by.

Gideon sometimes mentioned the lone farm at Menoudie corner, saying it belonged to an old man who lived there with his grand-daughter. The old fellow, he said, was one of the first settlers of the region. Matthew saw the man, gaunt and tall, standing by a pair of oxen, his mouth agape.

"Stop right where ye are," the old man shouted. "Where's yer britches?"

"In water," called Matthew. "Can tha lend me pair, and shirt, till I get hoam?"

"Where the devil do ye live?"

"House on left, 'cross water yonder. I'll coom back in boat."

"What ye doin' with that man ye've got hold of?"

"He's a deserter from fort. I'm taking him back."

"Stay where ye are, then. Sally's in the house gettin' dinner, but she's liable to come out any time."

The deserter stood as if indifferent to his fate, watching dully a flock of turkeys trailing into the yard.

The old man returned with a patched pair of breeches and a clean shirt. "I'll look up some greenhides for your feet," he said. "Come along in. Sally will have dinner ready in a lamb's shake."

"Fetch me a piece o' rope or summat," said Matthew. "I'll tie this lad oop afore I put on clothes."

The man spoke over his shoulder. "Needn't bother, unless ye want. I'll give my word I won't try to git away this side of the water, and Ned Barkness never broke his word to any man."

There was no whine or fear in his voice, and not much hope, but it had some quality of pride that decided Matthew.

"I'll trust thee," he said, and took his hand from the man.

He pulled on the shirt and breeches, though they were a tight fit, and they followed the old man into the house. "Here they be, Sally," he called. "Set the vittles on the table."

Sally was tending a bake kettle holding a savory roast. She was plump and hardy-looking as a partridge in the fall, her dark hair in shiny braids, her feet and legs bare, her dress of rough material that outlined her vigorous figure without modesty.

"Good day," she greeted. "Grandpa's kind of late tellin' me we'd have company, so you won't git anything fancy. The wash bench is around the corner by the rain puncheon."

Matthew walked to it without response, filled a wooden bowl with water and began sloshing his face and neck. The deserter looked at Sally. "My name's Ned Barkness," he said. "I'm obliged to ye for givin' me dinner. I ain't et since yes'day mornin' and that's why my insides are rumblin'."

"Were you lost?" Sally stared at him.

"No, ma'am. I skipped from the fort and they were huntin' for me. I couldn't risk a move till after dark and then had to be careful on account of dogs in every barnyard on Fort Lawrence ridge."

"You mean you deserted?"

"That's right. I quit bein' a sojer."

"You tell me about it," said Sally. "I never hear nothin' but grandpa talkin' about crops and shad."

"What you want me to talk about?" shrilled the old man.

"Never mind now. I'll tell you when we ain't got company. It's lucky I did plenty of potatoes, and this roast's a good size."

It was really a fine meal. A heaping dish of greens covered with butter, plenty of potatoes and new peas, meat and rich gravy, hearty wheat bread and deep strawberry pie. The deserter gave all his attention to his eating, getting full savor from every mouthful.

He sat back with a sigh of content. "That's best I've had since I left Massachusetts."

"Then you're New England?" said the old man.

"I were raised there by my uncle. We had a good farm, too."

"How come you left it, then?" Sally was watching Barkness intently.

"Had no choice. The village was set to fight the British and I had to drill with them or be tarred and feathered. So I drilled. One night when we were out on a skirmish a dozen of us were picked up by the redcoats. They packed us off to Halifax and I were locked up half the winter till they offered to let us go if we'd 'list. We were near starved, so I 'listed, and up we come to these parts."

"This is good country," said the old man. "I've got a clean farm."

"It's good land all right," shrugged Barkness. "I ask no better."

"Tha should have stayed at fort," said Matthew. His conscience twinged him a little; the man sounded honest.

"I might have," said Barkness, "if we had had some decent sojers. They're the poorest I ever saw. If fifty farmers come from New England they'll take the fort easy. Then what would happen to me?"

"Ye mean them at the fort won't fight?"

"The Colonel'll try, all he kin. But he ain't got a dozen he kin trust outside the fort. They're jailbirds and Swiss and riff-raff off ships. They ain't even got decent clothes."

"But where were you goin'?" asked Sally.

"Anywhere. I figgered I'd get in some back settlement and work for somebody till everything's quiet again."

"Ye couldn't do better," said the old man. "I'm Noah Peaman. I come here with not much more than an axe and shad net. Why it were three years afore I had cut enough trees down to be able to see the top of that hill yonder. But look at the place I've got now. When I quit workin' I'll be dead—and I'll want to be."

"Grandpa's opinionated," said Sally. "He brags about this farm on account of it was him picked it. He found water so he's proud of his well. He talks about firewood because he's gettin' old and minds the winters."

"I'd say he's done mighty well," said Barkness.

Matthew enjoyed the talk. Some Sunday he and Gideon would row over for a talk with Noah. He liked Sally. She looked capable. He could see she had scrubbed the pine floor with lye soap. She had used sand and elbow grease on the cooking pots until they shone. She was a worker all right. It took courage, too, to stay in such a lonely spot."

Then he remembered the musket.

"I'm goin' back to get the musket tha dropped," he said to Barkness. "Will tha stay till I coom?"

"Yes," nodded Barkness. "I reckon I won't git any place as nice as this again in a mighty long spell."

"Come and see my well," said Noah. "It's not ten feet deep and has never gone dry a day since I dug it."

It was a neat well, walled with field stone, the water raised by bucket on a sweep. Noah pulled up a bucket and let Matthew drink. It was as clear as though from a spring.

"I've got sweet land, too. Not a sour acre on the farm. Got a grove of maples at the back to give me firewood, and sap in the spring. I cut them all, and burn them, the different woods, I mean. A woman needs birch and poplar for a fryin' blaze, maple and oak for bakin', and ye can't beat old beech for a back log in the winter."

Matthew went along the road and picked up the musket. Barkness had cut his initials in the stock, but it was well oiled and new.

"We ain't got a firearm in our house," said Noah, eyeing the musket. "I loaned my old one to a man who left the country, and took it with him."

He rummaged in his loft as they returned to the house and found Matthew a pair of ox-hide moccasins.

Ned looked at the musket. "I hope you'll hand that in to the colonel," he said. "They'll give me extry lashes if you don't."

"Lashes!" Sally flushed. "Do they use whips on you?" She and Barkness were sitting on the same bench.

"Fifty, maybe more. I knew it afore I tried to git away, though."

"You must have been des'prit." Noah shook his head.

"I'd hate to be there and get took," said Barkness, "with Injuns helpin' the other side."

Matthew stiffened. "Do tha mean t' savages will fight wi' them?"

"Certain sure. There ain't a Injun 'round here now."

Sally looked at the new musket. "Would you sell it to us?" she asked Matthew. "Didn't you say you're a neighbour, 'cross the point?"

"Aye. I've been thear four years. Tha goes through oor field to t' village?"

"When I go." Sally looked at him with an indefinable quality of impersonality that irked strangely. "Will you sell us the musket?"

Matthew twisted uneasily. They had used him well and he wanted to please her. "Ned says he'll have more lashes if he don't hand in musket."

"Why," demanded Sally, "do you want to take him to the fort? Are you paid by the sojers?"

"Noa, lass. But he pushed me in water, boots and all."

"Man, I didn't want to," broke in Barkness, "but I had to get away while you were wading to the bank."

"Now, you see, why can't you let him go?" Sally was afire with resolve.

Matthew said, abruptly. "I'll sell musket."

"And Ned? Will you let him be?"

"Aye. Tha can marry him if tha will." He slapped her thigh in great good-humour.

"That's a bargain," cried Sally, but she stepped from his

reach and there was that in her eye which told Matthew he had misjudged her. "What's your price?"

Matthew thought of his old breeches, his shirt and boots. "I'll ask thee a pound, and tha can pay when tha will."

Sally flashed up the loft ladder with a twinkling of strong bare legs and was back with a gold sovereign. "There you are. Leave grandpa's shirt on the bank."

"I'll say nowt to ony man about tha being here," said Matthew to Barkness. "Tha better stay."

Noah followed him to the field. "Things happen queer," he said. "Sally's gone past twenty and she never let on she hankered a man. If the Injuns come he'll be handy to have about. Leave them moccasins, if you can walk up your field."

Matthew found his clothing stuck on a weir. He carried the oars up the lane.

"Where have you been, man?" shouted Gideon, meeting him. "We've looked here to the village."

"I had a swim," grinned Matthew, "and tide took my shoes."

"Bust my barrels! You had a swim! You had your wife worried."

"I'll not go again," promised Matthew. "I nigh lost my breeches as well."

"It'll larn you not to go alone," vowed Gideon. "Now put this in your mind. There's so many rumours folks has built brush heaps for signals in case them rebels come. I've built one for us, just other side of our brook. A man never knows what's ahead of him."

IV

Arson

TRISTRAM had never been nearer happiness. He had sowed his crops early and the weather had favoured him. He could almost see his peas and beans grow. The upland timothy was tall as his waist. Jeannie and Jacky were healthy as young pups. Delia was a wonder in her kitchen or out of doors. She was as good as two women.

Then John Lacey came over, with Melody. "I'm sorry to bring you hard news," he said, "but you will have to move. I have a deed to this farm."

The blunt statement numbed Tristram's thinking. He had forgotten that he held no title to the land he tilled.

"We will pay you," continued John gently, "for the barn you built, and the pens. You can take the crop you planted as well."

"I'll do nowt." Tristram fairly strangled his words. "I'll stay, and pay for land." He glared at them and his hands clenched. "No man will move me," he shouted. "I'll pay fair price, and no more."

Melody eyed him scornfully. "Shouting will gain nowt," she said sharply. "Tha can't scare John. Sometimes I'm shamed that tha art my brother."

"We've warned you," went on John, "and we mean every word of it. We will not sell, and if you do not move Healey will come from Amherst with constables and you will be the loser. But we do not want it that way. We will help you move or do anything we can to make things easy for you. It is best for all of us if we are friends."

Tristram's fury was so great that he left them, and they rode from the yard. He went to his barn and stared at the thick

244

plank flooring he had laid, at the loft where he would pile his fine grain. He went outside and gazed at his sheep pen, his poultry pen, pig pen and well shed. Then he walked over to Silas Plumley and told his story.

"It seems hard," said Silas, "but t' land is not yours. Tha will not find a better than John Lacey, either, and he is thy own kin. Man, tha must move."

Tristram hunched himself doggedly and rode over to the cabin they had built for Shubad Knapp. He walked about and made decision. He would move there. No one had claim to it. There was enough land cleared to make a start.

The next day he began moving. He knocked down the pens and sheds and hauled them over on his cart for setting up again. He took over his stock, his tools, his table, beds and benches, the bucket from the well, hay from the barn, his wood from the yard, leaving nothing that could be used in house or stable.

August came in with warmer weather. Delia and the children went daily to get vegetables from the garden. The men of the settlement helped haul planks and timbers from the mill. They gathered one day and raised a small barn. The roof was shingled and the floor laid. Tristram could board in and make the stalls.

He felt ugly as he began the next day. The smallness of the structure irritated him. He kept looking over the intervale to the fine barn John would have without it costing him more than he wished to pay.

There was a day of extreme heat, and the air boded storm. At night the sky blazed with lightning. Tristram took his tinder box and went out without Delia seeing him. He had made a terrible resolve.

It was dark but he knew his way across the fields without going by the cart trail. When he reached the yard he could not resist going into the house he had called his own and standing there in the shuttered darkness, dry and full of vague old smells of smoke, worn timbers and daily living. When there was a rustle of mice overhead he thought it was Judy whispering to him.

The idea startled him. He pushed her from his mind, but

she returned. He thought he could smell her hair as she tossed it free for combing. He turned and went out, making sure he latched the door.

There was some old hay left in the barn. He carried it to a stall, knelt beside it with dry punk. He struck his flint and the punk burst into tiny flame. He pulled wisps of hay over it, fed it. Then threw an armload on the blaze. It flamed high. He went out of the barn, leaving the door open to give a draught.

He ran. Looking back in the dark he saw the glow from the door dilate into wide sheets of flame. Soon the entire barn became a furnace of fire. Great drops of rain pelted him. Then a deluge began. Simultaneously a light flared on his left. The lightning had struck Plumley's sheep pen and it was aflame.

Delia was asleep when he reached the cabin and stripped from him his soaked shirt and breeches. She roused and peered out at the fires.

"It's where we lived!" she gasped.

"Aye, house or barn," he whispered, careful not to wake the children. "It's well we wur moved. I wur 'round to look at cattle, and rain coom."

She accepted the explanation of his absence without question, and they saw men about the fires. Finally Delia went back to bed.

"That were a neat house," she yawned. "It's bad luck for thy sister."

"Aye," agreed Tristram. He echoed her yawn. "They'll have to build."

When she was sleeping again he raised and peered into the darkness. Both fires had died down. There was a pelting rain. John's house would not burn.

In the morning the sun was shining again and the weather cleared to cooler air. They looked over the intervale. "It weren't house after a'," exclaimed Delia. "It's the barn that's gone."

Tristram nodded soberly and said he would go and see Silas Plumley. He found Silas clearing away the debris of the fire. He had lost two sheep only and it would be easy to replace the log pen. "T' Lord is merciful," said Silas. "I might have lost dozen sheep. Look at t' barn yonder. If tha had had hay in it tha would have lost it. Now tha have thy hay in stack."

"Aye," assented Tristram. He was pleased to find the old man accepting it as nothing extraordinary that two buildings had burned in the same area. He went home feeling avenged against those who would take from him the results of his work, and stilled his conscience with the argument.

At noon a gaunt man walked into his yard and rapped at the door as they ate dinner. Before he could rise the man had opened the door and entered.

"I'm yer brither, Donald Ferguson," the man said to Delia. "I've ma discharge from the army. I've been wounded bad wi' a musket ball."

Delia kissed his leathery cheek as if he were young and handsome, and he patted her shoulder. "Ye look a bonny lass," he grunted, "same as last I saw ye."

"I'm so glad to see ye," said Delia. "I was feared ye'd never bother to find me again. I hope yer wound will better."

She introduced Tristram. "Yorkshire, eh," Donald seated himself wearily after a brief handshake. "Country's full of them. Decent folks, too. Mostly wi' hooses." He gazed around him. "Ye ain't been long in the country?"

Delia explained their circumstances. Donald made no comment. He washed at the bench and took his seat at the table without waiting an invitation. "I'll bide wi' ye till fall onyway," he announced. "My hurt's a nagger but I can do chores."

Tristram's thoughts were chaotic. He had not dreamed of such a situation. If Donald were a vigorous man, he thought, he could help me with clearing the land. But he is far from strong. He's a dour man as well, a tight-mouthed Scot who will take everything for granted.

Donald appeared to make little of the children or of Delia, yet by bed time they had accepted him with a warmth and readiness that Tristram could not understand.

Each morning Donald did small chores, mostly helping Delia. He walked about when in the mood or rested on a bench in the sun. By the end of the week he was an established member of the family. He watched whatever Tristram did with a critical air, yet said nothing, and his attitude irked Tristram more than any speech could have done.

An officer from the fort rode to Bathol and offered good prices for fat cattle. He bought from every farmer, and was last at Tristram's house.

"They tell me you are the leader here," the officer said as he concluded his buying. "Mind what I say. We only accept the cattle at our pasture. If you have trouble getting them there, and lose some steers, that will be your problem."

"We'll coom wi' them," said Tristram heavily. "Tha be ready to pay."

He arranged the drive for the last of the month. The weather was kind and ripening grain gave the country an appearance of burnished gold. Fall dandelions and five finger garnished the road sides and wild carrot spread its lacy blossoms in the hay stubble. Brilliant fire weed added its colour to the scene.

There were twenty men with the cattle, each carrying a musket or rifle, and no one tried to stop them. The officer at the fort paid in gold.

Tristram, satisfied with the weight of his money, walked into the fort to see Ezra Hodge. Ezra had gone to work as a carpenter and it was rumoured that he earned a large wage. He had taken his wife along and they lived in a small house beside the barracks.

Ezra was on the roof of the officers' quarters, making it tight against rain. "I get two shillings more than t' soldiers," he said. "Do tha want job here?"

Tristram started to refuse, then considered. He had his hay in stack, and part of his grain. Donald would stay the fall, and the fellow was a trial. If he could earn good money and escape Delia's brother at the same time, it seemed a clever move. He would go home by October and gather his late grain and root crops. Meanwhile, Donald would have earned his keep.

He saw the colonel. "Send word back by your neighbours, and stay now," urged the officer. "Every fine day counts."

Lancelot agreed to take the gold to Delia and explain to her, so Tristram stayed. He worked till dusk, then ate with the Hodges as he was to live with them. The soldiers, off duty, sang bawdy ditties in their ramshackle quarters. They did not seem to care about the condition of the fort or possible danger, and he disliked them. He prowled about and saw the fort ditches were uncleaned, that timbers were rotted in the walls.

In the morning he told the colonel he should be working at the defences instead of patching roofs. The colonel assured him that everything would be attended to in good time.

"Best let them be," advised Ezra. "Tha art making good money."

"When I go to put in roots," said Tristram sourly, "I'll not coom back."

"Tha can't do that." Ezra stared at him. "Tha joined wi' fort. They would send soldiers to fetch thee."

Tristram gazed at him, dismayed. He had paid little heed to else than the amount of pay offered when the colonel talked with him, and had no idea he had signed to defend the place.

"T' Americans won't coom," cheered Ezra. "We'll be hoam Christmas."

From his vantage point on the roof Tristram could see the rain-washed gullies that seamed the glacis, flocks of geese on the marsh, soldiers' wives picking blueberries along old trenches. There was a farm not far from the fort. It belonged to a widow, Sethella Mullins, Ezra said, and her son was a half-wit. Tristram eyed the cattle in the fort pasture. They were fine stock. He picked out the steers he had sold. A new thought struck him. "Happen they want more cattle," he called to Ezra, "I'll sell rest o' mine."

V

In The Night

JUDY SCURR tired of working for Titus Green. She prepared his meals, did his washing and looked after his cow and poultry. He had no favours from her, for she disliked the man. She was lonely at River Hebert, and wondered where Reuben was living. During the summer her loneliness increased until, in August, she left.

Her decision angered Green. He paid her wages due and would not give her a lift by horse or cart to the river. So she took her bundle and walked the trail. The day was tiring and toward night the air grew close so that she did not mind wading at the ford.

It was dark soon after and the intervales seemed endless before she reached Tristram's place. Then it began to thunder and the lightning was violent. She hurried. Green had told her of Tristram marrying the widow and she thought he would give her shelter for the night. In the morning she would look for work.

She reached Tristram's yard and found the house in darkness. She rapped at the door and there was no response. Finally she opened the door and went in, feeling warily for the table and stools.

She encountered nothing. The room was stripped bare. Tristram and the widow had vanished. She went up the stairs to her room and saw, by lightning flashes, that her chest, the bed and table, were gone. Exhausted from her long walk, she sank to the floor, made a pillow of her bundle and tried to be comfortable. Thunder crashed overhead in long rolls. Then, in a lull between, she heard the door below being opened.

It closed again and there was no sound. Alarm hoisted

her to her knees. She waited, listening. The lightning flashed again. She saw dust on the window sill and knew the house had been vacant for some time. Then the door creaked open. Someone went out and closed it after him.

She made her way down the stairs as quickly as possible, waited a moment, then went to a window. Lightning zigzagged across the sky and she saw Tristram going to the barn.

Her heart beat rapidly. The mystery of his coming set her to trembling. She watched for his coming from the barn but did not see him. Rather she heard the heavy pounding of his feet as he ran.

His running frightened her more. She went up the stairs again. Light flickered into the room, wavered against a wall. She ran and peered. The entire barn was in flames!

She was outside in a hurry. Rain drops beat against her, warnings of a downpour. She heard shouts at Lancelot's house. Someone came, running. She made out Lancelot. He stared at her. "Judy! Tha didn't set. . . ."

"Noa," she said sharply. "It wur Tristram. I saw him."

Swiftly she told what had happened. They tried to find a ladder Tristram had made but it was gone. Sparks were showering them but the rain pelted hard.

It was a deluge that drummed on the house. It drove them inside. Lancelot introduced the man with him as John Lacey, Melody's husband, and in the stale darkness she told them of her leaving Green and of her intention to find work somewhere.

The barn roof tumbled in. Flames leaped high for a time, then lost their fierceness. Steam began to mingle with the smoke and blaze.

"No more will burn," said Lancelot. "I'll help tha, John, to build another barn, and we'll say nowt in t' place?"

"Not now," said John, "but some day I'll tell him that we know, and that I will brook nothing more from him."

Lancelot touched Judy. "Tha coom wi' us," he said kindly. "Thear is plenty o' room. When John and Melody move tha can be wi' my wife. She is new here, from Boston."

Judy went gladly, crying silently in the darkness as she went. The women received her with warm welcome and she did her full share of work. One day she went up to the big willow stub. Asa had told her she would find a fortune if she ever dug by its roots. She remembered how she had laughed at him about it, and now she probed idly with a stick.

Something yellow was exposed. She grasped a coin, wiped earth from it, peered, incredulous. A moment later she sat back, breathing deeply. At her feet was a pile of gold coins. There was enough to build a good house, she reckoned. She gathered them into her skirt, carried them into the woods and hid them under the roots of a great gnarled hemlock.

VI

Do Tha Want to Hang, Woman?

PATIENCE listened with a pulsing heart to young Asa playing with blocks his father had whittled for him out of dried pine. It had been a mild September. The kitchen was so warm with the cooking fire at noon that she had left the door open and now she could smell the tide coming in. Tide, and marsh. They seemed the life of the Point. Gideon was down on the marsh putting his broadleaf in stack. She would soon go to gather cranberries.

Asa tired of his play and when she peeped from where she was paring apples he was asleep, his head pillowed on an old jacket of Gideon's he always wanted beside him. He had one sleeve clutched tightly in his hands.

She put him to bed on the wide kitchen sofa and went back to her work. Apples being ripe always made her think of the winter ahead. They were getting in the beets and carrots. With the first frosts they would get in the turnips. There would be wild geese overhead, and bright moons, then November winds whistling over the flats. December would freeze the ditches. In pens, pigs would climb each other's back for warmth and snow would pile over the fences.

No sense letting her mind drift like that. She shook herself as if her clothing were sweated to her body. If only the Americans did not come marching from Saint John she would never mind the winter. Rumours were bad, though, about a trail blazed from Shepody, and Gideon had sold his fat cattle to the fort. He had seen Tristram there, signed on as a carpenter and regretting it, soured about his wife's brother.

Patience went out to drop her apple peelings for the poultry. She had quartered and strung more than three bushels of

253

sound fruit.   They had vegetables in plenty, crocks of butter, a barrel of salt shad, crocks of mince meat, onions, a side of beef and maybe more, to start the winter with, and the thought was comforting.

She started.   A strange woman was coming up the slope, finding the path past the apple trees, a sturdy young woman who came with assurance as if her presence were justified. There was nothing fancy about her linsey dress or moccasins, but she had dignity just the same, and her voice was as cool as her glance.

"I'm Noah Peaman's daughter from over there," she said, pointing over the water to where a strip of cleared fields nudged the shore line.   "We've got a boat and I come this way to buy things at the village.   My name's Sally."

"I'm glad tha get over," said Patience, wondering why the girl had come to her.   "Will tha stop in and rest a bit?"

"I haven't time to stay long," said Sally, and she hesitated, plainly needing encouragement.

"Was thear something tha wanted?" asked Patience.

"Yes."   Sally looked at Asa asleep on the sofa, and back at Patience.   "I want you to ask your husband to let me be as I come up through the field."

It was so different a request from what Patience had expected that she was unable to make reply.   She simply stared at Sally.

"I don't want to hurt anybody," Sally went on, "and I know by your look that you've never knowed what he's like. But he's been botherin' me twice now, tryin' to trip me by his hay stack."

Patience nodded.   She felt as if she had been swimming a long time and had just placed her feet on solid ground. "Are tha sure it's him?   Does he wear red-hide moccasins?"

"Yes, it's him all right.   They're steer red."   Then Sally's eyes filled.   "I'm decent if I do live over there," she said. "You tell him."

Patience drew a long deep breath.   Matthew had worn red shanks all the fall but Gideon wore old moosehides with most of the hair worn off.

"I'm terribly sorry," she said.   "I promise thee I'll tell

him and," she added strongly, "he won't bother thee more."

"He musn't," said Sally, almost whispering. "He can't. I'd—I'll kill him, sure." She rose to go, then sat down. "Do you know your husband was over to our place this summer?"

"Noa," said Patience. "He never said. What did he go for?"

Tersely, trustingly, Sally told her everything. "Ned and me is same as married," she said, her eyes imploring understanding. "We give our promise to grandpa same as if he were the parson, and that's all we kin do till the war's over. The fort parson'd have Ned back there and lashed, if he knew where he were, and wouldn't marry us nohow. But Ned's my husband just the same and I—I love him as much as a woman kin."

She rose to go and Patience put an arm around her. "Don't tha worry ony more," she said. "I'll tend to things."

"Thank ye," said Sally. She was soft and eager and strong—yet touchingly awkward—as they kissed. "You're good," she whispered. "I've never knowed any wimmen. Grandpa's raised me."

When she was gone Patience went outside and looked toward the marsh. Matthew was on the trail, coming with his oxen. She looked inside the kitchen and Asa was still sleeping, turned in a huddle like a young puppy. She flung on a shawl and went across the field, picking her steps.

Matthew swung his cattle next to the line fence, for he knew she would not try to climb over in her condition.

"Did tha want me?" he asked.

"Aye." She scanned his face. "Did tha see Sally coom oop from boat a while back?"

Resentment crept into his eyes. "Happen I did, what do tha want?"

"Thee are my brother," she spoke slowly, picking each word, but all her anger was to the fore, "and we are neighbours here to stay, but I want thee to keep from Sally. Let her be. Don't tha put hands on her no matter whear tha see her."

Matthew came over and laid his hands on the top rail of the fence, strong, thick hands, covered with black hair.

She could see rage arching his chest, flushing his neck a dark red. "I'll do what I want," he said harshly, "ony time, and tha will tend thy own man and be done wi'."

Her gaze met his fairly. "Did tha ever know me to tell thee a lie?" she questioned.

He shook his head. "What's that to do wi' it?"

"This. I'm telling thee that if tha put hand on Sally—I'll shoot thee wi' Gid's rifle same as a dog."

"Tha art a fool!" he snarled, greatly stirred, for there was no fear in her eyes. "Do tha want to hang, woman?"

"I'll hang afore I'll let thee touch Sally."

"Tha art crazy!"

"I've towd thee God's truth."

"But tha will hang."

"She coom to house and towd me, thinking I wur thy wife. It's God's blessing Sylvia does not know."

Matthew's jaw dropped in amazement, then tightened as his doubts gave way to fury. "T' devil wi' both thee and Sally!"

"Steady, man. Ye sound excited." Patience had not seen Gideon come across the field. "What's the mess?"

For a moment nothing was said. Patience tried to calm herself but Matthew was roused beyond reasoning.

"Tha can hear what I've said," he blazed. "Her coom," he pointed at Patience, "and threatened to shoot me. T' devil wi' her, I say, and keep her from my field if tha want no trouble."

Patience felt herself trembling. Intuition told her she had started something now beyond her control. Gideon was beside her, his hands on the top rail, as big and strong as Matthew's, his face suddenly hard.

"You are talkin' to my wife," he said coolly, "and to your sister. Them words ain't fitten for either, and best thing you can do is tell her you are sorry," his voice quickened, "here and now."

Patience thought, glancing at Matthew, that his eyes were like those of an animal gone ugly. His lips parted over his strong teeth in a grin that had no mirth. "If tha think tha can do aught about it," he challenged. "Get over t' fence."

Gideon let no change into his voice. He turned to Patience. "You better go to the house," he said quietly. "I reckon this had to come some time or other, and it's best you don't see."

She shook her head, feeling her blood pounding as if she had run uphill. "I want to stay, Gid," she said.

He did not look at her again. He put his weight on his hands and went over the rail as if it were no trick at all, tossed away his reed hat and faced Matthew. "Sonny," he said softly, "you've a bad streak in you that needs to be knocked out so it won't come back—and that's what I'm going to do right now."

The look that settled on Matthew's face made Patience cringe. It held calculated cruelty and determination. He rushed with a ferocity that startled her but he did not quite reach Gideon. A longer arm than his own shot out and a bony first cracked him stunningly on the cheek, sending blood gushing from his nose.

Matthew shook his head, sprang again and tried to grapple. He met another jolting blow, weathered it, plunged in doggedly, taking a blow on the neck, got his hands on Gideon and surged in mightily to get a bear hug.

It seemed he would succeed, so quickly did Gideon's body go in toward Matthew's, but Gideon's hard bony knee was driven upward with terrific force, knocking the breath from Matthew, almost paralyzing him. His hold weakened and Gideon wrenched free.

Not a word was spoken. Matthew's gasps and sobbing swallows of his own blood were the only sound as he stood away, and Gideon waited. Then Matthew rushed again, and when he was near he tried to kick Gideon in the groin.

He was too slow, and awkward. Gideon was in close before he knew and both hands crashed through Matthew's defense, the right-hander cracking with a sickening crunch on his jaw. Matthew staggered back, tried to clinch, and Gideon hit him again, with his weight behind his fist, rocking him back and away.

There was no more fight to it. Matthew was stubborn as a mad bull but Gideon's fists were battering rams that beat him back over the ground until he could neither see nor sense direction, and a final swing knocked him to earth like a poled ox. He lay there without motion, beaten to a soggy, bloody coma.

Gideon squatted down beside him. He was breathing fast and his face was wet with perspiration but he had no bruise of any sort. He looked around at Patience. "I'll stay and bring him 'round," he said gently. "Maybe Asa'll be wantin' you."

Patience could not stop her chin trembling. "Coom," she whispered. He went to the fence, his love for her so evident that it took the sag from her body. "I'll tell thee what angered him."

It took her but a moment and Gideon understood. "Don't you worry," he patted her arm. "He's got plenty of good in him. He'll be sour a week or so but that's only natural. His kind don't take a lickin' easy and it's humblin' to know the man ye throwed in rasslin' kin handle you when there's need. When he's had his sulk you'll find him steadied and sorry, and I'll gamble my britches that he'll let wimmen be."

Matthew roused slowly after the fight, and was sick before his senses cleared, retching forth the blood he had swallowed. His face was a mass of pain and he groaned as he put a hand to it.

"You've had quite a sleep, sonny," said Gideon's voice near him. "It's gettin' cold out here, too. Think you can reach the barn?"

Matthew inhaled deeply. Fragments of what had happened began to eddy in his thinking and then to jell in one piece. He kept his eyes closed. Gideon had beaten him, had hit him again and again, and he had not been able to get in one good blow. Terrific man, Gideon.

"Up you come, sonny. I don't want Sylvia to see you until I've washed you up a bit."

Matthew stood. His stomach still nauseated him. His body seemed on fire. He could scarcely move his mouth.

"You wouldn't quit," said Gideon cheerfully. "I had to knock tarnation out of you."

They reached the barn and Gideon brought a bucket of

water and cloth.   He washed the blood from Matthew's face and though each touch was painful Matthew marveled that the big man could be so gentle.

"I told Sylvia that we had the devil's own row over nothin' at all, gettin' serious when we hadn't intended," he said in the same easy tone, "and that you slipped and I hit you harder than I knew, so that your handsome nose will be swelled for a time.   What she thinks I don't know, and neither will you, but it's a good enough story.   See that you stick to it."

"Aye," groaned Matthew.   The agony in his head had settled to a steady throbbing.   "I'll get to bed."

He saw Sylvia watch, white-faced, as Gideon took him up the stairs and then he lay and suffered until sleep came. Sometime in the night he awoke and realized he had absorbed a terrific beating.   It made him wonder if he would be any good again to face a man, and depression was on him like a weight.

In the morning he was morose.   He peered into a mirror and saw how badly his face was swollen.   Sylvia asked no questions, patiently waiting for him to explain.   At noon he had not seen Gideon and he forced himself to mutter, as he ate dinner.   "We can't do that again.   Gid hit me like a horse kicking when I didn't dodge."   He paused.   "It wur no fault o' his.   We're friends t' same, but thear will be no more o' it."

"What wur it over?" asked Sylvia curiously.

He was prepared for the question.   "Line fence from t' marsh."

She asked no more and when Patience came over in the evening with a cranberry pie the two women talked as if everything were normal.

Matthew walked out to his barn and waited for Patience to leave.   He met her at the path.   "Tha can tell Sally I'll not trouble her more," he said, and looked anxiously toward his house.   "Will tha tell Sylvia?"

"Not if I can help," said Patience.   "She's a good wife to thee.   Tha be good to her."

"Aye," he said thankfully.   "I will."

He sold his fattened cattle to the fort and went with others to draw firewood for Colonel Goreham.   The pay was excellent for a man and oxen and it was a chance to work off the sullenness that had gripped him.   The first touch of frost had come.   The hardwoods were wildly coloured with the dying passion of fall and women waved to him from a cranberry bog. He did no more than acknowledge their salute; he had made his resolve to have no more to do with women who might cross his path.

He made two trips a day, his cart creaking and groaning under green, sap-filled logs, the tired oxen lifting their knobby knees with reluctance at the end of the last journey.   During the second week his lunch was stolen from the bush where he had placed it.   The men with him muttered about deserters, then they closed in gradually, like beaters trying to flush a patridge, and routed two of the riff-raff from the fort who whined and begged for mercy as if it were their second nature.

Matthew and another marched them to the fort.   The colonel was grateful and gave Matthew a pound for his help, praising him before his officers.   It made Matthew feel good and he looked for Tristram, found him building a platform for cannon.

"Americans are cooming," muttered Tristram.   "Do tha know?"

"Cooming?" Matthew stared at him.

"Aye.   T' colonel sent men to watch over at Shepody."

They turned as one man and gazed over marsh and water to the distant blue Shepody hills as if they could see there the soldiers on watch.

Matthew shrugged and looked at the platform.   Outside the parapet was a line of pickets about ten feet high, placed by a shallow ditch, and they seemed the only defence of the fort.   The fort spur, containing the powder magazine, officers' quarters, a carpenter shop and buildings in which the garrison slept, had only a palisade to defend it.

A flock of wildfowl passed overhead and the men pounding new pickets in place stopped work and gazed after the birds, then discussed them as if nothing else in the world mattered. Other men clearing a bush-filled ditch shouted they had found a woodchuck hole.

Matthew turned away. He knew he would desert such a place if he were in it, and with the thought he drove his oxen from the wood yard, then headed back on the trail. First thing when he went home, he decided, he would bury his money in the garden back of his house. The Americans could not get his fat steers, for he had sold them to the fort. He would stay on his farm and sit tight. In the spring there would be soldiers from Halifax.

He shouted at his cattle and hurried them, his ego suddenly excited with the thought that he had managed better than Tristram in everything.

VII
The Army of Invasion

LANCELOT liked the autumn. It gave him an urge to go tramping in the woods. He sniffed the air and noted the fall haze from settlers burning brush as he went to the house. It was warm and snug. From a pot on the crane came pungent odors of molasses and spices and baked beans. June had brought the idea from Boston.

She smiled at him as he entered, making him notice, as he always did, that her nose was the merest trifle short and that the tiny puckering in her cheek made a lovely dimple when she laughed. "I'll put tallow on my moccasins," he said, "and get thee some partridge in morning."

They had no more than finished their supper than there was a rapping at the door. Obed Muncie stood there, with Michael Healey. They rubbed their hands and stood before the fire. "Coolish ride," said Muncie. "We'll soon have snow."

"Tha didn't coom to tell us that," observed Lancelot. "What's t' news?"

"The Americans," said Healey bluntly, "are on their way to attack us."

June stared at him. Melody went to sit by John. "Oor fort?" she asked.

"Yes. The fort that defends this country, including Bathol." He looked at Lancelot. "We want you to help us."

"I'll not leave hoam," said Lancelot quickly, glancing at June.

"That's bad for our side," said Healey. "Francklin gave us your name. We want a scout to go into the woods and warn us when the rebels come."

Lancelot felt a flush of pride. "We've been working on t' barn for t' other house," he said, "and I'm a married man."

"Most of us are," answered Healey, looking at June, "and to be honest I must say I don't blame you for not wanting to go."

"Right always wins," said June suddenly, "if we'll only believe it." She looked at Lancelot. "I want you with me, but I think you had better go. I'll pray," her voice shook a little, "that you'll be safe, and I believe you will be. John will look after us here."

Lancelot looked at her, warmed a little to her thin fire of faith, and shook his head. It was an hour before he would surrender. "Tha may be reight," he said to Healey at last. "I'll go."

When the men had gone June stood with him, and faced the others. "We were to tell you later," she said to Melody and John, "but now it cannot wait. This is our wish. We want you to live here and let us take the other place. This is your house, Melody, and it is right that you should stay here. Nothing will please us more, and I know you want us to be happy."

Melody gazed at her, speechless, her eyes filled with tears. "I cannot agree to ony other plan," said Lancelot, his arm about June. "It's oor own choice. Tell us tha will stay, Melody, and I'll ride away to fort content."

"Tha art too good." Melody clung to John, her face radiant behind her tears. "I will speak fair wi' thee and say thear is nowt else could make me so happy, but to have tha two for oor family, and by us, is more than most ever have in life."

Lancelot thought of her happiness as he rode to the fort the next day. The country looked brown. There seemed fewer gulls on the mud flats and the sun went down early, touching drab roofs and chimneys with glorious tints. It seemed a diabolical thing that intruders wanted to come and molest people who had never in any way molested them. The Yorkshiremen had planted their roots in this new soil and strong growth had begun. They had acquired flocks and herds, houses and barns and implements, built dykes and put in bridges, such a foundation of the future as they would not lightly let go.

The next morning he was on his way in a canoe toward Shepody. At noon a scared voice hailed him from bushes on shore. He paddled in cautiously, and saw a bearded settler, haggard from hard travelling. "Eddy's men are in the woods," the fellow gasped. "Leastways they took the post at Shepody, every man jack of them."

"Did they head toward t' fort?" queried Lancelot.

"I think likely," nodded the man. "I put to the woods so I wouldn't be caught. I didn't really watch which way they took."

It was useless to question the fellow further. Lancelot dragged his dugout to a safe hiding and threaded his way inland. He could not go with a warning until he had made sure that the invaders were coming.

A young moose raced along an opening and plunged into a thick stand of spruce. Lancelot looked back the way it had come and went quickly up the nearest hillside, zig-zagging to keep tree boles behind him as the moose had done. He looked all about him, then went on, watching, guarded against surprise, his gaze sweeping the infinite multiplicity of the half-naked hardwoods. He did not see details, but if a detail were wrong he would see it.

Swinging westward, he covered three or four miles without resting. He discovered a path and followed it, for every aspect along the way was innocent; little glades were open and candid, stretches of sunlit grass were still green and red pigeon berries abounded. In full stride, he drew back as if his foot were descending on a snake. A fresh moccasin track was printed across his path.

In a matter of minutes he had found an old Indian trail that had been heavily tramped by a party, he reckoned, of not less than one hundred men. He kept on toward the coast. It would be harder going along the marshy area, but safer. It was possible that a second party might follow the first.

He climbed a tall pine until he could see over the nearer trees and as he watched, a hawk sprang suddenly up from the tree tops of the next hill and climbed the air. No idle impulse drove the strong wings upward at sunset; every beat was to put the bird a safe distance from danger.

Lancelot's mouth opened slightly in his intensity of listening. Through all the little sounds of falling leaves and running water he listened for loud talking—a party halted to rest. What he heard made him recoil.

It was the clop-clop of horses on the hardwood path, and in a moment he saw them under the trees, at the head of a line of plodding men who had kettles tied to their belts and blankets strapped on their backs. They trudged in silence, the second party; he had miles to make up if he were to get ahead of the leaders.

There was one way it might be done. He would reach the marsh area and camp there. Tide channels made it too risky for night travelling, but in daylight he could save miles by choosing a path.

Skirting a lake, he kept going until the moon was up, then squatted in a recess of dry ground on the marsh and ate his evening meal. Great skeins of geese came from the north and filled the air with the rushing of their passage, brant and mallards and pintails and black ducks. He spent the night enduring the loneliness and smell of the salt-laden cold, heard the marshes sighing beneath the tides, listened to the jabbering of settling wildfowl, the circling winged shadows in the night and, while his teeth chattered with chill, the rushing of the dawn flights.

The sun was slow in appearing and he was well over the marshy district before the mist had cleared. He found a trail and for ten miles held to steady jogging. Then reached the old Indian path. One glance sufficed. The first party had gone along and every track had been dimmed by dew. He was still behind. Eddy and his men had reached Sackville in the night.

An hour later he rapped at the door of a farmhouse in Sackville and asked if he might be served with a hot dinner for a shilling. He had had no breakfast and his stomach rumbled without ceasing.

The farmer and his wife served him boiled meat and potatoes. "Eddy come in last night," said the man, "and made the people feed him and his lot. I'm glad they didn't come here."

"Tha art not wi' them, then?" quizzed Lancelot.

"Neither are you, Yorkshire," grinned the farmer, "else you wouldn't stop here."

They peered out as loud shouting started dogs to barking. Men were straggling to the road, falling in at the orders of an officer wearing a blue coat with gilt buttons. Not a man hurried and a lone drummer pounded his summons slowly as if he, too, were not wasting any energy in haste.

Lancelot counted forty Indians in the fields and pasture. There were at least twenty Acadians, lugging ancient muskets. The others numbered forty-five or fifty. If they could surprise the fort, and had good leadership, they would capture it at first try.

Scouting Indians watched the marsh road and Lancelot had to use stacks of broadleaf on the marsh as a screen for his movements. It took him a long time to work around to a spot near the river crossing but he was well over the marsh, and thought luck with him, when a flock of crows flung into the air. They had been near the dyke and their clamor was enough warning for the Indians.

Lancelot ran. He jumped the dyke, slithered into the river channel on greasy mud, waded through, climbed the bank and was away. Behind him he heard a thin cry. He had been sighted and he knew the chase was on.

He tore off his jacket, glad that he had left his rifle with the Sackville farmer. A man running wanted to travel lightly. He felt overheated and tore his shirt from him. The cooling air struck against his skin deliciously. He gulped for breath, swallowing exhilarating lungfuls.

There had been five Indians in the party but as he lengthened his stride toward a stout pole-and-brush fence at the foot of the ridge three of the redskins fell back. The other pair were sprinters and they were running hard, bent forward, hatchets in their hands.

At Banfield, Lancelot had jumped fences by making a long hop to touch the top rail with one foot, and then soar on. He decided to try it and settled his pace for the long step.

He rose easily, and trod the rail. It yielded but was supported by a stouter pole below and the spring gave him impetus. Then, with a leap, he swerved sharply to his left.

The move saved his life. He heard the swishing of a hatchet as it shot by him. Then he sprang to catch up the weapon. The Indian saw his move. His features contorted in rage and disappointment as he turned and fled.

At the top of the ridge, Lancelot looked back. The Indians were grouped by the fence. They would make no further attempt to overtake him.

He reached the fort at dusk and was able to enter the gate without being challenged. He was tired, and furious at the laxity of the sentries, as he faced the colonel. There was action within moments. The officers rushed to their posts. The garrison was hustled to arms. Sentries were doubled.

"You saved us," said the colonel. "Eddy will wait for his other party and that will give us time to unload the supplies that have come by schooner." He gave final orders to an officer. "Make the rounds every hour and give the men an issue of rum. Give this man an order on the stores for a shirt and good jacket. Give him anything else he needs. We owe him everything."

VIII
Taken Prisoner

TRISTRAM calculated he would have enough money to buy a span of horses by the time he left the fort. He talked about their worth at every meal time with Ezra Hodge.

"They've gradely horses over at Windsor," he would say. "Harness will cost summat more than yokes, but horses will out-step oxen twice over. I've trace chains now, and horses will be champion to break new land. I've much to do."

Charity, Ezra's wife, agreed with him. Her father had owned horses in Yorkshire, she said. She considered his idea progressive.

Tristram liked her talk. Now and then when she had clean dress on he would look at her in a way that made her blush. But there were hours when he did not think of horses, or the land he would clear. Shubell Cutlip had joined the fort garrison, and the fellow was more or less insolent. His account of the way he had been trapped into fighting with the disadvantage of a small stable was known to half the garrison.

When the cannon platforms were completed Tristram felt more confident of the strength of the fort. The arrival of the supply schooner heartened him more. He saw there would be plenty of flour and beef at least for the garrison. He felt that if he had word from Bathol, assuring him all was well with Delia, he could be content. He was keeping away from the dour Scot, her brother, and was earning a snug sum for himself.

On the day after Lancelot returned, at dawn, the colonel asked him if he would go to the schooner and help check supplies as they were being unloaded.

"The sergeant I sent can't do simple arithmetic," the colonel

fumed, "and I doubt he's honest. Give all the hand you can
and see if you can find any shoes for the men."

Tristram was glad of the errand. It would be a pleasure
to tally the sacks and bales, the kegs and bundles.

The morning was thick with fog, and chilly. Tristram
joined a party going to do the unloading. Captain Barron
was in charge. Parson Eagleson joined them, the chill and
moisture in the air maintaining a steady drip at the end of his
sharp nose.

They filed silently down the path, trying to avoid wet grass
on either side, their heads bowed to the drifting mist banks.
Tristram was behind the third man as they reached the water
side. The tide was well in so they had to watch their step
on the slippery planks leading to the schooner's side.

"Surrender, or be blowed to bits!"

The low cry hit Tristram like a jab in the middle.

He jerked to attention, saw muskets aimed at them from
the deck, saw a party rise from reeds beside the shore to cut
off their one chance of escape.

"See where yer at," jeered the voice as Barron looked around
hastily. "Step along, or you won't be able."

Captain Barron stepped. There was nothing else to do.
No one of them was armed. They had meant to go on with
the work of unloading, not bothering with weapons for an
armed guard had been stationed on the schooner since its
arrival.

"How many does this make?" grinned the lanky woodsman
in charge.

"Thutty-four, Tom. One's a parson, by the look of him.
His hide ought to fetch more."

"Sure it will. Take extry care of him. There's sure to be
a bounty on a snout like he's got."

"Git aboard," snapped an order. "We're floated clear of
mud. Pray for wind, everybody, afore this fog h'ists."

Captain Barron and Parson Eagleson were hustled below to
be jammed into already crowded quarters but Tristram and a
burly oldster were ordered to give a hand with the ropes.
Tristram responded willingly. Anything was better than
getting shoved below before he knew what was going on.

They raised all sail but there was not enough air stirring to take up the slack of wet canvas. Up at the fort sounds of a pair of teamsters arriving with oxen filtered through in a muffled manner as if they were remote. Then carts could be heard rolling down the trail.

A vagrant puff of wind caused the main sail to flap idly. The fog began to swirl and eddy and dissolve. A persevering sun pierced it, and with its arrival enough breeze swung toward the Basin to start the schooner moving sluggishly along the channel.

"Whoa, Buck! Whoa, I tell ye!"

The teamsters' shouts were filled with wonder. The men began running toward the fort, leaving their cattle on the trail. The mist rolled over the upland and revealed an excited group of soldiers emerging from the fort. Their shouting filled the morning. And all the while the schooner was edging its way along the creek.

A party of men came down the slope, headed by an officer. They halted and waited for a cannon, one of the six-pounders, to be trundled down the road. Frantic work rolled it part way and there activity ceased. It was of no avail. The schooner was out of reach.

Tristram gazed at the ruffians about him and wondered when he would see home again. He thought of Delia, and the money in his chest at the fort.

"Ye don't look a soldier," said the nearest rebel.

"I wur doing carpenter work at fort," said Tristram.

"Carpenter, eh. We kin use ye, likely." The man had a twang in his speech. "Ye ought to be proud ye ain't a sojer. Them lads ye left on board here give all their time to a keg of rum they tapped. We could have walked on with lanterns and never been stopped. Most of them is cold sober now, though, hunched down below like coons in a hollow log."

Tristram thought of Colonel Goreham. The party he had sent to Shepody had been taken prisoners in a house, asleep. Here was a worse fix. Captain Barron and two sergeants as well as twenty-odd soldiers. There would not be one hundred and sixty left to hold the fort.

"Ye a Tory?" barked the man called Tom.

"I'm not onything," said Tristram gruffly. "I work where I get paid."

"I told ye that, Tom," said another of the rebels. "Half them at the fort won't fight. They're jist hired to work."

The schooner sailed into the Basin and Tom began shouting orders. Tristram pulled on ropes as he was told, obeyed every order, and was immensely relieved when they changed course and came back to a small river near Amherst village, putting the Fort Lawrence ridge between them and the fort.

Sails were lowered and they anchored near a pole bridge. Four prisoners were taken ashore and marched off to bring drinking water. Another party went for food and returned with loaves of bread, cooked meat and cheese.

"There's a tight lot in that village," swore Tom. "We'll have to make them another visit. They wanted hard cash for every bite we borried. They didn't want to even feed them that's come to give them liberty."

He looked at Tristram. "Git on the bank and make a fire," he said. "Cook us some taters and bile tea. Jim, ye keep an eye on him. He's Yorkshire, and Eddy says ye can't trust one of them."

Tristram built a fire and drove stakes as supports for his pots and kettles. He soon had the food ready. The rebels came ashore in turns and ate on the bank. Then the prisoners were served. Not a person came near from Amherst village.

When it was dark they had a final meal and after the kettles were washed Tristram was ordered back on deck. It had grown chilly and after Tom and a trio went to the village those on guard of the deck served themselves real hookers of rum from the tapped keg. They said it took the chill away, and each had a second mugful. They even offered Tristram an issue, but he refused.

"Do ye mean to say ye don't tech rum?" they demanded. "Then we'll take it for ye as we can't pour it back in the keg." They chuckled at their wit and drank again.

It was an hour later and tongues were wagging freely when Tom and his mates returned and shouted for a plank to be pushed out to the bank.

Tristram grabbed it and ran it out. He had been thinking of what he would do.

"Where have you lads been while we've been freezin' here?" bellowed voices on the schooner. "Is there a tavern open?"

Tristram kept hold of the plank. As it sagged under Tom's weight he twisted and lifted with all his strength. There was a wild yell and tremendous splash. Tom had fallen into the water between the schooner and land.

The other men on the bank shouted for a light. Tristram righted the plank and ran ashore on it. He was there before those on the deck had wits enough to shout for him to stop. A man on the bank loomed before him. Tristram seized him and heaved. There was a second splash. He reached for the plank, pulled it from the schooner and ran away in the dark, found the pole bridge, crossed it and was free on the marsh.

"Halt—you!"

There was plenty of profane shouting from the schooner. Then a musket roared into the night. Tristram heard the ball strike sod somewhere in the darkness. He kept on running. When he was well away from the stream he looked back. Lanterns were bobbing over the schooner's side. Dogs in Amherst, aroused by the musket shot, were barking.

In an hour he was across the marsh and over the Fort Lawrence ridge. Then he wished he had headed for Bathol. There would be no opportunity for the colonel to send men after him. Yet the shame would be with him of his running away, and, most important, was the matter of his money, and wages due him, at the fort. It were better, he decided, to return to the colonel.

Then he thought of the river between him and the fort upland. Eddy's men would be posted at the bridge. It would be better to get wet and muddy than risk capture.

He left the trail and went to his left, took off his shoes and clothing, made them into a bundle and waded into the river channel. The slimy mud was treacherous and when he slipped into icy water he hurled his bundle to the far side. The effort cost him his balance and he went down with a great plopping like a heavy frog.

When he reached dry ground on the far side he pulled handfuls of grass and cleaned himself as best he could. His bundle had reached safety and he dressed, shaking with chill, beside the dyke. He was moving away, beginning to hurry, when he saw the glow of a fire just inside a grove at the foot of the upland.

It was the rebels!

He veered to his left and moved as quietly as possible. The moon was only a dim glow but a thin skimming of clouds slid away and released stars so that the light became stronger. He reached alder clumps and made his way among them, was almost to a spruce wood when dried sticks snapped beneath his tread.

He halted, and listened. He was no longer cold. There was a low call from somewhere in the distance. Startled to action, he hurried to the wood and was pleased to grope his way onto a trail of sorts. It was a path that led from the ridge farms, a cattle road to the marsh. He drove up it at all speed—and crashed solidly into someone coming toward him in full stride.

The impact was terrific. The other man was knocked down and he dropped to his knees. He made no sound but a musket clattered against a stone near him. He grabbed into the darkness, found it, rose with it, gripping it by the barrel. The other person was struggling up, making grunting noises. Tristram swung the musket in a wide sweep.

It struck flesh and bone with a thud that jarred his arms. The man he had hit dropped on the ground, groaning. Smell of him reached Tristram's nostrils. He had encountered an Indian. He threw the musket from him into the bushes and began running.

A dog barked in the distance and soon he could see the outlines of farm buildings. He was near the premises of Sethella Mullins, he reckoned, and made his way to the road.

The sentry who admitted him stared as if he were seeing a ghost.

"How'd you git off the schooner?" he demanded.

"Walked off a plank when they got drunk," said Tristram, feeling important. "I want to see colonel."

He heard the fellow talking behind him as a sergeant took him to Goreham.

"Did ye ever hear sich a damned liar?   Says he walked off the schooner, jist like that.   And it on the way to Boston? There ain't one of them Yorkies acts like they was human."

The colonel paced the floor as he listened to Tristram's account.   "So the men on board were drunk!" he sighed. "After the warnings I gave that sergeant.   Anyway, I'm glad to see you back, and to know where they have the schooner. You are a good man, Crabtree, and I'm glad to have you with me."

IX
The Looters

WHEN a man rode from the fort ridge and said that the rebels had come and were camped three miles away Matthew did not become excited. He went to a corner of his garden and buried there the gold and silver he had in his possession. He smoothed the ground over, burned pea vines on it to hide traces, and went on with his work.

Two days later came rumour that the rebels had captured the supply schooner in a fog and that they had sailed it to the river beside Amherst village. That night he and Gideon kept sharp watch. They heard some shooting in the village but next morning the schooner sailed to the Basin and vanished.

"I reckon that's end o' it," said Matthew.

"Let's ride into the village and see what happened," suggested Gideon.

Sylvia heard him without making comment, but when Matthew gave her a conscience-urged kiss she said. "Tha'll not be long? Thear will be none but Patience here if ony coom."

"Noa," Matthew assured her. "We'll soon be back. Don't tha worry. Ship's gone."

She nodded, watched them ride away, then sat down to finish an apron she was working with a zigzag cross-stitch. It was to be a Christmas gift for Patience. Young Adam had fallen asleep and she was able to have some quiet. She thought of the brush piles that were to be lighted in case of any danger, and wondered if she could carry a brand to the pasture back of Gideon's.

Strange voices outside roused her. She peered out. A group of rough-looking men, armed with muskets and knives, were coming up the path at the rear of the house, and she saw boats they had come in. She went weak for a moment, then bolted the door, picked up young Adam and went up the stairs.

Too late, she remembered the brass kettle on the fire she had just tended. If they looked in the window they would know someone was in the house.

But there was no rapping. There was a coarse hooting outside, some rough jests about poultry in the yard, then a hand lifted the latch.

"What the devil! The door's fastened—and folks callin'? Ain't these Yorkies got any manners? We'll have to teach 'em."

"Teach all ye want," roared a voice. "Git yerself in first."

"Stand away, then. I'll get in."

Sylvia heard the speaker make a little run, then his shoulder hit the door with solid impact and it squealed with splintering shrillness as it tore hand-wrought nails from the bolt hasp out of the jamb, and flew wide open, bumping against the wall.

Sudden anger stiffened her as she saw the damage done, and she went down the stairs. "What are tha doing?" she demanded. "Art tha robbers?"

"Robbers, eh. We-ell, we might be, at that. We're at yer service, though, ma'am, as long as ye keep a civil tongue in yer head, and if ye will tell us where things is kept we'll save ye steps."

"What do tha mean?" she shrilled. The men were staring around her kitchen. They were dreadfully dirty and they smelled little better than Indians.

"Mean, ma'am. Why we're going to help ourselves, don't ye understand, and save ye the trouble of waitin' on us. Ain't that bein' real friendly?"

One man poked at the bake kettle, swung it from place. Sylvia's cat sprang from where it had been lying, arched its back and spit at the intruder. The man tried to pick it up and had himself clawed for his effort. He swore viciously and kicked the cat across the room. It shot out of the door like a black streak and the other men roared their merriment.

The noise woke young Adam. He bawled lustily at sight of the strangers and Sylvia could not soothe him.

"Take the brat outdoors," ordered one of the men. He was pawing into dresser drawers like a curious child.

Sylvia put her baby down, ran to the man and snatched from him the silver forks that had been Aunt Amelia's. "Get from my house," she cried. "Tha art worse than Indians."

The man caught her a slap on the face that threw her against the dresser. Then he kicked her feet from under her so that she dropped heavily to the floor.

"Tame the slut," yelled one of the men delightedly. "We'll get blankets to carry this stuff in."

Sylvia rose slowly from the floor, sickened to agony. Her baby was screeching like mad. Men were coming from the cellar with crocks of butter. Two men picked up Adam's big box cradle and carried it into the yard, child and all.

While they were gone Sylvia reached for Matthew's musket. He kept it loaded and she knew how to attend the priming. She laid the weapon across the table and as the first man entered she pulled trigger.

The explosion was tremendous in the room. The men jumped backward and smoke billowed after them. The ball had nicked one man's arm enough to draw blood.

Men swarmed from the other rooms and the cellar, shouting to know who had been shot. One snatched up Matthew's musket and pulled Sylvia from the table. "Watch out she ain't got a knife," yelled another.

Two men grasped her arms and rushed her outside. She sank to the ground, groaning, as they released her. The hurt man explored his wound, swearing viciously. "I'm goin' to burn this place down around her ears," he yelled. "I've a mind to fasten her and the brat inside."

"No need," offered voices. "Look at her on the ground. She's heavy with calf and. . . ."

"Look! Smoke!"

They stared. A brush heap somewhere in the next field had been fired. Its smoke spiralled high in the still air.

"Sylvia!" They heard a woman cry the name and saw her, also heavy with child, come into the yard and go to the one writhing on the ground. "What have they done?"

"Let 'em be," said a man. "Git the stuff from the house. Like as not that brush fire is a signal."

Matthew and Gideon met Thomas Cutlip, the cobbler, mounted on a black mare. He had sent word to Muncie. The rebels had been at his house the night before, he said, and, not content with taking a ham and his bread, had made foul remarks to his daughter, Ann, who had had to defend herself with a knife.

"Give us twenty men," yelled the cobbler, "and we'll ride over and peg their hides to the ground, the scum."

Matthew's interest was aroused as he listened. He felt that Shubell Cutlip's sister must have courage, though he remembered her as deaf and going always with a bonnet over her ears so that she would not catch cold.

They lingered, talking, until they saw Obed Muncie riding with a dozen men. Each carried a rifle or musket. "Look yonder," they shouted. "What's the smoke?"

Matthew swung about, saw a column of smoke rolling lazily into the air. "It's Gid's brush heap!" he shouted, and kicked his horse into a run.

They thundered along the cart trail in a string. Then Matthew shouted with rage. His house was on fire. Flames licked from every window. They saw men about it. Some were pointing and yelling, as if amused. Others were tying up bundles on the ground.

Matthew was like a madman, but neither he nor Gideon were armed. When he saw Sylvia on the ground, with Patience beside her, and saw young Adam wailing in his cradle, he gave no heed to the shouts of rebels who pointed muskets at him.

"Sylvia, lass!" he cried, leaping from his horse.

"Quick, Matthew," gasped Patience. "Carry her to our house."

He knew the worst from her tone and rage swept over him so blackly that he could scarcely see where he went, but he picked his wife up and carried her along the path between the farms, Patience following him with the baby.

"Kill," he shouted at Gideon. "Don't tha let one get away."

The looters were bunched like dogs facing a larger enemy. They had dropped their bundles and crocks and tubs, and a leader stood in front of them.

"Stop where ye are," he shouted. "We're the Army of Freedom."

"Army of dogs!" bellowed Gideon. "You're a cowardly pack of squaw men. Git off this farm afore we send ye to the devil."

Every man with Gideon slid to the ground and made ready for action. The looters looked at each other. Their leader stooped to take up a bundle he had put down.

"Noa, tha don't." Cutlip aimed his musket. "Not a skunk will take a thing wi' him. Get from here."

The men began backing away, edging toward the river. The man who had been shot was last to go.

Matthew came running into the yard. He was near before the rebels saw him. He struck the cat-clawed man full in face, knocking him backward so that he dropped his musket. Then he grappled the man who had been wounded, throwing him to earth like a child.

A third ran to help. Matthew seized him, wrenched his musket from him, swung it about without aiming and pulled the trigger. The weapon missed fire. In that heart beat the raiders started to run. Matthew clubbed the musket, then hurled it after them. The whirling butt struck a man and sent him sprawling. Cutlip yelled and fired. His shot struck earth beside a looter.

"Look, Matthew," yelled Gideon. "Your pig pen roof!"

A blazing brand had alighted on it. Matthew climbed on the low roof. Someone brought water from the well and after brisk action the blaze was extinguished.

The looters were running for their boats. The Yorkshiremen watched them go, then returned to help Matthew. Water was raised and buckets brought from Gideon's were filled. When the house chimney fell, taking down the roof and walls, there was no further danger. There was saved the loot dropped in the yard and Adam's box cradle.

Someone fetched O'Conner from the village. The doctor worked as if his own life were at stake. Finally he came to the door and spoke with Matthew.

"Be quiet as ye can," he warned. "Don't excite her in any way. She's had a bad time and her baby's dead. I'll stay the night and if she wants ye, I'll call."

It was the next morning before he let Matthew see Sylvia, and Matthew went in on his toes, as quietly as he could. He knelt by the bed and kissed Sylvia's feverish cheek. "It's cruel hard on thee, lass," he groaned. "Will tha forgive me for leaving thee?"

"Thear is nowt to forgive," she said weakly. "I love thee more than ever."

She seemed too limp to say more. Tears ran down her cheeks and he wiped them away, clumsily. After a time he kissed her again, and left the room.

He took his musket and powder horn and bullet pouch from the barn where he had put them. The musket was one the looters had left behind and better than his own. The bullet pouch and the horn he had found wrapped in looted blankets. No one saw him go. He walked down his field and kept from the road. By night he had found a man in the village who would risk rowing him to the fort and they set out as soon as it was dark.

The man put him ashore at a point beyond the creek mouth and Matthew made his way over wet grass and stubble to the fort.

"I've coom," he said to the colonel, "to handle a musket wi' thy soldiers. They've burned me oot and murdered my babe afore it wur born. I know t' man that sent them to my house and I'll settle wi' him if I do nowt else."

"They're a bad lot," agreed the colonel. "We're glad to have you."

"A devil named Meekins is worst o' t' lot," said Matthew doggedly.

He slept until noon, then Tristram wakened him and showed him where to get a dinner. He told of the burning of his house and Tristram listened with horror strong on his features. "I hope tha catch Meekins," he said.

His sympathy warmed Matthew. There was a call for men to make repairs on the fort ditches and Matthew worked with vigour. At night he thought of Sylvia, then his mind began calculating his loss by the fire. He was trying to remember how many crocks of butter there had been in the cellar when he fell asleep.

X
In the Fog

THE REBELS had no stomach for fighting. They made two half-hearted night attacks, fired buildings outside the ground and sniped at extreme range at night. Tristram used a musket and became accustomed to quick loading. He had been put in charge of the Yorkshire men and was amazed to find Shubell Cutlip among them. Shubell treated him with a mixture of contempt and friendliness, but he was one of a party that offered to go with Tristram and a sergeant to visit the farmhouse of Sethella Mullins. It was within cannon shot and the gaunt widow had refused to leave.

A dozen men went boldly down her lane, the sergeant saying he had been there often in the summer, that the widow had a wit refreshing as hot toddy and an uncanny knack of raising turkeys.

Sethella answered their rapping. She said some of the rebels had visited her but that they seemed afraid of her dog and soon left. She thanked the sergeant for his interest in her welfare.

A thick fog drifted in from the Basin overnight and in the morning was like a blanket. Water beaded on the fort pickets, dripped from the eaves. Men shivered as they stood sentry. Tristram rose early and walked about, uneasy, listening.

He had sickened of fort life. The constant alert against attack, the varying rumours, Matthew's bitterness and Shubell's indifference frayed his nerves. He hated the inaction. He detested the discipline. He despised the majority of the rag-tag weaklings and drifters serving as garrison. Each day he worried about his farm and Delia,

282

cursing the impulse that had led him to sign the colonel's papers.

Some odd noises came from the fog. Tristram started. "Thear is summat bothering t' cattle," he said to a sergeant. "Will tha coom wi' me to have a look?"

The mist made all sounds unreal. Even the crowing of a rooster over at Sethella's farm had an eerie quality. They slipped out of a gate and were hardly away from it before they heard a voice cursing a stupid steer. Eddy's men were there all right, trying to drive the fattened fort cattle from hay stacks just outside the defences.

Tristram hurried back with the information. The colonel said he was afraid it might be an ambush. He sent a party with a captain in charge and warned them to be on the watch for treachery.

Thirty men were in the force. They went out at a jog, their boots squelching wetly in the soaked grass. Tristram stood with Matthew, listening. There were sudden shots. Then a burst of shouting. Another rattle of fire. A steer bellowed as if in pain.

"Get another party ready," ordered the colonel. "We've got to back those men." He looked at Tristram. "You Yorkshiremen ought to be good with cattle," he said. "Will you go?"

"Aye," exclaimed Matthew. "I'm ready now." He had his musket with him, freshly primed. Tristram nodded, and hurried to fetch his own weapon. The party was formed when he returned and he fell in at the rear as they went from the gate.

They passed the stacked hay, men swearing as they slipped in fresh cattle droppings. Legs were soon wet to the knee. Suddenly there was shooting to their right and they could see a distance. The fog was lessening.

A trio of steers galloped into view, tails over their backs, racing back to the stacks from which they had been driven. There was more shooting. They could see men running on the slope above the marsh, headed towards a clump of alders that fringed the low ground.

"Run, lads," shouted an officer. "I think we have some of them cut off."

Cattle were facing in every direction. The rebels were retreating toward the woods on the far right, making but a small show of resistance. The first party was trying to get ahead of them, and were shooting and reloading as they ran. Far down the slope, beside the marsh, a dozen rebels still tried to herd some steers ahead of them.

Tristram ran in their direction. Anger hustled him when he saw that two of the cattle were red and white steers he had fattened.

"I see t' red devil!"

The shout came from behind him, and Tristram recognized Matthew's voice. Then his brother ran past him, making terrific pace for a heavy man. Soon he was ahead of everyone else in the party.

Tristram tried to follow Matthew but his legs were too stiffened with hard labour. The party began to break up, some men running toward the first group, others chasing lone rebels who were ducking from view among the alders. Watching as he ran, Tristram finally saw Peter Meekins. The young man's flaming red hair was unbound and he was hatless. He was chasing cattle and he could run faster than any of the others.

The parties became more separated. There was a brisk exchange of shots as the rebels drew near the woods. Tristram slowed his running. He saw one rebel drop his musket and fall forward, pressing his arms across him as if he were seized with colic. Another slid to his knees and rested there a moment in a most difficult pose, then toppled over. A soldier near Tristram threw down his musket. "I'm hit," he yelled. "In my shoulder."

The captain in charge of the first party began shouting to his sergeants. They signalled a retreat. Men stopped running and looked around. A rebel fell near the marsh and rolled in the grass. Meekins ran to him, looked at him briefly, then shook his fist at the nearest soldiers.

Tristram took quick aim and fired at him—his first shot. Meekins turned and ran. "Get him, Matthew," Tristram shouted, not knowing where Matthew was, and running as he shouted.

He stopped to reload, dropped his ramrod in his hurry, fumbled with his powder. He adjusted his priming, looked for a target. Something struck him hard in the ankle, knocked his leg from under.

He fell forward, dropping his musket, and sprawled on his face in the wet grass. Red-hot pain shot through his leg, lanced upward into his body. He rose to his hands and knees, and fell back. The pain was too great. It sickened him. He tried again, wondering what had happened. Agony seared him. He collapsed in the grass.

For a moment he lay wholly still, his heart pumping loudly, his senses whirling. Pain seemed to eddy in his body, reaching all over him. His leg was on fire.

Finally he gripped the grass and pulled himself into a sitting position. Every move hurt him. He stared about him, dumbfounded. It was incredible. Not a man was in sight, rebel or otherwise. There were a few steers out on the marsh. Nothing else could be seen. The only sound was the faraway barking of a dog. And the fog was thickening again.

Another period of dizziness put him flat on the sod and when it had passed the torture in his leg was exquisite. He groaned and was sick. After a while he felt for the wound, managed to roll down his thick grey stocking, twisted about and had a look.

He groaned deeply. A musket ball had smashed his ankle so that his foot was turned inward. His shoe was filled with blood but the bleeding had slowed to a small seeping. It was the ugliest wound he had ever looked at and his pain took on the rhythm of his pulse, a steady throbbing.

He had another dizziness and when he recovered he was shaking like a chilled horse. No one had come to look for him. He raised on his hands and knees and began crawling.

Each time he moved his shattered ankle he perspired. Some steers came from the marsh. He heard their hoofs on the sod near him. They came through the fog, snorting and blowing when they found him, then ran off. Something dark blocked his way. It was one of the rebels. A bullet had torn a hole in his neck.

Tristram rested. He was tired in a way he had never been tired before. His exhaustion made him stupid. He lay beside the corpse for some time before he rose to crawl on. Dully he noticed the dead man's shabby breeches, brass buttons sewn on a homespun jacket, a belt of rawhide, a knife in a sheath. Finally he saw there was a flask in the jacket pocket.

It was an effort to tug the flask from place. He pulled the cork with his teeth, tilted the neck to his mouth and let a fiery liquor gurgle between his lips. It eased some of the torture in his leg, gave him strength. He probed the pocket again, found a packet smelling of rank tobacco, a rag soaked in sweet oil for cleaning a rifle. There was a handkerchief, too, holding a taint of green soap, and it made him think of fresh-washed clothes on a line in a whipping wind. He wondered where the fellow had stolen it.

A voice muttered complaint about the cold and wet. As he listened he heard it shouting for some one to come, and was amazed to discover it was himself who called. He had another drink from the flask, tried to crawl again, and slumped to the grass, unconscious.

Sharp pain restored him. He was being carried and each jolt set liquid fire leaping through him. "I thowt tha wur at fort," Matthew was saying. "I didn't miss thee till dinner. Is't hurting bad?"

"Aye," groaned Tristram. "I thowt tha would never coom."

He scarcely knew when they carried him in at the fort gate. There was still a mist in the air, and smoke from the barracks chimneys swirled low, mingling with odors of boiling meat and baking bread. They placed him on straw in quarters that had a fireplace, beside other wounded men.

One man moaned continually but Tristram was in a coma. They had bandaged his leg as best they could but the pain was overpowering, and the next day a surgeon who arrived with reinforcements was summoned by the colonel. He had one look at the smashed ankle. Then he called in a pair of stout helpers and made a quick amputation. It was crudely done but Tristram pulled through.

XI

The Woollen Text

THE DAYS that followed were, to Tristram, a life time. An orderly told him that a schooner had brought two companies of soldiers from Windsor, and that the rebels had been scattered to the four winds, but he gave scant heed. His flesh had burned from him in the first days of his suffering and he lay as if he had lost the power of speech, eating what he could of the food brought him, asking nothing, saying nothing.

Cattle by the fort stacks bawled dismally in the increasing cold. Some of the soldiers became drunk each night and wrangled with each other. A flock of geese in Sethella's field trumpeted noisily when the day was still. Sleet and rain came with a thaw and set the eaves dripping, the roof to leaking. But he remained mute.

Lancelot came with a cart and moved him from the barracks to Sethella's house, arranged with Sethella for his meals and her attention, and induced the fort doctor to promise he would attend the ankle dressings each day. But Tristram would not talk with Lancelot. Neither would he talk to Gideon when the big man visited him.

They had taken his foot and he was a cripple for life. The thought swung around to meet him in all his pondering. It dominated him. It gnawed at his courage. It held him in a depressed mood as evil as an illness. Everything he had tried to do had turned against him. He defied any man to prove it were not so.

Each day after Sethella brought him his breakfast she built a cheerful fire in his room, and tried to set him to talking. It

287

was useless. He would grunt responses to her questioning and stare at the ceiling.

In his mind he went back to the days at Banfield when his father's thinking had become impaired and he had taken charge. The seeding he had supervised, the hoeing, weeding, harvesting, the prices he had obtained at market, the praise his mother had given him on Sunday mornings when they would sit and review the week's work.

It came to him that his mother had not had much out of life. She had worked hard. She had kept a close watch of every expenditure. She had nagged her sons and husband to greater effort. But they had not grieved when she died. They had come to Nova Scotia knowing she would have fought such a move to the last. Life did not add up. It did not seem worth while.

Sethella increased her efforts to cheer him. She never let her half-wit son enter the room and she would talk to him an hour, any time he would listen, about the tricks of getting good growth from any kind of seed. She explained the need of warming buckwheat before sowing, and the corn one could grow by placing a handful of hardwood ashes and a smelt in each hill.

"Smelts rot easy," she told him, "and fish soft-rotted is the best manure you can put in the ground."

She freshed his room with vigorous sweepings, changed his pillow and hung a sampler by his bed. It was worked in coloured wool and the text bothered him. It read: "If your heart is wrong the world is against you."

"Eddy raised more trouble than a plague around here," declared Sethella, "and this part of the world's ag'in him, and will be. He don't dast ever come back to his home. They've got some that were with him in Halifax jail. Others were sickened in the Shepody woods, with only Injuns to tend them."

Each day she brought him some tidbit of rumour, and when nothing else would stir him she repeated her story of feeding her dog to a Maine sergeant. Tristram appreciated the tale more than anything else she told him. The sergeant had taken her winter's supply of butter and some of her poultry. One night she let her dog out and prowling rebels killed it while the sergeant sat in her kitchen.

"He said he'd come back the next night for a decent meal, and I said I'd have him one." Sethella's bony features would look less grim as she recited. "I got the dog from the barn-yard where they left it, and cooked it for 'em. Three came with him, and they four cleaned the meat till there was nothing left but bones. It weren't long afore they left, and the next night one of the men came over. 'What was it the sarg'int et?' he wanted to know. 'Dog,' I says. 'The one his men killed.' 'Gosh a'mighty,' he says. 'They're all sick.' 'Shouldn't wonder,' I says. 'I never did know what that dog et.'"

The wool text was on the wall where the first daylight touched it. He could read it before he could see the door latch or the stool by his bed. Some days he tried to ignore it but usually he stared at it with defiance. He did not let on to Sethella that the text irritated him; he did not mention it at all.

When he grew stronger and his leg healed he made a crutch with a rest for his knee which he padded well with wool, and he began moving about on it until he learned to tuck it under his arm and balance himself while he used both hands. He began doing little chores outside. The fort doctor made a final examination and said the stump had healed perfectly. Tristram was somewhat encouraged. He made Sethella a table which she said was worth all her work of attending him.

He had some callers on Sundays. People from the nearest farm came over to ask curious questions about his stump. Healey visited him. O'Conner came to criticize the amputation. One day Shubell Cutlip walked in. He flushed at Tristram's lack of response to his greeting.

"I've thowt o' thee lying here," said Shubell, "and coom to tell thee I'm sorry we had trouble. Will tha shake hands and forget?"

Tristram stared at the wall, and the text seemed to quiver. He put out his hand with a decent grip and said there would be no hard feelings.

"Tha did good work," said Shubell.   "T' colonel says tha would make a champion soldier."

His words cheered Tristram more than anything Sethella had said.   He began to regard his misfortune as a contribution to his country, and decided it would be an advantage in his getting rid of Delia's brother.   His wound was more serious than Donald's.   Surely the fellow would not stay with a man who had been crippled in battle.

His first move was to Amherst Point.   When he had rested there he rode home on Matthew's horse, Gideon going along with him to take the nag back.   He had his crutch slung to a rawhide over his shoulder, and felt quite a man again when he was mounted.

Delia met him quietly, her glance going to his stump in spite of herself.   "I couldn't leave the children," she said, "else I'd been to nurse ye."

Jackie peered at him shyly but Jeannie came to him with a rush.   "I don't care if ye have both feet off," she cried. "I'll love ye just the same."

He showed them how he could use his crutch, then kissed Delia.   "Tha have been good wife," he said.   "I knew things would do wi' thee to tend."

It was the highest praise he had ever given her, and delight shone on her face while he visited the stable and pens and sheds, observing how neatly they were kept, and how saving she had been with firewood.   Donald stood in the background. He offered no sympathy and he gave Tristram no more than a civil greeting.   He looked more gaunt and morose than ever.

"I thank thee for staying wi' Delia while I wur away," said Tristram.   "Now I've coom home to stay."

"Ye should," said Donald drily.   "Ye'll not do much running aroond wi' that stump."

Gideon rested his horses, then rode over to Lancelot's for the night.   "Man," he boomed, as he was leaving, "anybody with a crew like you have will get along.   It's worth havin' a foot shot off to have wimmen folk soft on you at home."

He rode away and Delia began getting supper ready. Tristram thought he had never tasted better beef stew.

They sat around the fire in the evening and he told them about the fight for the cattle.

"Hoo mony men did ye lose?" demanded Donald.

"Three, wi' myself," said Tristram.

"Then," snorted Donald, "ye saw no real fight. We lost a hundred in one morning, and half them died. Did ye kill a rebel?"

"I wur not signed on for soldier," said Tristram harshly, and he would not say more about it.

It was hard enough, though, to hold his peace while Donald sat and smoked his pipe in a smug manner as if he had won the argument. Still, it was worth keeping quiet. Delia was his loyal wife, no doubt of that; there was equally no doubt that she was loyal to her brother. A man with one foot off could never hope to get another woman to live with him, so Tristram put his thoughts together and curbed his temper.

When they were going to bed Delia patted his arm. "Tristram," she said modestly, using his name as if she liked it. "I've news for ye. I'm wi' child."

He stared at her as if he had not heard, then great jubilance welled into one of his infrequent smiles. "Thee have given me best word," he said gently, "I have ever heard spoken."

XII

The Sail Boat

LANCELOT settled more snugly in the hay of a barn behind the house Eddy was using as his headquarters. It was a mow directly over the stable for horses. He had slit a neat hole in the boards with his knife and could see every person arriving at the house. There seemed to be more callers than Eddy wanted. Some of the unwanted ones were irate farmers, furious about having their cellars raided by Maine woodsmen.

"Do one more errand for us," the colonel had begged at the fort. "Find out when there's to be another attack. If we can get a messenger to Windsor we'll have reinforcements in jig time, but it's the next few days that worry me most. Will you try?"

Lancelot had hoped to get home to June, but he promised to do what he could. Luck had been with him in the night and he had reached the barn unobserved.

Peter Meekins rode into the yard with some young men of his own sort, and Lancelot thrilled. Here was the man the Yorkshiremen were blaming for the burning of Matthew's house.

"Any word of attack?" shouted Meekins as a man came from the house.

"None." The man spoke as if he did not care who heard him. "It's my honest belief that they'll never make one."

"Then we'll go and take the fort ourselves." The young men began laughing at Meekins. "The British in that old tumble-down are shaking in their shoes. There aren't a dozen good men in the fort. What's the matter?"

"Far as I can make out," roared back the answer, "all that

come are a bunch of bloody thieves, with no stomach for fighting."

A door was flung open and Eddy stepped outside. "No more of that," he cried sharply. "You're talking treason to our cause, man. I've told you that we can't do anything on bright moonlight nights. In less than two weeks we'll make the attack, and we'll take the fort. You fellows in this district have been small help. If we had two hundred good men to help us instead of half that number we could do something."

"You'd have twice as many as you've got," Eddy's bluster could not scare the farmer who faced him, "if ye'd been able to handle the mob ye brought. Who the devil's going to stand for having his cellar robbed and his wife insulted by them supposed to be on his side? Another week of what's been going on and you'll have the ones you've got now turned against you."

"You're plain speaking." Eddy closed the door as if he did not want those inside to hear him, "and I'll be the same. If you and others of your kidney don't back me up you'll not have houses to rob. I've been hard put to hold the Indians in check."

The farmer stared. "Jonathan Eddy. Do you mean to stand there and try to frighten decent folks with Indians? If ye do, man, you've lost the respect of every neighbour you had, and I'll tell ye more. I've fought Injuns afore, and can again, and no bloody talk like you're handing out will change me."

He jumped to the back of his horse stiffly, swung about on his stomach and kicked a leg down each side of the nag to get upright.

"The best thing ye can do," he added with plenty of acid, "is head this crowd you brought back to where they come from, and wait till you can bring a decent army good men will want to help."

Eddy made no reply and the man rode out of the yard. Meekins had untied his horse from the hitching post. "Say the word," he urged, "and we'll soon change that old rooster's mind."

"No." Eddy shook his head. "Let him be. We're making more enemies than friends through some of the work you've done. Who are watching that no messengers get through to Windsor?"

"We've ten men watching the river, and Injuns on the marsh."

"Indians?"

"We had to use them. White men'd freeze out there at night."

"But we can't depend on Indians. I'm surprised at you. If a sail boat gets away in the Basin we're finished. Have our own lads out there tonight."

Meekins shook his head. "They won't go and you might as well know it. Fact is, a lot of them are growling about getting no pay. It's colder'n the devil out by the dykes."

Eddy entered the house without another word, slamming the door behind him.

"He's got his dander up," grinned Meekins. "He doesn't like the truth. I hope he didn't think I'd go out there tonight. There ain't a man in the fort with guts enough to try and get to Windsor."

"Yup," agreed one of the young men. "A couple tried, with a dugout. They were scared to death when we caught 'em."

"Come in the barn and have a nip," invited Meekins. "I know where there's a jug hid in the straw. Leastways some of them think it's hid."

Lancelot heard them enter the barn, and listened. "I've a mind," boasted one, "to go to the fort and offer to take a letter to Windsor. They'd pay well, which is more'n Eddy'll do. There's a sail boat by the creek mouth and I'd have her out in the Basin and around to Windsor by this time tomorrow."

"Ye mean ye'd try," jeered a voice. "Them's Maccan Injuns at that post. They know about that boat good as you do. Ye'd have yer hair lifted, 'stead of sailin' the boat."

"He wouldn't need to fear," broke in Meekins' scornful tone. "Them Injuns is just about quittin.' They'll be gone home any time."

The group argued and sang. Presently they filed out of the barn and headed for the house. "We'll dinner here," bragged Meekins. "We're good as any Maine hay shakers."

Lancelot slid from the mow and stole out at the rear of the stable. It was a short distance to the woods and no sentry was posted there. No one gave any heed to a man walking with a rifle on his arm. He reached the woods and long before dark he was back at the fort, making his report.

"If someone will coom wi' me tonight," he offered, "I will have them away in t' boat at high tide. I know t' Indians."

Three men volunteered. They set out at dark with Lancelot leading the way. There was a slight mist and the air was clammy with chill. At the marsh Lancelot kept well in advance and found a path leading to the dyke. The men at the barn had said the sail boat was pulled well in from the shore, on rollers, and its mast had been removed.

The rank grass dripped with moisture. They could hear the lapping of water as it entered tide channels, and dank exhalations reached their nostrils. Lancelot watched a musk-rat climb a bank, wander along it, then move toward the incoming tide. It was clear that no Indians were there.

The sail boat was at the mouth of a small reedy creek. He followed along the dyke until he smelled smoke, then went on boldly enough until a head and shoulders loomed above the grass and an Indian ordered him to stop.

There was no mistaking the voice. It belonged to Tomas, the brave who had accompanied Joe Paul during their first hunting trip. Lancelot gave him a greeting in Micmac, climbed over the dyke and found a small fire around which a trio of redmen squatted.

"Is Joe Paul here?" he queried.

"No," grunted Tomas. "He's gone home." He put his musket down and piled more wood on the fire. A green ox hide was staked around the windy side of the blaze to prevent sparks being blown about, and to retain heat for the squatters.

"Hoam? To Maccan?"

"Yes," shrugged Tomas. "Many go."

"I'm glad," said Lancelot. "T' English are cooming in ships so I coom to tell him not to be wi' t' Americans. Else he will be blamed for making trouble. No Indian will have trouble if he is at Maccan."

In the glow of the fire he could see the Indian faces plainly. They were utterly unreadable, blank and closed and grim.

"Thear are many ships," he added. Tomas muttered the news to his mates. They talked rapidly a moment then relapsed into grim silence.

"We are taking t' sail boat now," continued Lancelot, "to meet t' ships."

Tomas glanced at him. Lancelot took from his pocket a packet of tobacco he had secured from the fort stores.

"Divide this wi' others," he said, "and tha better go hoam."

The Indian accepted the tobacco eagerly. "We friends," he grunted.

Lancelot went back to the three men and led them to the boat. "Don't tha look at dyke," he warned. "Tha can get away afore they change their mind."

They stepped the mast into place and rigged up the sail, fumbling a long time with ropes in the darkness and using a heavy wooden bailing scoop to clear out rain water. They made sure the tiller was in working order. It was impossible to move without noise. They had to pound wedges in place to hold the mast. But no Indian came near.

Water-logged poles served as rollers and the craft was pushed to the water. It stuck in the muddy bank but Lancelot used a timber as a lever and got them afloat. The men hoisted sail and the wind caught them. They called a low farewell and headed out into the Basin.

Lancelot walked back to the dyke. The fire had been kicked apart. No voice greeted him. The green ox hide had been taken away. There was not an Indian to be seen. He stared into the darkness over the marsh and grinned. Then he slapped his rifle under his arm and started at a stiff jog to get warm. He would reach a farmer's barn at Fort Lawrence and sleep in the hay the rest of the night. Then he would go to Gideon's for his horse and ride home.

XIII
Three Women Alone

MELODY'S flaming hair fell over her shoulders, shimmering in the firelight, and her eyes were tender with sleepy love. She was watching John thread a needle and she was proud of his skill with his fingers. John was a man, she felt, of the type all women wanted, at once masculine and gentle.

"Tha art clever," she said, yawning. "Will tha ever go to bed?"

"Soon as I'm finished stitching this moccasin," he said, and a grin walked slowly across his mouth.

"Tha art stubborn," she said, with more pride than reproach. "I'll fix it in morning."

She scanned him appraisingly. He was a big man, blond of hair and brown of skin. When he smiled little wind lines crinkled at the corners of his blue eyes and made him look curiously young.

It was well, she thought, that he was stubborn, if he were to be a farmer. Farming was a risk and a man needed stiff-necked faith in himself and his judgment to stand against the hazards of a settler's life. Once a man began to be uncertain he would be a failure.

There was a shuffling of feet outside the door, startling her so that she barely smothered a cry. June and Judy had been to bed an hour and it was late. A hand knocked in timid fashion and John opened the door.

"Ma's got cramps," said a boy's voice. "She wants to know if you'll come over."

It was one of the Garrison youngsters, a lanky lad sprouting surprisingly from his cowhide shoes.

"John, that's first call tha've had to doctor." Melody thrilled to his importance. "Tha had better take over herbs tha fetched from Amherst."

When he was gone with the boy Melody went to bed. It would be that way many times, she reflected, but it was something above the average to be a doctor, and she was sure John would be a good one.

She was not nervous as she blew out the tallow dip. Some women in the settlement barred their doors and lay at night with straining ears and nerves, imagining furtive hands were trying the latch, but she was not one of them. None of the invaders had come to Bathol. It was remote from the war.

It was the next day that the looters visited River Hebert. A man came riding for John, and Melody marveled that word of him had reached so far. He was an oldish chap with quaint manners, doffing his hat when Melody opened the door and extending his hand. She shook it readily but his fingers were hard and dry and cold like a turkey's foot. He said two men in the river settlement had rebel bullets in them and a doctor might save them.

Melody was glad that John had brought a probe and lancet in his small packet of instruments. She made him a hot meal, fed the man who had come for him, and watched them ride away. He said he would not be home until the next day, and maybe not until the evening.

It would be a good thing, Melody decided, to ride over and see Mrs. Garrison. The big woman had recovered from her cramps but she seemed nervous. She wiped her fire-reddened face with the hem of her apron and put out her hand but her shake was limp as if she cared nothing for the custom. "It's dull weather," she said. "Our taters ain't keeping good."

Her husband tried to be cheerful. He poked at the fire and began making talk about his youth. He said he had had forty days of schooling and spoke of it as, Melody thought, Noah might speak of the forty days of flood. Then his wife began fiddling with hairs at the back of her neck. She seemed to be scratching around in her mind for correct words of some statement she wanted to make.

"What is tha have on mind?" blurted Melody, while a slow fear moved, small yet distinct, somewhere within her.

"Ma!" protested Gabriel. "Don't you. . . ."

Mrs. Garrison no longer looked as if she were trying to clamp on words that weren't handy. Her flush had faded and left her flour-white. "I wouldn't be Christian," she said, "if I didn't tell you same as I'd want you to tell me. I know your man's gone but I can't help it. Melody, there's skulkers 'round."

"It's like as not she's 'magined 'em," put in Gabriel. "I didn't see a sign of them myself." He wrinkled his brow, visibly bringing his intellect to bear upon the problem.

"It don't make any diff'rence what you saw," said Mrs. Garrison, shaking her head. "I seen 'em. But I can't let Gabe go over. All we can do is pray nothin' will happen."

Melody rode home at once. She discovered that she was trembling all over, like a wet dog. She put Annabelle in the stable and forced herself to explore all the sheds and outbuildings. No skulkers were there. Then she took down John's rifle from its rack. "I'm walking oop t' hill," she said to June, trying to be casual. "Happen I'll see moose."

June nodded, paying little heed as she busied herself with baking a pudding, but Judy turned from her chores and said she, too, would walk up the hill.

"Have they coom?" she asked quietly when they were outside.

"It could be," said Melody, and she told her, briefly, of Mrs. Garrison's alarm.

They went up the hill and peered into woods openings as if they were looking for a beast that had strayed. It was very still under the trees and Melody felt a prickly sensation creeping up her back as they returned to the house. Judy was calm but said, softly, before they went into the house. "Thear is summat in bush. I can feel eyes watching."

June had become an excellent cook but Melody had no appetite for supper. Judy made more pretense of eating, and at last it was dusk, the outside chores were finished and they had lighted the candles. Three women together, June said, laughing, were poor company, and if they did not mind she would go to bed. She liked to lay there and think of Lancelot coming home, she said.

Melody smiled brightly and said goodnight. Then she replenished the fire and sat in the shadows so that she could watch the windows. The room was warm and neither woman spoke. Soon she began dozing at intervals, rousing with starts, thinking she had heard someone outside.

"Noa," said Judy, watching her. "Thear has been nowt."

A stick fell to embers and Melody, watching the window, saw a face rise into view. One heart beat it was there; the next it was gone.

The nails of her clenched hands dug into her palms as she sat. Strength seeped from her, left her helpless.

"Tha saw someone?" breathed Judy.

Melody managed to nod. "At window," she whispered.

Judy stood and reached for John's rifle. She opened the door and walked outside as if she were to deal with some vermin disturbing the barnyard fowl. For a moment Melody could not move, then she found her feet and followed Judy.

There was a weak moon and the sky was sprinkled with stars but all objects were indistinct. A cold wind came from the intervales as they stood by the end of the house, and Melody coughed. She tried to muffle the sound by putting her mouth to her jacket sleeve but the spasm shook her. Then Judy pointed.

"Someone is by elms," she murmured. "Tha stay here."

Melody could not have gone had she wished. The situation was too tense. She saw Judy walk to the trees, her rifle raised as a man would do, heard her speak with challenge.

A figure glided forth, and gave her low answer. Then Judy came back to her. "It's t' Indian, Joe Paul. He wur looking for Lancelot."

"Joe!" Melody grasped his arm. "What do tha want wi' him?"

"Me no longer with Eddy men," said Joe. "Many come from them. We are back at our camp. We are your friend." He smiled so that she could see his teeth in the darkness. "Me sorry to look in window. Sartin would not if Joe knew you 'lone. Joe go now. Come back soon, one day, two day, for hunt with Lancelot.''

They watched him go with his cat-like tread, then they went to the house. "Judy," quavered Melody, "I was so feared I could do nowt. Tha art champion.''

"Noa," said Judy tightly. "It would not matter if summat happened to me, but wi' thee it is different.'' Then the emotions she had pent too long erupted. Judy bowed her head to her knees and wept with such abandon that Melody was hard put to quiet her.

When she did Judy sat back with decision. "Tha have been kinder to me than ony other,'' she said. "Thear is summat I want to tell thee.''

It was the story of the gold coins she had found by the stub's roots, and when she had finished her tale Melody was strongly stirred. Where the money had come from she could not guess. She recalled Tristram's talking of gold he had had, and knew that if he had buried it the money was not rightly his.

"T' money is for thee," she said firmly. "Don't tha tell ony other. If it wur put thear by father I know he would want tha to have it. He wur fond o' thee and tha wur kinder to him than most.''

XIV

The Reckoning

MATTHEW was vastly disappointed when Meekins escaped him on the morning of the fight for the cattle. His desire for vengeance was doubled after the doctor had removed Tristram's foot.

When the soldiers arrived from Windsor he was anxious to be in the attack. It was decided that an attempt would be made to surprise Eddy's forces before dawn the next morning. The men were given a thumping big supper of hot beef and potatoes, topped off with a hearty tot of rum. At five o'clock they were on the move, having eaten a hasty breakfast in the dark.

There had been a sharp frost and old grass was slippery underfoot. Matthew got extra slices of beef from Ezra's wife, and a half loaf of bread. No one could say where they would be by noon.

The surprise was a failure. Cattle were disturbed in the bush and their rush to the open woke men sleeping near Eddy's farmhouse. A musket was fired. Its report set dogs to barking, then the attack was on.

Matthew advanced without hurry. It was too dark to see clearly and he had become separated from his fellows. When he reached a farm men were back of a fence, shooting at the house.

One man had gone through a gap where bars were let down. He was lying on his back a few yards on, still gripping his musket, his face turned upward, dead. Someone fired from the house and the ball struck a fence rail, breaking it in half. A soldier fired in return and Matthew heard the bullet thud solidly into house timbers. No one spoke. Some hens

302

fluttered about the yard. A pig squealed discordantly in its pen.

A door of the barn was opened from the inside. There was a shot from the house immediately. Then cattle rushed into the yard, a pair of oxen and a horse. A curl of smoke issued from the barn eaves, became larger every minute. Soon smoke poured from the door, thick and grey.

"It's going to rain by night," remarked one of the soldiers by the fence. "It always does when smoke hangs low that way."

The smell of burning grain permeated the morning. The horses snorted in fright and galloped away on a cart trail. Steam rose from the frost-wet barn roof and smoke mingled with it. A party of rebels burst from a window at the back of the house and ran desperately for cover.

Matthew stood up and fired. The muskets along the fence erupted a ragged volley. Two of the running men went down. One stayed still. The other sat up and held his leg with his hands. None of his mates looked back.

The barn roof burst into flames and the crackling noises of the fire filled the air. Matthew reloaded, and found himself alone. The soldiers had gone along through the pasture in pursuit of the fugitives. One of them had taken the musket of the wounded man.

"I'm bleedin'," he groaned when Matthew approached him. "Give a hand, will ye? There must be some rags in the house. Get me a sheet, anything. Don't let a body lie here and die."

"Tha should have stayed at thy hoam," said Matthew severely, "and thear would be no need o' bleeding." A woman came from the house. Two children followed her, both whimpering with fright. She knelt by the rebel and began bandaging his leg.

The fighting had spread more than a mile along the settlement. Smoke from another burning building billowed upward to hide the first sunlight. Scattered shooting sounded from many directions but there did not seem to be any organized battle. Matthew went on slowly. The cleared fields were smaller and he judged they belonged to Acadians.

A prolonged burst of shooting started him running toward a

brook hollow. He saw some soldiers running after a party of the rebels. They vanished on a slope of mixed growth. Later some of the enemy crossed an open space. One was without a hat and he had bright red hair.

Matthew ran until his heart jarred his ribs. He plunged into the grove where he had seen Meekins and found gaps where trees had been cut, and winter roads for hauling. Underbrush was littered about. He burst into a glade where a squirrel scolded furiously and, winded, sat on a felled tree left by the woodcutters.

Then he stiffened, and cocked his musket. The back of a jacket showed behind the log.

"Coom from thear," he said fiercely, "else I'll shoot."

The figure squirmed from the hiding place and rose. It was a woman and she had a baby in her arms. Her hair hung in untidy braids and she was a slovenly creature, but her china-blue eyes stared at him and her mouth sagged open.

"Matthew!" she gulped. "Are ye a sojer?"

It was Polly Clews.

He turned from her in disgust but she ran after him and tugged his jacket.

"My man is here, Matthew. He's hurt. Help me get him out."

He let her pull him around for her begging was pitiful, and saw an Acadian. The fellow was cowering in the brush, holding a hand to his side.

Matthew examined the hurt. A bullet had creased the man's ribs but no great harm had been done. A path led to a cabin and the fellow went to it, gibbering with fright. An officer and soldiers were in the yard. They listened indifferently to Matthew's story and said the Acadian could stay in his home. Then they ignored him and sat on a bench in the sun.

Matthew went back to the woods. Nothing had gone as he expected. There had been no battle. They had tramped miles in a vague pursuit, shooting wildly at running men, burning some buildings. That was all. Someone on the road began blowing a whistle. It was a recall but he went into the grove until he found a stump to sit on and there ate his bread and meat.

Bluejays shrilled in a thicket beyond and he went to investigate. Gideon said jays were fake alarms half the time, but nobody knew which half.

He saw the cause of their noise. A man had crawled under the trees. He now lay face downward on a carpet of yellow leaves, one leg drawn up as if he wanted to go further. A tiny pool of blood had formed below his chin. The man was very still and his hair was red.

Matthew stood and gazed until the jays had flown away to other business. He dropped to one knee and turned the body over. The face was pallid under its tan so that Peter Meekins looked little more than a boy. Matthew felt queerly. He picked up his musket and went away. He hated war and there was nothing more he wanted.

The afternoon was dark and a rising wind kept the embers of the burned buildings smoking. Cattle bawled in the fields as if they sensed disaster. Drops of rain rode on the increasing breeze. Every beast without a roof would have a miserable night.

Matthew trudged doggedly until a downpour began, then took refuge in a house occupied by several soldiers. A woman served them supper, went to bed and barred her door.

In the morning the sun was bright. The woman made them a pot of porridge that put heat into their stomachs. Matthew let the soldiers go on without him. Then he cut across fields and headed homeward over the marsh.

Gideon and Patience were sat in their chairs when he arrived at their house. The two babies played on the floor. He glanced at them briefly, looked at Patience.

"Whear is Sylvia? How has she been?"

Patience looked at Gideon, nodded for him to speak.

"You left sudden," said Gideon. His voice was neither hard nor soft. "O'Conner was looking to find you all the afternoon you were in Amherst village."

Matthew stared at him. "Tell it, man. She's not. . . ."

"She is," said Gideon, interrupting his shout. "She asked for you an hour after you'd gone. When we couldn't find

you she worked herself into a fever. O'Conner came back
with a tale of you heading for the fort. She give up, then,
in spite of all we could do. Last thing she said was 'What
made him go?'"

The youngsters on the floor, frightened by Gideon's tone,
ran to Patience and she soothed them. She looked at Matthew.
"We buried her 'longside Uncle Malachy, in my best dress wi'
t' lace on t' collar. It's all we could do."

"Did you find what you went for?" asked Gideon.

Matthew gazed at him, inarticulate. Black grief descended
on him like a stone. He could not speak; he merely shook his
head.

"Then," said Gideon calmly, "you lost out all the way
'round."

Matthew turned toward the door as if he could not see.
Young Adam toddled across the room, reaching up baby
hands, but Matthew went outside without a word, closing
the door behind him.

XV
Return of Judy

LANCELOT AND JUNE were comfortable in their own home. They found the house warm enough in winter and it was fun to visit back and forth with John and Melody. The two men joined forces in getting out their year's supply of fuel, and John helped with the building of pens and sheds.

It was a grand spring. The Yorkshiremen had spent a nervous winter, keeping their ears open for rumours from the fort. Relief was immense when word came that there was no danger of another invasion. The fighting around New York had worn out both sides. The majority declared that the war was as good as over. It seemed incredible that nothing much had happened at the fort. Eddy's Maine bushmen and Indians together with vengeful Acadians and many home supporters had failed to weld themselves into an efficient fighting force. They had had no stomach for fighting. The miserable garrison of jail birds and renegades, thinned by frequent desertions, had kept them at bay.

Silas Plumley said the hand of the Lord could be seen in the events and he held thanksgiving meetings in several houses.

There was nothing June loved more than to tramp in the woods with Lancelot. He knew every place of interest and he understood wild creatures. One Sunday he took her back of Nathan Hodge's fields to a small lake where wood ducks hatched.

It was imperative that they move silently. Wood ducks were among the pickerel weeds and rushes, their shrill "peet-peet-peet" cries breaking the wilderness quiet when they were

307

startled. June watched them until noon, then she and Lancelot ate lunch by a weathered windfall.

He pointed out a tiny island where black-backed gulls nested and in a maze of blowdowns found a trio of young horned owls that stared at them and snapped their beaks.

In the afternoon they idled around the lake, finding a colony of blue heron nests odorous with smells of old eggs, dead young and rotting fish, seeing a partridge with chicks. Then they headed for home on a trail that led to the river.

"Listen!" June tugged him to a halt.

A dog came running under the trees. It was a yellow cur and it wagged its tail briefly, then scurried back the way it had come.

"It's Reuben's dog," cried June. "He must be around."

The dog returned, then dashed away again. When they advanced they could not get near it. It seemed anxious to be followed.

"We'll go that way," decided Lancelot. "It's t' path by Nathan's house."

They were near to the clearing when they saw Reuben. He was lying on the ground. He said a weakness had overtaken him and he had been unable to reach his own cabin.

Lancelot hurried to bring Nathan with a crude stretcher and they carried Reuben to his home. Israel Hodge was there ahead of them and he had the bed ready.

"It's some seizure," he pronounced. "T' man wants bleeding."

Reuben mumbled something and Israel bent over him, then started violently. "Get from here," he cried to June. "Whear is John? Have him soon as tha can. Reuben has smallpox."

"Smallpox!" June gasped at the word. "But John has gone to River Hebert. It's a confinement and he won't be back until tomorrow."

"Then we must have t' Amherst doctor," declared Israel. "Tha ride, Lancelot, and see if tha can get someone to nurse him."

Reuben muttered about water. Israel held a cup to his lips. The sick man swallowed with effort. "Tell Judy," he grunted.

"He's burning wi' fever," said Israel. "Give him no heed."

June went to see Judy. "We found Reuben in the woods," she panted. "He's got smallpox."

Judy gazed as if she could not understand. "Lancelot's riding for the Amherst doctor," added June. "He'll try and fetch a nurse."

"Aye," said Judy. "It'll be hard to find one. Nobody wants smallpox."

"Lancelot will find someone," assured June. "Don't you worry."

Judy turned slowly. "I reckon," she said, "if ever he'd have me back it's now."

"No, dear." June tried to be tactful. "He wouldn't even know you. Why risk getting it?"

"Tha think I might spoil my looks," shrugged Judy, "and happen I do, who will care? I'm going to him."

She rode over with Lancelot, her spare clothing in a bundle, acting with such calmness that Israel shook his head. "She don't know what she's doing," he whispered.

Lancelot rode to Amherst for the doctor. O'Conner put his owlish head out of a window after Lancelot had almost kicked his door in. He was so drunk that he let his head sink to the sill as he listened to Lancelot's request.

"I'm tight," he orated, "as a pair of new shoes. I couldn't bleed a cat. I can't as much as see good. Ye'll have to wait till tomorrow."

He was in such a mulish mood that Lancelot had to ride away to Gideon's and spend the night. In the morning O'Conner looked ghastly, groaning in self-pity as they rode. By the time they had reached Reuben's cabin he was bowed with fatigue.

Judy met them as though nothing were out of the ordinary. She had put a clean shirt on Reuben. The cabin was swept clean. A pitcher of fresh water was on the table. The way she stooped over Reuben to speak to him made Lancelot think of an angel in a religious picture he had see at Backfall.

"He's been bad wi' fever," said Judy, "but he's rested this morning. I gave him gruel for breakfast."

O'Conner grunted. He drank thirstily of the water, rinsed

his mouth, grimaced and spat out of the door. Then he squinted at Reuben closely as he opened his shirt.

"By the bogs of Dunderry!" he blurted. "Smallpox! The man has measles! Haven't ye a granny in the settlement? She'd have seen the spots first off. He's sick because an adult has them harder, that's all."

Reuben opened his eyes. "I'm better," he said grumpily. "Put yon shouter ootside. I want none o' him."

"It's the doctor," cautioned Judy, "coom from Amherst."

"Send him back," insisted Reuben. He looked up at her. "Are tha staying wi' me?"

Judy gazed at him as if they were alone. "Do tha want me?"

"Aye, Judy." Reuben settled comfortably. "I'd be sick again to have thee coom."

O'Conner blinked his watery eyes and led the way outside. "The good Lord," he said roughly, "never put a crazier people on this earth than Yorkshire."

XVI

Jackie's Pup

THE HARROW was a home-made affair of eight crossed planks fastened with iron spikes. The heavy teeth were shaped to suit Tristram on Knatchball's anvil, and were so spaced that each turn up and down the field needed no more than a half-lap on the previous one. Seed grain was buried perfectly and the earth left soft and loosened.

Tristram found it hard to travel back and forth on the mellow soil, and he often rested while Jeannie walked with the cattle. She was growing fast and would be a big girl, taller than her mother, and with the same glossy hair.

There were occasional showers at night, but June held to lovely weather. Tristram finished the planting of his small field and tried to be content. He could not do more. Long hours at swinging his crutch tired him more than heavy labour had done. He tried not to look along the river to the many acres Plumley had seeded and to take his enjoyment from the good season and the good earth. Nothing stirred his pulses like the sound of a plow cutting virgin soil, the aroma of freshly-turned furrows, the reek of sweating cattle and the jingle of his harrow chains.

The day after his planting was finished he made his way to an old beaver meadow included in what had been Shubad Knapp's holding. The meadow had been uncovered by a shrinking of the river, and rank grass grew richly with the coating of life-giving silts that had been spread over it by spring freshets. He had only to spade a low dyke to maintain the meadow as a fertile field, and once the idea was formed he let it force him to new hobblings as he broke the ground.

311

"There's no need," protested Delia. "Be content with what you have in crop."

"I'd be stark giddy," declared Tristram, "to let sweet land bear nowt but wild hay. We've had bonny weather and thear will be champion crops."

"Ye will overdo and be sick," warned Delia.

"I'm ommost done," he answered, and she let him be.

Solomon Smith came over that evening. He looked at Jackie and said his errand was a pleasant one. "I've three pups," he said. "Your lad can have one. Let him come over in the morning and take his pick."

Jackie looked at Tristram and his pleading was in his gaze.

"Aye," said Tristram, glad to do something for Jackie. "We'll get t' pup tomorrow."

He liked Jackie. The youngster looked lonesome at times, being left much in Donald's company. Donald's health was failing rapidly. He sat in the sun a great deal and seldom talked with anyone.

There was a river crossing beyond the meadow that Tristram was seeding. A hewed timber reached to a stone in the middle of the stream, and a second piece extended to the far bank. From there it was but a short distance over the fields to Smith's mill but Delia had never let her children use the tricky footbridge.

In the morning Jeannie stayed indoors to help her mother with a baking. Tristram insisted on it. He noticed that Delia had become slow on her feet, that the knotting of her petticoat strings had become a long process. She no longer tried to hook her whalebone and hickory stays. "Save thy steps," he urged. "Let t' lass give a hand."

Jackie went with him to the meadow and Tristram watched until the boy was safely across the river. "Stay yon side when tha coom back," he ordered, "till I get here to watch thee."

He watched the lad race over the field to Smith's mill, then went back to his work. It would be great, he thought, to have three or four such sons on his farm, to have them grow to man size, hard, strong, durable as whiffletree oak. They would clear the trees back to the hardwood hills, draw the stumps when they had rotted. There would be fat cattle in the pastures, flocks of sheep. They would build the biggest barn in Bathol.

Flies bothered his oxen. He was twice as long in finishing the field as he expected. He forgot Jackie entirely until he saw that it was nearly noon.

He hurried to the river, perspiring hugely. Jackie was not there. He shouted. A kingfisher darted from its perch on an alder, flitted upstream. But no cry answered him.

Jackie set out eagerly to Smith's mill. He had never seen a pup but his mother had told him enough to make him more excited than ever he had been over anything he had seen. The fact that the pup was to be his own added to his anticipation.

The mill was idle. No one was about. He could hear shouting from far out in the fields where Solomon was planting. The thought occurred to him that the pup might be in the mill shed. He peered in, saw new planks in a neat pile, glimpsed the big saw. There was a heap of fresh sawdust that would be grand to play in.

He edged around the corner to see the huge water wheel. The front of the dam dripped water that flashed in the sun. There were water slugs in crevices, green slime on old timbers. It was a perfect place to investigate but he went to the house. He wanted his pup.

The kitchen porch was interesting. No other house in Bathol boasted one. Only a mill owner could afford to put a roof over the outside space where his wife stored her buckets and brush brooms. Something stirred in one corner and Jackie cried out in delight. Three tiny dogs were sleeping beside their mother.

One pup scrambled up, emitting little woofs of surprise. Mrs. Smith opened the door. "I never heard thee coom, Jackie," she said. "Are tha for pup?"

He nodded, his eyes shining. "Mother said I was to tell ye 'thank ye.'"

"Tha art a bonny lad," said Mrs. Smith. "Take thy pick."

Jackie pointed to the one that had woofed at him.   It had a white nose and paws.   "Him," he giggled.   "Can I?"

"Aye.   Have a barley cake."

Jackie accepted the offering as he watched the pups.   He began eating mechanically as Mrs. Smith took the dog family indoors.   Then she handed out to him the pup he wanted.   "He'll be lonesome at start," she said, "but he'll soon be champion.   Feed him bread wi' milk."

"Thank ye," said Jackie.   He took the pup in his arms and grinned as it slobbered a wet tongue on his cheek.   Then he was on his way.

"Pup!" he piped breathlessly as it snuggled in his arms. "You're mine.   I'll get ye something to eat soon as we're home.   You'll have all ye want every day."

He giggled whenever the pup nuzzled his face and was almost to the river before he let it down on the ground.   It gamboled about him then made little whining noises.

In an instant Jackie caught it up again.   "Don't ye cry," he whispered.   "We'll play when we get home.   Just you and me."

He looked for Tristram but no one was in sight.   No one waited for him; no one came for him or called.

It did not look far across the timber but Tristram had given him strict order not to attempt a crossing.   "We've got to stay here," he confided to the pup, "till a man comes."

The pup squirmed restlessly in his arms and he let it down on the bank.   Then he pretended to be asleep and the pup licked his ears until he rolled over.

"Pup, oh, pup," he cried.   "You are funny."

It was so warm they both became tired.   The pup, panting hotly, climbed into Jackie's lap as he sat on the river bank. All at once it scrambled from him, dropped from his reach. It fell into the water, making a small splash.   The cold made it yelp.   Jackie cried out in dismay.   He slid down after it, waded into the river to his knees but the current carried the struggling animal out of his reach.

Wading deeper, he tried to catch the pup further on.   It was a vain effort.   An eddy swung the tiny struggler from him. Jackie lunged recklessly. He managed to catch the pup but was swept off his feet. Before he could make an outcry he was under water.

He rose once, near a tree root, but to grab for it meant to relinquish his pup, so he sank once more, kicking to find something solid to hold him, his pet firmly held in his arms.

The hewed timber was an awkward bridge for a man with a crutch and Tristram had to cross over on his hands and knees. The river bank was soft sod. The grass was pressed down, showing where Jackie had sat a long time. There were marks where he had kicked his heels against the turf. Just below the spot a stone had been dislodged, making it look as if something had slid down the bank.

Startled by such evidence, Tristram hurried to the first turn of the river. There, stranded on a gravel bar, was Jackie's little cap that his mother had knitted for him. It was held firmly by a stick, a pathetic signal, bobbing in the slight current.

In places the river was five feet deep so that a small boy would be carried along unless he could catch hold of something. Trying to pray, Tristram hobbled on, peering into each pool, dreading what he would see.

Someone hailed him from the cart trail. It was Peregrine Knatchball. "Art daft, man?" he cried. "Tha'll break neck, going at such pace wi' crutch."

"Coom!" Tristram shouted in anguish. "Help look for my laddie. He's fallen in river."

Knatchball climbed the pole fence at once, ran ahead to where freshets had gouged tree roots bare of earth. There, snagged on a stick, they found Jackie, still clutching a tiny pup with white nose and feet.

Knatchball lifted the lad out, his blacksmith hands, horny with handling metal, gentle as a woman's as he wrung water from the soaked clothing. Tristram knelt beside him, his face contorted with emotion. He would never know what had happened. At any rate—the thought seared his conscience—it would never have happened had he thought of the youngster instead of dreaming of a bigger farm. He was responsible.

Knatchball carried Jackie home. Tristram followed without a word. When they reached the yard Delia came to the door. Tristram tried to say something but his words would not form coherently. He could only put an arm clumsily about her. Jeannie cried out. She dropped to her knees beside the pitiful little bodies.

"Jackie!" she wailed. "Don't look like that. Don't be dead! I want you, Jackie, I want you!"

XVII
Ann's Bonnet

WHEN he had finished the chores about his barn Matthew became restless. He had his seed planted. His ground was in excellent order. He had cleaned the debris from his house cellar. The stone wall was as good as ever. The Maccan carpenters had agreed to come the next week. They were to build a house exactly like the one that had burned. He had cut the main timbers for it in the winter. They were in his yard, cleanly hewed, ready for framing.

He saw Gideon, carrying little Asa, go with Patience among their apple trees. Their baby was probably asleep in its cradle. It was another boy, named after Gideon, a healthy little chap, filled with vigour.

The day was quiet. Swallows twitted at the barn eave. Crows cawed on the marshes. Otherwise there was a gentle Sabbath stillness.

Matthew became more restless. He had a fine farm, there was no denying it. The grass was so rich that his cattle were heavy in flesh with feeding. His oxen were in grand fettle; he had not lost a lamb in the spring. His gold had been saved in the spot where he buried it. Yet he had no pleasure in life.

His thinking pictured Sylvia as she had moved about his house, so sure and cheerful. He groaned inwardly, was filled with self-pity. A man had to have a wife. There was no joy to be obtained unless he fulfilled the injunction of every land—increase and multiply.

The dropping of a rail by one of his sheds roused him. He saw that his great white sow had rooted out a corner post of

317

her yard fence, collapsing the poles. Now the big animal ran loose, followed by a swarm of squealing youngsters.

He had a tedious time getting her back in the yard when he had made repairs. A pig could not be driven like a cow or horse. Neither could it be lured or coaxed. Then the young ones had to be caught. It was long past noon when he had everything in order and in that time he had made a decision.

He would not live alone; he would get himself a wife.

One by one he thought of the unmarried young women of the district. Many were desirable but there was not one without an ardent suitor of her choice. It was useless for him to think of them. He was candid with himself, owning that he looked ten years more than his age, that he was too dark and glowering to be called attractive, too slow of wit to be company for the majority of women.

His thinking swung to Ann Cutlip. She was about his age and a big hearty girl. She had courage, too, coming with her father to a new country, knowing he would have to leave her alone while he was away with his cobbling. Her mother had died while she was in her teens.

Thomas Cutlip had a head on his shoulders. He had arranged for Ann to work out here and there while he was away in the winters. It kept the girl from being lonely, earned extra shillings. Soon she had become adept to the ways of the country. If her hearing had been good she could have taken her pick of the young men but as it was she had been left single. The average man did not want to shout his words when he was courting, then talk loud the rest of his life.

Matthew had scarcely known her. He had not seen her a dozen times until April. Then, by chance, he had discovered that it was Ann who had written to Unity about Tristram's fighting with his brother. Ann, it seemed, had not forgiven Tristram for his trapping Shubell in Paddy's stable.

In April he had seen Ann on an errand to a neighbour's. She had responded quickly to his hail, talked as long as he wished. She spoke in the loud tones of the deaf but was witty enough in what she said. After that he had stopped several times to chat with her as she worked in her father's garden. It was apart from the nearest house so that no one could hear what he said.

He had had no trouble discovering that Ann was keen enough to get married. After their fourth or fifth talk he would have proposed to her had not her deafness discouraged him. Then he had thought to go to O'Conner.

"No," said O'Conner "There isn't a thing I can do for her hearing. Nor can any other doctor. It's an ailment she got as a child. She wears that deep bonnet over her head indoors and out, afraid she'll take cold and be worse. Truth is, it never helped her any. She'd be better if she went bareheaded."

Matthew had shrugged, turned to leave.

"You're wanting to marry her, I see," added O'Conner. "Ye could do much worse. She's sound every other way, easy satisfied, too, else she'd never have stayed alone so much. Once she gets to read your lips you'd have no trouble with talking. Fact is, she's a bargain."

It was a fine Sabbath evening. Matthew waited until it was nearly dark, then went to call on Ann. He wondered if she had heard how he had acted with Sylvia's child. There was nothing he could do about it, if she had. He would not have young Adam back to please any woman. Every time he had looked at the child's red head he had felt sickened.

He was surprised to find Ann on a bench in her garden. "Good even," he shouted. "I've coom to see thee."

She smiled. "Father's away onyhow." She pointed at the bench. "Sit thee doon. It's first time I've had a man to keep me company." She laughed, a hearty, infectious good humour.

"Do tha get lonely?" he asked.

"Eh, me?" She peered at him from under her wide bonnet. "At times I do, same as ony. Do thee?"

He moved impatiently. She was not so simple-minded as he had thought. "Some," he acknowledged. "I'm living alone. Did tha know?"

She nodded. "I've been towd. Thy wife died while thee wur at fort."

"It wur rebels hurt her," he said fiercely. "I wur trying to catch them that did it."

"Did tha?"

"Noa, but others did. T' chap were killed."

"Then tha had better stayed hoam."

"Aye," he admitted, realizing the trend of her talk. "It would have been better."

Ann kicked at the grass with the toe of her shoe. Matthew, watching, saw how well her father had cobbled her footwear. It would be a smart piece of work to have a cobbler in one's family.

"Did tha coom to court me?" she asked with disconcerting directness.

The day had been warm and she was not wearing many petticoats. He could see the outlines of her legs. They were stronger-looking than Sylvia's had been. Her hands, too, were shaped for work.

"Aye. If tha will let me?"

She smiled, showing fine white teeth. "Nowt would suit me more. When do tha want to marry?"

Her frankness warmed him. Why beat about the bush when the girl was willing. "Next week," he said daringly.

Her eyes searched his face. "Tha have no house yet?"

"Noa, but I'd like a wife to help over at Gid's wi' cooking for t' carpenters."

"That will be champion," said Ann. "I know thy sister. Coom in house. I'll show thee my dress for marrying. Father said I wur a fool to make it wi' no man wanting me, but now I'm glad I did. Shubell said it wur all right. He said he wur sure I'd be married, and he would not let ony man play unfair wi' me."

They went into the cabin together. It was neatly kept with every piece of crockery shining when Ann lighted a candle. Matthew could see that she was flushed with excitement.

She took the dress from a trunk in which she kept it, smoothed its creases, then held it up for his inspection. It was an attractive shade of green, trimmed with lace.

"It's champion," he shouted. "Tha will look a queen."

Her cheeks were more rosy as she smiled at his compliment. "Don't tha shout too loud," she chuckled. "I'll soon catch thy tone. I hear father easy."

He admired her as he watched her put the dress away. She was quick with her hands, smart on her feet. She carried her chin up, walked with some style. Man, but they would have fine children.

"Do tha know," he cried, "I've never seen thee wi'oot a bonnet. Take it off."

"I'll do," she answered. "When we're married I'll not wear bonnet at all."

She undid the strings, whipped off the bonnet and faced him, then smiled.

Matthew shut his eyes to the candle glow, then looked again. Her hair was a bright foxy red. It was the exact shade of young Adam's.

His lips moved without forming words.

Ann smiled again. "Try louder," she said.

XVIII

The Funeral

NEWS of Jackie's drowning spread through Bathol. Delia, going about like a sleep-walker, said the burial would be in the glade where the Knapps were buried. There was plenty of room for a small boy alongside.

Lancelot made a fine pine coffin that June lined with blue camlot. Solomon Smith took planks from his mill to Tristram's yard and set them up on stakes to serve as seats. Every man, woman and child of the settlement arrived for the funeral, the majority going early to have a look at the lad before the lid was fastened on the casket.

The coffin was carried to the centre of the yard where Silas Plumley had taken his stand. The Crabtrees led the singing. Everyone joined in with fervour. It was the finest singing Bathol had ever heard, strong and steady, in slow meter and with grand harmony. The hills gave back the last notes in long echo.

Knatchball sat with his huge hands hooked over his knees, staring at the ground. Solomon Smith gazed at the coffin as if he could see Jackie through the wood. The Garrisons were there to the last baby, with Mrs. Garrison sniffing audibly until the singing began. The three Hodge families were grouped as if they would shelter Ezra's wife, who was heavy with child.

When the hymn was finished Silas Plumley made a prayer more effective than any they had heard Parson Eagleson offer.

"We coom to Thee, Lord, in t' broad field, seeking Thy favour as ever man has done. Knowing Tha have said in Thy book that whear two or three are gathered, Thee will be also. Oor hearts are heavy wi' sorrow this day. . . ."

He prayed without hurry. The reverence in his voice awed even the smallest to utter stillness. The Sabbath was perfectly quiet, the air warm. No breeze stirred the foliage. The silence was spread over the intervales like a sheet of gold-green, shimmering and tremulous. Even the river seemed to run softly.

Tristram sat on the front bench with Delia beside him. He had not slept more than a few hours since the drowning. Jeannie's wild grief had cut him bitterly but he had been able, finally, to calm her sobbing. With Delia it was different. She had not accused him, yet there was something in the way she dressed Jackie for the last time, making each move with a tenderness more poignant than tears, that tore his emotions asunder. He would have welcomed blame, accepted it; it was her silence that unnerved him.

Silas Plumley did not attempt a sermon. He talked, rather, of their need for greater faith in submitting themselves to ways they did not understand, confessing that they were weak in misfortune. In his rambling talk he went back over the years since their arrival at Bathol, spoke of what they had accomplished, of the peril of war that had menaced them, of their gratitude that the peril was past.

He made Melody think of her father working at his coach. John Lacey thought of the morning he had met Melody. Each listener had elbows against a neighbour yet it was as if they were alone, each remembering some episode that had been imprinted deepest in their memory.

When Plumley was finished the people followed in procession those who carried the coffin to the grave. They sang another hymn in the glade, then filed back to their seats as Nathan Hodge stayed behind to fill in the small opening with soft earth and tamp it smooth.

"We'll sing again," said Plumley. "T' Lord has given us a fine day to praise him."

When the hymn was finished there was a pause. No one seemed to want to move. They were startled when Tristram rose suddenly. He turned awkwardly on his crutch to face the assembly.

"I want tha to listen to me," he cried. "I've been a sinner and t' day's coom to make confession."

Garrison's dog ran in from the field, looking for the children, but scarcely a person looked at it. Every eye watched Tristram. There was not another sound until a rooster crowed near the stable.

"T' Lord help thee," intoned Plumley. He made his way to a seat beside his wife.

Tristram groaned aloud. He looked a man in torment. "I'm cused wi' sin," he began in a choked voice. "I've worked harder than most o' thee know, all wi' thinking o' nowt but gain. It's bigger fields I've wanted, more cattle, bigger barns—to gloat over like a marchant wi' his money."

He rested, shifted his weight on his crutch, looked at Delia.

"Afore thee all," he went on, "I'll tell my wife I'm to blame for her laddie being drooned. I towd him to bide by t' brook till I coom—and forgot him. He wur seated thear long time. T' marks wur plain in t' grass. Forgie if tha can. I cannot blame thee if tha don't. I wur planning more land I'd have years to coom—and Jackie wur waiting—a bonnie, bonnie lad."

His voice broke so that he could not go on. He was torn with sobbing. Mrs. Garrison joined with him in loud weeping. Then, for the first time after the drowning, Delia wept, flooding her cheeks with tears.

Tristram grew quiet. He faced the people again.

"I set fire to t' barn on John's place," he shouted. "It wur no lightning struck. I wur mad wi' leaving t' place. I wur crazy mad. I went over at night when storm wur bad. I set fire in t' stall wi' straw. No one could know, but I tell thee now before t' Lord."

His voice had a note of despair. His excitement was enormous. When he stilled there was a hushed whispering, like a wind in evergreens.

"I hated my brothers," he shouted. "I hated all in settlement. I sinned in God's sight. I've been a champion wretch. Now I ask thee all like I'll ask t' Lord—will tha forgive?"

"Aye, man," responded Plumley. "T' Lord help thee."

"Aye, we do. Aye, we're glad to forgie thee."

Assent came from everyone, it seemed. The events of the afternoon had strung emotions to high pitch. Women sobbed. Some men shouted "Amen!" Tristram trembled violently. He looked suddenly old, exhausted. "I'll sin no more," he vowed.

"Amen," pronounced Plumley.

"Pray for me, Silas," cried Tristram, in torment. "Pray now."

Every person heard Tristram's plea, saw him drop on his knees. They watched him there, were more deeply moved. None of them could have said afterward how Plumey opened his prayer, or how he prayed, but more than half the assembly said "Amen" with hearty accord. Then they were standing, the women talking with Delia, going with her to the cabin. The men, taking careful turns, began going to Tristram. They shook his hand, told him they admired his courage and honesty.

"We'll coom to harvest thy crop," roared Jacob Cornforth. "Tha have suffered enough, man."

"He has that," agreed Israel Hodge. "Every man forgies thee."

"It took a good heart to say all ye did," praised Garrison. "I know how ye feel, too, gettin' about on a stump."

Their encouragement buoyed Tristram, raised him from the agony that had wrenched from him his confession. The rough compliments began to elate him. He felt almost heroic.

"We'll help thee build a better home," said Hodge.

"Noa," returned Tristram, "I'll be content wi' cabin we've got, but will build more rooms to it."

"Tha are a good man!" Mrs. Cornforth's voice had a carrying quality. She spoke as if she were pronouncing a benediction. "Whatever wrong tha have done, tha have suffered for't. Tha can count on us to help thee from now."

Other women came to him. Every person seemed his friend. A sense of triumph seized him. He was being admired. He would be remembered in the settlement, pointed to with pride. Mrs. Plumley said she would remember him in her prayers. Delia came and kissed him. "Ye made me cry when I couldna," she whispered. "Now I feel better. I forgie ye aboot Jackie. Let's say no more o' it."

There was a diversion. A couple came along the trail with a small child. The women moved across the yard for a nearer glimpse.

"It's Reuben Scurr."

"It's Judy wi' him."

"He looks a new man since she went back to him."

"Aye. It's wonderful whear he earned so much money. They are to build soon, and he has paid Solomon for every timber—in gold. He has bought Judy pots and pans and t' like."

"He has bought all t' land next Nathan Hodge, and best oxen in Maccan."

"Judy's like a new woman, too, having a lad in her house."

Tristram wondered as he listened to the comment.

"Whear did they get t' lad?" he queried.

"It's thy brother's lad—Matthew's little Adam. He would have nowt to do wi' youngster since t' mother died."

Tristram went nearer to the trail. He watched people talking with Judy as though she had never left Reuben, as if she were a good woman. Reuben hoisted the child on his shoulder so they could see what a bonnie lad young Adam was, and how neatly Judy had dressed him.

"Reuben's worked every day since they got t' lad," said Nathan Hodge. "He's clearing ground. He'll have a champion farm. He paid gold for't."

Judy had never looked better, Tristram thought. She had flesh on her frame again. There was a dash of the old colour in her cheeks.

"She makes a champion mother," said Mrs. Cornforth. "Judy is a good woman."

Tristram turned toward his cabin. He could not understand why people considered Judy a changed woman. She had not made a confession. Then he began to wonder where Reuben had obtained his money.

Lancelot came near him.

"I'm glad I towd about t' fire," said Tristram humbly. "It wur on my conscience."

He expected Lancelot to put out his hand eagerly, expressing approval, but it came to him that neither he nor Jonathan had joined the other men in exclaiming their admiration of his stand.

"Aye," said Lancelot. "It must have been."

His manner pricked Tristram's thinking.

"Did tha know before?" he asked.

"Aye. Judy wur in t' house when tha put fire in barn. She saw thee. That wur night she coom to my place."

"Did others know?" Tristram's lips were suddenly dry.

"Noa," shrugged Lancelot. "Just John and Jonty."

"Tha towd Jonty?"

"Aye. He knows thee same as we do."

Lancelot's words stunned Tristram. He fought back resentment.

"What do tha mean?" he asked.

Lancelot looked around warily before he answered.

"Jonty wur wi' me when we saw squaw by t' brook tha wur meeting. He has bark cover for rifle tha dropped when tha shot Indian in Solomon's woods."

Tristram stared at Lancelot as if he were unreal. The fields seemed to revolve in the sunlight. His mind was a chaos. Then Delia joined him and he struggled to grasp what she was saying. The women surged back from the trail as Reuben and Judy went home. He tried to collect his wits, gazed at Lancelot.

"Good day," he called. "Coom over when tha can."

"Aye," returned Lancelot, his face blank as a shuttered window.

The men began to join their wives, standing in groups, talking in subdued tones. Tristram could not steady himself. He saw that his cows had come to the bars, were waiting milking time. He saw that many of the people would still talk with him if he gave them chance. Then Jeannie came to him.

"Will Jackie have his pup in heaven?" she inquired.

He led her to one of the plank seats. "Aye," he said gently. "He'll have chosen a name for't by now."

She gazed up at him. "You'd never tell a lie to any, would ye?"

He looked at her quickly as he shook his head. They were sitting there together as the people started homeward, Jeannie snuggled against him, making them both pathetic figures.

When everyone had gone he went to the house. Donald extended a thin hand. "Shake, mon," he said gravely. "I'm prood o' ye."

Tristram was surprised. His gaunt brother-in-law had not troubled to talk with him at any time.

"I've been a sinful man," Tristram said heavily. "I'm sick o't."

He looked out the door to where the crowd had gathered. The grass was scuffed bare in spots. The land was poor; too much gravel. He would never have a proper crop in a field near the cabin.

"Muster Muncie's comin' the morrow," went on Donald. "I talked wi' him. The Croon has seized the Meekins place at Maccan. I'm takin' it."

"Taking it?" Tristram stared at him.

"I am that. Read this paper and ye'll understand."

Tristram noted the paper's official seal as he read:

"Headquarters. Bofton. 18 Dec, 1775.

"The Bearer hereof

Donald Ferguson,

having voluntarily engaged to ferve His Majefty in the Royal Regiment of Highland Emigrants (raifed and eftablifed for the Just and Loyal purpofe of oppofing, quelling and fuppreffing the prefent moft unnatural and unprovoked and wanton Rebellion) conformable to the Orders and Directions of His Excellency, the Commander in Chief, and agreeable to His Majefty's Moft Gracious Intention, fignified by the Earl of Dartmouth (Secretary of State for America) That fuch Emigrants from North Britain (as

well as other loyal subjects) that fhould engage to ferve in the
aforementioned Corps, fhould be confidered in the moft
favorable light:—And after the completion of the prefent
unhappy civil War (to which period only they are obliged to
ferve) be entitled to a Proportion of Two Hundred acres vacant
(or forfeited lands) for every Man or Head of Family, together
with Fifty Acres more in addition for every perfon the family
may confift of, the whole to be Granted and Patented without
any Expense to the faid Grantee—AND MOREOVER to be
free of any Quit Rent to the Crown for twenty years.   I DO
THEREFORE with the confent and approbation of His
Excellency the Commander in Chief, Certify and Declare,
that the faid Donald Ferguson is, at the Expiration of the
prefent trouble, or when Disabled so as to Merit a discharge,
entitled to receive as a Juft reward for his fpirited loyalty, the
beforementioned grant of lands, in confequence of the Orders
and Directions of His Majefty.

"Given under my Hand and Seal, Time and Place as firft
abovementioned.   John Small
                                       Lt.-Col. Commander
To all Concerned   Royal Highland Emigrant
Civil and Military: Regiment."

.Tristram re-read the paper before he saw Delia was watching him as if she knew its contents.
"It's champion farm tha will get," he said slowly.
"Wull ye tak' it?"
"Take it!   Do tha mean that we. . . ."
"Ye ken well as I do mysel' that I'll not live to see end o'
the year, but if ye'll move now, paying sixty poond for the
buildings as agreed by the Croon, I'll mak' my wull proper
and ye wull hae it a'."
It was too much for Tristram to assimilate at once.   He
saw himself established again, with good earth, fine stock,
a proper house, with Delia at her work, with children, sturdy
boys, playing about, with neighbours admiring him for his
possessions, respecting him as a Christian.
He wetted his lips with his tongue.   There would be the
tending of Donald to his finish, a need of catering to his every

whim. But after that there would be just he and Delia!

"Wull ye be happy there?" asked Delia, patting his hand.

"Happy! Thear is nowt could make me more content. Donald is working wi' t' Lord. He has blessed me more than I deserve."

He tried to speak humbly but his elation had returned. The chores he helped do enabled him to regain some control of himself. He was decently sorrowful when he spoke of Jackie as Donald took his candle to retire for the night.

Tristram could not sleep soundly. He woke more than once, trying to visualize the width of the intervale fronting the Meekins holding. The upland above it, he was sure, needed more rotation of crops. The fence needed repair. But it was a grand property, with at least thirty good acres on the other side of the road. It was, in fact, the biggest cleared farm on the river. The house, too, was of good size. There were plenty of outbuildings.

He tried to think of some passage of Scripture Plumley had read on the Sabbath, but all the words jumbled. Delia moved restlessly beside him, held to his arm tightly for a time. Then he drifted off to sleep again.

In the morning he was up early, energetic in his chores. Some Indians trailed by with their dogs, carrying bundles, going back to their summer camp after salmon fishing at the head of the river. He glanced at them casually. His cattle were near the trail and he hoped the Indian dogs would not molest them.

One of the squaws looked at him. She was younger than the others. She had a child by the hand but when she saw Tristram she picked it up, carried it so that he could see. The child's skin was very light, indicating that its father was a white man. He did not notice it. He was watching the dogs. They had come near the fence, barking at the cows. He shouted at them. The curs slunk away as one of the Indians shouted imperatively.

Tristram turned away with relief. There would be no trouble. It was going to be a fine day. Muncie would be there by noon to fill out the necessary papers.

It did not strike Tristram's thinking that the Indians would be camped beside the Meekins farm at Maccan. In fact he did not think of them at all.

He resolved, as he fed his calves, to have Jeannie read from the Scriptures each Sabbath. It was a good thing to hold favour with the Lord, and Donald.

His piety slackened. Donald had come into the yard. He walked slowly, revealing feebleness. Tristram watched him narrowly and began to calculate how much longer he would live.

After the funeral Jonathan and Unity went over with Lancelot and June for supper. In the evening John and Melody joined them.

"Let's go oop t' hill to father's grave," said Jonathan. "I've not been this spring."

The grave was in neat order. There was not a weed in its blanket of soft grass. A heart-shaped plot of pansies in the centre was in bloom.

"It's lovely," cried Unity. She looked at Melody. "Do tha tend it?"

"Noa, it must be Lancelot."

"Tha are wrong—it's Judy. She's ony one knows what father meant when he carved words on stump. She says he helped her more than ony other man."

"Here Stays Good Yorkshire." Unity spelled the words out, stood on her tiptoes, peered. "Look!" she exclaimed. "It's growing!"

They gathered around the stub. Sturdy shoots of green willow were growing from the very heart of the stump.

"I wish father could have seen," said Jonathan. "He would be sure it meant summat."

"I'm sure it does," declared Unity. "It's a sign o' perpetuity or t' like. My father would have made a sermon oot o' it."

"See! Stand here and look at the way the sun hits it." John pulled them back a distance as he pointed. They stood together gazing in silence, awed by the unusual lighting.

The last rays of the sun came over the tree tops of the slope, catching the upper part of the stump, bringing out vividly the bright green of the sprouting willow, then reaching to the lettering. Every letter was caught in the glow. Below it there was but the outline of an old stub.

There was not a sound in the evening air; it was as if the valley held its breath. They stood in a group, watching, until the light had faded. It held to the lettering until all else seemed indistinct, then vanished. Then, without speaking, they glanced upward. The first stars had appeared.